SOUNDING
DRUM

SOUNDING DRUM

LARRY JAY MARTIN

KENSINGTON BOOKS
http://www.kensingtonbooks.com

KENSINGTON BOOKS are published by

Kensington Publishing Corp.
850 Third Avenue
New York, NY 10022

Library of Congress Card Catalog Number: 98-075065
ISBN 1-57566-368-6

First Printing: June, 1999
10 9 8 7 6 5 4 3 2 1

Printed in the United States of America

To
Walter Z., for the perfect acorn;
Kate D., the visionary, who saw past the warts;
and always, Kat, my everything . . .

PROLOGUE

Dank.

Suffocating.

She steeled herself, forcing herself to take a deep breath and become one with it. It wasn't as if she hadn't experienced the feeling before.

She half expected bats' wings to brush her—she had always hated bats near her hair—but knew the cave must have been sealed for hundreds of years. No acrid bat guano seared her nostrils, only the musty and, to her, enticing—even seductive—odor of time.

She laughed at herself, realizing the suffocating was because she was holding her breath.

If only a low rumble occasionally threatened them, it would remind her almost exactly of a dig she'd been on years before on Maui. As if she'd willed it, the earth quivered underfoot, but this low rumble was less ominous than the one emanating from an angry Peli.

Then again, a New York subway is in many ways far more dangerous than a mere volcano.

After almost twenty years in the diggin' trade, almost nothing surprised much less astonished her. Now she stood, a curious image in a deep and ancient cave, still dressed in street clothes, a miner's lamp glowing like Cyclops on her forehead. In her low-heeled shoes and knee-length skirt, she leaned forward, mouth agape, eyes wide, reading what she could see between the curls of the four-hundred-year-old roll of foolscap. It had been cradled in a Canarsee basket, at the apex of two crossed Haudenosaunee war clubs with intricate carved heads.

A document she'd carefully extracted from that crumbling basket in an alcove of the granite cave.

A document she held tenderly, fearing it would crumble to dust in her hands. It was rolled, tied loosely with rotting cord woven of bark, composed in a fine hand with a quill pen, its ink faded but still partially legible with the help of the powerful light on her forehead. The light cast eerie dancing shadows into the nooks and crannies of the musty cave. Shadows, images, moldy smells, reminding her of times and beings long dead.

Had she been deep in the Valley of the Nile, on a high Andes peak, or in the Mongolian outback looking for the grave of Genghis Khan, she would have been pleased at another significant discovery. But as a Native American and full member of the Kootenai tribe of northwestern Montana—albeit a sandy-haired, blue-eyed one, long transplanted to the city and academia—she was both fearful and elated with the importance of her discovery.

But the shadows, and the feelings permeating to the innermost center of her being, were not nearly so strange as the document's contents.

Strange—and exciting.

If ever there was a document spirits, kind and kindred, would want known to the world, this was the one.

If it was real, and it must be. . . .

It had to be.

So she would take it where it would do the most good. Take it to Stephen Drum as soon as she extracted herself from the cave next to the basement of the Andrew McGuire Building in the center of Manhattan.

Three of her students who had responded to her emergency call worked nearby in the half-light forty feet below Manhattan's streets. Volunteers they were, receiving only a small stipend for their labor but gaining great respect for having worked under Dr. Fox.

David Greenberg, the sharpest and most alert of the crew, cut his eyes to where she stood half inside an alcove, giving only her back to the rest of them.

"You find something interesting?" he called out to her.

Both Patricia Elridge and Ingrid Petersen glanced over. Paula shrugged, brushing sandy hair away from her forehead, hiding her quivering excitement. "Naw, standard stuff, nothing yet." She wanted his attention turned elsewhere. "We need to get a grid set up here. Can you handle it? As of now, you're officially crew chief."

The girls glanced up with only momentary irritation, then went back to their delicate work.

"I've got to clean up a few things back at the office," Paula continued, "and I need to get into my dig clothes before I can concentrate."

"You know I can handle it," David said with confidence, thrusting his receding chin as far forward as he could under the circumstances, centering dark eyes on her, then turning back to his work with new fervor.

And he was right, Paula knew he could. She concealed what she was doing, carefully placing the parchment in a black plastic bag.

Waiting until the others were intent on their work, Paula carefully cradled the bag and its precious contents in her arms and headed for the rift in the foundation wall. David Greenberg and both girls looked up, curious about what she was carrying from the site. But before they could ask, she'd moved out into the basement and was ascending the stairs.

CHAPTER ONE

Steve Drum rested, chin in hands, deep in concentration, his mind on one of the most pressing problems he'd ever faced. His thoughts turned to his youth and maternal grandfather as he threaded his fingers through his straight black hair, now grown to the collar as he was no longer subject to the rigors of a big law firm.

Swinging his highly polished crocodile boots a little to the left, he dropped long legs from where he had them propped on a credenza to the forest-green wool carpet. He rose from his matching hickory desk, shook out perfectly tailored Armani slacks, and strode across his office to a pair of nine-foot windows peering down on Wall Street, twenty-two stories below. Draping an arm across the wing of a pedestal-mounted bronze of a bald eagle centered between the windows, he studied the city.

It was a view he loved almost as much as the one of the Mission Mountains from his home in Montana, one he would have never imagined having when he was back on the "rez." Across Wall Street, the four-story Grecian columns of the New York Stock Exchange guarded the entry to the world's most powerful financial institution, one Steve had put to good use over the past six years. In front of the columns a pretzel vendor worked his stand, hawking his wares to the passersby.

Both extremes of the free enterprise system only feet apart.

He liked the image, thought it the best of the United States Constitution at work. He knew well the worst of it.

His attention returned to his problem. Often, when he reached a seemingly insurmountable obstacle, as he did now, he turned his thoughts to the man he still regarded as the wisest of any man he'd had the pleasure of knowing. Charley Standing Bear, his grandfather.

Were Charley here, he'd know what to do.

This was not the first time Steve's life had been threatened since he had taken on this job, his consulting position to a number of tribes on Indian gambling, but this was the first time he had been told where and when he would be killed. He felt the hot breath of the bear waft over his face.

He consciously toughened his resolve.

It wasn't as if he hadn't felt it before.

The message had been mailed to him from the Mohawk Nation, a reservation in northern New York State unique in that it crossed the border between the United States and Canada. He was due there in a week to evaluate the existing management of several small casinos. The Mohawks had been in a war between themselves and the gambling faction of the tribe and the government, a shooting war at times. The threat to Steve's life could have come from existing casino management, from those on the reservation opposed to gambling—and there were many—or from the white men living near the reservation who hated the fact the Indians were gaining great economic advantage.

Or, hell, from damn near anywhere.

There was still his problem with his old mentor, sometimes friend, and oftentimes enemy, Aldo Giovanni. Don Aldo Giovanni, of Saddle River, New Jersey.

Whoever it was, it was a problem that had to be thought through.

One that could mean his very life.

So he appealed to the wisdom of his elders, as he often did. And mostly, to his old, long dead but still revered grandfather.

Three conversations with Standing Bear, who had been in his eighties when Steve was only coming into his teens, were engraved deeply in Steve's mind. Now he recalled one of them almost verbatim. It was a conversation, or more correctly a soliloquy, that had centered his early thought processes on a common thread and was the basis of much of his business acumen.

His grandfather had been carving a small bear charm from a

chunk of ponderosa pine with a hand-held adz—how he made his meager living—and he hadn't raised his deep-set eyes to the youth seated cross-legged on the dirt floor before him for many minutes. Wood chips all around him, Steve hadn't thought of moving as his grandfather's resonant voice cast an almost hypnotic spell.

"Man is unlike other creatures that walk the earth, swim the waters, or pass before the sun in the morning sky," he said, pausing occasionally as he took a particularly delicate cut. "He is of two faces.

"One, like the oyster, clings to the rock and waits for life to come to him." A chunk of wood flew, and Steve, known then and even now to his tribe as Sounding Drum, could begin to make out the eye of the two-foot-high bear.

"The other, like the eagle, seeks what he needs and conquers it.

"Too many men here on the reservation have become oysters." He raised his old hooded eyes for the first time in minutes— sharp eyes belying the wrinkles around them—and looked deep into those of his grandson, a gaze boring into his very essence. "Remember, in all you do, be an eagle." He dropped his gaze again and carved for a few moments while Steve contemplated what he'd been told.

"Study men, Sounding Drum. Know what rules them, what drives them, what they hunger for, and you will know where lies their weakness and how to obtain what you need." Old Standing Bear set aside the adz and stretched, working the kinks out of his stooped shoulders. "One thing you should understand above all else . . . prejudice is ignorance. Know the spring from which it wells, and it, too, you will rise above. If you do not, it will drown you as sure as the river floods in spring."

The old man cleared his throat and walked over. Steve stood, and his grandfather placed a wrinkled but still firm hand on his shoulder. "Always work from a position high in the sky, above all men in your honesty, above all men in your inner strength, no matter what they might do or might have done to you. Always, in all things, look past your anger. Look past foolish pride. Rise above, and you will stay above."

Steve couldn't help but smile as the years-old image of his grandfather seemed reflected in the tall windows, staring back at him, willing him to understand, willing him to rise above other men. Willing him to watch from on high.

With his grandfather's image before him, he sat down on the floor and crossed his legs as he had done as a boy, and contemplated the business problem, the life problem, he faced.

He would look past anger at receiving the threat to his life and past foolish pride. He would not be frightened of the bear's breath in his face.

Paula Fox waved down the first cab to pass and gave the driver the address of the Red Ace Corporation, 40 Wall Street, almost at the very end of the island. Wall Street, the financial center of the world.

She settled back, but was unable to relax, keeping the black bag in her arms in front of her, treating it as tenderly as a newborn. Still, even nervous and distraught at her impulsive action, she was comforted by the fact she knew exactly where and to whom to take it.

She didn't hear the calliope of automobile horns, or even the cursing and ranting of her cabdriver as they moved down the island. She was completely spellbound. This discovery transcended her job, her responsibility even to those who funded her digs and paid her salary. She felt a deep responsibility to those who believed in her. She'd been taught as a child to "dance with who brung you," . . . but she felt a deeper responsibility to her ancestry.

She was a fervent student of New York history, actually of the history of anyplace she found herself, as well as a practicing anthropologist and full professor at New York University. So, knowing exactly how to treat a new discovery of almost any kind, it saddened her, grated against the very grain of her being, to move the document like this. It should have had the benefit of a specialist from the university or, better yet, the Smithsonian even before it was exposed to the raw air outside the cave—but it was too late for all that.

Too late because this document *could not* fall into the wrong hands. Greedy, self-serving hands, she knew from past experience, would most certainly defame and decry it.

She didn't want anyone knowing what she held, even those most in her confidence, as was David Greenberg.

No one other than Stephen Drum.

The cave itself had been discovered while a construction crew expanded a steam line servicing the building. The side foundation wall had been broken into, and the granite beyond caved in, decomposed like sand—and a cavern opened before them. A hand-held light of the crew chief, who luckily was standing almost next to the rift, shone into the opening revealed to him alone a number of Indian artifacts guarded by a few prostrate skeletons. Had the crew chief not also been a chief of the Oneida Nation and a reverent man in his own right, work would have continued as usual. But Thad Wintermoose stopped work immediately and ushered his crew away. He alone returned and set up barriers, fabricating a story for his crew, his bosses, and the building management. His foul-air tester, a soil-vapor extraction unit—a small, hand-held device he kept holstered on his waist when working below ground—had beeped, revealing hazardous and highly explosive methane gas in the cavern, and now probably filled the basement.

It was a lie he knew would keep them clear of the site until he could act.

No one was willing to die over a steam line.

Then he called Dr. Paula Fox from the building's foyer pay phone, having heard her reputation. A reputation regaled and even revered among many Native Americans.

Paula Fox immediately appealed to the New York State Anthropological Site Protection Agency, and work, as a result of a phone call placed to a very irritated contractor by the almost omnipotent agency, was suspended until the site could be properly evaluated.

The cab stopped at the impressive entrance to 40 Wall Street, and Paula paid the fare and climbed out. She stood staring up at the building, holding the black plastic bag carefully in front of her, wondering if she was doing the right thing. Finally, gaining confidence, she strode toward the wide bank of glass doors.

The image of Standing Bear in the tall windows melted away and Steve's contented half-smile faded as the intercom buzzed, jerking him back to the present.

Sally, his secretary, sounded bored as usual as her singsong voice echoed from the speakerphone. "Paula Fox is here . . . she doesn't have an appointment, but says she *has* to see you."

Steve rose from the floor and walked to the door to greet his old friend without bothering to answer his overdramatic secretary. Sally, though happily married, went out of her way to protect Steve from any woman she judged might be interested in him. It was not one of her job responsibilities, Steve thought, and smiled, knowing that Paula did not fill the bill of an interested woman. She was merely the oldest of friends and shared a mutual respect for heritage.

The fact was, the only woman he was interested in, in truth head over heels in love with, was, of course, one he couldn't have—one unknown even to Sally. He valued Sally highly, nonetheless. Sometimes her overprotectiveness came in most handy. He opened one of his eight-foot-tall double doors.

"Paula, come on in here. It's been far too long." He smiled broadly, and the smile worked its way up his angular face to penetrating dark eyes, but never quite erased the intensity in them. When he saw the creases between Paula's pretty, intelligent blue eyes, he knew something was dreadfully wrong. He stepped aside, letting his smile fade and forgoing the usual hug as she passed, carefully carrying a black plastic garbage bag cradled in her arms—held as if it contained the Holy Grail.

She walked straight to his desk, stopped, collected herself, and took a ragged breath before she spoke, centering worried eyes on his. "I'm going to show you something, but promise me you won't touch it. It's terribly fragile, and if I'm right, beyond value to you and me, and every Native American." She carefully removed a rolled brown paper, seemingly very old. Using the bag to keep her own skin oil off the parchment, she placed it in the center of his desk.

Paula, unusual for her, had no underlying humor in her voice and consequently Steve's undivided attention.

As she began explaining her find and its apparent contents, he began to wonder if the lives of the million Native Americans in the United States would ever be the same. The faded document on his desk could be the beginning—or the end—of the reservation system if not handled with the most delicate approach. It could cause a white backlash that would scar every Native American—if it was factual. Deep down, he doubted its authenticity.

But if authentic, it portended a change for the better, or possibly far, far worse.

If Paula was even close to right as to what she had, she had lain a magic carpet at his feet, or placed an iron yoke around his neck and the neck of a million others.

Even his experience as a Wall Street attorney for a half dozen years and the head of the Red Ace Corporation, which controlled a good chunk of Native American gambling in the United States for the past five, gave him no real background for the uniqueness of this find. *If* it was legitimate.

He had no way, at least not yet, of evaluating where this discovery would lead them.

It looked like there was a chance, albeit probably a very remote one, that Native Americans had a legal claim to an island.

Manhattan Island.

The next morning, his appointments canceled and death threats long out of his mind, the parchment disguised in a sealed hand-tooled metal canister emblazoned with the universal warning marked in bright red RADIATION, MEDICAL—DO NOT OPEN and casually packed in his carry-on bag among books and a paper authored by Dr. Stephen Drum on atomic medicine, he left his fourteenth-floor condo on the East Side.

Tuffy Jefferson, the doorman, hailed him a cab. Jefferson, a wide smile as always lighting his dark face, held the door for him. "No Town Car today, Mr. Drum?"

"Not today, Tuffy. I'm off for a few days. Watch the home front for me."

"You got it, Mr. Drum. Have a nice trip."

Steve liked Tuffy. He reminded him of some folks he knew back on the rez. Tuffy had put four of his kids through City College by tending doors, and Steve always overtipped him. And he was well repaid with service.

As they headed out of the city, Steve had some second thoughts about the trip. He and Paula had immediately concluded that the two of them, at least for the time being and until both agreed otherwise, would be the only ones to know of the discovery.

They also agreed that the only impartial observers to see the document—they had to have experts to flatten and decipher it—would be those with no ax to grind either way. Someone well outside the sphere of influence. Someone, they eventually concluded, outside the country. Most of the night had been spent determining who and where these experts would be. Finally, they decided they would go to someone with only a monetary ax to grind—a group of private experts who would be well paid.

Steve carried his own passport, along with a card identifying himself as Dr. Stephen Drum, Atomic Medicine, Johns Hopkins University. It was nice that New York had more than its share of sympathetic Native Americans in many skilled trades, including printing—and Steve Drum could call on them at any time of the day or night. It had been after midnight before this particular call had been made, with a deadline for the documents of six A.M. They had not let him down, had complied without questioning his reasons.

Steve patted the passport in his jacket pocket. By using his own name he was guilty only of impersonating a medical doctor.

He boarded a seven-thirty A.M. flight to Boston, then the nine-thirty A.M. Concorde to Paris. The ticket agent, as he had expected, made him check his carryon so the "dangerous" medical package would be in the cargo hold. He apologized profusely and proclaimed his ignorance. It went as planned. By late night Zurich time he would be in Switzerland and the document would be safely in the hands of specialists at Sotheby's Zurich office, who would, for a very large fee, flatten the foolscap without damaging it.

And then, and only then, with it flattened and protected in a sealed glass vacuum case, could he decipher the whole thing, again with the help of a specialist. But this time he would return to London and on to Oxford, and to a friend, another Native American, Patrick McGoogan, a professor of the history of comparative law who dealt with old documents routinely. Patrick had been a Harvard classmate of Steve's. His hobby, Steve recalled, was the five tribes of the Iroquois. There they would begin to judge the document's true value, if any.

If it was as genuine as he hoped it was, the real work would begin.

Proving it.

It was signed by a signature and a mark. One, he hoped but knew would be nearly impossible to prove, was the mark of a Canarsee chief, Onnegaha, and the other was Governor John Quinton Williamson, whom they could only pray had some authority in New York.

If it could be proven . . .

He knew it was a very, very long shot.

He settled back into the deep seat of the Concorde and sipped the Glenlivet scotch the stewardess had delivered even before the jet engines began to hum. It was the one and, normally, only drink he allowed himself daily, so he savored it. In this, he didn't want to follow in his father's footsteps. Stephen smiled and the stewardess who passed smiled back, but his smile wasn't for her. It was for the thought that passed through his mind.

He was wondering how the mayor of New York, and millions of New Yorkers, would react should he be able to hand them . . .

A three-day notice to "pay rent or quit."

CHAPTER TWO

Paula Fox returned to her apartment and tried to sleep after driving Stephen Drum to Kennedy Airport, but she was too excited—sleep wouldn't come even as exhausted as she was.

Finally she rose, showered, and dressed in her dig clothes. Hiking boots—lightweight for summer, mostly canvas—khaki shorts, short-sleeved shirt, and slouch hat. She gathered up her tools—a set of dental picks, a loupe, and a larger magnifying glass. The larger tools, sifters and digging implements, would already be on-site, knowing her able assistant, David. Hers was an outfit she normally packed for some remote location, along with three other changes, not dressed in while still in her Greenwich Village apartment.

Before she headed out the door for the subway, she noticed the flashing answering machine light and poked the button. She was not surprised at the half dozen awaiting calls. The first two were from David Greenberg and the next four from Peter Lund, the head of her department at NYU. The first two Lund calls were concerned, but the last two rang with irritation. She decided it would be best just to head for the dig, overcoming his first complaint by her presence, and return his call from there.

Paula had always had a tenuous relationship with Peter. Tall and imposing, cocksure, Lund had made a few semi-subtle yet clumsy passes at Paula her first and second years at NYU—she was now in her third—but she had skillfully sidestepped all innuendoes and kept her relationship purely professional. More and more he tried to lay the crap details on her—a petty vendetta for her lack of interest, she'd concluded, and determined it would be in her best interest to merely ignore it.

He'd been more than just a little irritated when she'd responded to Thad Wintermoose's call and gone to the discovery site without finding him first. She'd called, but luckily he was giving a lecture at the Metropolitan Museum. It gave her secret pleasure to leave him out of it. All he could be was irritated, since she'd taken the proper action. Still, he was peeved, and probably vindictive, at not being in on this fascinating discovery from the very onset.

To her surprise, as she exited the elevator into the garage level and headed for the stairway to the subbasement below, she ran into him.

"Hi, Peter," she said, trying to sound as normal as possible.

He seemed to collect himself. Wearing hiking boots and rough pants with a blue work shirt and maroon NYU-emblazoned tie, he appeared the proper head of department on-site—even though she'd always suspected him of being a tad color-blind because of the odd combination of colors he wore. He spoke with a tight jaw and eyes sparking with embers. "You look like hell. I've been trying to reach you since yesterday."

"I—"

"I understand you left the discovery to get your dig clothes, and no one has seen you since."

"I had a personal—"

"And I was informed you left the dig carrying a black plastic bag. I presume you found something you weren't prepared to share with your students, but, of course, you took it straight to the department."

She wondered which of the three student helpers had been so eager to report her leaving and the possibility that she'd left with something of value. "No," she managed to say.

She had sworn a blood oath with Steve that no one not directly involved in its restoration would know of the find until its worth, its cultural worth if nothing else, was evaluated.

"No, you didn't find anything, or no, you weren't prepared to share what you found and of course have taken whatever it was directly to the department for our joint study?" He eyed her like a pit bull at a pork chop in the butcher's window, his jaw clamped, awaiting her reaction and answer.

She sighed deeply, too tired to continue bantering with her overly officious, now glowering boss. "Peter, I didn't find anything. I came straight to the dig when I got beeped. I had a shopping bag with some things I picked up—"

"I think that's bullshit, Paula. I think you left this dig with something of value, and I'm very disappointed in you."

"Then I guess you just have to be disappointed if that's what you choose to believe."

"No, that's not all I have to be. That is not my only option. I suggest you turn yourself around and leave this site, and be in my office at nine in the morning. David Greenberg is in charge here until Robert gets here to take over."

Robert Wallis was the only other qualified field archaeologist on staff at NYU.

Paula shrugged, turned, and headed back to the elevator. But the fact was, she had to get back to the site. There was something there critical to the proof of their find.

Lund's voice rang after her. "Remember, Paula, you don't have tenure."

She didn't grace the remark with a response, but, rather, punched the elevator button and waited, giving only her back to Peter Lund.

She allowed herself the luxury of a cab back to Greenwich Village, but instead of going to her apartment, she had the driver let her off in front of her favorite deli, Mama Gold's. It was only eleven, but she was in need of a bowl of chicken soup. It usually cured almost anything that ailed her, including a little guilt and depression.

When she finally returned home, she was not only too excited to sleep, but too anxious.

She loved her job at NYU. But she loved this find even more. And she *had* to get back on the site, if only for a moment—she'd promised Steve she would. She knew it was absolutely imperative to their objective.

She prayed Stephen would call before her meeting in the morning, for moral support if nothing else.

Nuzzling her head deep in her pillow, she closed her eyes. It always relaxed her to think of the Mission Valley, and her teaching there. She took a deep breath, and recited:

> "Ko-es may-yestwh yetl-wha skal-halt,
> ko-es chi-test-tewh, ko-es t'hom-stewh,
> ko-es ch-shee-e-pi-lestwh,
> Ko-mee e-tse-hyl."

Then she repeated the prayer in English:

> "Teach me today,
> guard me, keep me straight,
> guide me.
> Amen."

As always, it calmed her, and she slept.

Thad Wintermoose also had a call on his answering machine when he returned to his Brooklyn Heights apartment. More than just a call, it was a demand. He was to put in a command appearance at his employer, the Manhattan offices of East River Contractors and Demolition at eight A.M. The call didn't surprise him. He knew he was in Adam's-apple-deep shit when he had fooled his coworkers with his methane gas trick, and had fooled building security to the extent they had evacuated the building. He'd stood watching with his chin on his chest, mouth agape, as a building full of eight-to-fivers filed by.

He'd mumbled his surprise aloud. "Chicolini may look like an idiot, he may sound like an idiot, but don't let that fool you—he really is an idiot. Groucho Marx, *Duck Soup* . . . and so am I." Thad mimed flipping the ash from his cigar.

Thad Wintermoose was a movie buff with a collection of over a thousand videos and was seldom stuck for a line. He thought this one particularly appropriate for this mass exodus. He had no idea how much it cost in time and actual dollars to shut down a midtown Manhattan ten-story building, but he knew it was a hell of a bunch.

He smiled to himself since there was no one to share it with in his little apartment, knowing it really wasn't funny. Still, he viewed it as an act of respect to the entombed Native Americans in the cave below, even if the hundreds of building occupants didn't know they were filing by the bier. There should have been a dirge playing, both for the remains and for his job.

He was resigned to the fact he might have to go back to high-iron work. He was as sure as a Missouri mule is stubborn, he was about a dozen hours from being fired. And to tell the truth, he didn't blame them a damn bit.

As stubborn as that proverbial mule, he verbalized his thought. "Frankly, Scarlett, I don't give a damn."

He'd protected a part of his Native American history. Kept a possible holy place from being desecrated as had so many before. That was enough for him. There were jobs everywhere for a man who could walk the high iron—he'd done it before. He could do it again.

Besides, by far the best of all of it was the fact he'd gotten to meet Dr. Paula Fox.

What a woman!

Luckily no one sat beside Stephen Drum on the trip from Boston to Paris, so he got almost two hours sleep. He was not so lucky on the Lufthansa flight from Orly to Zurich.

The thin man with the window seat, receding hairline, and quick, piercing blue eyes wasted no time in making conversation in a heavy accent. "You look like the American film star . . . Smits. Jimmy Smits."

Steve merely smiled, and shook his head.

It didn't quell the man. "I do much business in China. You are part Chinese, Eurasian perhaps?" While mopping a perspiration-gleaming brow, he asked the question in Mandarin Chinese to Stephen's surprise, since Mandarin *was* Stephen's second language. While at Harvard he had studied the language extensively, believing that with a billion and a quarter people, China would soon take Japan's place as the strongest Asian business power. He even kept a Chinese houseboy whom he ordered not to speak English, only Mandarin, while at the condo. Conversing with him kept Stephen's Chinese sharp.

The question was one Stephen had been asked before. His high cheekbones, complexion like a deep reddish Caucasian suntan, fooled some.

"I'm not Eurasian, not for the last ten thousand years or so," he answered in almost perfect Mandarin, hoping that would keep his seat mate busy thinking for a while, but no such luck.

"You're American," the man surmised, and Stephen was disappointed, knowing his Chinese must be steeped in an American accent. "I'm from Antwerp myself. So you must have Chinese ancestors . . . are you from San Francisco?"

Stephen smiled. He really didn't know his heritage for quite ten thousand years. "Could be some Chinese in there somewhere, if ancient Americans truly came across the Bering Sea ice pack. I'm Salish." Again, he hoped that would shut the man up. He wanted to sleep, to help adjust to the time change.

"Montana, at least the Pacific Northwest," the man stated, switching to English. He was so thin, his predominant Adam's apple bobbed when he spoke, and his eyes bulged slightly, but he was obviously well educated. "Do you speak German?"

"No."

"Too bad. You know German is the language of Zurich. I go there often for business. My German is excellent. A very civilized and efficient place, Zurich."

Stephen grunted his agreement.

"I've fished the Flathead River near the Salish reservation," the Belgian continued. "I'm an expert fly fisherman, and an accomplished outdoorsman."

Stephen could picture this guy on the creek. He would be Orvis's "dream fisherman" with every possible tool and toy to go along with his thousand-dollar fly rod and reel. But rather than pursue it, he said quietly, "I hope you enjoyed Montana," trying his best to be polite but put an end to the conversation.

"Yes, very much. I have never understood the American treatment of you natives."

For a moment Stephen thought the man sympathetic to the Native American cause. Then the man flashed a condescending smile.

"Why your government thinks it must have sovereign nation-states within its borders is beyond my comprehension." He eyed Stephen, obviously hoping to get a rise out of him.

Stephen was too tired to banter. "Is that so," he said, and turned away from the man, fluffing a pillow and closing his eyes.

"Yes, that is so. And the gambling issue . . . I enjoy gambling. But for one group of Americans to have such an advantage over another? It seems to go against your American idea of democracy."

Stephen sighed and turned back, getting out of his slouch and sitting up straight. "Any state can approve gambling for or by any of its citizens, if it so wishes, by a majority vote of those citizens, as has Gary, Indiana, or haven't you heard of rust-belt roulette; Nevada, of course; New Jersey; and several others. The Mississippi is covered with gambling boats again, as is the Gulf Coast. Some don't think it right for them, and I for one respect their wishes and beliefs.

"Do you know of our loss of the buffalo, of a way of life?"

"I know American history." The man's attitude about his knowledge of history and politics seemed about as humble as his opinion of himself as a fisherman. "And I understand democracy."

"Actually," Stephen managed to say, stifling a yawn, "the United States is a republic. A federal system with a lot of divisions of semi-autonomous areas, mostly states, and possessions, and, yes, reservations with sovereign rights gained . . . granted by God . . . long before any European graced the shores of North or South America. Long before there were any United States or possessions. Of course those rights have been 'protected' by a hundred broken and dishonored treaties, since most Native American lands were stolen from the indigenous peoples who had claimed them for three hundred or more generations. It's not commonly known, but some native North American cultures lived in cities almost as impressive and sophisticated as the pyramids of Egypt or Mexico. They farmed, carried on trade from the Pacific to the Atlantic . . . while your Flanders, by the way, was still in the deep throes of the Dark Ages in mud and wattle huts."

The man didn't seem impressed that he knew Belgium was formerly Flanders, but Steve continued anyway.

"We, as Native Americans, were starved into a temporary submission. As to gambling . . . we prefer to think of our right to enjoy gambling on sovereign reservations as . . . the return of the buffalo."

The man smiled tightly, unfazed. "The other side of the question is the right of the victor. And you were, after all, a conquered people. And, of course, there is economic dominance . . . what I saw of the reservations was not so impressive."

"Then I'm sure you didn't see much of the reservations. And to a great extent, that is the way the world works today. Do you know how a Native American was judged before the Europeans presumed they had the right to do so?"

"I imagine I do. As a warrior, of course. But you enlighten me."

"As most civilized nations *should* judge men, and be judged themselves. Not by whom he's conquered or what he possesses, but, rather, by what he's *given away*. Think about that. And if you know the history of the United States, do you know of the Trail of Tears and the theft of land and well-developed European-style farms of sixteen thousand Cherokees? Or Wounded Knee? Or the good Christian Chiverton's raid? Or Sand Creek? Or the Dineh's long walk where those women and children who fell behind were shot by white soldiers? If you don't, then you know little of the history of the *Native* American, only the history as written by people of European descent. And I can tell you that written history is seldom objective, or fair."

That quieted him for a moment. But it didn't last. "That's a noble thought, being judged by what you give not what you have, but hardly one that works in today's world. Again, I say, the spoils belong to the victor."

"Yes, and it's true the Anglo *was* the victor in westward expansion, at least in the first three centuries of our relationship with them, in the *first* battles. The next century is yet to be judged, and what has happened in the past . . . is prologue. The *war* is now an economic one . . . and long from over."

The man's bulging eyes centered on him coldly, as if he were a few cards short of a full deck, which irritated Stephen, so he added, "Nevertheless, how would Belgium know so much about the right of victors, at least in this century?" That caused the man's sunken cheeks to redden, but at least shut him up, and Steve was able to doze.

Zurich lay at the north end of Zurichsee, a beautiful deep blue quarter-moon-shaped mountain lake, and the moon itself cast a long line across the lake by the time the plane arrived. The Lufthansa jet swept low over the blue-black water as Steve awoke to the stewardess making a fasten-seat-belt-and-raise-your-seatbacks announcement. For a second, as he focused out the window on the sun setting over the high Alps, he thought he was landing at the Kalispell Airport in Montana.

But these were the Alps, not the Rockies. And this was Zurichsee, not Flathead Lake.

He'd been in Zurich twice before. He knew that upon clearing customs he could have his bags checked directly onto the finely tuned electric train without having to bother with them, but he was in no hurry. He hailed a cab, loaded his two small bags, and took a leisurely drive into the city.

Hotel Franziskaner, Niederdorfstrasse 1, Zurich, in the central city, had been recommended to Stephen by Patrick McGoogan, his friend at Oxford. Steve was pleased at its old world charm, central location, and modest price, since he was looking for a place only to park his body for the night.

He waited until ten P.M. to call Paula Fox, then did so from his room, surprised to find her home in New York's midafternoon. He'd expected to have to leave word on her machine. "Hey, how are you?"

"Wonderful," she said, deciding not to worry him with her problems with Lund and the university, and the fact she had no idea how she was going to get back onto the site to do what she'd agreed to do while he was in Europe. "More important, how are you and your . . . your *paperwork* doing?"

"Great. I have an appointment midmorning, as you know. I'll call again as soon as I finish and know something."

"I'll probably be right here."

"Is something wrong?" he asked, suddenly concerned at her worried tone.

"No, absolutely not. Just tired." She reaffirmed her decision not to clutter his mind with her troubles. "I imagine you're as beat as a stepchild in a foster home."

"That's a stepchild or a foster child, not both."

"Oh."

"Actually I'm ready for bear. Don't know how I'll be in the morning, or if I can sleep. But I'm so wound up that it probably won't catch up with me for days."

There was a long silence before she spoke. "Call me when you're out of . . . out of your appointment."

She was being particularly cautious, a wise decision, Steve decided. "I will. Get some rest. Tomorrow could be a red letter redman's day, or another Wounded Knee."

CHAPTER THREE

Steve awoke shaking his head in disgust, wondering what the hell he was really doing in Switzerland when he had work to do all over the United States.

He'd left with the enthusiasm of a teenager mugging in the backseat with a girl for the first time and now had a sour taste in his mouth about the whole affair. If it hadn't been for Paula . . . He felt like a man who'd bought a treasure map in a curio shop for fifty cents, thinking it real, but just discovered otherwise.

He'd know soon enough.

Sotheby's Swiss branch was a three-story rococo building located on Rue du Gustave in Zurich's Lindenhof section on a hill above the Limmat River, a longish cab ride from the hotel. The leaves were turning along the river. It was old-world breathtaking. He was happy he'd allowed time to enjoy the view.

Sotheby's location was as solid as the permanence of time, and as old as the Mississippian city of Cahokia that he'd partially described to the thin-faced Belgian. The upper floors of the building overlooked the old quarter, an ancient Roman settlement.

Steve departed his cab and glanced at his watch: ten A.M., right on the money. He stood for a moment admiring the building and its surroundings, half expecting a huge cuckoo bird to appear out of one of the upper windows and tweety-tweet out the time.

Americans, and he at one time had been as guilty as the rest, often thought of the United States as an almost omnipresent, omnipotent country. Europeans, he had learned after many trips abroad—this was his third here to Switzerland, although the prior two had been to ski—thought of the United States as a Johnny-come-lately for whom only time would prove worth, or not. After his first trip to Europe, he could understand that feeling.

Particularly now, as he looked down upon a twenty-century-old settlement on the banks of the Limmat River.

He smiled. It was not like him to engage in deep thinking, caught up as he was in the day-to-day, even hour-to-hour hubbub of gambling. Maybe the document he held in its aluminum tube would lead him to think again, and far more seriously, of his past and his people.

In typical Swiss fashion, Herr Frederick Grindelwold kept him waiting only seconds, then escorted him down into a dark basement, along a narrow hall, then into a well-lighted room with glass tubes and white worktables resembling a medical laboratory. Three spotlessly dressed white-uniformed men worked over various antiquities and artworks.

"Would you enjoy coffee, Herr Drum?" his short, balding, slightly effeminate host inquired.

"Actually I had more than my share at the hotel, thank you. How long do you think this will take?"

"I presume this tube contains the document and not some deadly virus?" He smiled, though tightly.

"Yes, the medical markings were only a precaution . . . prying eyes and all that." Steve handed him the tube.

The Swiss antiquities expert took the tube, seemingly used to such precautions in the moving of documents and artworks from one country to another. Many times such transfers were strictly illegal.

"It is not vacuum sealed?" Grindelwold inquired.

"No, there wasn't time."

"Then we can begin right away. Do you have flight reservations?"

"Actually, no. I had no idea what your timetable would be, and I intend to wait with you . . . with the document . . . until you're finished."

"I understand. I am sure you will be able to make an evening flight. Foolscap is a size and parchment a material we are accustomed to working with. How do you Americans say, it will be a snap of the fingers."

"Yes, a snap."

Steve watched with interest as the document was removed, placed on a sterile surface, then carefully sprayed with a fine mist that smelled of alcohol or resin of some kind. Ever so carefully, waiting and spraying in between, the technician began unrolling the foolscap. Before Steve realized it, two hours had passed, with the technician only half finished.

Herr Grindelwold had returned to his office, but stuck his head back into the lab and called to Steve, "Herr Drum, I would be pleased to have you accompany me to take lunch."

"No, thank you. I'm not leaving the document. If someone could bring me something back?"

"As you wish."

When the technicians in the lab broke for lunch, which they took from paper sacks and enjoyed across the room—brown baggers even in Switzerland—Steve had a chance to study the writing now exposed through a powerful magnifying glass. But it was almost nonsensical to him, written in Old English. He knew it would make perfect sense to his good friend, Patrick McGoogan at Oxford.

They finished by four P.M., with only the tech working directly upon the document taking an untold interest in its content. He assured Steve that he spoke but read no English. Steve had to assume if he read no English, or that even if he read a little English, he certainly read no Old English.

Steve paid the fifteen-hundred-dollar fee in cash.

This time it was an Air Italia flight he caught at just after seven P.M. He landed and was out of Heathrow and on his way to Oxford by ten.

Paula Fox slept like the proverbial rock through the clanging of her alarm, and was barely able to make her meeting at NYU.

Peter Lund; Arnold McTavish, NYU's director of personnel; and, to Paula's surprise and chagrin, a Lieutenant Oliver Michael Toole of the New York City Police Department awaited her.

Overdramatically, Lund introduced the police officer, whose red-blotched face was obviously not from his too-tight collar. They all took seats at the conference table opposite her. It was clear to Paula that sides had been drawn long before she arrived—and she was literally and figuratively alone on hers.

Before Lund could continue, Paula interrupted. "It would seem if you feel the need for a police officer, I should feel the need of an attorney."

Lund cleared his throat. "You are accused of taking something from the dig site at the Andrew McGuire Building."

"And just who made this accusation?"

This silenced Lund for a moment. He glanced at both other men. "It really doesn't matt—"

"Maybe it doesn't matter to you, Peter, but it certainly matters to me. Since when do you *not* get to face your accuser in this country?"

For the first time since being introduced, Toole spoke up. "This is not a trial, Ms. Fox. I was invited here to hear your explanation. You're certainly not under arrest, but if you feel you need an attorney, I suggest you summon one."

Paula could feel the heat rise to her cheeks. "I not only don't feel the need for an attorney, I don't feel the need to sit through some stupid sophomoric inquisition." She rose and pointed a finger at Lund. "You, sir, had best walk on eggshells. To risk a cliché, those in glass houses should not cast stones." Even though Lund's flinch at this was a tiny motion, she could see it well enough. It gave her more than a little satisfaction to note his knee-jerk, eye-twitch response. And she could hardly keep from smiling when the Irish cop looked at Lund with some interest.

NYU had already had its share of sexual harassment suits, and even though she'd never consider taking that kind of action because of his clumsy passes, it seemed, as Stephen Drum had said many times, the best defense was a good offense. Particularly when she knew for a fact that this time she was in the wrong. At least as far as the law was concerned. But she was on a roll now, so she continued her tactical advance.

"This smacks of some kind of McCarthyism. I have a mind to go directly to the teachers' union and *The New York Times*."

"Don't you think you're being a little dramatic?" Lund asked, beginning to redden.

"No, I don't. I think you're being a little dramatic having a police officer at a personnel hearing. . . . In fact, having a hearing at all, since there's nothing to be heard." She spun on her heel and made for the door.

"Don't you dare run out!" Lund snapped behind her.

She spun back. "I am not running, Lund. I'm walking out on you and these silly tactics. You can ask Dean Williamson to call me if this discussion is to be continued. Otherwise, I'll be back on the dig in the morning."

"No, you won't—" He was cut off by her slamming the door.

As she made her way to the car, she wondered which of her students had been the one to report her carrying something out of the dig. Neither of the girls seemed to be interested in anything other than their grades and getting out of school and on to some exotic location.

It was fairly common to find very valuable artifacts when a discovery was made, and common for all involved to be suspect. She wondered, for the first time since she had become involved, if she wasn't more likely to be a suspect since her people, Native Americans, were the subject. She had to choke back the notion of being persecuted, then smile because the "persecution" was well deserved in this instance.

Still, it paid to know thy enemy.

David Greenberg, unlike the girls, was a journalism major and an archaeology minor. He wanted to *write* about archaeology, not practice it, even though he'd proved to be very good at the practical aspects of a discovery. But writing was his real forte. He part-timed at some Greenwich Village exposé rag.

She'd always trusted him explicitly, but now she wondered. Hell, all press people were basically muckrakers. It seemed to go with the territory.

Still, she'd be truly disappointed . . .

She spent the afternoon at the Metropolitan Museum. She'd considered going straight to the dig and trying to brazen her way in. She *had* to get back to that dig. But she decided against it, as she knew Lund would have cautioned them against allowing her on the site. And she didn't want to put David on the spot in case he wasn't the guilty party who'd ratted her out. She had to find another way.

She hadn't taken the time to enjoy the Met since she first came to New York. It took her mind off her problems. Then she took in an old Cary Grant, Rosalind Russell movie, *His Girl Friday*, at the Art Nouveau theater near her apartment. At three bucks she could afford it, at least for a few days she could afford it. It was after ten before she allowed herself to go back to her apartment. She had a stiff shot of brandy while soaking in her old claw-foot tub before she pulled on a flannel nightgown and crawled into bed.

She dreamed of Cary Grant and smiled in her sleep.

Steve's home phone rang and the machine's speaker echoed throughout his vacant condo. "Hi, Steve Drum here. Leave it and I'll get right back to you." The beep signified it was time to record the message, but the only sounds were the simple tones coming from the machine: one, two, three, being punched in. His messages replayed. "Message one, nine forty-five A.M. Wednesday," the machine said, then a sultry woman's voice came on. "Hi, just checking up on you. I'll be in the city on Friday. When do you want to get together?" Then the machine again, "Message two, four forty-seven P.M. Wednesday." This voice was much gruffer and muffled, as with a hankie over the phone. "You prick, stay away from St. Regis and our casinos or we'll tack and dry your hide on the outhouse wall and use it for butt wipe." Then the machine again, "Message three, eight-twelve A.M. Thursday," and another male voice. "Steve, Alex Dragonovich here. My people told me what a great presentation you made. I've decided you can help us with a negotiation at Shiprock. Give me a call."

The man surreptitiously checking Steve's calls sat in a dark sedan in Central Park, making notes, a cell phone to his ear. He closed his notebook as the machine announced that the previous call was the last, then started the car and roared off.

He slapped his palm against the wheel hard enough to make it reverberate and uttered only one word aloud, "Bastard," then gunned the car, swerving around the vehicles blocking his angry route.

At the same time his calls were being usurped in New York, Steve awoke in Oxford to the sound of someone rapping on the door.

"That'll be Mrs. Coddington with morning tea and scones."

Patrick's deep voice brought him back to where he was. He raised his head from his crossed arms on the table.

"What time is it?" he asked, rubbing his eyes.

"Must be six-thirty if it's tea and scones. Trust me, you'll like her scones."

When Steve's eyes cleared, he could see the scroll still in its protective box, and the sight of it refocused his attention on why he was there. Beside it lay several sheets of paper bearing his learned friend's large printing.

Patrick returned from the door with tray in hand. "Are you a strawberry and heavy clotted cream fan? You must have made a good impression on my landlady."

"You get clotted cream for a good impression? What do you get for a bad one?"

"You'll like it, you backwoods bumpkin."

"I'd eat roadkill this morning . . . it seems I've forgotten a few meals since I left New York." He rubbed the kinks out of the back of his neck with one hand. ". . . So, I fell asleep during the most exciting part. What's it look like to you?"

"You'd better get something in your belly first."

Steve's spirits fell, presuming it to be bad news, but Patrick caught his expression. "No, *compadre* . . . I should say yes. It's the damnedest document I've ever had the pleasure of interpreting. I've got to get to the library and deep into the archives, and possibly to the Hag's files in Amsterdam, but if it's legitimate as to time and place, and as to the signatures . . . it's a treaty, and a damned complicated one at that. But the long and short of it is, the treaty gives this Canarsee chief and his people rights to a hell of a chunk of the north half of Manhattan Island."

"Why the Hag?"

"The Dutch settled New Netherlands and founded New Amsterdam, now known as New York—you ignorant Montana dolt."

Steve smiled sheepishly. "What tribe are the Dolts?" Then he laughed. "You mean a Native American actually got a piece of land *back* from the white-eye?"

"As wild a thought as it is, yes. It seems that's what this is all about. Seems these ignorant Europeans messed their own nest and there was a cholera epidemic in the Dutch camp at Fort Orange . . . that was way on up on the west bank of the river, where Albany now resides. This Canarsee chief took pity on the

Dutch and English and brought his people back from Long Island, where they'd retired after selling Manhattan for such a huge sum twenty-five years before. Anyway, the Indians fed and nurtured the camp until a few of the Dutch recovered. The tribe was not spared, however, and almost half of them ended up lost to the disease.

"And the Dutch patroon, John Quinton Williamson, asked the Canarsee—"

"What are you talking about, Dutch? This thing is in Old English, and *Williamson* sure as hell isn't a Dutch moniker. If the Dutch were in control—"

"True, but this Dutch patroon had an Englishman running the fort, ol' Captain J. Q. Williamson. They were all sailing men, and some of the best were English. The Dutch would turn a dollar, or guilder in this instance, any way they could—hell, they'd deal with the devil for half a guilder. Anyway, what he wanted for this kindness, the old chief, I mean, actually he was called a sachem . . . it seems the old patroon's daughter was one of those nursed back to health by the chief himself . . . and this Canarsee wasn't bashful. He obviously believed in your philosophy; if you're gonna be a bear, be a griz." Patrick laughed a deep guffaw. "What the old chief wanted was to return to the island of his birth and become a neighbor, and this treaty grants that right."

Steve seemed puzzled. "I thought Manhattan was named for the Manhattan tribe who occupied the island?"

"I don't recall studying that, but even if that's true, the tribes moved around, just as they did in your part of the world. Manhattan Island consists of more than one watershed, and like the West, the tribes tended to occupy a particular drainage, or more than one adjacent watershed if they could hold them from interlopers. Actually, there's some thought that Manhattan, or *manna hatin*, as two words, is actually an Indian phrase meaning 'place of the whirlpool, or island of the mountain' . . . there's disagreement on even that among the so-called experts. You did study a little Native American history, didn't you, Steve?"

Patrick guffawed again, then turned serious. "I won't know how much land until I can refer to some old maps and landmarks, but it looks like a hell of a lot. It appears that this patroon at Fort Orange must have owned some major portion of Manhattan . . . at least let's hope so. None of those folks at that time, including our New York cousins, were bashful about selling something in which they owned no interest." He rubbed his chin thoughtfully. "I want to spend some time in the bowel of the Bodleian Library. There well could be some correspondence there that might just help establish this as a factual document. And of course I need to dig up some documents with the old patroon's signature and that of his provisional governor."

"So, what's a patroon?"

"Let me get cleaned up, which wouldn't hurt your cause with the ladies, and we'll make a pass by my office so I can straighten up some things and get loose for the afternoon. Thank God for my light, autumn schedule. By that time it'll be noon, then we'll head to McGillicuty's Pub and I'll accept lunch in trade for a history lesson on New Netherlands over a mug of good ale and some fish and chips or kidney pie . . . after I finish in the loo." Patrick headed for his tiny bathroom, which certainly wouldn't hold the two of them.

He turned back and said in all seriousness, "I think, if this treaty is not contradicted by the takeover of the English in 1664, and if there's no record of the old chief trading out his interest for a few shekels sometime later, and—the big *if*—if you can find some descendants for whom to stake a claim, then we can write a hell of a Supreme Court brief to establish some rights here." He shook his head, laughed in amazement again, then closed the loo door.

CHAPTER FOUR

"My God," was all Steve could manage to his friend's broad back as he closed the bathroom door behind him. Steve sat for a moment, spread some of the heavy cream on his scone, but merely stared at it, his thoughts in Manhattan.

He hadn't really allowed himself to believe truly that this document, this treaty, could be legitimate. If it hadn't been Paula Fox who brought it to him . . . Even so, he'd treated it in his own mind as a lark. But now he was beginning to see its far-reaching possibilities.

If it was legitimate, it was merely a chip on a no-limit table that had a six-pack of other players who held piles of chips, and stacked decks—but as a Native American he was used to poor odds.

How could this be used to the advantage of his people?

He'd been among the first to see the great advantage gaming could bring to the reservations and he'd capitalized upon it. Not only for his own economic benefit, but for the many reservations that now had cash flow for schools, housing, child care, and job creation.

For Native Americans, gaming truly was the return of the buffalo.

But unlike gaming, which took place only on sovereign reservations, this chip was a key to a chunk of the richest island in the United States . . . hell, maybe in the world.

The Indian Gaming Regulatory Act of 1993 had prohibited gambling on reservations that didn't have a compact with their respective states. Even Steve's own reservation, the Confederated Salish and Kootenai Tribes, had had problems and only recently been able to reopen casinos, and they were entitled to little more than other Montana gaming establishments located all over the state, with poker and lotto machines in almost every bar. The white-eye was continually chipping away at Indian gaming rights.

It was Steve's belief that there was only a limited window for Native Americans to strike at the economic heart of gaming. And they'd best strike fast while the iron was hot.

As the Belgian on the plane had pointed out, the United States was a democracy, less of a republic all the time, and eventually the rest of the country would realize this and tire of the Indian economic advantage and would vote themselves equality. There are two hundred fifty million of them, and only a million of us.

He had to figure a way to continue the advantage for all Native Americans.

And he knew this treaty was only a chip, only a wedge to drive into the status quo—a wedge that would have to be *so* cleverly used. One million Native Americans could benefit from what he had sitting before him on a small chrome and Formica table. And so could he.

But every step had to be exact.

Every move calculated.

He remembered what his grandfather had taught him the summer they hunted together after his father had been killed. Steve was used to hunting with his dad, who was strictly a meat hunter . . . but to old Standing Bear hunting was an art, almost a religion. He'd taught Steve patience. Steve remembered his exact words: "Step once, look twice." That was exactly what he must do now.

And he must be clever.

He had to get the opposition working against themselves. A buffalo jump. He had to get them running pell-mell to their own destruction. Still, like every buffalo hunt where the Indian had possessed only a yew stick, a string of sinew, and a handful of flint-tipped painfully straightened branches, it would be hard fought. Whatever it was he decided to seek, no matter how small a concession—he was setting out with a long, hard-shouldered, slick-rock mountain to climb.

He decided to call Paula and tell her the good news. At least it was news she wanted to hear . . . he hadn't yet decided if it was good news. It was damn sure exciting.

But first he had to call his answering machine. There was one person in his life who would call him only at home. He had been remiss in not seeing if her call had come in.

His machine answered with the message "You have no new calls," so he hung up, then wondered if he'd forgotten to listen to his messages the night he'd left for Switzerland . . . Hell, he'd check it when he got home. And then he wondered if he'd missed the call he really wanted. But he couldn't do anything about it until he was back in New York anyway.

He dialed Paula's home phone, knowing it was almost eleven P.M. in New York.

"I hope this is important," her groggy voice answered.

"Caught you sleeping?"

Instantly her voice was normal. "Hey, I hoped you'd call."

"Do you want the good news or the bad news?"

"The good."

"It seems as legit as an Indian agent is crooked."

"It couldn't be that good."

"So far we can't find a flaw, but Patrick is on his way to some library where he thinks he might find some documents with this Williamson's signature. Then he's worried it might be negated by the English takeover in 1664 . . . you might have mentioned that the Dutch controlled New York when this was signed."

"I didn't want to discourage you—good old practical you."

"Thanks. Anyway, if that didn't happen, his exact words were, 'We can write a hell of a Supreme Court brief.' "

She sighed deeply. "That's so good, I can hardly stand it. Now I know I won't be able to go back to sleep. What's the bad news?"

"There isn't any yet, which worries the hell out of me."

"You're such a bloody realist. Give your wings to the wind, my red brother."

"Give your head to the pillow, sis. I'll be on my way home as soon as I have a few more hours with Patrick. He's in the loo, or I'd put him on."

"The loo? You'd better get home before you start wanting tea and crumpets every afternoon."

Even with the light conversation, he noted something strange in her voice. "Are you okay? You sound worried."

"You know the old term, cheese it—"

"It's the cops." He finished for her. "You don't mean . . . ?"

"Wouldn't you know it, the cavalry is after us already. Peter Lund, my illustrious boss, called me on the carpet and had a bloated Irish cop in tow when he did."

"So, what happened?"

"Nothing yet. I did a Steve Drum and accused Lund of being everything from a mass murderer to a pedophile. . . . I even resorted to the old cliché 'Those in glass houses . . .' He'll think twice before he chucks any rocks, but he may be forced to. It seems one of my loyal students ratted me out for taking something from the site."

"Well, circle the wagons, your white knight is on the way home."

"Don't mix metaphors, particularly centuries apart. I'm in the middle of a Cary Grant dream, so I'll see you soon."

"At least it's not John Wayne."

"Remember Greasy Grass," she said, and he laughed.

With that they broke off.

Steve found the only overstuffed chair in the two rooms of Patrick's flat and sat with his tea and scone. It worried him that New York's Finest were involved, but with only the observation of a student in a darkened cave to go on . . . Still, Paula's taking the treaty from the site would have to come out sometime. It was the only way they could establish its validity, tying it to the dig, which meant admitting she'd taken it.

Hell, he'd cross that bridge, and her defense, when he came to it.

Worried that his expected call hadn't been on his phone, he dialed a New Jersey number and let it ring, but the wrong woman answered—at least it hadn't been a man's voice. Steve hung up, rude but necessary, then turned to Patrick's handwritten notes.

All Patrick had done was expand the tiny writing on the document to a legible size, but it was still in Old English filled with ye, hither, yon, and other more common words with a lot of Ys where consonants normally were and ending with extra Es. Even not understanding the odd sentence structure, he was able to get the gist of the document, and the gist appeared to be a hell of a chunk of the north half of Manhattan Island.

Patrick interrupted his study by turning over the loo to him. As he traded places with him, he agreed to meet Patrick at his office, then showered and shaved.

In a light pullover, khaki slacks, and Reeboks, he was ready for the fall English countryside. Before he walked out the door, he tried the New Jersey number again. This time the right voice answered. He knew she'd be near the phone if she was home, after his hang-up call. He smiled then asked, "Is Greta in?"

"No Greta here." He could hear the humor in her voice.

"Rats, I'm calling all the way from London."

"London! My that must be expensive. Sorry, no Greta here, Mr. Friday."

"Thanks, that's just fine. I'll probably be a little jet-lagged . . . but fine."

As he hung up, he heard her mother's voice in the background. "Angela, who's on the phone?" He hung up, knowing she knew where he was, and that she would meet him Friday in New York.

He decided to while away a couple of hours walking around Oxford, enjoying the ancient architecture and a few bookstores. Stopping in a tea shop, he took advantage of another cup and a biscotti, then, nearing noon, headed for Patrick's office.

Patrick greeted him with a gloomy face. Steve sighed deeply, knowing it had been too good to be true. Patrick said quickly, noting the sigh, "I called the research librarian at the Bodleian. He informed me after a quick check of the index that there was very little in the way of correspondence from New Amsterdam and no treaties between the Dutch and the Canarsee. But don't get nervous yet. I'm a great fan of Amsterdam and I'll take a couple of days and go see what the Dutch have in their libraries . . . ." He unlimbered from his chair. "Let's go eat, and I'll give you that history lesson . . . of course the charge is lunch and all the ale I can drink."

"I didn't bring my life savings," Steve said with a less than enthusiastic smile.

"I'm telling you, don't worry. I'll find us enough to have the New York government reeling and crying for a settlement."

"Don't underestimate these city boys. New York City government is gristle tough. Probably the toughest rough-and-tumble bunch of double-talking hard-asses in the country, if not the world. And New York State is no less. They've seen and heard it all. This looks like it's gonna be a long, hard fight."

Patrick pulled his office door open and waved Steve through, and he said with a hard tone, "It's been a long hard three hundred years, so what's new."

"True, my red brother. True."

Steve and Patrick drank the afternoon away, something Steve seldom did anymore. Patrick brought him up to speed on New Amsterdam history, then they caught up on old times.

Thad Wintermoose reported to his company's office on the East River in Manhattan.

His boss actually called him a bastard, to which Thad replied, "Yes, sir. With me, an accident of birth. But you, why, you're a self-made man."

While his boss furrowed his brow and tried to figure out what Thad had said, Thad walked out, in his mind thanking Lee Marvin and the writers of *The Professionals.* One of his favorite old films. Actually, Thad knew his parents well and was satisfied with his birth status, but he couldn't resist the line.

He was there for only fifteen minutes and left with his final check in hand, including a little over ten thousand for six years of funded retirement—thank God he'd made it past five, or he would have received nothing.

He took a deep breath of the warming morning air and wondered what he would do to kill the day. He wasn't ready to look for another job, though he'd have to before the month was out. He didn't want to use up what little retirement he'd managed to sock away.

Before he'd walked a half-block, and after considering taking in an old movie, he knew exactly where he was going. He wanted to check in with Dr. Paula Fox to see if laying down his job for the Native American cause had come to anything. He'd be real disappointed if those skeletons were a bunch of Puerto Ricans who'd been planted to hide the bodies.

He laughed, then thought aloud of Paula Fox. "Not much meat on her, but what's there is choice," he muttered, pronouncing the words in his best Spencer Tracy Brooklynese. He pondered over what film it came from as he hailed a cab and headed for NYU.

Unexpectedly he got a very cold reception when he finally found the archaeology department. He was informed by the secretary, with a cold tone, that Dr. Fox was not in and not expected.

He wandered out, again lost for a way to kill the day, then realized she must be working at the McGuire Building, or maybe at home. He spotted a pay phone. To his surprise, her number was listed. And more to his surprise, she answered her home phone.

"Hi, it's Thad Wintermoose. I just wanted to check and see if that hole in the basement came to anything."

"Haven't you been back to check it out?" Paula asked with a warm feeling for this man who'd had the foresight to protect what might prove to be the most valuable archaeological discovery ever in New York State, maybe in all the states. Maybe in the world, at least so far as Native Americans were concerned.

"No, to tell the truth, my company . . . I should say, my *old* company . . . wasn't quite as happy about it as you seem to be. I got canned this morning."

"You're kidding?"

"Another nice mess you've gotten me into," Thad said with a laugh. "Actually, I was tired of that job anyway. I don't suppose you'd have time to tell me about this hole in the ground . . . I mean, is it a find worth finding?"

Paula felt a little guilty. "Where are you?"

"I'm at NYU. I came by your office—"

"I'm not sure it is my office any longer . . . I may have gotten the ol' boot also."

"You're kidding? All good things must end. As was said in a fairly decent film long ago, 'In the morning of my race I have seen a winged ship arrive, bearing the white men who are to become the masters of our land, and before the sunset I have seen the last of the Mohicans.' "

"Actually, it was the *passing* of the last of the Mohicans."

Thad was silent for a moment, stunned, then he recovered his composure. "Bull. I never miss on old movies."

"Well, you missed on this one, Wintermoose."

"Let's have coffee and settle it like two civilized Indians."
Paula paused a moment.

Thad Wintermoose waited, sensing that the first to speak lost.

A thousand thoughts raced through Paula's mind. The last thing she wanted was to become involved with a construction worker. But she owed him the courtesy of at least a cup of coffee, after what he'd done. "You name the place to powwow."

You lose, I win, thought Thad, and gave her a place. She countered with Mama Gold's deli. He got the address and got off the phone before she could change her mind.

When he hung up, he was still shaking his head. A woman who knew her movies, and was fantastic in other ways as well. Maybe she was too damn smart for a hardheaded high-iron man!

No guts, no air medals, he decided, unconsciously quoting another old movie line. He'd find out soon enough.

He left the pay phone and headed for a cab. A silly grin covered his usually stoic, wide face, for a man who'd just lost a six-year job.

Joseph Bigsam reclined in a deep padded chair with his eyes on the bank of one-way mirrors lining his office on three sides. From his comfortable perch high above the casino floor he could see most of what was happening with the play below. If he wanted a closer look at a dealer or pigeon, he could unlimber his large frame and take one of three walkways traversing the forty-thousand-square-foot gambling establishment, twenty-five feet above the tables. In addition, the place featured an adjacent twenty-thousand-square-foot bingo parlor with ninety-thousand-dollar payouts, four hundred times those offered by regulated parlors in Syracuse, two hundred miles to the southwest.

Consequently, both Canadians and New Yorkers flocked to the rez to gamble, not to speak of residents of Pennsylvania, Vermont, Massachusetts, Connecticut, Ohio, and Michigan, who had regular bus gambling junkets set up now that Bigsam had built a two-hundred-room motel across the road.

Big Sam's International Gaming Pavilion was the Akwesasne-St. Regis Reservation's largest. And, he was sure, its most profitable.

Joe Bigsam's eyes were on the mirrors, but his thoughts were

on his troubles. All the casinos on the New York side of the shared
New York/Canadian reservation had their problems. The extent
of them was evidenced by the twenty AK-47s in the rack on the
wall behind Bigsam's desk. They'd been removed from their racks
more than once, including one time when over one hundred FBI
agents had stormed the place trying to confiscate the casino's slot
machines.

Bigsam and his men had faced down Washington's finest.

And they'd had their share of internal strife, with many hurt
and three killed. Usually, it was the antigambling Mohawks, the
Bible thumpers, who tried roadblocks and power outages or any
other way to shut them down. But hell, money always won, and
that was one thing of which they had plenty.

Thank God, the rez and the casino operators had what all causes
need most—zealots.

The Warriors, an unofficial police force of young Mohawks,
employed by the gambling interests, had faced the Fibies, the
FBI, down and won the everlasting respect of their long-dead
ancestors—at least that's what Joseph Bigsam and the other casino
owners had told them. There was nothing like a bunch of young
hotheads to put at the front of a siege, or a siege standoff. Particularly when you backed them in their butt-legging operations, as
cigarette smuggling was known on the rez, and fed them enough
dough to keep them in booze, cars, and broads. Hell, any young
man would respond to that combo.

But now the siege was a lot more ominous in its insidiousness,
more subversive. The tribal council—with the endorsement of
the Canadian-side Mohawks and, of course, the antigambling
Mohawks on both sides of the border—had hired an outside
consultant to come into the casinos and offer advice. A consultant
who was well recognized and had the endorsement of a dozen
reservation tribal councils across the country, and contacts in the
Department of the Interior and the Bureau of Indian Affairs in
Washington.

The first bit of good news was that the consultant was an Indian
himself and was involved in gambling. The bad news was he'd
been hired by the traditionalists and the antigambling Mohawks,
who'd forced the casino owners to cooperate by threatening an
all-out war. A war would keep customers away, even though
Bigsam and his cohorts were sure of winning. Wars, too, were

won with money. The second bit of good news was the man had canceled his inspection of the casinos that had been scheduled for over a month. Canceled it after one small threat via an anonymous note in the mail and a single threatening phone call. Hell, this was going to be too easy.

Bigsam and the other owners had a hundred-million-dollar-a-year business at stake, and they would brook no interference from anyone, particularly an outsider . . . even if an Indian one.

The casino operators agreed, in secret council, that first they'd try to simply scare him off. Unless he had giant cajones, that would work. If it didn't, they'd agreed to leave their options open after letting him wander around and see for himself how good the casinos were for the rez. Hell, anyone who wanted a job had one, not like the old days.

The consultant would learn little. Joe Bigsam, like the other casino operators, shredded the day's receipt reports at six each morning—right before he called it a night. No one but Joseph Bigsam knew the true results of the casino and bingo operation.

Still, if he's not scared off, if he showed, then Joe knew he would have to make a decision.

If he doesn't see it our way, Bigsam thought, then he'll see the highway, or . . . the bottom of the seaway.

They had too much at risk.

Stephen Drum flew with the sun on the way home, arriving at Boston at noon on Thursday, then at Kennedy by three-thirty. He was back in his office at five P.M. He was surprised that he could reach Paula at neither her office nor home. Deciding he'd try from the condo later, he returned all his calls waiting at the office, including one from his apparent new client, Alex Dragonovich, chairman of the board of International Consolidated Oil and Mining.

Steve had worked hard and waited a long time for this particular client to come calling. He'd made half a dozen presentations to Dragonovich's underlings hoping to get this call.

And now he had it.

He'd even gone so far as to rent space in the same Wall Street building as his hoped-for customer. And it had worked.

Sally stuck her head in his office door for the second time that morning. "I canceled your meetings in St. Regis. Do you want to reschedule them?"

"Yes, anytime next week," he said, knowing he must keep up with his workload. And that he must face the threats coming from the Mohawk reservation. As his old grandfather, Standing Bear, had told him many times—face your problems head-on, like a charging bison, or they'll never go away.

Sally eyed him for a moment. He knew she was curious about why he'd suddenly canceled everything to run off to Europe, but he also knew she wouldn't ask. She knew she'd learn as soon as he wanted her to know.

He walked to the tall windows and stared out at nothing in particular. He'd waited a hell of a long time to *again* meet Alex Dragonovich. Although Dragonovich would not remember meeting Steve before—in fact, Steve *counted* on Dragonovich not remembering.

When Sally gave him the notation of the call, he had thanked her, then asked her to give him a little time alone so he could think.

He'd relaxed at the big hickory desk and put his feet up on the credenza. This call, as much as he wanted it, came at a bad time. Steve's mind was consumed with both the problem and threat of the Mohawks, and with this new opportunity—if a three-hundred-fifty-year-old document could be called new. His time, he feared, would be dominated by both, but he had to make time—nothing could stand in the way of his gaining the complete confidence of Alex Dragonovich.

Twenty-five years before, when Steve was only twelve, he had met Dragonovich for the one and only time.

Then it was the Calico Mining Company who employed Dragonovich, the talented mining engineer and administrator. Since then Calico had been bought out by Golden Orb Mines, and Golden in turn by International Consolidated Oil and Mining, a company formed and substantially owned by Dragonovich.

Even as a teenager Steve had closely followed the career of the mining executive. And a meteoric rise it had been, over the financial carcasses of dozens of men and the actual carcass of at least one—Bob Lee Sounding Drum.

Steve had not let revenge dominate his thinking, but it had

niggled at him like a tick on the back of his neck—always there, dug in deep to the spine.

Steve returned to his tall windows, watching the city streets far below begin to fill with the afternoon rush.

He got a sudden taste of bile in his mouth as that long-ago afternoon's memories, that terrible afternoon, flooded his mind.

CHAPTER FIVE

Bob Lee Sounding Drum was a great father and a decent rancher . . . when he was sober.

That same morning Bob had discovered a half dozen sick and dying steers and heifers on the three hundred twenty acres he ranched a dozen miles east of Ronan, Montana. Bob's grandfather before him had been allotted eighty acres of marginal farming land as his tribal right, and added another eighty of grazing land he bought from a broke neighbor with all his savings just a year before his grandfather passed on. His father, Steve's grandfather, had added another one hundred sixty of grazing land until the little family could almost make a living from the ranch.

Three hundred twenty acres wasn't much, but it would grow hay for the winter, and the Drums' cattle could graze it and some adjacent tribal land.

But Bob Drum was partial to the bottle, and when he started to drink, it was sometimes a month before he got so deathly sick, he had to stop.

He started again, for the first time in over six months, when he found a fourth of his little herd on their knees, bloated, or prone on the ground, glassy-eyed with protruding tongues. And he knew what the trouble was.

Two miles up Cache Creek was the Calico Mining Company's Cache Creek Gold Mine, and the shaft deep in the mountain was running shy of ore. Money that had been used to tend the tail ponds was put to other uses—the pond's liners were deteriorating, leaking hard metals and arsenic into the stream.

The same stream from which Bob Drum's little herd drank, the same stream he used to water his fields, and the same stream that undoubtedly fed the aquifer supplying the house well.

Months before, two of those dying calves had come early, actually late in a hard winter, and Bob had gone out into a driving blizzard to carry them, one at a time, hugged to his chest, over a mile back to the barn. He'd saved them, but almost died himself.

The more Bob Drum sucked on his Jack Daniel's bottle, the madder he got. By the time Steve arrived home from school, he found his mother stone quiet. Suspecting the reason, Steve walked out to the log barn and discovered his father pitching hay, and stopping between every forkful to tip a bottle of whiskey.

Steve choked back a tear. "Pop, why don't you come in now. Mama got a bunch of venison sausage cooking and a pot full of greens—"

"Get the truck, boy. You're driving me to town," his father commanded, and Steve knew better than to argue. Not when Bob Drum was drinking.

A burning knot rose in Steve's throat when his father walked from the barn carrying his old Smith and Wesson .38 in its worn and scarred holster.

Steve had been driving the old '62 Chevy pickup since he was ten, but mostly on the ranch. He could tell why he'd been ordered to drive as his father stumbled his way across the barnyard, then dropped the revolver in the old scarred holster on the truck floor.

"Drive, boy" was all he said after he managed to climb into the passenger seat.

Steve started down their long, dusty driveway. Glancing at the rearview mirror, he could see his mother standing in the doorway, a dish towel in her hands. Steve watched as she dabbed at her eyes.

"Pa, let's hang around and eat—"

"Drive, boy. Don't mouth. I've had about as much mouth and trouble as one man can tolerate."

"Pa, what's going on?"

"Damn mine's poisoned the water. I talked to the tribal office and all they said was that they'd contact the county. Hell, the whole damn herd'll be buzzard feed long before anyone gets around to doing anythin' about it . . . if'n they're not dead as an Indian agent's heart already. I'll be damned if I'll let some greedy bunch of white-eyes run us off'n our land . . . and that's what'll happen we lose the cows."

It was the longest speech Steve had ever remembered his father making. His father didn't like to rely on anyone and came by that honestly. Neither had his father before him, nor had Steve's mother's family. They relied on one another.

As long as Steve could remember, his father had never asked the tribal office for help. For him to do so had required choking on a big chunk of pride. Then for the tribal office not to be able to do anything other than call a county office, a bunch of white-eyes who were the descendants of those, after the Indian Allotment Act, who'd stolen most of the Salish-Kootenai lands . . . It was the same federal act that had opened Oklahoma to the land rushes. Another broken treaty, another lie . . .

Had it not been for those thieving politicians and the wave of Easterners who took advantage of that broken treaty, the Drums would have been heirs to maybe as much as two thousand acres— still, a tiny fraction of what the Salish-Kootenai had occupied for many thousands of years.

It had been something Bob Drum could never quite forget while fighting to make the little three-twenty pay.

"What are you gonna do, Pa?" Steve made himself ask, being as how the whiskey seemed to make his pa so talkative.

"You drive, little Drum. I'm gonna see what . . . big bosses will do about our problem. Someone owes me for twenty-four cows, 'cause I know damn well they're all going down . . . now ish time I took 'em to market."

Steve could see his father was beginning to slur his words. He was real drunk, and Steve had a very bad feeling about him going to town at all, much less going while hot under the collar over his herd. "You want to go to the sales yard, Pa?"

"Can't sell no *dead* cows at the sales yard. The Long Bar."

Steve knew there was no buying and selling of cows at the Long Bar—though there was a lot of talk about cows and a lot of other things. There were two pool tables, and whiskey, and a lot of white-eyes at the Long Bar. It was where the white-eye farmers, ranchers, miners, and loggers hung out after work. The only Indian Steve knew who hung out there was Jack Longears, and he was the swamper.

The Indians had their own place across town.

"I think you oughta go to the Bearpaw Bar, Pa. Or back home. Ma is gonna have dinner ready."

Bob tipped the bottle of Jack and took a long draw. "The Long Bar, boy . . . and no more of yer lip."

"Yes, sir."

The Long Bar had a neon Olympia Beer sign glowing through the soot-covered window, encircling a clock. It was four P.M. when Steve pulled into the forty-five-degree parking in front of the place. He parked between two shiny new pickups. His pa's truck had a broken windshield, and hadn't seen wash water since the winter mud gave it a good coat. Steve slunk down in the seat behind the wheel, ashamed of his father's drunkenness, afraid of being seen driving the truck. He watched his father stagger to the front door, strapping on the revolver as he went.

It wasn't uncommon for a man to have a gun on his hip in western Montana, but it wasn't common either.

The clock ticked on, and Steve prayed his father would pass out before he got into trouble. After a half hour Steve slipped from the truck and made his way to the door, but opened it only an inch and put an eye to the crack. His father sat alone at the bar on the stool nearest the door. A lot of men lingered at the rear around the pool tables. Steve slipped back to the truck, hoping his father would soon cool off and leave so they could go home. Steve was hungry, and Ma had some good venison sausage and fry bread waiting.

Shortly after five the truck next to Steve pulled out, and a green truck with a Calico Mining Company emblem on its side slipped into the parking place. It was a new Ford with a winch on the front, a truck Steve thought was about as fine a thing as a man could own. The man behind the wheel made a few notes on a pad, then slipped out and headed for the bar. A big man with wide shoulders and a handlebar mustache, he moved easily.

The man hadn't been in the bar ten minutes, when the roar of a gunshot slapped Steve across the face. Steve's spine went rigid, then turned to mush as he slunk deeper into the seat. A rush of fear overtook him, and he jumped from the truck. He was afraid to run and afraid to stay. But fear for his father overcame his own and he had to go inside that bar to see if his father was all right.

He pushed the door open and sucked in a deep breath of dank, smoky air. A group of men crowded in a circle in the center of the barroom. It was strangely silent.

As his eyes adjusted, Steve began to shove his way into the center of the crowd. With a murmur, the crowd parted before him.

His father lay on the floor on his back, his legs strangely askew, a callused hand covering the bubbling hole in his chest. "Deep Purple" played on the saloon's scratchy jukebox, but the only deep purple in Steve's mind was the color of the blood pooling on the floor beside his father. Steve felt as if the floor had opened and swallowed him. He was sinking to the center of the earth, the center of creation. He couldn't breathe; he couldn't speak.

Bob Lee Sounding Drum's eyes followed his son as the boy bent over him.

"I—" was all he got out, then a track of frothy blood wormed its way from the corner of his mouth down his cheek to float on the growing puddle. Then the gurgling stopped and Bob Sounding Drum's eyes glassed over.

Jack Longears angrily shoved the men aside and put his arm around Steve, ushering him from the bar just as a sheriff's deputy burst through the door.

"It was an accident . . . crazy, drunken Indian," rang out from several white-eye bystanders.

The last thing Steve remembered seeing as he looked back was the man with the handlebar mustache handing Bob's gun over to the deputy.

Later, at a county inquest, Steve learned from the testimony of several white-eyes that his father had been waving the gun around and threatening Alex Dragonovich, the manager of the Cache Creek Gold Mine. They struggled and Bob Sounding Drum was shot in the chest by his own revolver.

Jack Longears had little to say at the white-eye inquest, but told Steve and his mother in the shade of a cottonwood tree outside that Bob had never pulled the gun. Jack explained that Dragonovich had taken a swing at Bob when confronted with the fact that the mine was poisoning their water and in a very quiet voice demanded three hundred dollars a head for twenty-four steers. They'd rolled around the barroom floor, gouging and swinging. When Bob began getting the best of Dragonovich, two other miners stepped into the fray, one landing a solid kick to Bob's head as he sat astride the larger man. In moments, Bob was beaten badly by the three men. Dragonovich had jerked Bob's gun from its holster. Bob had grabbed for it, but gotten only the barrel, and a gunshot to his chest for his trouble.

It had been anything but a fair fight, and Bob had died.

At his father's funeral, the last tear Steve Drum would shed in his childhood rolled down his cheek. He swore aloud on his father's grave and those of all his warrior ancestors to revenge his father's killing. But his mother's father, old Standing Bear, pulled him aside and told him all good things happen to those who wait. The day after the funeral the old man took him deep into the Mission Mountains for a month, camping, hunting, and fishing.

Later, together, the three of them saved the ranch with a lot of hard work and the help of a loan from the tribal council.

Old Standing Bear stayed with Steve almost constantly, living at the ranch in a barn room until he died quietly in his sleep two years later, when Steve was in his first year of high school.

Steve and his mother worked the ranch and repaid the loan after the county forced the mine to control its tail pond seepage. But the mine had polluted the area so badly that the ranch, Stephen Drum's only legacy from his parents, had little value.

Still Steve remembered and savored his grandfather's words— *all good things come to those who wait.*

He tried Paula Fox again, and again didn't get her, then returned Alex Dragonovich's call.

Yes, it would be a pleasure helping International Consolidated Oil and Mining with their problem negotiating with the Navajos at Shiprock.

A far greater pleasure than Alex Dragonovich would know or probably ever understand. *Yes, Standing Bear, waiting was a good thing.*

Steve usually stayed in the office until past seven, but, with a long-desired result accomplished, he decided to leave an hour early. Besides, something was gnawing at him about the condo, and he didn't know what.

He normally had a driver with a Lincoln Town Car pick him

up and drive him to work in the morning, so he could work in the car, then back to the upper East Side in the evening, but he'd failed to call Litcomb's Limo, so he hailed a cab.

Where he lived was three-quarters of the way up Manhattan; he picked the location at 84th and Madison because it was so far from Wall Street. He had his fill of financial types by the end of the day, and his condo was about as far as he could get from the now-digital-nonticking ticker tape and still have a comfortable drive. At six A.M. going to work, and seven P.M. returning, he usually missed most of the traffic.

At six P.M., a little earlier than normal, it took him longer than usual getting home.

The condo seemed as he'd left it. Li Chung, his Mandarin-speaking houseboy, who normally left at six, had obviously been called by Sally and informed of his return. There was a casserole on the kitchen island with instructions as to its time in the oven. A mixed green salad awaited in the refrigerator. Steve smiled at Sally and Li's efficiency, then turned the oven to three-fifty to preheat it, per instruction.

He went to his answering machine in his small condo office, actually the smaller of its two bedrooms, and noted the flashing digital readout. Six calls. Poking the play button, he listened to them one by one, making notes. He wondered why he hadn't been able to get his messages when he called from England, but thought little of it. Electronic gizmos were out of his realm, and he paid little attention to any of them other than the computer.

The call he was most interested in was the second call from his lady, who informed him she was coming into town tonight in case he happened to get back, and would be at the Peninsula Hotel just off Fifth, where she usually stayed. She could easily afford it.

The third call was another threat about his consulting job at St. Regis. For a second, he whiffed the foul breath of the bear standing over him, then it passed. He would rise above . . .

He poured himself a finger of brandy in a snifter and flopped down in a Charles Eames chair next to the phone, hit the control to the fifty-inch television in the wall, and poked in the financial channel. With the news in the background, he called the Pen.

"Angela Giovanni, a guest, please."

"Yes, sir, Miss Giovanni has checked in, I believe," the voice said, and on the first ring, she answered.

"You still in London?" she asked, her voice pensive.

"Nope, in my Eames easy chair right here on easy street."

"Out or in?"

"In, if you don't mind. There's a great-looking chicken and mushroom casserole ready to go into the oven, a mixed green in the fridge, and a bottle of excellent chardonnay awaiting milady . . . and a little something wrapped in fancy paper to prove I was thinking about a fancy Italian lady and not just bird-watching in jolly old London town."

"You shouldn't have, but then again, if you hadn't . . . I shopped til I dropped this afternoon, so if you don't mind, I'll spend a little time cleaning up and be there about seven-thirty"—her voice dropped an octave—"it's been two weeks . . ." and his loins reacted as they always had to her voice, her smell, her glance.

It was maddening to him that she should affect him so. "Two weeks is thirteen days and eleven hours too long. Shall we eat at seven forty-five?"

"How about nine-thirty?"

"You're my kind of fancy lady."

He hung up, then decided he would shower before she came and be waiting in his robe. Two weeks was far too long for both of them.

As he showered, he thought back over their longtime relationship. They'd been together, off and on, longer than most Manhattan married couples.

He remembered the first time he'd seen Angela ten years earlier, almost as clearly as the last time only two weeks ago. It was at her father's estate, where she still lived, in upper Bergen County, New Jersey.

Years ago Steve had been invited there because he was a great swimmer and, propitiously, as it turned out, happened to be at the right place at the right time.

With a long weekend and a group of friends from Harvard Law School, he'd rented a sloop, blowing a week's part-time pay, and they'd met at a friend's parents' house near Annapolis to go day sailing on Chesapeake Bay.

"Jesus, look at that," one of his classmates said, and Steve, at the helm, glanced over to see a large powerboat and smaller speedboat bearing down on each other. The driver of the speed-boat was obviously not paying attention, and even though the much larger cabin cruiser tried to bear off, he hit the cruiser a glancing blow, broaching the speedboat, keel up, and knocking the powerboat off course. Its skipper, in a position at the helm on the flying bridge, flew out of his captain's chair and down the ladder to the cockpit below. His head did not reappear, so he must have been out of commission.

The powerboat continued away at a slow speed from the badly damaged speedboat.

They were only a hundred yards from the sloop, but directly downwind, and all Steve could do was swing the helm into the wind and back the sails.

He could see someone in the water, floating facedown.

CHAPTER SIX

It would take far too long to try to bring the sloop about and tack back to the wreck.

He kicked off his deck shoes and dove into the water, stroking with all his power and concentration toward the victim, his stroke strong and sure from high school and collegiate swimming. He'd won the state in high school in the butterfly, and was a tenth of a second from making the Olympics in college. In fifteen seconds he reached what proved to be a young man about his age. Rolling him over, Steve began a one arm sidestroke with the unconscious victim in tow. Had it not been for the foam life vest the man wore, he probably would have already drowned. As it was, he was unconscious, probably from the impact, head streaming blood from a deep gash, and repeatedly coughing up water.

Steve thought about towing the young man the few yards to the broached speedboat and waiting for help, but it lay upside down in the water and seemed to be getting lower every second.

So he headed for the sloop. As he stroked he was just as glad the man was out cold, since he might have fought him, as drowning victims are prone to do. Steve's friends had managed to bring the boat a quarter of the way closer to the wreck, but they were inexperienced sailors. Even so, in less than five minutes from the impact, Steve was at the side with the young man in tow.

His friends tried to haul Steve into the boat after taking the man aboard, but Steve yelled, "See if you can pump the water out of him. Did anybody call—" Then he remembered the rented sloop had no radio. Still, a half dozen boats were aimed at the wreck, but the closest was still a quarter mile away. "I'm going back," he said, and stroked away again. One of his schoolmates worked over the man while the other continued to attempt to maneuver the sloop closer.

Before he reached the wreck site, the speedboat slipped under, leaving a floating ice chest, beer cans, and a few cushions.

Steve tried diving, but found no one else. He hoped the man was alone in the speedboat.

Another speedboat reached the scene before the sloop, and Steve remembered the big powerboat as the couple in the just-arrived boat pulled him aboard.

Out of breath, he managed to say, "That big . . . powerboat . . . in the distance . . . you can just see her transom. Catch her. She was the other boat . . . in the wreck and her skipper fell from the flying . . . flying bridge with the impact. He may be out cold in the cockpit below."

The man gunned the fast inboard, and it literally hit only the wave tops closing the three-eighths of a mile to the big power-boat. They drew alongside the retreating stern of the vessel, and Steve leapt to the swim step and climbed aboard.

As he suspected, a man in a blue blazer and white duck pants lay unconscious in the cockpit. He bled profusely from a chest wound. Steve noted blood on a stanchion, and surmised the man had fallen chest-first on the sharp railing.

Steve waved the speedboat over and called to them, "Can one of you come aboard and compress this wound while I drive this thing in?"

He helped the woman aboard, then said to the man, "Can you pick up the injured man on the sailboat? He needs medical attention."

The man driving the speedboat seemed reluctant, so Steve said, "I'll get him with this big tub," and to his surprise the speedboat driver just nodded his head. The cruiser was clean-lined and modern, anything but a tub—under any other set of circumstances Steve would love being aboard her—but he was irritated. They headed for the sloop with the woman tending the injured man in the cockpit below. Steve searched the control panel and found a cellular telephone. He was confident the accident had been reported, but called 911 anyway, and was assured the coast guard boat was on its way. Even though they were only a few miles offshore, when Steve said he was unfamiliar with the boat and the bay, the operator sent a coast guard helicopter to lead them to the best docking spot for the ambulance.

Steve managed to come alongside the sloop without colliding and pick up the injured man he'd pulled from the water. Shoving both throttles to the wall as the helicopter circled overhead, then began leading the way, he headed for shore.

He had better control in the open water, but managed to give the dock a good rap when he pulled alongside, marking the hull as he docked. In minutes both men were loaded in an ambulance and on their way to the hospital.

While the sloop was closing the distance to the dock, Steve gave the coast guard the best report he could of the accident.

In an hour he and his friends were sailing again.

It was the following week when he received a call at his tiny apartment in Cambridge.

"Mr. Drum?"

"Yes, sir," he said to the man with a deep voice and slightly foreign accent.

"I'ma Aldo Giovanni, and I'd like to see you."

"Sir?"

"I'm the papa of the boy you pulled from the Chesapeake. I woulda like to thank you in person."

"Well, sir, no thanks is necessary. I did only—"

"My son would be dead if it wasn't for you. Please, Mr. Drum, allow me to thank you ina person."

"I hope your son is okay?"

"He's fine. Probably no smarter for the rap on the head, but fine."

"Again, sir, it's not necessary, but I'm free the rest of the day."

"Good. Please meet me at Allendi Aviation, the executive terminal at the Cambridge airport, at noon, if that's convenient."

"Sure, how will I recognize you, sir?"

"Wear a suit and tie, young man, and be prepared to be gone the rest of the evening. We will find you."

"I've got a report in international law due tomorrow, sir. I can't spare—"

"Wear a suit an' tie, young man. While we're talking, I'll have someone take care of your report."

Steve's curiosity was piqued, so even though he might have to stay up all night to finish the report, he replied, "As you wish, sir. Noon, at Allendi Aviation."

He dressed in jeans and sneakers—his only footwear—with a tan corduroy sport coat, light blue button-down dress shirt, and blue and tan striped tie. He owned no suit, and only the one tie and dress shirt, and that he'd purchased after being accepted to Harvard Law.

Steve could not have been more surprised when he was approached in the Allendi waiting room by a ravishing young lady in a nondescript gray-trimmed black uniform. "Mr. Drum?"

"Yes, ma'am."

"Nice to meet you. Mr. Giovanni is waiting in the Gulfstream."

"Gulfstream?" Even after a tour in the Marine Corps, and exposure to a lot of aircraft, Steve had no idea what a Gulfstream was.

"Yes, follow me, please."

Steve's jaw dropped when they rounded the corner of a nearby hangar, and the sixty-foot-long ultramodern Gulfstream jet painted black with gray highlights awaited like a huge raptor ready to spring off the runway. He followed the young woman up the ladder and paused at the hatchway. The black, gray, and smoked-glass interior was as nice as anything he'd ever seen in his life. He was awestruck as she moved forward into the heart of the plane. She turned back, and smiled at him, seemingly understanding his dropped jaw. "Nice, yes?"

"I think *incredible* a better word."

"Come on, Mr. Drum, Mr. Giovanni is eager to meet you."

The center of the plane was done like an office, with an eight-seat conference table extending out from the rear, facing the front of a small but elegant desk. A full communication panel with a thirty-five-inch Sony television lined the wall behind the desk. A classical piece, Steve thought Vivaldi maybe, emanated discreetly from the speakers around the cabin.

A tall, thin, impeccably tailored man seated behind the desk in dark suit, shirt, and tie lifted his eyes from some paperwork and rose as they entered. He extended his hand. Steve closed the distance between them and heard the engines begin to wind up.

"You could live in this thing," he managed to say, eyeing the man and taking his hand, surprised at the strength in the slender fingers. His thin face was kind enough, but his quick, dark eyes seemed remote and distant—a little reptilian.

"Actually," Giovanni said, "you could live-a comfortably here. There's a full bathroom, a queena size bed in the rear, and a gourmet galley and bar."

"They're starting the engines," Steve said, then felt a little foolish.

"Yes, they are," Giovanni said, a small smile almost rising to narrow eyes. "I'm Aldo Giovanni, Tony Giovanni's papa."

"Yes, sir, I'm sorry, I'm a little bewildered—"

"Don't be, Mr. Drum. It'sa just glass, metal, and plastic . . . it's flesh and bone that's important . . . and blood. Come this way." As the stewardess disappeared to the rear of the plane, Giovanni led him forward to a smaller area with four deep, comfortable gray leather seats facing two and two with a cocktail table centered between. He motioned Steve into one. "Take a seat and fasten your belt." He smiled, and Steve did as he was told.

"We're flying somewhere?" Steve said, and again felt a little foolish.

"Yes, young man, to Kennedy. To be truthful, I'm a fella who hates to fly . . . but there's not a decent Italian place in all o' Cambridge. I want you to have a decent meal . . . you've earned that and more."

"So we're flying, in this monster jet, to New York, so I can have a plate of spaghetti?" He had to laugh.

"Spaghetti is American food, Stephen . . . may I call you Stephen?"

Steve nodded as the plane began to move.

"Anyway, I got this little favorite place down on Eighth in Manhattan, and I like to eat there every once in a while. It's good Sicilian food. Lotsa squid and shellfish. Is that okay with you, Stephen?"

"Yes, sir, my paper's not due until ten A.M."

"It's okay. The dean of the law school is a friend of a friend, a big donor to Harvard. You've been given a couple extra days for the paper . . . since you're a hero."

"Hardly, sir, but a couple of days is fine with me," Steve said, unable to wipe the smile off his face.

Before they were in the air, he had a vodka gimlet, his drink of preference at the time, in hand, and a plate of antipasti in front of him, and Aldo Giovanni was politely grilling him about his life.

"So, what kind of name is Drum?"

"Actually my true surname is Sounding Drum, sir. It's Salish."

"Salish? Where's this place?"

"Montana, sir, I'm Native American."

"You don't say. Like Indian? Like Custer and, what's that place, the Little Bighorn?"

Steve smiled again. "Yes, sir. Except we prefer to think of it as Greasy Grass."

"So, you kicked the crap outta them at Greasy Grass."

"Yes, sir, we did. Although that was the Sioux and a little before my time."

Aldo Giovanni laughed aloud for the first time.

He continued to politely grill Stephen as the plane winged its way to Kennedy. He knew almost as much about Stephen Drum as Steve knew about himself by the time they landed.

A black stretch limo was waiting at the executive terminal, and Aldo Giovanni continued to learn about Steve while they entered the city until they pulled up at a shop on 54th, in the center of town.

"You're not hungry yet?" Giovanni asked, stepping from the limo. The black suit- and hat-clad, wide-shouldered driver held the door.

"I'm fine, sir. I had enough on the plane."

"Good. We're gonna get you some-a clothes before we go to dinner. Probably the blue jeans would not work so good."

"We can go somewhere—"

"You letta me handle this, Stephen."

"Yes, sir."

They entered an exclusive men's shop and immediately two clerks and another slickly dressed Italian who proved to be the owner were at their sides. In seconds Steve had three men measuring every angle of his body, and in minutes he had a complete outfit, including alligator shoes off the rack, and they were out of the store and on their way to an early dinner.

Steve was back in Cambridge by midnight, flying alone with only the ravishing stewardess to keep him company. She made several sexual innuendoes along the way, but Steve was too naive to understand that her duties went beyond serving antipasti and drinks. Later, he kicked himself when he thought of the things she'd said, and that he hadn't at least made a pass. The limo had driven Mr. Giovanni back to his estate in New Jersey. A town car had been hired to drive Steve back to the executive terminal at Kennedy.

Steve went to bed that night with the silly grin still on his face, a new suit in the closet that probably cost a month's pay, and his belly full of the finest Italian meal he ever imagined—he'd been served no spaghetti.

In his wildest dreams that night, he couldn't have topped the day.

A week later, three hand-tailored suits—dark blue pinstripe, black, and dark gray pinstripe—three pairs of handmade shoes, a dozen tailored shirts, and a dozen ties arrived by UPS.

He realized then he had no address to send a thank-you, nor even a telephone number. Trying Aldo Giovanni in the telephone book for Saddle River, where he'd mentioned living, Steve was not surprised to find there was no listing.

He found the number a day later, when the grants and scholarships office of the law school sent him a message in class and asked him to report.

He entered, a little apprehensive since he had received a scholarship from the Confederated Indian Scholarship program. It paid only half his tuition and none of his books, so he still had to work waiting tables weekends and special events at the Harvard Faculty Club, even with what he received from the GI bill. He hoped to hell nothing had happened to that scholarship, or it would mean laying off school at least every other year to work. He'd be twice as long completing law school.

An officious little man in a paisley bow tie and bottle-bottom glasses came out of his private office and waved Steve in. "You're Stephen Drum?"

Steve stood in front of the man's cluttered desk while the man took a seat. "Yes, sir."

"Sit, sit."

Only with the invitation did Steve seat himself at one of the two straight-back chairs in front of the man's desk.

"I'm Willard Evanston."

"Sir . . ."

"You know you'll have to give up your Confederated Scholarship?"

"Why's that, sir?" Steve asked, shocked.

"This grant. You can't have a hundred-percent grant and maintain a scholarship from the Confederated program."

"A hundred-percent grant?"

"Yes. All of your expenses, housing, et ceteras . . . and, unusually, a thousand-a-month in spending money has been provided."

Steve was awestruck. He searched his mind, trying to remember the dozens of grants and scholarships he'd applied for the year before, but none came to mind that offered anywhere near what had just been explained to him.

Evanston continued. "The first spending-money check is here. You'll have to sign for it. The rest will be direct-deposited if you'll fill in your bank and account number." He handed Steve a sheaf of a dozen papers. "All the rest of the blanks, please."

"But where did it come from?"

Evanston's mouth formed a constipated smile for the first time. "You didn't know this was coming?"

"No, sir."

"Must be a pleasant surprise. All I know is the check is from the Giovanni Charitable Trust, drawn on a bank in Atlantic City."

"Who do I call to thank?"

"Here's the spending-money check. The bank's name and address is on the check, of course. That's the only contact I know of."

It took Steve a half-day via telephone with the bank to run down the office of the Giovanni Charitable Trust, which happened to be a law firm in New York City. He got nowhere in trying to ferret out the address or telephone number of Mr. Giovanni, but did get the promise that his message of thanks would be passed along.

It was another week before Giovanni called and invited Steve to the Saddle River estate for the weekend. It was there, dressed in a new black suit, he met Angela.

Steve smiled at the remembrance of how clumsy he'd been and at how much he'd learned since—much of it thanks to the Giovanni family.

The water began to grow cold. He'd taken too long—it was a

bad habit, running the extra-large hot water heater out when he had something on his mind. He'd spent many hours over the years thinking about Aldo Giovanni; his son, Tony; and daughter, Angela.

As he was toweling off, the buzzer on the intercom rang. Naked, Steve crossed the living room to the small white plate with slots for the speaker and pushed a button. "Yeah, Tuffy?"

"Ms. Angela is on her way up, Mr. Drum."

"Thanks."

Tuffy at least knew Angela's first name and was the only person on earth, so far as Steve knew, who knew she occasionally came to call.

Grabbing a robe, hair still askew, he hurried to the door as the bell rang, pausing to take a deep settling breath before he opened it.

As always, the sight of her unsettled his breath—in fact, took it.

The same tall, slender build as her father but with kind, deep, all-knowing hazel eyes. She stood in a brown raw silk sport coat, shimmering gold soft silk blouse that clung to her ample breasts, tightly tailored brown slacks, and brown faux crocodile heels accenting her height. He knew them to be fake even never having seen them before. One of the few things they argued about was animals' place in the scheme of things.

He reached out, took her by the waist, and lifted her off her feet, pressing her body close to his as he carried her back into the entry and shut the door with a kick. She sailed the brown Gucci bag she carried into the condo, uncaring where it fell. The scent of orchids caused his breath to catch.

He set her down, stared into her eyes for a moment, stroking her arms in long, languid movements, drinking in the feel and look of her. They came together in a crushing embrace, lips meeting, the kiss deep, hungry, insistent. In moments, neither of them yet speaking a word, they were leaving a trail of clothes behind on their way to his king-size bed.

Twelve stories below Steve's condo, a black sedan sat double-parked on Madison. The man inside watched the windows high above. He was almost relieved when one of New York's finest blew his horn forcing him to move along. It physically hurt him to sit there and watch, waiting for the lights to go out, knowing what must be going on there.

He'd been tailing Angela Giovanni and was not surprised when she led him to Stephen Drum.

A Nikon with a 300mm mirrored lens rested on the seat beside him.

As he drove away, he glanced at the camera, wondering what use was the best for the pictures of Angela Giovanni entering Steve Drum's apartment building.

He would have to destroy them if he decided to kill the sleazy bastard right away, something he truly wanted to do. They would be incriminating if discovered. Then again, they might be worth something first. Hell, they may be worth a lot ... and he was never one to turn down an easy buck.

And he needed the money, thanks to recent events in his life.

He got a tight smile thinking about extorting a chunk of money from Steve Drum. How much would he pay to keep Don Aldo Giovanni from finding out Drum had been porking his daughter for years?

Finally, he laughed out loud.

A helluva lot, he bet.

One helluva helluva lot.

Killing the son of a bitch could wait a while ... a short while, but a while.

CHAPTER SEVEN

Thad Wintermoose and Paula Fox walked out of the Emporium Theater in Greenwich Village, where a month-long Cagney festival was well under way.

Coffee had ended with a trip to the Guggenheim Museum, then lunch, then the Museum of Modern Art, then *Angels with Dirty Faces* with Cagney and Pat O'Brien. A real Cagney classic.

They'd talked, laughed, and argued about movies for most of the afternoon. As they walked from the theater, Paula glanced over at the big man. Like many Native Americans, he was barrel-chested, with enough belly for two men—but even without much muscle definition, she sensed he was very, very strong. And he would have the heart of a warrior. He'd worked on a high-iron erection crew for ten years, tossing red-hot rivets from beam to beam, across several hundred feet of emptiness below. Any man who'd do that work had to have plenty of heart and nerves of steel.

Still, a blue collar worker? She'd sworn that she'd never become involved with anyone who'd not been formally and extensively educated.

She'd known far too many men who had not been, back on the rez.

And Thad had admitted to only a high school education and poor grades at that.

What was she thinking, letting this go beyond coffee?

She turned to him. "It's been a great day, Thad. I've really enjoyed having the time off . . . even under the circumstances. But I've got to get home and get some rest."

"Okay, cab or walk or what?"

"It's only a short walk from here . . . you don't need—"

"Of course I do. Which way to your palace?"

"A humble apartment."

"They hounded us when we didn't want to live no more in those dumps they call houses," he said, imitating Cagney.

" 'They hounded us when we found we couldn't have the fine things all around us,' " she said, following the line.

But he corrected her, *"Get* the fine things, not *have."*

"You should be called Winter Bull, 'cause you're full of it."

He laughed. "You sure you have to call it a day? The night is young."

"We can stop again at Mama Gold's. She makes a mean pie."

"I love mean pie," he said.

Damn, I did it again, she thought as they walked along together. Pie, that's all. Then bed. Alone. Her thoughts turned suddenly to Stephen Drum. He was due back from Europe that afternoon.

When they reached Mama Gold's, she excused herself and went to the ladies' room, stopping at a pay phone on the way. Stephen didn't answer and she didn't leave word on the machine.

Steve sat across his inch-thick glass dining table from Angela. She'd donned his blue dress shirt, long bare flawless legs tucked under her, and picked at Li Chung's chicken mushroom casserole and salad. Steve, famished, had long finished his, but he still worked on a glass of Pine Ridge chardonnay. The odor of sex lingered in the air, and he felt a twitch in his loins again. He wanted her to stay, to be with him until he was so satiated he would want only to sleep. And it made the heat begin to rise in his back. Passion and desire gave way to smoldering resentment.

"How's your father?" he asked.

She eyed him carefully, a bite of mushroom suspended halfway to her mouth. She seemed to pick her words carefully. "You haven't asked about Papa in years. Are you hoping his heart is about to give out?"

Steve laughed less than politely. "He's got a heart of pure cold steel. It'll never quit on him."

"Please let's not talk about Papa."

"Okay. How's Tony?"

"Are you trying to pick a fight?"

He considered that a moment. "I don't know. Are you staying, or going back to the hotel?"

This time it was her turn to consider. "You know Mama will call me first thing in the morning. Even at the ripe old age of twenty-nine, she still considers me her little girl."

It irritated Steve, even though he knew it shouldn't, that Angela still lived on her father's estate. Her cottage was a quarter-mile from the main house on a beautiful pond. Still, it was Aldo Giovanni's pond. And the arrangement kept him from seeing her more.

This time his smile had a hard edge. *"Are* you her little girl?"

"You *are* trying to pick a fight. Didn't Europe agree with you . . . and what were you doing there that was so important that you didn't call before leaving?"

"I was working. And how the hell would you know if I called. Maybe Papa Giovanni or your mama answered. I couldn't exactly leave word. In fact, I did call on your machine and clicked the receiver three times, as you suggested. But you didn't return my call."

"It was months ago I suggested that . . . to answer your question. I think, considering your mood, it's better that I go back to the hotel."

"It would be better if you told Papa G to stuff it, and stood up on your own hind legs."

She replaced the fork with the bite of mushroom still uneaten on the side of her plate, carefully dabbed the corners of her mouth with her napkin, and rose from her chair. "He's my papa, no matter who he is or what he's done. And Mama's been sick off and on—"

"I'm beginning to wonder if that's a ruse to keep you in the fold."

"That's beneath you, Stephen. I'll never go against my family, you know that. You've known it for years. No matter how much I love you." She turned and headed for the bedroom.

Now he felt bad. He had been picking a fight. It always angered him that she had to go, and unless her family was traveling she would never even consider staying overnight.

Don Aldo Giovanni, whose interests included gambling in Atlantic City as well as running numbers in most neighborhoods in the State of New Jersey, still exercised almost absolute control over his family.

It irritated Steve enough that he didn't follow her and apologize. He wanted her to be clear about the way he felt.

After he graduated from Harvard Law, his last two years' expenses covered completely by the Giovanni Charitable Trust, Aldo Giovanni offered him a job. Not a job in the true sense of the word, since he was technically self-employed, but all the same, a job. Giovanni set him up in a small office suite in Atlantic City—Steve's own firm, in his own name. It was rumored that the city was going to try to legalize gambling, and Aldo meant to be in on the ground floor.

Steve's firm grew to three associates as he handled most of the day-to-day affairs of the Giovanni interests. In addition to how the family made their major money, the numbers business—a source of funds Steve was not made privy to until he'd represented the family for two years—they also owned a produce company, a trucking company, a heavy equipment company in New Jersey, over a dozen coin vending companies handling everything from cigarettes to candy to trinkets, and a fleet of rental cars.

Steve was kept busy with the legal operations. He was invited to the Giovanni estate for dinner parties at least once a month, and at least once a week had a meeting there to discuss business with Don Aldo, whom he now was invited to call Al. Many times he stayed for dinner and Mama's wonderful cooking.

Finally, during a long walk in the Giovanni gardens, he invited Angela to come to Atlantic City and go for a sail with him. His first extra money had been used to buy an eighteen-foot day sailer.

She accepted, and that Sunday showed up at two P.M., after she'd gone to mass with her mother. They'd sailed the day away, and had dinner before she'd returned to Saddle River. The following Wednesday was Steve's normal meeting day with Al. During the course of their conversation, and after they'd finished discussing a potential purchase of another trucking company, the sharp-eyed businessman stared out the tall windows of his study, then suddenly turned to Steve.

"I understand Angela was in Atlantic City last Sunday?"

"Yes, sir. We had a nice afternoon sail." For the first time, Steve considered that possibly Al Giovanni had not known about Steve's day with his daughter. Steve stood a little straighter. "I hope you don't mind."

"Mind? Why would I mind? She's a grown woman . . . you'll stay for dinner?"

"Certainly, sir, if I'm invited."

"As always. I'm going to rest awhile. You're welcome to relax here in the study, or walk in the garden."

Steve merely nodded, and Aldo excused himself, polite as always. After glancing through a *Time* magazine, Steve decided a walk in the garden was not a bad idea. In fact, he might just run into Angela there. He wandered out and made his way through the formal gardens to a path in the woods he knew led to Angela's.

But he stopped short in a thicket of chokecherries when he heard a voice raised in anger. It was Aldo Giovanni yelling at his daughter just inside an open window of her cottage, just steps from where Steve stood.

"I don't ever want you to see anyone without my permission, even someone as close to me as Stephen. He's eight years older than you. You-a understand?"

"Yes, Papa."

"And I don't appreciate your lying about it. I'ma gonna take it up with your mama and she'll take it up with Father Pistacorri, you-a understand?"

"Yes, Papa."

"Never again without my permission, unnastand?"

Steve seldom heard Al Giovanni fall back into a heavy Italian accent unless he was very angry. Steve wondered if his anger was only because it was him, because he was Indian. Had he been Italian, he wondered if Angela's transgression would have been so bad. But that was thinking that Steve seldom allowed himself. He didn't engage in self-recriminations or minority self-indulgence, as so many minorities did. If he had, he would never have gotten as far as he had.

No, Al was mad only because Angela had gone without his permission.

Angela had come back to Atlantic City almost a year later to see him. It was the fifth or sixth time when the confrontation rose its head again, like a cobra out of a basket. Steve had been so attracted to her, he hadn't asked if she had her father's permission—he'd been afraid to, not wanting to spoil their budding relationship—and he sure as hell never volunteered the information to Al during any of their business meetings or dinners. In fact, while in her father's presence, he treated Angela as if he barely knew her, even after he'd begun sleeping with her.

They'd just met at an Atlantic City boardwalk restaurant for dinner, when Al Giovanni entered with a pair of his bodyguards. The two no-necks took a seat at the far side of the oak and red-wool-carpeted room, leaving Al to approach by himself.

Steve saw him coming before Angela noticed and said quietly, "Your father is joining us."

She paled, then went rigid.

Al pulled up a chair, and polite as always, said to Steve, "You don't mind?"

"Of course not, Al. I'll call the waiter over—"

"No, thank you, Stephen. I'm-a not staying." He turned to Angela. "Anda neither are you."

She seemed frozen, with nothing to say.

Steve looked Al straight in the eye. "Is there anything wrong, Al? We were only having a quiet—"

"You go out with the boys," he said to Angela, motioning toward the no-necks, and she stood quickly, dumping her red cloth napkin on the floor as she left.

Al eyed Stephen for a long while before he spoke. "My daughter anda my family are not a part of my business. I don't appreciate you seeing my daughter. You shoulda come to me if you wanted to see my little-a girl."

"She's all grown up, Al."

"Don'ta you think I know how old my daughter is. I was at Mama's side whena she was born."

"I'm sorry—"

"You take care of the legal business, Stephen. I'll-a take-a care of my family."

"Okay, Al." Steve watched as Al Giovanni rose from the table, then he, too, stood up, and cleared his throat. "Okay. How about I come out to Saddle River and pick Angela up for a date, if that's okay with you and Mama Rosa?"

He eyed Al Giovanni carefully and thought he noticed his face reddening. He'd never seen Al lose his temper and had often been glad he hadn't. He'd heard rumors . . .

Al didn't speak for a long while, then he said in a harsh whisper, "You've-a been very close to us, Stephen. You saved my only son from adrownin'—"

"And you've been very good to me, Al."

"So I'ma gonna tell you plain. My daughter is gonna find a good Catholic boy—"

"I was raised Catholic, Al. I went to mass every Sunday until I was twelve. I can start again."

This time it was clear that Al's face was reddening. "An *Italiano* Catholic boy, Stephen. A gooda *Italian* boy."

Steve, too, was angry, but he knew better than to push this with the old man. It was, he'd discovered when the man who'd owned the boat and sued him and come to him with a broken leg, not good for one's health to push Al Giovanni too far.

Al poked a narrow finger in Steve's chest. "So you stay in Atlantic City and take-a care of business. Angela will stay with her mama at home. You unnastan'?"

"Yes, sir." But he couldn't quite help himself, and had to add as Al started away, "If that's the way Angela wants it."

Al stopped and turned back, his jaw clenched. "I take care of my family, Stephen. You take care of some of my business. I tell you now, Angela will stay on the place with her mama. You won't see her again, ever again, unnastan'?"

"As you wish, Al. Whatever you, and Angela, want."

Steve knew he was pushing it, but he just couldn't help himself.

Al turned and strode out without another word.

He paused only long enough for a few words with his men, then he, Angela, and one of the bodyguards left, while the other came across the restaurant and stopped at the table where Steve had returned to his seat. The man had dead eyes, a pug nose, and slick hair lapped over the collar of his silk suit. His knotted ham-sized hands stayed loosely at his sides, palms facing back like one of the great apes, while he bent close to Steve and spoke in a low, gravelly voice.

"I'm told you have been a good friend of Don Aldo's. Don Aldo takes good care of his friends. Stay a friend—"

"Even friends have disagreements."

"That's true. The important thing is, is this matter settled? It had better be."

Steve couldn't help but give the man a hard look, but he decided prudence wise, and said, "Seems as if it is."

"Good. I'll tell Don Aldo you said so."

"Good. You do that."

The man left behind Al and Angela, glancing back several times before he cleared the door.

Stephen was not invited back to the Saddle River estate again. While working at his office in Atlantic City, he continued to do his job as best he could—while Aldo Giovanni elected to conduct their weekly business meetings via the telephone.

Still sitting at the dining room table, Steve finished his glass of chardonnay, then ran his finger around the rim of the crystal until it began to ring a clear, constant tone, then he sat it aside. He'd been through a lot with Angela, and she'd risked a lot to begin seeing him again.

He owed her more than a little snippy anger at the fact that she wouldn't stay. Family loyalty was something he not only admired, but practiced. She appeared back in his bedroom door-way, fully dressed. He rose, threw his napkin in his plate, and walked to her.

"I'm sorry. I acted like a snotty little kid who couldn't have his favorite toy."

She smiled. "I like being your toy. I wish I could stay."

"Maybe after old iron heart goes to meet his maker."

Her eyes hardened. "Don't say that, Stephen. I love and respect my father, and wouldn't do anything to hurt him, ever."

"You've got your row to hoe and I've got mine."

"I don't consider my family a 'row to hoe.' "

He walked to her and pulled her close, pulling her head to his shoulder and whispering in her ear. The fragrance of orchids mingled with the slight musk of sex, and emotion flooded him with heat. "I don't want to come between you and your family. Someday we'll find another way."

"Breakfast?" she asked.

"I've got to be at the office early, so unless you're near the Street . . ."

"Early is not on my agenda."

"Then I'll see you the next time you get to town."

"Next time, my love," she said, putting a slender hand behind his head and pulling him to her mouth. She kissed him deeply, then headed out the door.

The kiss was passionate, but, to him, sad. He wondered if she felt the same.

"Next time," he said quietly after the door had closed. Another time, another place, he thought.

She was long gone when he remembered he'd forgotten to give her the diamond and ruby earrings he'd brought all the way from London.

Maybe it was just as well.

The man waiting a few steps from the tall, brass-trimmed condo building doors dropped the camera to his waist, spun on his heel, and started away as Angela left the building, obviously not wanting to be seen. It was enough that the big black doorman had been giving him the evil eye. Stopping by a deli window, he kept his back to her and studied the salads displayed there. The doorman waved a cab down for her, but the man didn't hurry to his parked car to follow. He turned from the window and merely watched her being driven away, then moved to his car, glanced back up at Steve's window, shook his head in disgust, and left in the opposite direction.

He spun the wheels on the black sedan, cutting in front of traffic, and sped away.

CHAPTER EIGHT

Paula Fox called Steve shortly after six A.M. "I'm glad I caught you."

"Me too. I'm loafing this morning," he said, but actually he was on the treadmill, trying to stay in shape.

"Late night?"

"Not really. Actually I was in the sack at ten. You're the one with the late night. I called just before I hit the hay."

"I spent some time with Thad Wintermoose . . . you know, the guy who protected the document."

"Sure, I remember the name."

"What the heck is that noise?"

"Treadmill. Got to keep the Greek-god body."

"Good luck, Achilles. Watch out for the spears. Anyway, I wanted to talk to you before I talked to Thad. He got the boot from his boss for doing what he did—"

"Send him over to the office. I'll find something for him . . . can he do anything?"

"He was a construction guy. He did high-iron work, or so he said."

"So says every Indian within five hundred miles of New York. It seems to be an ethnic claim to fame."

"This guy can be believed," she said with conviction, and a wink at the subject of the conversation who had just walked out of Paula's bedroom to her kitchen, looking for a cup of coffee.

"If you say so . . . send him over. How did you do with getting what we need?"

"Lousy. I'm banned from the site."

"Banned? The thing with the cop?"

"Just general principles, I guess. Anyway, I've been thinking about how to get it done, and I'll come up with something."

"I'll hold you to it. You know this treaty won't be worth a damn unless we have proof of direct descendency. We may have to blood-test every red man east of the Mississippi before this is over. It's imperative you get back on the dig." He changed the subject. "Do you know anyone in forensics, anyone expert in DNA?"

"I don't . . ." He sensed she placed a hand over the receiver, and he heard a muffled "The coffee's in the upper cupboard," then she was back. "Anyway, I don't even know if DNA will work after three hundred and fifty years."

"Hell, I read somewhere that it could work after thousands of years." He smiled, then asked, "Who's making the coffee around your place these days?"

"You writing a brief, counselor? It's my maiden aunt, come to stay with me."

"You don't have a maiden aunt, Paula. This is Steve you're talking to."

"It's not my Chinese houseboy making the coffee, like around the Drum pad . . . enough said unless you're trying to embarrass me."

"You're a big girl."

"I'm petite, thank you. Anyway, I'll have us an expert in DNA forensics before you break for lunch."

"I'll hold you to it, but it won't do us a damn bit of good unless we have some DNA to compare to."

"They'll have to circle the wagons, 'cause I'll storm the ramparts if I have to."

"And now it's you mixing not only metaphors, but centuries again."

"I'll get the goods," she said emphatically.

"Call me, and send Thundermoose around. Have him bring me a cup of coffee."

"It's Wintermoose. Good-bye, nosy."

Steve was laughing as he hung up the phone. Paula was one

of the most private people he'd ever known. He hadn't pictured her bringing a man home unless she'd known him for months. Most of them were intimidated by her intelligence and sassy wit long before that. He was looking forward to meeting Wintermoose.

Just after he finished reviewing his past week's trades on the market—a habit of his every Saturday—he got a second call from Paula. His mood darkened.

"They what?" he asked her, astounded.

"They fired me. The notice came in the mail . . . that chickenshit, Lund. Can I have Wintermoose's job? He can get on somewhere pounding iron or whatever it is they do."

"No, you can't have his job, if I have one for him. I've got some ideas for you, so come along with him. What about the forensics person?"

"I've got a call in. Seems Meredith Spotted Fawn is a molecular biologist specializing in DNA at Michigan State. And she's also a Potawatomi. I left word on her home machine."

"When are you coming in? Are you all right with this, Paula?"

"The Great Spirit works in mysterious ways. Yes, I'm fine. But I won't be if you don't keep me outta jail, my red brother."

"Get in here by ten. And bring Wintermoose and bring me a cup of coffee . . . if your houseboy has it made."

She hung up without responding to his badly timed humor.

He could give them a half an hour if they arrived by ten. He had another meeting at eleven. The meeting was only a few floors above his office, but he wanted a few minutes to get his head on right before he came face-to-face with Alex Dragonovich for the first time in over twenty-five years.

Paula and Thad Wintermoose arrived exactly on time. Sally showed them in while Steve finished a phone call. He'd run a recent check on Dragonovich and International Consolidated Oil and Mining, and this phone call was the detective he'd hired. Oscar Petersen of Stanley Reporting Service, actually an investigation agency, gave a verbal report—just the one Steve wanted to hear—and said he'd have a written report in by the following day. As Steve suspected, Dragonovich was the majority owner of ICOM. The company was his one and only asset and investment. If he lost ICOM, he'd lose everything. And better yet, Dragonovich had borrowed heavily against his personal stock. Should that stock fall below its loan value, any prudent bank would call the loan. Steve hung up the phone all smiles. He rose and extended his hand to the big man across the desk.

"So I hear you're out of a job, Mr. Wintermoose," Steve said, wiping off the smile.

"The big bosses didn't see the humor in that McGuire Building being vacated in the middle of a workday." Thad smiled as if it were no big deal.

"You work there long?"

"Six years. Long enough so they had to pay my retirement."

"Great. We don't have a lot of employees around here. In fact, up to now it's just been Sally and me . . . but there's always something."

Thad's look hardened. "I don't need any handouts. I'm healthy as a bull moose. I can probably get on about anywhere."

"It wouldn't be a handout. What have you done in the past?"

"Started out on the farm upstate, then the navy. I was a shore patrolman for five years, then did some rent-a-cop work around the city while I was waiting to get on the high iron." He seemed to sit a little higher in his chair. "I walked iron for six years before I got laid off . . . due to lack of work . . . then I got on as day labor in general construction and moved up to foreman at the last place."

Steve had his answer. "I was going to hire some outside help . . . actually bodyguard help. Are you licensed to carry a firearm?"

"Damn straight I am. I even did some part-time work as an armored car guard . . . lousy pay but not a bad job."

"Can you handle yourself?"

Wintermoose grinned at this one. "I was number one in the state in high school as a heavyweight wrestler not so long ago. No one's tougher than a wrestler, in case you didn't know."

"A swimmer myself. But you didn't answer the question. Can you handle yourself?"

He grinned again. "You wanna try me?"

Steve laughed. "Yeah, in a hundred-yard butterfly."

"No thanks. What'll this bodyguard thing pay, and why do you need one?"

Steve thought the latter a particularly fair question. He explained the threats on his life, that he might be setting out on a new venture that would cause half the State of New York to want his hide. He asked what Thad had been making, then matched it.

Thad Wintermoose continued to smile, then asked, "When do I start?"

"How about Monday morning? Come to the office ready to travel for a couple of days on a minute's notice. If you're legal with permits and all that, come carrying but out of sight. Shoulder holster or back or something . . . whatever you prefer. I'd suggest you study up on personal protection . . . it'll give you something to do while you're sitting around waiting for me."

"Sounds all right."

"You're Mohawk?"

"Oneida. On the rolls but not active in the politics."

"Just as well. You know anyone on St. Regis?"

"Probably a few who worked around the city, but none I can recall offhand."

"We're going up there pretty quick, and a few of those folks don't seem to want to see me coming."

"That'll be their problem. . . . And you?"

"What?"

"What tribe?"

"Salish, from Montana."

"Plains tribe?"

"Not really. Rocky Mountains . . . the Bitterroot Valley and parts west . . . but a buffalo people."

"Good."

"Monday morning, then." Steve stood and shook hands with Thad. "How about waiting outside while I finish up with Paula?"

The big man excused himself, and Steve turned to his old friend and shook his head as if concerned. "Sorry, old friend, but *I* don't have a job for you."

She looked a little crestfallen, and Steve laughed. "But the Native American Improvement Coalition has one."

She eyed him curiously. "I thought I'd heard of all the Native American groups around the country."

"You probably have. I just incorporated this one yesterday afternoon. I made a few phone calls and have one tenth of one percent of the gross of several Indian casinos around the country committed to the cause, and I've just begun. I wouldn't be surprised if you'll have a budget of well over a quarter of a million a year to begin with. Probably a lot more after I get hold of a few of my other clients."

Paula smiled finally. "That's nice. A budget to do what?"

"To lobby for Native American gaming in Washington, and to lobby *against* all other forms of legal gambling on a state level all around the country. You'll have enough to do. I've made an offer on some space down the hall. We'll be neighbors . . . and I'm on your advisory committee. You're not shed of me yet. And, of course, between you and me, there's this new opportunity . . ."

"I've never lobbied."

"You've politicked plenty. It's the same game. If I recall, you got Paul Nighthawk elected to the State Assembly when you were still at the University of Montana."

"I didn't say I'm not game. What's this job pay?"

"Same as you were making, whatever that was."

"And when do I start?"

"Tomorrow. You need to go furniture shopping and hire a secretary . . . now I've got to haul ass. I've got a meeting I've been waiting for for a long, long time."

She rose and headed for the door, then turned back. "Thanks, my brother."

"You're welcome, my little blond redskin sister. But don't be so hasty. You may not thank me after you get into this thing chin-deep. You're going to be at the vanguard of this treaty thing if it comes down like my dream last night said it would."

"Did you filter it through a dream catcher?"

"One's hanging right over the buffalo robe where I sleep."

"Water bed would be my bet."

"Shows how little you know, little sister. Now, go . . . and let's both give our wings to the wind. Right now I've got to use all my coyote wits on this next meeting."

She got up to leave, but paused as she reached the door. "Not to seem petty, but where's the document?"

"London bank, in a safe deposit box. If anything happens to me, by my instruction you'll get a letter and key from them. Patrick has a copy and he'll be sending along a full translation when he finishes it."

"Probably a good idea . . . the deposit box in a foreign country, I mean."

Steve buzzed Sally as Paula left. "Give me a few minutes to

cogitate, please. Then I'm off to climb the ivory tower of International Consolidated Oil and Mining."

"That's fine. I just made a tentative appointment for you in St. Regis for Monday afternoon. The casino managers and owners have agreed to meet with you. . . ."

"Confirm it," he said, feeling the sour breath of the bear brush his face.

"And, by the way, you just received an invitation from the mayor's office. You've been invited to the Rainbow Room on Thursday night . . . along with three or four hundred of the mayor's other intimate friends, to celebrate New York's ethnic diversity. The First Annual Rainbow Dinner. Congratulations, you're now among the in crowd."

"Sounds like a pain in the proverbial ass, but one I'd better bear, pardon the pun. I presume you booked a return trip from St. Regis."

"A proverbial ass must be one trying to tote a wise man, or some such. If that's not the ass you refer to, I hope you don't plan to moon the mayor."

"Hardly." Steve chuckled.

"As to your flight, this is Sally, your efficient secretary you're talking to here, you're scheduled back Wednesday night."

"Right, thanks. Get Wintermoose on the same flights. Now, give me a few minutes. . . ."

He sat quiet with his eyes closed for twenty minutes, having a silent spirit talk with Standing Bear. Then he rose and walked to the small bathroom off his office to run a comb through his hair.

He'd become hard as flint on the inside while preparing himself for the coming meeting, and slick as calf slobber and smiling on the outside. He took one last look in the mirror, turned, and walked out into the hall to the elevator foyer. He punched in the twenty-seventh floor.

International Consolidated, known on the Street as ICOM, leased four floors of the building, twenty-seven through thirty. The elevator deposited him in the company's outer sanctum, the reception area. It was all mauve and gray, with oversized chrome-framed pictures of drilling rigs and mining equipment on the walls, each with an individual recessed spotlight flaunting the company's hard iron and steel assets.

Steve smiled before he turned his attention to the striking receptionist. Smiled because he'd found out only that morning there
was a crack in the armor.

The bleached blonde with more than ample accoutrements
looked up and smiled as he stepped in front of her rosewood
desk. "Good morning, you're here to see . . . ?"

"Mr. Dragonovich."

"Have a seat, please. You must be Mr. Drum?" He acknowledged with a smile and nod as she continued. "Coffee or something else to drink?"

Her smile rang as phony as her crisp British accent, or at least
as fake as her bulging breasts—he couldn't help but glance at the
ample cleavage. If they weren't the result of an old boyfriend's
twenty-five-hundred-dollar investment, she'd been born with
forty double D's—come to think of it, maybe a five-thousand-
dollar investment—that stood up proud and sassy. She flounced
away, her fine muscle tone amply demonstrated in the gluteus
maximus region, when he said black coffee would be fine.

As he thumbed through a recent issue of *Mining Journal,* he
couldn't help but notice that she waited twenty minutes before
calling to announce that he was in the lobby.

He presumed the twenty-minute wait to see the great man was
obligatory. As soon as she placed the phone back in the cradle,
she smiled at him. "You can go up now, Mr. Drum. The far
elevator is for our four floors exclusively. Please press the ICOM-
four button. Miss Callahey will greet you in the ICOM penthouse
lobby."

"Thanks, and thanks for the coffee," he said, making his way
to the prescribed elevator. He hesitated a moment after she said,
"Anytime," and turned back.

"What's your name?"

"Melody."

"Thanks, Melody." This time her smile seemed genuine. She
looked him up and down as he headed for the private elevator.
She was a tune he wouldn't mind playing . . . particularly if he
wanted to learn something about ICOM. *Can't do that,* he chastised
himself. *You've got a deal with a certain Italian lady, an exclusive deal,*
he reminded himself.

The top-floor receptionist flashed a perfect pearly smile under
a tease of red hair—she was equally endowed. He decided the

twenty-minute wait must have fulfilled his homage. The redhead escorted him directly to a pair of heavily carved doors, probably stolen from a centuries-old church in some far-flung country where ICOM had a drilling concession.

Seated behind his desk, Alex Dragonovich was the picture of a highly paid executive. He kept his head lowered, studying some legal-sized document. The redhead escorted Steve across the twenty-five-foot office to directly in front of the desk, also heavily carved. When she cleared her throat, Dragonovich looked up and flashed a hard smile, then stood and extended his hand—the hand that had held the gun that killed Steve's father so many years earlier.

Steve's insides hardened to flint. With a coyote smile, he took the firm hand and shook.

"Please, sit, Mr. Drum . . . glad to finally meet you in person. I've heard a lot of good things from my people."

The years had been kind to him, Steve decided while lowering himself softly into the deep chair. Hair a lot grayer but still thick, eyes clear. The mustache was gone. Steve wondered if he'd had his teeth capped, then decided yes, he had. As he remembered, young Dragonovich's teeth had been on the scraggy yellow side.

"It's great to meet you, Mr. Dragonovich."

"Please, call me Alex."

"Yes, sir . . . Alex."

"Now, my people tell me you have some influence in the Native American sector."

"Some, yes. At least I hope so."

"Do you know why I asked you here?"

"No, sir." Actually, Steve knew exactly why.

"As you probably know, we're heavy into mineral exploration. To be honest with you, we've been approached by a Native American who's made a discovery that's partially on a reservation. We need a negotiator to make a deal with that reservation—a hard deal, Steve. One that's to our advantage. Is that something you can do? Set aside your Indian affinity and negotiate on our behalf?"

Steve's demeanor turned serious. "I work by the golden rule, Alex." Dragonovich looked disappointed. "The man with the gold makes the rules." Steve laughed. "I work for the man with the money," he said, lying easily.

Alex Dragonovich nodded, and smiled, seemingly satisfied.

Steve sat back in his chair, deciding to let Dragonovich play all his cards. As Standing Bear had told him many times, you don't learn anything by talking.

Dragonovich eyed him, studying him, seeming to read through his cavalier attitude for a moment. He cleared his throat. "You're sure this is something you might be interested in? Something you can do even if the deal is one-sided our way?"

"I've negotiated a lot of deals. I'd say it's right up my alley, so to speak." And I'm an old alley fighter, Steve thought, and know the value of throwing the first punch. And it's already been thrown. "So, what reservation might this be?"

Dragonovich smiled and sat back in his chair. "We have to have a nondisclosure executed first. Our deal with the Navajo prospector who brought us the discovery is conditioned upon our being able to deliver the tribal council. We can't discuss the details until you've signed a nondisclosure."

"That's no problem. I'm not working on any oil or mining deals at present, so there couldn't possibly be a conflict? Where's your agreement?"

Dragonovich leaned over and punched a button on his phone. "Gretchen, did Rostinburg get that agreement up here?"

"Yes, sir."

"Mr. Drum will pick it up on his way out."

"Yes, sir."

Steve rose, smiling tightly. "I think we've forgotten one little item."

"And that is?"

"Compensation."

"I was told you billed at three hundred an hour. Is that right?"

"For legal work, yes. This is agenting, and I expect to work on a commission when I act in an agency posture."

"Fine, then you can have one percent of the deal if it comes down, and, of course, nothing if it doesn't."

Steve smiled. "The oil and mining business must be different from other industries I've dealt with. Five percent would be more like it."

This time it was Dragonovich's turn to smile. "Had you originated the deal, yes, five percent would be fine, but you did not. The deal has been found and already partially evaluated. You're acting only as a closer. One percent is more than fair."

"Two and a half."

"One and a half, and that's my final—"

"Two will work for me," Steve said before Dragonovich could spit out his ultimatum.

He gave Steve a disgruntled look, then broke into a smile. "It's a small deal for us, so I'm not worried about a pittance. Two percent it is. You drive a hard bargain, Steve."

"Five's normal, I got two, and you say *I* drive a hard bargain." But Steve was secretly laughing. He knew it was a deal that would never go through. His compensation would be far greater than Dragonovich could even imagine.

Dragonovich smiled a little like the cat who ate the canary. "Read the contract, make your changes, sign it, and we'll have a deal, presuming you're not one of those attorneys who belabors every comma and period."

"I'm a deal maker, Alex, not a deal breaker, and I'll make this deal for you if anyone can." *Actually I'm gonna break this one right over your steel-gray pate, with any luck, and my father looking down and smiling. Better than that, I'm gonna break you along with it.* Steve smiled like a boy with a new puppy and shook the tall executive's hand. "It's a real pleasure to finally get to do some business with you, Alex."

"Get this one put to bed, Steve, and there'll be a lot more."

Steve continued to smile all the way to the elevator. He had the agreement back on Dragonovich's secretary's desk within the hour, with only the compensation clause changed. By that afternoon the secretary had called to make another appointment for Monday morning, where the details of the deal would be discussed. It wasn't really necessary. It was a deal Steve already knew intimately.

Monday morning with Dragonovich, the culmination of years of quiet planning against the man who'd killed his father, and Monday afternoon on his way to St. Regis, to face a death threat of his own.

The Great Spirit, as Paula had said, did indeed work in mysterious ways.

CHAPTER NINE

Monday morning with ICOM went smoothly, with Steve being relegated to a couple of Dragonovich's subordinates and given the details of what ICOM referred to as the Hovenweep gold, silver, and lead discovery, including a list of deal points that would make or break the deal.

Steve was to contact and arrange to meet Hector Alvarez, a member of the Navajo Nation, then, together, meet with the tribal council of the Navajo Nation as soon as the meeting could be arranged. Finally, he was to assist Alvarez in arranging for a core rig to visit the site and take "independent" samples of the find.

Steve smiled as he left the ICOM meeting. He knew two things critical to the coming negotiations: first, Hector Alvarez was actually Hector Rodriguez, and Mexican, not Navajo, and second, there was no discovery. He knew Rodriguez, but Rodriguez didn't know Steve, which was just the way Steve had planned it.

He still hadn't formulated how to take the greatest advantage of his setup, but he had an inkling. It all depended on how committed ICOM became to the project. And how tenuous their financial situation really was. Those facts should be forthcoming after he received another report from the firm he had hired to investigate ICOM.

But for now he had to put it out of his mind. He had a short meeting with Paula, then he was off to St. Regis to meet with the antigambling faction who had hired him as a consultant, then with the casino operators.

He got off the elevator on his floor, only to be met by a squat, wide-shouldered man in the hallway in front of the Red Ace office door.

"Hey, you're Stephen Drum," the man said with a tight smile.

Steve saw the man's hand extend and thought he was going to shake, but, rather, he thrust a manila envelope into Steve's extended palm.

"This is for you."

Steve presumed he'd been served papers for a lawsuit, but then realized the envelope was only five inches by seven, much too small for legal documents.

He looked up, but the man was disappearing into the elevator. Shrugging, he carried the envelope inside and waved to Paula to follow him into his office. Thad Wintermoose rose from his chair, but Steve motioned him to stay. He pulled the flap from the envelope as he rounded his desk.

Removing several pictures and a note from the envelope, he sighed deeply. The pictures were of Angela Giovanni entering his condo building, then coming out hours later. They would have been innocuous, harmless, except the address was clearly visible on the building facade and the pictures had a date and time imprinted in a lower corner. The note was simple. "What would you pay to keep Aldo Giovanni from knowing that his daughter was porking a dirty Indian." There was no question mark at the end of the crude printing.

"Fuck!" Steve collapsed in his chair.

"He exclaimed," Paula said, then asked, "Or was that a pass?"

"Hardly, that would be incestuous. Just another problem. What would a day be without another kick in the balls?"

"Whoa, is Steve Sounding Drum, Indian warrior, feeling sorry for himself? Let me see those."

Steve stuffed the envelope in a desk drawer. "Personal. And no, I'm not feeling sorry for myself. It's a problem for someone else more than me."

"Good. You don't need any more."

He seemed eager to change the subject. "Have you done any good with the DNA thing?"

"I'm waiting here for a call from Meredith Spotted Fawn. We've been playing phone tag, and I left word for her to call me here at eleven. Now, about the furniture—"

"No matter how good she is, she can't work without material from the site."

"I'm working on it."

"Paula, if you want me to handle it—"

"You gave me the responsibility. I'll handle it."

"I don't want you in deeper kaka with the university."

"Getting the material is my assignment, and I'll—"

"Okay, okay. Just don't hang yourself with the rope I'm giving you."

"Have you heard from McGoogan?"

"Not yet. I called him yesterday and got no answer. I hope he's in Amsterdam, deep in the bowels of the Hag."

"That's bowel, not bowels. Bowel is plural. Now, about the furniture—"

In less than twenty minutes he was finished with Paula. After he locked the pictures in his personal safe in the credenza behind his desk, he and Thad were on their way to Kennedy to catch a commuter flight to Albany, then on to Messena, the closest airport to St. Regis, the Mohawk Indian reservation.

While in the town car, he made a call to his home answering machine. He'd brought his bag with him to the office so there would be no need to stop. Concerned about how he and Angela had left things between them, he wanted to hear from her. As he hoped, there were two messages. "Hi. I'm going with Mama and Papa for a short trip to France and Papa's hometown in Italy. We're leaving Friday . . . so I won't be in the city. We'll be gone almost two weeks. I'll try and call from there, if I have a chance . . . we, you and I, could probably use a little break, so maybe it's for the best. . . . I don't mean that like it sounds. I know I'll miss you terribly." There was a long pause, then, a quiet, "Love you." The click of her hanging up echoed through his skull, as loud and lonely as a midnight tom-tom.

As first he felt a little angry, then decided to judge her, as his old grandfather had often suggested, when he'd walked a mile in her moccasins. She had her own family problems. The second message was more direct but the caller nameless. "I hope you've had a chance to think about what those pictures are worth."

That, too, was a problem more affecting Angela and her relationship with her family. Then again, it was Aldo Giovanni who would be more than merely upset by the pictures, and Don Aldo could certainly make it Steve's problem if he was angry enough. Don Aldo was not a man to upset if you could help it.

But the first call troubled him far more than the second, try as he might to understand, try as he might to put himself in her shoes.

And that crack, *being apart will do us good,* or whatever it was she'd said. Hell, they were hardly ever together as it was. The *love you* she'd closed with echoed inside his head.

She could have made sure she talked to him, or saw him, alone, before she left for two weeks. He would have liked to make love to her before she left, and he felt an obligation to inform her of his problem with the stalker photographer.

It was her problem too.

He had the sudden impulse to call her at home, but that would only cause more trouble.

A very bad taste danced a dirge on his tongue.

They rode the rest of the way to Kennedy in silence. In the car, he sat back and closed his eyes, thinking of the first time he'd known someone to cross Aldo Giovanni. Two months after he'd saved Tony from drowning, he was walking back to his room, when a man stepped out from the bushes near his porch, called out his name, and handed him a sheaf of papers. He spun on his heel and left without another word. Steve carried them to his room before reading them. He was being sued! He'd never been sued, and he was amazed as he read the documents. Some jerk named Trevor Whitcomb had named him as a defendant in the damage of his yacht. He was accused of ramming the boat into the dock while driving it without the owner's permission.

Steve sat, mouth open, astounded. The man he'd risked his life to save was suing him for damaging the boat. He claimed damages of sixty-seven thousand dollars.

Well, he wanted to become an attorney, so he guessed this would be some practical experience for him. He spent all his free time for the next week preparing an answer in pro per, without benefit of an attorney he couldn't afford.

When he was about to put the answer in the mail, a knock came on his door. The man standing there untangled his hand from a crutch and extended it, introducing himself as Trevor

Whitcomb. His left leg was encased in white plaster from ankle to thigh.

At first Steve was confused, since in the boat accident the man had sustained an injury to his chest, not his leg. Whitcomb sheepishly explained that he'd been in error filing the lawsuit. It was a stupid and ungrateful thing to do, and he begged for Steve's apology and said the suit had been dropped. Steve accepted the strained apology, then inquired about his leg. Whitcomb's eyes flashed anger for a fleeting second, then he composed himself. With gritted teeth he explained he'd had another accident.

Later, when he inquired about the man to Mr. Giovanni, he'd been told that the man was ungrateful and the ungrateful often have accidents. This man had carelessly run into a baseball bat. Steve left it at that, but he pictured some no-neck goon having a long chat with Trevor Whitcomb.

It was the first of many times he suspected that Papa Al's methods were from the old school—the old Sicilian school.

Later, when they tried to purchase a trucking company, and the owner reneged on some negotiations, the man turned up missing. He'd never been found. Papa Al now owned the company, buying it from the man's estate for much less than the original price.

Steve had no proof of Al's involvement in the man's disappearance, but it seemed prima facie.

When they arrived at Kennedy, Steve was surprised to see Thad check his small carryon along with his two-suit bag, and questioned him about it as they hurried to the gate.

He flashed Steve a sly smile. "It's no easy task to board a plane with a firearm, even if you have a permit to carry. It's much easier to just check the piece."

"I thought they had radar or X ray or some damn thing?"

"They do at some airports, and for some flights in particular, but not usually for commuters. Even then if the piece is checked and discovered, it can be explained away a lot easier with a permit. Human nature, and the will to survive being what it is, they X-ray all *transferred* bags from flight to flight and any bags checked *without* passengers accompanying them . . . Most of these zealots causing airplane problems lose their zeal when they're going to be blown up with the rest of us heathens. So bags without passengers attached are particularly suspect."

Steve watched the big man move easily through the busy terminal, keeping pace with his own fast stride, avoiding bumping into others, never seeming to need a breath. So far, the man had impressed him. Of course, he hadn't been tested. Steve laughed quietly to himself. He hoped his new bodyguard *never was tested!*

He wondered what the real extent of Thad's experience was. "Sounds like you've been down this rosy path before . . . with guns and air flight, I mean."

Thad laughed. "I have, and believe me, checking is a lot easier. These airport cops seem to believe, like Bogie, who said, 'My, my, my, such a lot of guns around town, and so few brains.' "

"Bogie?"

"You know, Steve, Humphrey Bogart."

"Oh, yeah, I agree with that too. The fewer guns, the better, at least this side of Montana. Where we're going is proof of that. The Mohawks have had their share of shootings . . . "

"You anti-gun, Steve?"

"No, not at all. At least, not from a legal standpoint. It's just that I believe in the Constitution. I wonder what the anti-gun folks would think if Cambridge, Mass., or Duluth or Topeka passed a local ordinance banning Jews, or Catholics, or Germans. Or banning the local paper from writing about politics. You know, freedom of religion, all men created equal, and freedom of speech . . . in my mind, the right to bear arms is the same. *Guaranteed* under the Constitution. If they continue dicking with that right, what about the others? If they want to screw around with constitutional rights, then they should *change* the basic document by amendment . . . as provided for in the Constitution. Rather than try to reinterpret it by twentieth- or twenty-first-century standards."

"Why don't they try to change it?" Thad asked as they neared their gate.

"Because they know they can't. The basic strength of this country is the fact it's a federal system, as diverse as every city and county, every ethnic background; made up of states, counties, cities . . . and yes, reservations. Local law prevails . . . *so long as it's constitutional.* Two-thirds of this country is going to have to agree to a constitutional amendment." He had to dodge a group of nuns, and, being Catholic, did so with special reverence and deference. Then he continued. "Knowing they can't get that agreement, the anti-gunners circumvent by local ordinance. And

those local ordinances get passed not because they're constitutional, but because we read continually about some child shot by
his schoolmate when it's the parent who carelessly allowed access
to the firearm whose *sentence* we should be reading about. It's a
knee-jerk reaction to an inanimate object. It's easier to deal with
a firearm than with a distraught parent.

"We seldom read about the sixty-year-old grandmother who
defends herself, and maybe survives, by shooting, or, more likely,
merely waving her gun at some punk burglar with a knife . . .
not because it doesn't happen more often by far, by twenty or
maybe a hundred times, than the accidental shooting, but because
it's page-ten news, not front-page."

"Is that bad," Thad asked, "local ordinances against guns, I
mean?"

"Would it be bad if the ordinance said no Indians allowed in
Duluth? Both rights are clearly in the Constitution."

"I see your point."

They made the plane on time.

Paula stopped by her apartment on the way to shop for furniture. She wanted to change out of the heels she wore and get
into something more practical for trekking around the miles of
furniture store halls she knew she had to face.

Her answering machine was blinking, so she poked the button.
"Dr. Fox, I was shocked to hear about your being let go. Please
call me." It was David Greenberg. She dialed the number he left,
and he picked up on the first ring. She agreed to meet him for
lunch at Mama Gold's.

If it was David Greenberg who'd ratted her out, was he now
following his journalistic instincts and trying to find out what
she'd left the site with, or worse, was he spying for Peter Lund?

It should prove to be an interesting lunch.

She visited two stores, then caught a cab to the deli. She was right
on time, and he was already seated, picking through a generous
stainless steel bowl of pickles on the table. Thin-faced but topped
with a generous mop of black hair, with a runner's lean body,
almost chinless, David Greenberg arose when she approached.
He mopped pickle juice from his hand with a paper napkin,

replaced his gold-rimmed half-glasses on his nose, then offered both his hand and a generous smile.

"I'm glad you could join me, Dr. Fox," he said, waiting for her to take a seat before he regained his.

"I'm glad you invited me."

"This is a great place. My first time here."

They ordered. Paula, her usual chicken soup, this time with matzo balls, and David, gefilte fish. Both had herbal tea.

After the tea was served, there was a short silence. He finally cleared his throat. "I'm really sorry that you're not still on the dig. I'm sorry that schmuck Lund canned you. I can't believe it!"

She weighed her response a moment. If he was there on Lund's behalf, she wanted him to believe she was on the attack. "It's not over. I have several courses of action—"

"I want you to know that I didn't say a word about your leaving there with that bag. It was none of my business, and to tell you the truth, you probably had . . . have . . . a greater right to what's at that dig than the university . . . at least a moral right, if not a legal one."

Paula smiled coyly. "Of course, you're presuming I had something in the bag other than my laundry, but thanks for the thought. Why would I have a 'greater right'?"

"I heard your lectures regarding the bones of your ancestors being improperly entombed in the cold and dusty file drawers of hundreds of museums rather than in the holy ground to which they were consecrated. Had this dig been on Masada, I might have felt I had rights also. So in many ways I agree." He seemed suddenly steeped in moral indignation. "It wasn't your laundry, Dr. Fox. It was a rolled parchment, tied with woven bark. I'd glanced at it earlier, and it was gone after you left."

Again Paula smiled, but this time a plastic one concealing her shock that David knew exactly what she'd taken. "I'm sure Lund was very interested to get this information."

She was sorry they were interrupted by the waitress serving their food before he could respond with other than a wounded look.

When the squat bleached blonde left, David eyed her over the gold rims of his glasses. "You have no reason to believe me, Dr. Fox, but I was not the one who squealed on you. It was Patty Elridge. If you don't mind my saying so . . . and for lack of a more descriptive or accurate word, she's a cunt."

At that, Paula smiled. "I don't mind a bit, under the circumstances."

"All she saw was you leaving the site with the bag. She had no idea what was in it, she just wanted to make brownie points with Lund. To tell the truth, I think the old boy is schlepping over to her apartment and slipping the kabossa to her. Again, if I can speak frankly, she'd dick a dead dog for a D, and he's been giving her A's for the past two years in every subject she's taken from him . . . and she was completely pissed you gave me the dig chief position."

"You are frank, David. That's interesting information, nonetheless."

"Lund is a dizzy bastard trying to pin the tail on the donkey. He has no idea what was taken from the dig. I didn't tell him, and the girls don't know. I don't think Ingrid would say if she did. She has, as I do, a great respect for you." He forked a big bite, but paused before it reached his mouth. "I hope you found something of great value, and I hope you put it to good use. I know whatever it was, it wasn't for personal gain."

He chewed as she eyed him, considering his sincerity.

"You really believe that, David?"

"Yes, ma'am. Oy vey, this is great. Eat your matzo balls before they get cold . . . and try one of these garlic pickles."

She decided to take a chance. "If you really believe what you've said, and you really believe in me, then there is something you can do for me."

He swallowed, but eyed her for a long time before he responded, dabbing a napkin at his mouth. "I'll tell you what I'll do. I'm a writer, as you know, an aspiring journalist, and I hope to make my mark writing about archaeology, which is an avocation, not a vocation, with me. If there's a story in this . . . and not just the discovery, I mean. I want the first crack at it—if there's no chance of my going to jail, or ruining my career before it starts, shoot. I'll do anything I can, given those conditions."

She leaned forward, pushing her soup to the side, and spoke in a low voice.

"That's fair enough, about the first story rights, but only if you'll agree not to publish anything until I give you the go-ahead."

"Done." He reached over the table and they shook hands. Only then did he ask, "And jail?"

"Damn slight chance, I'd guess."

"I hope you're a good guesser, Dr. Fox."

"Please call me Paula, David. When are you back at the dig, and have they moved the skeletons yet?"

"This afternoon, right after lunch, as a matter of fact, and no, they haven't moved anything yet."

"Now, here's what I need from the site—"

Neither of them finished their lunch, which Paula paid for, overtipping the waitress. She was thrilled her problem could be solved without her returning to the site. They left, agreeing to meet at her apartment at six P.M.

It was all she could do not to apologize to David for doubting him. But she didn't. It was probably better he didn't know.

When she arrived home early that evening, David sat on the granite porch in front of her building. He carried a small paper sack. She waved him after her, hurried up the three floors of stairs, unlocked the door, and entered. He followed, unrolling the top of the brown paper bag as he did so, and extending it in both hands.

She took it from him and peered inside. Three digits, each from the hand of a different skeleton, rested inside.

"Oy vey," Paula exclaimed, and David laughed.

"Now, can you tell me what was in the parchment?" he said, biting his lower lip in anticipation.

"No, I can't. Not yet. But I can make you a cup of tea."

"Is it my last before going to jail?" he asked, only half in jest.

"No one saw you remove these?"

"No one. I was scared shitless, to tell you the truth."

"Then, David, my young friend, I will swear I took them the same time I took the . . . the other item, if it comes to that."

"So, what *was* the other item, exactly?"

"Sit down, David, while I fix you a cup of herbal. And think of something else to fill your busy little head with. How about your forthcoming article in *Smithsonian* magazine . . . when this is over."

"Thanks for the thought, but I'd much prefer a Pulitzer Prize–winning book."

Before she could get to her small kitchen, her phone rang. She answered and smiled as she heard the voice on the other end announcing who she was. It was Dr. Spotted Fawn, calling from Michigan State, and now she was ready for her.

CHAPTER TEN

Steven Drum was escorted directly into Joseph Bigsam's office and invited to wait there. He entered the building without Wintermoose at his side, instructing him to wander around, play the slots, and act like a customer . . . but to keep as close an eye on Steve as he could.

He'd been met at the airport by Rollie Hendricks and Thomas Mackelbee, both Mohawk leaders of the opposition to Indian gaming on the rez and Steve's employers on this job. But the pair had elected not to enter Big Sam's casino or attend Steve's meeting with the acknowledged but unofficial leader of the gaming interests.

The office walls, those that were not mirrored, were lined with memorabilia and artifacts. A beautiful collection of wooden and corn-husk masks—false faces of the Iroquois—the finest Steve had ever seen, adorned the office, lined up high on the wall out of reach. A number of small frames below the masks enclosed quotes, many by Indian leaders.

With his hands folded behind his back, Steve bent to read one; to his surprise, one by an Englishman.

> The Iroquois laugh when you talk to them of obedience
> to kings; for they cannot reconcile the idea of submission
> with the dignity of man. Each individual is a sovereign

in his own mind; and as he conceives he derives his freedom from the Creator alone, he cannot be induced to acknowledge any other power.

John Long, England, 1645

Steve smiled. Then went on to the next frame:

If they are to fight, they are too few.
If they are to be killed, they are too many.
Thoyanoguen Hendrick,
Mohawk, the French and Indian War

and to the next:

Why do you complain that our young men have fired at your soldiers, and killed your cattle and your horses? You yourselves are the cause of this. You marched your armies into our country, and built forts here, though we told you, again and again, that we wished you to remove. My Brothers, this land is ours, and not yours.

Shingas and Turtle's Heart, Lenape

Before he read on, he heard the click of the door, but not before he'd concluded that Joseph Bigsam was an interesting man.

Bigsam entered his office through a door behind his desk, a hidden door in the walnut paneling Steve had not realized was there. Flanking the door on either side were rows of semiautomatic weapons.

The man was big, filling the door frame. Without smiling, he rounded his desk and extended his hand. "You must be Steve Drum. You're interested in Indian wisdom?"

Steve smiled, shook, then followed the wave of Bigsam's hand indicating he should be seated. He took a leather wing chair, one of a matching pair facing the big desk, while Bigsam took his leather chair behind the desk.

"Not only Indian quotes," Steve said. "I see at least one by an Englishman."

Bigsam smiled for the first time. "Only when they accidentally spoke truth, even if in regards to their prejudice, did I bother to

hang them with the others. You might notice that out of the thirty
or so framed, only three are those of white-eyes."

Steve laughed. "I can't argue with the odds, which brings me
to the subject at hand. You know I've been hired as an outside
consultant—"

"Hired by those opposed to gaming."

"True, but I took the job only if I could give recommendations
I felt were for the good of the rez as a whole. For all the people,
without taking sides or making moral judgments."

Bigsam began to tap his fingers on the desktop. Steve sensed
he was already bored with this meeting and would pay little
attention to anything he had to say.

"Well, Steve, that's an interesting approach for the doomsdayers
to take. Maybe they're getting smart."

"I presume there are smart people on both sides of the issue.
There usually are, or there wouldn't be an issue."

"So, what can I do for you?"

"You can show me around your operation . . . and maybe we
can get to know each other a little better."

"That's fine, but I don't know what good it'll do you or your
'cause.' "

"My cause is only what's in the best interest of the Mohawk
as a whole. And you should know, I believe in the return of the
buffalo, but only if it benefits all Indians."

Bigsam rose and walked around the desk. "Come on, I'm proud
of my operation and wouldn't mind showing you around. But
don't expect anything to come of it."

"No expectations." Steve rose to follow.

Bigsam paused, then pointed to one of the quotes on the wall.
"Read that one before we begin."

Steve walked to the small frame and read:

> When I look upward, I see the sky serene and happy;
> and when I look on the earth, I see all my children
> wandering in the utmost misery and distress.
>
> Mashipinashiwish, Ojibway

When Steve finished, he merely nodded.

As Bigsam walked to one of the one-way-mirrored doors leading to a walkway over the casino, he grumbled, "When I got into

this gaming in the first place, it was admittedly to help myself, but also by helping myself I felt I could help my people. It's been the Christian minority on the rez, not real redskins, real dumbskins, who can't see that they no longer wander in quite so much misery because of what I and a few others have accomplished."

"Like I said, Mr. Bigsam, I believe in the return of the buffalo and the benefit to all *skins*."

"Good, then come on and I'll show you the finest Indian gaming operation in the country." Then he laughed, a deep, resonating echo like a bellowing bull. "Of course, when my people, my dealers and croups, look upward, they see only mirrors, not the sky serene and happy. But they know that Joe Bigsam is looking down, watching. The eagle in the sky."

"That's the way to run a railroad," Steve said, following.

Steve was surprised and pleased that Joseph Bigsam showed him the entire operation, including the counting room. He took him from table to table, even introducing him to his floor bosses. All, Steve noted, appeared to be Indian.

Thad Wintermoose stalked them, staying a couple of aisles away. Steve thought another man stayed on their heels, then realized it was two men. A pair of twin Indians, dressed identically, each equally as large as Bigsam and Thad Wintermoose.

They returned to Bigsam's office, and the man again invited him to be seated. Opening a desk drawer, he broke out a bottle of Knockando scotch. "Care to indulge in a white-eye weakness?"

"Don't mind if I do. That's a damn good bottle of scotch."

Bigsam looked smug. "You have a bodyguard along. Big doofus guy, a skin, cowboy boots."

"Yes, I do. I'll mention to him you think he's doofus-lookin'." Steve got an equally smug look. "And you have a couple of boys shadowing you around. Twins. Butt ugly, dog dumb. Probably Mohawk."

Bigsam laughed so loud, the mirrors shook. He settled into his leather chair, took a sip, and eyed Steve for a moment. "So, what wonderful suggestions do you have, now that you've seen my layout . . . besides the obvious, that I should close it down and let the redskins who bought into the black-robe book, the Bible thumpers, have their way?"

"That's the last thing I'd suggest." Steve savored his own drink for a moment. The solution to the rez problem came to him in a flash. "You know I know quite a bit about running a casino—"

"And I don't?"

"Not at all. You're doing a hell of a job here . . . but I could increase your gross by fifty percent, and your net by two hundred or more."

Bigsam guffawed. "That's horseshit, Houdini."

"No Houdini to it, just a little refinement."

"So, if you could, what's in it for you?"

It was Steve's turn to laugh. "Actually, all that's in it for me is a job well done. I'll give you a few tips, if you'll commit a lousy twenty percent of your *increased* net to fund specific rez projects."

Bigsam studied Steve a moment, thinking before he spoke. He took the time to jam a big cigar into his mouth and light up. He pushed a desk humidor across to Steve, who shook his head no. "I've had a half dozen consultants here from Vegas. They seem to think . . . and I think . . . we're doing a hell of a good job running our own dog and pony show."

"You are, but you can do better. What do you have to lose? Nothing, and a hell of a lot to gain."

"So, I suppose you'll want me to report my take to the Elder Council? That'll never happen. Nobody sees my take sheets."

"I see you have a shredder behind your desk. You won't have to show anyone anything. I can come back here as a consultant for the council and tell in a few hours if you're holding out on them."

"Bullshit. No one can do that."

"Oh? You're running two thousand seats down there. You're grossing two million a month, probably a little less in the winter months, when the access is tough due to the weather, but you make up for it in the summer. If you've got a twenty-percent hold on the poker machines, twenty-five on keno, and fifteen on the rest of the slots, like you say you do, I can tell you within five percent what you're netting, unless you're overpaying salaries or promos or something."

Bigsam was silent for a long ten count, then he laughed. "You've been studying my operation for a whole lot longer that just this afternoon—"

"My first time here, Joe. No one's told me a thing about your place other than it's the biggest here."

Joe again fell silent. "So, what kind of rez programs?"

"On the ride in I found out there was no child care center here, no truly effective youth drug and alcohol programs, and damn few scholarships."

"Bullshit again. I have a child care center for my employees—"

"That benefits you and your operation and employees, Joe, not the rez as a whole. How about the Mohawk girl who wants to go to school to improve herself but can't because the old man's abandoned her, or in jail for butt-legging or peddling something worse, and she's got two papooses at home. Commit twenty percent of your *increased* net, and I'll show you a hell of a lot of ways to increase the net . . . and make you a hero to your people instead of a surrogate white-eye." Steve leaned forward in his chair. "And I want you to join the Native American Improvement Coalition. That'll cost you one-tenth of a percent of your gross, but it'll come back to you in a hundred ways."

Joe clamped down on the cigar and spoke between clenched teeth. "Don't insult me, Mr. New York City, I'm no surrogate white-eye, and none of my people think so." He spat a bit of leaf on the carpet. "It would take a dumb-skin not to take you up on that, Drum."

"Great. Can we write it down, a short form agreement?"

"You do it and send it to me . . . but first, give me one measly suggestion that'll increase my take." He sat back in his chair and raised a bushy eyebrow. "Just one."

"Okay, what's fifteen percent of a dollar?"

"Don't insult me. It's the Bible thumpers who are the dumb-skins. It's fifteen cents."

"Now, what's ten percent of five dollars?"

"Okay, I'll play along. It's fifty cents."

"So, increase your number of five-dollar machines to ten per hundred from the one per hundred you have now, and reduce the hold on them to ten percent. . . . Your gross will go up by over seven percent, and your net by two or three. Your players will keep hearing those five-dollar machines pay off. Your crowds will grow bigger, as will your gross and your net."

"I'm not sure—"

"Try it and see. I'll guarantee it. And increase the number of fifteen-hundred-dollar keno payouts. Even though you don't report winners to the IRS, your clientele is used to playing at houses that do, and they'll play the fifteen-hundred-dollar nonreporting payouts two to one, increasing your take by twenty percent."

Bigsam studied him for a minute. "Draw your agreement, with my right to rescind in six months if your New York city-slicker ideas don't pay out."

"You got it. You'll be hearing from me." Steve killed the last of his Knockando, then rose and leaned across the table to shake hands.

"By the way, what the hell is the Native American Improvement Coalition? Another do-gooder save-the-wretched-Indian group?"

"No, it's a new group founded by Indians for Indians to lobby for Native American gaming and against the growth of gaming in the white-eye sector . . . although that part of it is not common knowledge. Actually, they're looking for someone to sit on their advisory council, and you'd fill that bill."

"Not interested, but I'll join . . . *if* we come to an agreement." As Steve headed for the door, Bigsam called after him. "You're an attorney, a Harvard-educated one, I understand?" It was the first time Bigsam gave any indication he knew anything about Steve. Obviously he'd done his homework.

"That's true," Steve answered.

"So you believe in the white-eye law . . . even though at good ol' Harvard they probably called you a blanket nigger behind your back?"

"Yeah, actually I do. I think the Constitution has served us well . . . us being the real Americans, I mean, as well as the immigrants."

Bigsam eyed him skeptically. "I guess that's right, to a great extent. I wouldn't have this place if the boys in black, the nine scorpions in the bottle, hadn't finally ruled in favor of rez rights."

"The only thing wrong with the Supreme Court," Steve said with a smile, "is the fact they have no real Americans among the scorpions."

"True." Bigsam's smile tightened, and his voice lowered an octave. "Do you believe in the Declaration of Independence?"

"I don't know a hell of a lot about it, and I haven't given it a lot of thought. It's the Constitution that deals with the law. . . ."

"Maybe you should know a little more about it." He motioned to the wall with his head. "Read that one in the black frame before you leave."

Steve paused then walked to the framed quote at which Bigsam pointed.

> ". . . the merciless Indian savages whose known rule of warfare is an undistinguished destruction of all ages, sexes, and conditions."
>
> *United States Declaration of Independence*

"I've never read that," Steve admitted.

"A document highly revered and believed in by the white-eye. I don't expect *our* agreement to result in any additional government interference in my operation. I'd hate to break out the AK-47s again and prove the merciless Indian savage part."

Steve nodded. "True. I'm sure a lot of white-eyes believe in the Declaration of Independence; however, most of them know about as much about what it says as I do. They believe in the concept. But it's the Constitution I agree with, *properly* interpreted. Let's keep moving forward, and we'll have a place among the scorpions." Steve waved as he left. "You'll hear from me with a short form agreement. I'll know what you're increased net is, and I'll expect it to be reflected in your donation to rez projects. It's my only upside out of this other than a pittance from the other side."

"A deal's a deal."

Steve paused and turned back. "By the way, I've had a few threats on my phone and in the mail . . . and even handed to me in the hall outside my office. I presume that's some of your overeager cohorts here on the rez?"

"I wouldn't be surprised," Bigsam said, gnawing on his cigar with a corner of his mouth turned up.

"Call them off . . . even if *you're* them. I don't scare."

"I'll mention it the next time we get together."

"Good. Come see me the next time you're in the city, and I'll repay the scotch."

"I'd like that."

Steve nodded and closed the door behind him.

He spent the rest of the afternoon and the next day visiting the other casinos on the rez and meeting the owners, but did not engage in any more negotiations. He figured if Bigsam went along and he was able to increase his net, even with an agreement that would benefit the rez, the rest would follow.

On Tuesday night he had dinner with Rollie Hendricks and Thomas Mackelbee.

At first, after hearing his plan, they suggested that he was creating a feather-bed job for himself. When he said he'd recommend three other gaming specialists who could equally well do the required inspections, they backed off and admitted it was a plan that could benefit all. They accepted his recommendations.

The next morning he and Thad flew back to Kennedy.

He spent most of the trip home worrying about Angela and how he'd left it with her. He was glad that at least he'd solved the problem with the stalker-photographer. At least he hoped he had. There was little doubt in his mind that the man had been from St. Regis, and probably worked directly for Joe Bigsam. Who else would be giving him a hard time?

It had to be connected to St. Regis. Now he wouldn't even have to worry Angela with the matter.

He guessed she'd call from France, or maybe Italy.

CHAPTER ELEVEN

Early Thursday morning in New York, very late Thursday night in Amsterdam, Steve received his eagerly awaited call from Patrick McGoogan.

"Are you sitting down?" he asked Steve.

"Yes, and holding my breath."

"Inhale the polluted air of New York City, my friend. It seems the good governor John Quinton Williamson is well documented here at the Hag, and had full legal rights to return the land described to the Canarsee. In fact, it was land he personally owned."

"And the signature?"

"I'm no handwriting expert, and I suggest we get the jump on the opposition and employ one, but it looks authentic to me."

"Great news."

"I'm getting copies of everything in the files with Williamson's signature, and a lot of other documents and correspondence I didn't have time to read. I'll have a file box full of reading material. My Dutch is a little weak, but I've got an associate back at Oxford who'll be thrilled to interpret for us."

"Great, keep me informed."

"You got it."

Steve sat back in his deep chair for a moment, shaking his head. He hadn't really believed it until then. And now that he believed it, what the hell was he going to do with it?

He walked out of his office, past Thad Wintermoose, who sat reading up on personal protection, waving him back down into his seat as he passed, then headed down the hall to the new offices of the Native American Improvement Coalition. Paula had already hired a secretary. A round-faced, rotund, serious Seneca girl, Alice Blackrock, who was a recent graduate of City College and well qualified. She assessed Steve as he entered, not yet quite sure who was who around the coalition.

"Is Paula in?" he asked as he walked past Alice's desk to her door. In a leap, Alice was on her feet barring the door to Paula's private office.

"I'll tell her you're here."

Steve laughed. This girl would do. "Okay, you tell her I'm here."

Alice stuck her head through the door, careful to do so in a manner where Steve couldn't see into the office. She announced him and stepped aside so he could enter, offering him a now-cherubic smile. "Would you like coffee, Mr. Drum?" she asked.

Again Steve laughed. "Yes, ma'am, please."

He sat and explained Patrick's findings to Paula.

As he spoke, he could see her emotions were as mixed as his.

When he finished, she sat back thoughtfully, then studied him expectantly. "Okay, now what?"

"You know, I don't have any idea where we're going with this. When we get the DNA information, I guess we'll try to prove some direct descendency from the Canarsee. Then make some kind of claim and see what falls."

"It'll probably fall right on our head."

Steve laughed, but this time more seriously. "I'm still thinking about it. Old Chief Onnegaha has been waiting over three hundred years. I guess we're in no hurry . . ."

He rose and walked out, feeling like he was about three feet off the ground.

He returned to his office. As he passed through the outer office, Sally looked up from her work. "You remember it's bib-and-tucker night tonight."

"What?"

"You're invited to the mayor's Rainbow Dinner at the Rainbow Room. You do have your tux pressed?"

"Call Li. He should be at the condo. Then call Litcomb's and get me a ride in a stretch . . . just to the dinner, so I arrive in style. I'll cab it home."

"You got it. You know the invite included 'guest.' I took the liberty of RSVPing for two."

He waved her off with a smile and entered his office. It made him think of Angela for the hundredth time that morning, and the fact he had not heard from her since the call announcing she was off to France and Italy with her parents. And reminded him that *she thought* they could use "some time apart." That was the bad news.

The good news was his conversation with Joseph Bigsam must have worked. He'd heard nothing more from the stalker-photographer. Bigsam had been good as his word and called him off.

For the hundredth time, he was going somewhere alone. He was almost pissed enough at his situation with Angela, or lack of one, that he wondered, a flashing thought, who he might call to go to the dinner with him . . . but he didn't, he wouldn't. He still had an understanding with her, and he would honor it until they agreed, mutually, to cancel it or, far better yet, to acknowledge and solidify it. But he was beginning to doubt, to wonder if that would ever happen.

When he arrived at the condo, his houseboy, Li Chung, was gone but his tux was waiting, creases sharp as a flint war ax, on the cherry-wood valet in his bedroom. He passed it by on his way to check his messages, and his stomach felt as empty and dry as a shed snakeskin when he found no message from Angela.

He took his time showering and dressing, listening to an old Cal Tjader disk, then a little Bach, just to get him in the mood for a staid dinner with New York's diverse ethnic community.

He'd met Mayor William Patrini only one time, and that in passing at a Democratic political fund-raiser to which he'd been invited. He'd never taken part in politics in New York, preferring to play hard to get and not to get swept up in the bullshit. There was no Native American party, and probably never would be.

As he dressed, tying a neckpiece of black and white porcupine quill, elk tooth, and bear claw in place of a black bow tie, and clipping beaded black and white button covers over the pearl studs on his shirt, he inserted beaded cuff links and smiled. If they wanted him there as a representative of Native Americans, he'd give them representative. He wished he had a well-tanned elkhide tux, but Armani didn't make them.

Still, he felt a little like he was to be the main dish rather than a guest at a Pilgrim Thanksgiving.

Alone, dressed and knowing that the limo was waiting down at the curb, he poured himself a scotch and soda, walked to the window, stared out over the city, and listened to Johann Sebastian Bach's *Jesu, Joy of Man's Desiring*. As if in response to Johann's suggestion, he desired Angela's company. He slammed down the scotch and soda, and against his normal restraint, poured himself a stronger one. Neat this time.

Finally, he steeled himself with a deep breath and the last of the double scotch, and left.

It was seven-ten, ten minutes late, by the time he arrived at Rockefeller Center, at the GE Building, and the limo dropped him off. International Broadcasting Company, whose offices occupied most of the building, had installed a giant TV screen on the face of the building overlooking the ice rink. A bit of Times Square in Rockefeller Center. It could be seen even from Fifth Avenue. Usurping their normal broadcasting were scenes of the mayor's Rainbow Dinner, on the building's sixty-fifth floor. Giant speakers on either side of the screen, which was actually several dozen large TV screens put together to form one, emitted a Glenn Miller tune.

Even though a few minutes late, Steve took the time to wander around and enjoy the murals and statues. Pausing at the entrance, he studied a limestone relief of a man holding a compass and the words etched below, WISDOM AND KNOWLEDGE SHALL BE THE STABILITY OF THY TIME. Not disagreeing, he walked on until he reached a stairway to the mezzanine, and noted a large mural of five men kicking and fighting for a ball representing the earth. The plaque explained: "The five races of mankind, Caucasian, white; American Indian, red; Mongolian, yellow; Malay, brown; and Negro, black; are shown with the world as a symbolic football using war for the supremacy of the world."

Pleased to note that old John D. Rockefeller, Jr., and the artist acknowledged that red men existed, he moved on to a stairway at the other end of the mezzanine. Pausing again, he studied another mural obviously by the same artist. Five men again, this time with hands clasped and a broken cannon. The plaque below stated: "Their ire and venom spent and problems solved, the five races are now shown clasping their hands in brotherhood. The symbolic silent and broken cannon is seen in the foreground." A noble thought. It moved him, and he studied it for a long while before going on.

Steve entered the elevator with a group of East Indians, the men in tuxes and the women in beautiful, glimmering silk saris dripping with jewels. They quickly rose sixty-five floors to the top of the Rock.

The Art Deco Rockefeller Center had always fascinated him. Although he didn't know a lot about its history, he'd loved it and its Radio City Music Hall—particularly the Rockettes—since the first time he'd enjoyed a show there, and was happy he'd been invited. By the time the elevator arrived at the top floor, he made up his mind to enjoy the evening and have a good time.

He walked straight to the bar, set up outside the main area, and got himself another scotch neat. Walking through the foyer and a cloud of smoke from those wanting a last cigarette before entering, he made his way into the Rainbow Room proper, rather smugly flashing his invitation at the doorman. A full orchestra played a Glenn Miller tune, and the room teemed with guests of every skin color, many, like Steve, displaying some subtle form of their native dress.

The warmth emanating from the mayor's guests seemed to reflect the warmth of the dark wood walls, maroon carpet, and lights of the city beyond the huge window wall. The guests stood, not finding seats yet, trying to avoid the speeches they were sure to have to endure. They talked, mingling, but mostly in ethnic groups. Blacks and blacks, browns and browns, yellows and yellows. The rainbow's colors were well defined. Steve seemed to be the only redskin there.

He wandered from group to group, looking for someone he knew. Then he suddenly stopped short. He would recognize that bare back anywhere. He knew that mole, the shoulder blade, the sensuous olive complexion, the curve of that beautiful spine.

At first he felt a rush of enveloping warmth, then her back was encircled by an arm in a black tux, with a diamond-encrusted cuff link glittering, blinding, hypnotizing. He watched, unseen, an arm's length away as the man nuzzled and whispered something in her ear, then, as she glanced up at the suntanned male-model look-alike. A glance, a look, he'd always thought reserved for him, her eyes a dance across the man's sharp features, a caress.

A caress that had melted him many times, but now suddenly tempered him to cold steel.

A dousing of red-hot iron into cold, congealed oil.

Then he melted in a different way. His stomach swarmed with worms, snakes. His mouth went dry. His first impulse was to wrench the arm away; tear it from its socket and beat the model's carefully coiffed pate senseless with his own appendage—then he realized he had no right, and it sickened him worse.

Starting to turn and walk out of there, Steve was stopped short by Aldo Giovanni's deep voice.

"Stephen, good to see you."

Robotlike, he extended his hand and shook with the man who'd done so much for him, but stopped short of the ultimate gift. Steve's eyes stayed on the tall, slick-haired man whose arm encircled Angela's waist, and who was now rubbing her bare back with a long-fingered manicured hand. Another diamond, at least four carats, flashed on the man's pinkie finger. Hearing her father's voice, she turned slowly, an arm's length from him, taking herself out from the enveloping arm of her escort.

"Steve," she said, and her hazel eyes went blank.

Mrs. Giovanni, Angela's comfortably rotund mother, stepped around her daughter, put a hand behind Steve's neck, and bussed him with a warm chubby cheek. He had to bend down to allow her to do so.

"It's so good to see you, Steve," she said. "Are you alone . . . maybe we can get you to join our table."

"It's assigned seating, Mama," Al quickly intervened. "Can I buy you a drink?" Steve imagined a smirk on his face, but it could have been a smile, one never really knew with Al. Then, almost as an afterthought, Al added, "This is Nick Masticelli. Nick, Steve Drum."

The man had turned with Angela and re-encircled her waist with a long arm. He had to remove it to extend his hand to Steve. His handshake was firm and strong; still, it was all Steve could do not to try and sink him to his knees with a vise grip. He didn't. He merely nodded.

"Nice to meet you," Nick Masticelli said, flashing perfect white teeth. "Great outfit," he added with what Steve also perceived as a smirk. He returned his attention to Angela. "Dance?" he asked.

"In a minute," she said, looking back at Steve, her eyes searching his for some reaction. He nailed her with one look, as hard and cold as slate. Getting some satisfaction from her Orphan Annie stare, he ignored her and turned his attention to Al.

"I'd love a drink. Let's wander out to the bar."

Steve strode away, not awaiting an answer. Al Giovanni followed a few steps behind. By the time he arrived at the bar, Steve had already ordered another double scotch neat, and a Campari and soda for Al.

They talked for a while, Steve not really hearing anything Al said, until he finally surveyed Steve carefully. "Is this the first time you've met Nick?"

He had Steve's full attention. "Yeah, I think so. You known him long?"

"Yes. He's a fine young man. His father is in the business in Hartford."

Steve knew that Al was letting him know that Nick Masticelli was connected, a "family" member.

"He's just a little older than Angela," Al continued, "and went to college near her. They used to date in college. Nick's an attorney, like you."

Steve forced himself to smile. "Old sweethearts. How nice for Angela."

"I have high hopes for them," Al said, watching Steve so carefully, Steve thought he might be counting the quills on his neckpiece.

"Good for Angela," Steve said, then changed the subject. "How's Tony?"

"Tony's the same. Tony will always be the same."

Steve merely nodded sympathetically. The band's trumpets played a reveille and went silent, and the crowd began moving back into the Rainbow Room. Steve nodded to Al and moved away to find his seat. He pulled his invitation from his coat pocket and found his table number, searching the table placards until he realized the direction they ran. He guessed he was not among the privileged as he moved to the back of the room and found himself seated against the rear wall.

Two blacks, natives of Nigeria, or so said their name tags, and four Asians, Taiwanese, shared his table. After he sat, one seat remained vacant; he presumed that was for his nonexistent date. The empty seat mocked him until he moved it away from the table and back against the wall. He felt like throwing it through the tall window, but the shards and chair itself might be a little hard on the innocent sixty-five stories below.

He hardly had time to introduce himself to his tablemates, his attention being consumed by his poor view of Al's table in the front of the room near the dance floor. His view of the floor was hindered, but the view was far too clear of Nick Masticelli seated there, winding a finger through a strand of Angela's hair, his face only inches from hers, before a thin-faced man took the podium from the bandleader.

"Good evening, I'm Terrence Thornburg with the mayor's office."

Steve threw down the remnants of his drink, then forced his attention to the speaker.

"I'd like to welcome you to the First Annual Rainbow Dinner, appropriately enough, here at the Rainbow Room in historic Rockefeller Center." The man went on for fifteen minutes waxing eloquent about Mayor Patrini and all the accomplishments of his tenure, finally introducing the mayor, who took the podium to resounding applause from those gathered to enjoy free food and drink.

As the orchestra began a very low and slow rendition of "America the Beautiful," the mayor waited in silence until the room finally quieted, relishing in typical political manner the echoing accolade. Finally, his deep voice resonated over low, almost hypnotizing amber waves of grain and purple mountain's majesty.

"Welcome, welcome, to this dinner, and more important, to the United States of America and the unequaled and unparalleled City of New York. I welcome you, *and myself,* and congratulate all of us. After all, all of us here are immigrants. All of us came to this country from Europe, Asia, South America, Africa—"

The hair began to rise on Steve's neck. All of *you* are immigrants. All of *us* were here to welcome you. And did.

The mayor continued. "As we marched across this land in the nineteenth century, almost all coming through Ellis Island to fill and farm and mine and timber this great land and—"

To pilfer and steal from Native Americans, to lie and kill, to rape and plunder, Steve silently added.

"We took a wilderness and turned it into paradise—"

A pristine wilderness, and turned it into a trash pile, denuding it of wildlife, of topsoil, of minerals, of its indigenous people.

"And we remembered our roots. No, not the roots in Europe or elsewhere, but our roots here, here in New York. Great fortunes were founded here. Immigrants who landed with nothing but hope founded the greatest financial center in the world, drawing wealth from the immense natural resources of this country."

I think I'm in the wrong place, Steve concluded. But he wouldn't get up and walk out, as much as he wanted to, much as he should.

He wanted to continue to watch the unfolding love story of Angela and Nick. Angela, the perfect Italian daughter. Nick, the Italian stallion. Nick, the "family" man. Nick the Tom Selleck look-alike, *sans* mustache. Nick, whose granddaddy probably came through Ellis Island.

The mayor finished and turned the program back to the orchestra. Steve watched Angela accept Nick's offer to dance, then they disappeared onto the overflowing dance floor.

"Where are you from?" He realized one of the Asians was talking to him.

Steve managed a smile. "I'm probably in the wrong place since I may be the only nonimmigrant here. I'm a *Native* American," he stressed the native. "I'm from Montana."

"Aw," the Asian said. "You are Indian?"

"Yes," he said, a little combative in tone. Then he realized it wasn't the Asian's poor judgment that left out any mention of those who had been there to greet the immigrant hordes with open arms. To feed and shelter them and help them through those first hard winters. To retreat from their relentless advance, to accept their purposefully smallpox-infected blankets . . . the Pilgrim version of germ warfare . . . and believe their lies for far, far too long.

"So, you're from Taiwan?" Steve asked, trying to be polite.

"Yes. I am an immigrant."

"So, has the United States welcomed and been good to you?"

The man smiled widely. "Yes, I guess you could say it has. It has been very good to me. This is not my best year here, but I came with nothing, and I am now an owner of real estate."

Steve nodded his approval, trying his best to keep up a polite conversation with the man, but continually glancing at the dance floor, not wanting to miss the saga of Nick and Angela.

"So, you've managed to save enough to buy yourself a piece of the dream," Steve said. "Only in America."

"Yes," the man agreed. "Only in America."

"Wonderful. Where's your real estate . . . a home, I presume?" Steve asked, again glancing over the man's shoulder.

"Actually, you're sitting in the crown jewel of my holdings."

This got Steve's attention. "Here. You own this restaurant?"

"No, and yes, I own the real estate . . . this is leased. Actually, I own this building."

Steve laughed. "You own 30 Rockefeller Plaza?"

"Well, my company does. This and other buildings in the Center. As you probably know, Rockefeller Center was originally composed of fourteen buildings, and grew at one time to nineteen, but this is the jewel in the crown. The Asian American Real Estate Trust bought this building, the lower plaza, the French Building, and the British Empire Building out of bankruptcy two years ago."

With sincerity, Steve introduced himself and learned Wilber Wong's name, then said, "Congratulations. I've long admired the Center, and particularly this building." He did not voice his thoughts that only in America would the site of the nation's most famous Christmas tree be owned by Taiwanese. He laughed at the thought of the tree being topped by a fat Buddha.

"Thank you," Wong said with modest sincerity.

Steve eyed him for a long while, then he had one of those flashes that was becoming common to him. He added, "I see you have several vacancies in the building."

"A few. Bankruptcies are always hard on a real estate complex, even one with a proud heritage. It has taken much longer to refill than we hoped. The market is not so good in midtown Manhattan."

"I'd guess you have at least twenty-five percent vacancy?"

He picked a figure out of the air, actually, he'd not thought about it at all, but slightly remembered an article in *The New York Times* about Rockefeller Center some time ago. The four Asians talked among themselves for a second, one making a rude remark in Chinese regarding Native Americans owning nothing but mud shacks, at which they all laughed. Steve acted as if he had no idea what was being said.

The man cleared his throat and returned his attention to Steve, but cut his eyes away as he spoke. "I wish our vacancy factor were that small. But it's getting better."

"So," Steve said casually, "is your interest in the Center for sale?"

"Oh, no," the man said quickly. "We at the trust are much better buyers than sellers. It is not for sale. We will work our small problems out." He looked disdainfully at Steve as if to say *Why would you care, you of mud huts*. But he didn't, he merely acted a touch condescending.

Steve smiled and shook his head. "I hope so," he lied.

Rockefeller Center. Now, there's a thought.

He turned his eyes back to the dance floor and caught Angela and Nick returning to the table.

Taking a deep breath, he again tried unsuccessfully to quell the anger that had been inching its way up his spine since he first realized she was there, and not on her way to France and Italy as she'd left word she would be. In all fairness, he realized, she had said "this weekend." And it wasn't the weekend yet, but she'd also said she wouldn't be in the city.

Still, she was here, and obviously here with the Italian stallion. That was *not* part of their understanding.

Steve traded business cards with the Asian, who was obviously ambivalent about doing so and did just to be polite, then Steve rose and made his way across the room to Al's table. He'd remember Wilber Ian Wong, president of the Asian American Real Estate Trust. Putting him out of his mind, he shook hands with Al and bussed Mama on the cheek, then extended his hand to Nick Masticelli. "Nice to have met you," he said, and got a handshake and nod in return. He never met eyes with Angela, then excused himself and started out of the room.

Again, the sound of his name stopped him short. He turned to see Alex Dragonovich waving him over. The tall, graying mining executive sat with nine of his employees at a circular table.

"So, you're a part of the Rainbow also," Dragonovich said.

"You bet. Actually, we Native Americans are the pot of gold at the rainbow's end." Dragonovich and his people laughed, and Steve realized his table was well adorned. The bleached blond receptionist who called herself Melody was in attendance. The orchestra, having progressed from the forties to the fifties, finished "Three Coins in the Fountain" then struck up an old Bill Haley rock and roll song "Rock Around the Clock," and Steve glanced over to see Nick and Angela rising to dance again. He couldn't help himself.

"Do you dance?" he asked Melody, who giggled and rose to take Steve's hand. To the obvious glare of Alex Dragonovich, Steve escorted her to the floor and danced as he had never danced before, working her near Angela and Nick, and actually bumping them in his exuberance. He caused them and several other couples to give ground as he deep-dipped the luscious blonde until her long tresses swept the dance floor. To his utter joy, Melody was not only delicious to look at, but exuded sex with every movement of her well-developed, overripe body, and every beat of the music.

Steve could feel Angela's eyes boring into his back as he pulled the girl close and buried his face in her neck.

Melody was obviously a little drunk, and giggled more than once as she thrust her pelvis against him—until he thought he might be bruised for life.

As the music stopped, he said loudly enough so all the nearby dancers could overhear, including Angela Giovanni, "You know, that's a great idea, I'll see you there, baby."

Melody looked at him with furrowed brows, having no idea what he was talking about, but he hustled her off the floor before she could say anything in reply.

Alex Dragonovich gave him a serious frown as he returned her to the table. He smiled and thanked the mining executive for allowing her to dance, then bent down and gave her a lingering kiss on the cheek, eliciting another glare from Dragonovich.

In a heartbeat, he was out of the room.

He had the cab let him out at an Irish pub two blocks from his condo, and in the wee hours was the last to leave, insulting the pubkeeper by drinking up a whole bottle of scotch and not touching a bit of the fine mist of the Irish bog.

Stumbling home at two A.M., leaving a footprint on the corner of the unaddressed Peninsula Hotel envelope peeking out from under his doormat, ignoring the blinking answering machine, he fell into bed, not bothering to remove his tux shirt and pants, and kicking off only one shoe.

His last thoughts were of Rockefeller Center, adorned with hand-painted elkhides and hair-on buffalo robes. Then the Center was suddenly decorated in white flowers, white blooms and lace everywhere. The look Angela had given Nick Masticelli slashed through his mind's eye, then they walked away, disappeared into the mist, and lace, and flowers, hand in hand.

He slept fitfully, dreaming of the bear and its foul breath for the first time in months.

CHAPTER TWELVE

Centipedes did tangos on his tongue, obviously after first taking a forced march through the chicken coup.

At least their millions of little feet were coated with something that tasted really, really bad. And they were up early, he noted through squinched eyelids, the sun just washing the eastern sky with a splash of dirty light.

He tightly closed his eyes again, then eased the effort because even that made his head feel as if a large blacksmith were shoeing horses there, between his ears. The hammer echoed, reverberated. Be kind to yourself, he chastised, allow yourself to awake slowly. But then, it would be a good idea to hurry the process as he felt the need to exercise some religion, and exorcise some poison from his stomach by kneeling before the white throne. But the twenty feet from his bed to the bathroom seemed as foreboding as the Dineh's long walk. It was not hard to recall why he'd pledged to himself not to take more than one drink a day. Last night he'd exceeded that limit by at least two dozen. And of course, Hoolihan's Irish Pub didn't have good scotch, so, like the fool he obviously was, he'd swilled their cheap stuff.

Cursing the Kennedys for ever importing the swill, putting one foot deliberately on the floor, he managed to sit up in bed, then knew that the contents of his stomach were about to revisit the light by the shortest possible route. It wouldn't do to puke all over his Armani tux, even though it already looked as if it had been through the Custer massacre and lost. He charged to the bathroom, knocking over the phone stand and the answering machine as he did so.

Fool, fool, fool, he chastised himself as he fell to his knees and rested his elbows on the toilet rim. Good old Li Chung, the water reverberated nicely blue thanks to some chemical insert. Then he remembered why he drank scotch and soda. He did not throw up, but, rather, just roiled and wished he could. Rising clumsily from worshipping the ceramic edifice, he undressed, then tried to turn the blue water green with the addition of a splash of yellow.

The one physical part of his Salish culture he brought with him to New York was the sweat bath, only in his apartment it took the form of a cedar-lined sauna, with petroglyph reproductions painted on its walls. He turned the heat above unbearable and sat in its corner, leaning his head against the wooden wall, cleansing every pore. Many times while there he'd chant a Salish spirit song, but now his head hurt too badly. He splashed water on the rock heater until it finally drove him out. Stumbling into the shower, taking his toothbrush and toothpaste with him, he first took a cold shower, then, adjusting the water to just short of scalding, he slowly ebbed to the floor and sat in the flood, trying his best to brush away both the taste in his mouth and memories of the night before.

Love story. The saga of Angela and Nick. Love is never having to say you're sorry, preppy. He spat a mouthful of toothpaste at the drain, wishing it were into Nick Masticelli's eye.

He felt the fool for drinking, but more the fool for having spent the last several years acting as Angela Giovanni's Indian lackey. Seeing her at her convenience, not imposing himself on her precious family. Striking an agreement, a pact, not to see others.

The fucking he got was not worth the fucking he was getting. He said it, then choked. It almost made him cry to do so.

Every caress she'd given him now echoed of sandpaper.

Fuck, he was a fool.

No more, he decided. Never again. He wanted to throw up. His head hurt, reeled. But the anger began to solidify his resolve.

Pushing himself up to his feet, he finished the shower, toweled off, then faced the mirror and hollow eyes glaring back, like two piss holes in the snow, and shaved.

He would think of Angela Giovanni no more. She was officially *out* of his thought process.

Now, what did he have to do today that was positive? Something that would move the sagging saga of Stephen Sounding Drum forward.

Angela, Angela . . . no, no, no, he would not think of her again.

Put her out of his mind. A wasted ten years, that's all Angela Giovanni is . . . was.

Move forward. He shaved. He mentally fortified himself. He would overcome his weak stomach. His weakness. He fell back into an old habit. As he shaved, then patted on his aftershave, then dressed, he conjured himself as one of the old warriors and envisioned himself among them. To the beat of the tom-tom, he was putting on war paint—only he was not going out to face the ancient and ferocious Blackfeet, but a more formidable enemy, the flood of financial immigrants, cavalry in sharkskin astride laptops. And his war paint was Polo aftershave, a Savile Row hand-tailored pin-striped suit, a hand-stitched broadcloth button-down shirt, a Harvard tie, and a pair of highly polished crocodile tassel loafers.

Thinking of the mayor's speech, his Rainbow speech, Steve's anger solidified his resolve even more.

All of those in that room were *not* immigrants. Some of us in the room, at least the forefathers of one of us in that room, *greeted* the immigrants. Some of us were here on Manhattan Island, fishing, hunting, weaving, growing, working in peace, loving the land, respecting the land, not desecrating it, for a hundred or more, maybe five hundred, generations before the *Mayflower* and its load of European criminals crept ashore.

There, in the Rainbow Room, high in Rockefeller Center, three hundred immigrants listened to a second-generation Italian mayor talk of New York being the center of the financial world, the center of immigrant fortunes. New York City, Manhattan Island, that had come to the immigrants for a handful of beads. New York, building its financial might on piles of mine tailings, of devastated forests, of raped and wasted topsoil all across the North American continent.

Rockefeller Center, from a fortune made from oil extracted from what—in all that was holy—was Native American land. From coal, off the backs of tens of thousands of coal miners. From railroads that brought the immigrants west—and from the buffalo hunters who came to desecrate not only a species, but a way of life. Fur became felt, hides became shoes, bones became fertilizer—all of it became New York wealth. Millions of noble beasts who fed and nourished two hundred or more nations of Native Americans became felt and brogans and fertilizer. And Native Americans starved, losing everything that had been theirs for five hundred generations.

Yes, it would be fitting, the completion of a full circle, should Rockefeller Center somehow serve to benefit the native people of the United States. All Native Americans.

Now, that was a goal worth accomplishing. The circle of life completed. Closed, to fruition.

And maybe a hell of a good chunk of Manhattan Island still technically, even under white-eye law, belonged to Native Americans.

Maybe he could give a few immigrants their walking papers. As he'd thought before, he'd like to give them all a three-day notice to quit or pay rent.

He laughed. It was still not a bad thought. Right now he was particularly not too fond of Italians, especially after one had filled his thoughts for the last ten years, to no avail.

He would think of *her* no more.

Even to *claim* half of Manhattan Island would be worth the fun of it. Worth the attention it would bring the Native American cause. He would sure as hell make the newspapers, the world's newspapers if he lay claim to half the richest island in the world.

He laughed again, but his stomach rolled. He had to get something in it to settle it. Even before he finished the thought, he heard Li Chung enter the front door and call out a greeting in Mandarin Chinese.

Steve answered likewise, then walked out of his study and asked Li for a couple of poached eggs, orange juice, hot tea, and dry toast. It was about as much as he thought his stomach could stand, if it could stand that.

He returned to his study, wondering if Angela had called or come by last night after her date. Old sweethearts, Al had said. At least he thought he'd said that. Angela and Nick. A good Italian boy. Fuck them, and the sleek black limo they rode in on.

No more.

He walked back into the master bedroom and picked up the telephone and answering machine, having to plug it back in since it had come dislodged when he'd stumbled over it. The phone rang immediately. He allowed the machine to answer.

Then he realized that if Angela had called, it was too late. After being disconnected, the machine was recording over any calls that had been on it before he'd accidentally unplugged it.

Good. To hell with her. He'd as soon not know. He couldn't stand to hear a bunch of lies . . . although he was sure she had never lied to him before. Of course, she'd said she was going with her parents to Europe. She hadn't mentioned going to the mayor's Rainbow Dinner with good old college sweetheart Nick. Omission was, most times, as foul as commission. Still, he would think of her no more. No more. *She* was out of his mind.

As the old chief had said, he would fight no more forever. At least not that fight.

The voice on the speaker was Paula's. He picked up the receiver. "Hi."

"Hi. I'm glad I caught you. I've had another command summons from Peter Lund at the university. Seems they want me to appear again, this time before the dean, 'to discuss the dig,' quote unquote."

"Did you ask if they were going to have a cop in attendance this time?"

"Yes, I did, as a matter of fact, and he said no, but he will have a representative of the university's legal staff, an attorney, there."

"Good, I'll go along as your counsel."

"I was hoping you'd volunteer."

"We're in this together, Paula. What time?"

"Two P.M., in the dean's office. I told them I'd call back if I could make it. So I guess I'll call back and confirm."

"I'll see you at the office and we'll prepare," he said, then realized he'd need some time to get his head and stomach right. "How about lunch?"

"I'm free for lunch."

He took his time around the apartment, doing paperwork until nine. He called a friend in the real estate business, an old client, Fred Alexander, and retained him to find out all he could about Rockefeller Center. As soon as that call was complete, he called a broker he often dealt with. Jonathan Noble III, of Winston, Winston, & Noble, was also a past client and had old-line contacts all over the Street. Steve requested a full financial report on the Asian American Real Estate Trust. His last call was to Stanley Reporting and Oscar Petersen, the investigator who had helped him with ICOM. He also retained them to dig into the Asian American Real Estate Trust and its officers' private lives.

Yes, the not-so-inscrutable Oriental, Wilber Ian Wong, had said the building was not for sale, but yes, he'd admitted it had over a twenty-five percent vacancy. It had to be costing millions a year to maintain. And everything was for sale. At least everything the immigrants owned.

Hell, he thought in a moment of weakness, that the seventy-story edifice had to be worth two hundred million dollars, maybe a quarter billion, even a quarter empty. His own five-million-dollar net worth wouldn't go far.

Still, it would be interesting to know more about it.

And there was always the O.P.M. method—other people's money. He'd employed the O.P.M. method before.

By the time he'd finished Li's poached eggs and toast, his stomach had settled.

He had to smile as he watched Li carry his tux, the pants in one hand, the coat in the other, to his small utility room and the cleaner's bag residing there. Each item held only by two fingers as if it were a smallpox-infected blanket given the Indians by the Pilgrims.

Li cut his eyes to the dining table, where Steve was finishing the last of his toast and tea, and made a comment under his breath in his impeccable Mandarin. "You wore this to a celebrity *rodeo* last night, and won first place in the dung throw." There was obviously no Mandarin word for *rodeo,* as it was spoken in English.

It was not a question but an accusation, so Steve ignored it.

He made another call. Talking with Oscar Petersen reminded him of ICOM and Alex Dragonovich. He'd probably lost an assignment and an opportunity he'd worked hard for due to his feigned interest in Melody. Obviously, she was more to Dragonovich than merely an employee. He'd have to try to repair that relationship as soon as he got to the office.

At least repair it temporarily; he planned to terminate it in a spectacular manner in his own good time.

It was time he cleaned up a lot of old business and got on with his life.

Alone, if that was the way it had to be.

CHAPTER THIRTEEN

Angela made the excuse she had to go to the ladies' room just before she boarded the Air France 747, and ran instead to the bank of pay phones. Only once in their long relationship had she called Stephen at the office. This would be the second time.

She was irritated with him for several reasons, one being the fact he hadn't given her even the shadow of a benefit of the doubt. He'd seen her with Nick Masticelli and presumed the worst. He of little faith. He of less confidence. Then he hadn't been home when she'd gone by his apartment as soon as she'd gotten rid of the man her father had foisted upon her. She'd had no idea her father had a date awaiting her at the mayor's dinner, or even that they were attending a dinner. She was as surprised as Stephen when she arrived to find Nick Masticelli awaiting with his suave manner and plastic hair. He reminded her of a dark Ken of Ken and Barbie fame. At least in appearance, if not demeanor. Her father continued his attempts to find her a "good Italian boy" no matter how many times she rebelled and was repulsed at his choices. Although she liked Nick as a friend, an old college friend of whom she had fond memories. And she'd been obliged to be at least decent to him, since he was her father's guest.

Even the mayor's dinner had been a surprise. She had thought they were going to dinner with her brother, Tony, before leaving for France and Italy.

She'd left word on Stephen's answering machine to call her at any time. Luckily the Pen had been out of suites and she had a room separate from her mother and father, but he hadn't called. She'd gone by his condo twice, the last time after two A.M. having to slip out of her room to do so. She'd finally left a long love letter under his doormat, explaining that if he'd only be patient, she'd work things out with her father within the next six months. As Steve had often told her, goals without time limits were only wishes.

But he hadn't responded to that either.

Jealousy heated her cheeks at the thought of the sleazy blonde and his display with her while dancing. Yes, she could understand him being a little angry. But did he really meet the blonde with the boobs somewhere after the Rainbow Dinner as his parting remark had implied?

He wasn't home, didn't answer the phone all night.

And they had a pact.

Was their pact a thing of the past? Her chest constricted at the thought of it. She knew she hadn't been fair, but she loved her mother so much, and her mother needed her too. And her father hated the thought of her being involved with anyone other than a "good Italian boy."

She hoped it wasn't over with Steve. She couldn't stand the thought. Not now. Now that she needed him more than ever.

Steve's secretary picked up the phone. "Mr. Drum, please?" Angela asked, her voice anxious.

"Sorry, but he's out on an appointment. May I ask who's calling?"

"Miss . . . Ms. France. Please tell him I called."

"Your number?"

"Can't be reached. I'll call back."

She ran for the plane, barely making the gate as the attendant pulled the embarkation ramp door closed behind her.

Steve, Steve, she thought, sinking into the plush first-class seat behind her parents, *please don't have gone somewhere and taken your anger out on a sleazy blonde. Please be patient a little while longer. I know exactly how we'll resolve this problem with my father, if you'll just be patient.*

If I'm right about what I think I am, even my hard-headed father won't be able to refuse us.
Mama will kill him if he does.
Or me.

Steve briefed Paula as if it were a deposition she was faced with. Don't volunteer any information. Don't answer anything you're not sure of without getting a nod from your attorney. Don't volunteer any information. Answer questions with a yes or no if possible. Don't volunteer any information.

Finally she said, "I understand, I won't volunteer any information."

And take on an attitude of righteous indignation. He'd said again and again.

With Thad Wintermoose in tow, they arrived at the university and headed for the administration building and the dean's office and were shown to a nearby conference room. Thad, large hands folded behind his back like a palace guard, waited, stationing himself outside the half-glass door.

Paula was immediately taken aback when she entered. Horace Williamson, dean of the anthropology, archaeology, and paleontology departments, sat at the head of the long table. A shock of white hair fell across his black-rimmed glasses, watery eyes, and puffy, mottled face.

To his left, Peter Lund, the archaeology department head, sat, cold blue eyes riveted on Paula. To his right, facing Lund across the table, was a slight, balding man Paula didn't know. Robert Wallis, Paula's peer and the archaeologist who'd taken over the McGuire Building dig; David Greenberg, Patricia Elridge, and Ingrid Petersen, the students on the dig, flanked them down either side of the table.

Steve stepped forward, introducing himself as Paula's attorney and extending his hand and nodding to each of them in turn. Paula noted the name of the man she didn't know, Alfred Swartz, representing the university's legal department. Steve pulled out a chair for Paula at the far end of the table, a half dozen chairs between her and the first of the others. He took the chair at the foot of the table, purposefully separating himself and Paula from the opposition, facing Williamson down its long length.

"Well," Steve said with some impatience, "we're here."

Dean Horace Williamson turned to the balding, watery-eyed but intense Swartz. "Fred, shall you lead off?"

Swartz cleared his throat, fingering a pencil atop a yellow legal pad in front of him. "Mr. Drum, Ms. Fox, we've asked you here to try to clear up some questions regarding the McGuire Building discovery and your role there."

Steve smiled wolflike. "I can't help but note that you folks were all nicely entrenched in your seats when we arrived. Has this meeting been going on for some time?"

"Just a few minutes," Swartz answered, a tight gash of a smile slitting his face.

"Since we were not privy to the first part of this meeting, do you have any notes or a recording of what transpired in our absence?"

Swartz shrugged. "We just engaged in some informal chatter while awaiting you—"

"So, counselor, if I have to resort to discovery in our pending discrimination lawsuit, I won't find you met here for an hour before we were invited so you could prime this rather imposing group to antagonize, deprecate, and intimidate my client?"

"Lawsuit?" Williamson seemed aghast. Lund paled.

"Of course," Steve said nonchalantly. "Your client dismissed my client without cause. She's been subjected to sexual and racial discrimination—"

Lund looked as if he were going to be sick on the table.

"Racial?" Swartz asked, glancing around the table, confused.

"You weren't aware that Professor Fox was a member of the Kootenai tribe of Montana?"

"She's blond . . ." he mumbled.

"And blue-eyed, and on the rolls of the Kootenais since birth. It sounds like you should have been briefed by your client as well as you obviously briefed them."

"Wait, wait," Swartz said, standing. "We asked you here in an informal and friendly manner—"

"I don't consider it friendly to have met and planned some kind of strategy for an hour before we arrived."

"A half hour," Swartz admitted.

"A half hour," Steve repeated. "If you have allegations about my client's behavior, then let's hear them. If not, then we're all busy."

Peter Lund seemed to steel his backbone and slapped the table.

"By God, she took something from the dig, and we want to know what it was."

"Peter, button it up. I'll handle this," Swartz said. Lund's backbone went to spaghetti again, and he sagged in his seat.

"Mr. Wallis," Steve snapped, "you've been heading this dig. Do you have evidence of anything missing?"

"One of the girls—" he tried to answer.

"Which one?" Steve snapped.

"Why, it doesn't matter which—"

"It matters to us. Which one?"

"Ms. Elridge."

Steve turned to the girl, who'd slunk as far back in her chair as possible. "Is that right, Miss Elridge? You've accused Ms. Fox of taking something from the dig. What, exactly?"

She didn't answer for a long while, then shrugged. "Something. A paper maybe."

"A paper *maybe*," Steve said, shaking his head. He turned to Swartz. "Counselor, a paper *maybe*. You're engaging in a witch hunt because you know your client has screwed up, and you know we have a good discrimination lawsuit and you believe the best defense is a good offense." He glanced at the ceiling and expelled a long breath, then turned his attention to the other end of the table. "I'm really sorry we graced this meeting with our presence. Time better spent preparing a lawsuit. I suggest your time would be better spent determining what amount you'd like to offer Ms. Fox to buy out the remaining contract she's been forced to abandon, with generous punitive damages, of course."

Steve rose to his feet. "Come on, Paula. You've got better things—"

"Wait," Dean Williamson snapped. "There's not only the matter of a missing artifact of some kind, but we've recently discovered some missing skeletal items."

This time it was David Greenberg who slumped in his seat.

Steve snarled. "Have you checked the bins and bins of Native American bones resting in the basement of your archaeology building?"

"Of course not," Williamson said, indignant. "The missing portion of the skeletal discovery never arrived."

"My ancestors' remains are 'skeletal items.' " Steve shook his head, seemingly astonished. "And I guess your undisturbed fam-

ily graves are the hallowed ground of your ancestry? So my ancestors' 'skeletal items' never arrived to join the desecrated remains
of the ancestors of thousands of Native Americans. Remains that
should be properly interred in sacred ground, as *were those* you
recently acquired from the McGuire Building ... before you
robbed those sacred grounds. I wonder"—Steve seemed suddenly
almost teary-eyed—"I wonder how you'd like it if my basement
were filled with bins of bones ... bones I'd dug up from local
cemeteries. Bones of your father and mother, your grandfather."
He seemed to suddenly see the light, and a cunning smile darkened his face. "Maybe there's a lawsuit here too."

"Mr. Drum," Williamson sputtered.

But Steve was pulling Paula to her feet. "Thank you," Steve
said as they headed for the door, "you've given me an idea for
a hell of a class action suit with all the Indian Nations as plaintiffs
... grave robbers would not incur the sympathy of a jury."

He paused at the door and turned back. "By the way, obviously
I'm not being paid to advise you, but I can't help but do so. Do
not call Ms. Fox back here to dwell on your 'maybe' accusations.
We'll be too busy working on our factual findings ... we'll leave
the maybes to you."

They were out the door with nothing but stunned silence behind
them.

Paula shook her head as they headed down the hall. "I'm sure
glad you prepared me so well for this meeting."

"Me too," Steve said absentmindedly.

"Did they try to trick you?" Thad asked her.

"Hell, I sat there like a stone, didn't say a word. Not one word."

"Sounds like you were properly prepared and very eloquent,"
Thad said, and they all laughed.

Steve turned serious. "I think you should give Greenberg a call
and find out what the real tone of the meeting was before we
arrived. All I did was slap them around a little. I could have set
them back so they won't step up again ... and I could have just
made them real, real angry. Fighting mad."

"Oh, good," Paula said, "so what now?"

"Put your head down and your tail up and go to work. Don't
worry about the cougar tracking you until you hear his pads on
the trail, feel his breath on the back of your neck."

"That's a comforting simile."

"Relax," Thad offered. "From what I could see snooping through the door, that Lund and his boss are cut from the same bolt." He went into his Cary Grant imitation. " 'To hardly know him is to know him well.' "

Paula puzzled. "You got me. What's that from?"

"You should know that one, Paula," Thad said with a condescending laugh. *"The Philadelphia Story."*

"Okay, but I like this one better at the moment: 'If there is ever gonna be law and order in the West, we've got to take all the lawyers out and shoot them down like dogs.' "

"Careful," Steve said, holding the door for the two of them.

Paula smiled as she walked out into the fresh air. "Not you, but I didn't like ol' bald Alfred. He worries me."

Steve waved at a cab. "He's probably okay. It's catching. He worries you because he worries. He's a Jewish lawyer. He's paid to worry."

The cab passed them without a glance, so Paula stepped out near the traffic and waved at another.

Thad scratched his head. "So Jewish lawyers worry more than goy lawyers?"

"Jews worry, which may be one of the reasons they're so successful. You ever hear about the Jewish mother who bought her son a couple of shirts for his birthday? He met her for lunch the next day and she studied what he had on, then she said, 'So, you didn't like the other one?' "

Both Paula and Thad laughed.

"The good news is"—Steve climbed in the cab Paula immediately captured—"with luck, he'll worry about what we're up to rather than what we took from the site."

"Let's hope so," Paula muttered, watching the NYU campus disappear behind them.

"The truth is," Steve said, looking out the cab window, "I hate all these frivolous lawsuits happening today."

"Some must have merit?" Paula questioned.

"Some," Steve offered, then added, "but generally, the plaintiff is someone who's gotten a half mil for spilling hot coffee in her crotch due to her own carelessness . . . those we used to call imbeciles, we now call plaintiffs. It exemplifies the worst of the legal system."

That brought another quiet laugh.

CHAPTER FOURTEEN

As they exited the elevator on their office floor, Steve's parting remark to Paula was, "I want to talk to Dr. Spotted Fawn the next time you do . . . maybe a conference call. And get in touch with Greenberg."

"Okay." She headed down the hall. Entering her office, Alice Blackrock looked up and without a greeting gave her the morning's calls. The first one was from Dr. Spotted Fawn. "Get the doctor's secretary on the phone," she instructed, "and Sally, too, so you can clear the time with Steve, and set up a conference call between her, Steve, and me. As soon as possible."

"Yes, ma'am." Paula almost expected a salute.

The next call, to her pleasant surprise, was from David Greenberg. He wanted to meet her at Mama Gold's tomorrow, Saturday, for lunch. She asked Alice to call and confirm; a face-to-face meeting would be better than a phone conversation.

Steve walked into his office to find Sally with the phone to her ear, glaring.

"No, you may not. Just a second," she snapped, poking the hold button. "Some SOB is on the phone. Won't tell me his name. I told him you were out, but he insists . . . says he's your photographer."

"Damn," Steve said, stopping short. Damn Joe Bigsam, he thought, but didn't verbalize it. Then he headed into his private office. "Put him through, Sally."

He walked to his desk, pausing for a moment to peer out on the street. What the hell is Bigsam up to? He promised to put a stop . . .

He turned and picked up the phone. "I thought I was through with you."

"Nick Masticelli sends his regards, Drum."

It was obvious the man was speaking into some kind of device that disguised his voice to a raspy Darth Vader quality. What could he have to do with Nick Masticelli? "So, big fucking deal," Steve said, sounding bored. But his mind was racing.

"It's time you tell me how much it's worth to you for me *not* to deliver those pictures to Papa Al."

Again he paused before responding. Who had he heard call Aldo Giovanni Papa? Not that it was uncommon among Italians. "Let me bring you up to speed, asshole," Steve said with a growl, then lied. "Angela Giovanni and I were never more than friends. And now we're hardly that. If you know Nick Masticelli, you know Angela's dating him. Go take some pictures of Nick and Angela."

"You fork over a quarter mil, chief, or I'm sending over the pics. Al will believe the worst of you. He always has, in case your dumb ass is too *stupido* to know it. If Al don't like my pics, and he won't, the quarter mil is chump change compared to him cuttin' your nads off and using them for sausage stuffin'."

"Look, let's meet somewhere and talk this over—"

"Fuck you, Farley." It was another term Steve had heard before, but he couldn't place where.

"Okay, then let's meet somewhere and I'll give you a down payment."

There was a moment of silence on the other end of the line. "Now you're beginning to make sense, monjo man." There it was again, another term from out of his past. But try as he might, he just couldn't place it.

"Tell me where, and give me a couple of days to get some money together."

"Fuck your coupla days and your squaw mama. Fifty thou minimum. This afternoon."

The hair rose on the back of Steve's neck with the "squaw mama" remark, but he maintained his calm. He needed to get shed of this thorn in his side. "Where?"

"I'll call you back about four. Be there for my call, or the pics are on their way to Saddle River."

"I'll be here, then I'll be wherever you want to meet."

He hung up and buzzed Sally. "Send Thad in, and have him bring the rest of my messages, please."

"Paula is setting up a conference call with Dr. Fawn. I told her anytime this afternoon, okay?"

"The sooner the better."

Thad appeared in front of his desk with a handful of messages and fanned them out before him like a deck of cards.

Steve looked up from being lost in thought. "Sit a minute." Thad wedged himself into one of the wing chairs. "I've got a problem—"

Explaining the fact he had a blackmailer working him, Steve did not expound on the details. Then he asked Thad to go to work to get the hardware—recorders, scopes, camera, whatever Thad needed—to find out who the guy was and to get ready to nail him when they met, probably that afternoon or evening.

"You don't give me much time, boss," Thad said, but was up and out the door before Steve could answer.

He buzzed Sally again. "Get me ten thousand in cash and put it in my black briefcase." Then he had another thought. "Make it twenty-five hundred, five hundred in twenties and the rest in ones. Get a whole bunch of extra two-thousand-dollar stack wrappers. There's a gym bag in my closet. Let's use it rather than my three-hundred-dollar case."

"Big night out tonight?" she asked in a puzzled tone.

"Just get it, please, Sal. Cut a check to cash and bring it in."

Among his calls, he paused when he came to one from a Ms. France with no return number. Could that be Angela? He stared at it wistfully for a moment, wadded it up, and chucked it into his wastebasket. He would think of her no more, forever.

Sally stepped inside, handed him the check to sign, and told him she'd be out of the office long enough to step downstairs to the bank.

The next call in the pile was from Joseph Bigsam. He immediately dialed him and snapped angrily when the casino owner answered. "I thought you were going to call off the dogs?"

"You're not getting any heat from anyone in St. Regis, counselor. Better bite somebody else's butt."

Steve paused for a moment. The St. Regis bunch had no reason to know Nick Masticelli. "Sorry," he said. "It's been a rough afternoon."

"Thought you were going to send me an agreement. I don't do biz with redskins who don't get biz done."

"Sorry again. I'm working on it. It'll be on your desk the first of the week."

"Okay, it'll be bad medicine if it's not. We've got a deal."

"We've got a deal."

"Just to seal it, how about another tip?"

"Hey, tips are what I get paid for."

"Getting your work done is what you get paid for, counselor. Another tip will quell my impatience."

"Okay, Bigsam. It's time you went to bill receptacles on your slots. With the slots accepting bills, you can cut your change girls down from a dozen to two."

"Bullshit, that'll cost hundreds of thousands—"

"And you'll get it back in increased revenue in four months. I've proven it at a dozen clubs . . . as much as a twenty-percent increase in the slots. But there's one thing . . ."

"Now the bad news?"

"Yeah, if you look at it that way. In the long run it'll be good news. You'll be cutting loose at least ten rez girls. But you'll be offering them equivalent paying jobs in the child care center you're funding, equal paying jobs elsewhere in the casino, or giving them interest-free loans to go on to college, with guaranteed jobs when and if they graduate with at least a two point grade average."

Bigsam laughed. "You're a hard man, Drum."

"But I'm a fair one. And you'll *make* friends by firing some of your help. Ever do that before?"

He hung up after getting Bigsam's agreement.

Sally buzzed him with his conference call. Paula introduced him to Dr. Meredith Spotted Fawn, and he immediately began putting her on the spot.

"Doctor, when will you have some DNA so we can go forward?"

"Forward with what, Drum?"

Steve smiled to himself. Answer a question with a question. She, too, was tough and efficient. "Let me back up," he said, his tone a lot less insistent. "Do you have a few moments?"

"Just a few."

"Those bones you have can help us establish a direct lineage that could be very important, financially important, to all Native Americans."

"What exactly does that mean?"

"I can't tell you exactly what it means . . . at least not quite yet. But the Native American Improvement Coalition and my company are working on a project, a highly secret project, that can help us all take another giant step forward."

Dr. Fawn paused a moment. "Is that true, Dr. Fox?"

Paula answered. "Yes, absolutely."

"So you want to tie these three- or four-hundred-year-old skeletons to some living individuals?"

"Exactly."

"Then we're talking mitochondrial DNA typing . . . looking for genetic concordance."

Steve smiled. "If you say so."

"The Hardy-Weinberg Equilibrium . . . identical D-loop sequences will have to be established."

"I'm not surprised," Steve said, and Paula laughed.

"Are these Native Americans you'll be comparing with?" the doctor asked.

"Of course. Yes, they are, and it'll be Native Americans with some preponderance of Native American blood to whom we'll be trying to tie the skeletal remains."

"A substructure. It's sometimes difficult to prove direct descendency with such a small group."

"Seriously?" Steve asked, presuming the opposite.

"Seriously. More chance for mutations in an intermarried, closely interbreeding substructure . . . and other problems you're not interested in hearing. But it can be done, and I can do it."

Paula spoke up. "So you've been able to get the material you need from the bones?"

"That was no sweat. We've extracted DNA from four-thousand-year-old mummies. These remains must have been in a dry, relatively stable environment to offer such great material."

"That's super news, Dr. Fawn," Steve said, relieved. "What now?"

"You need to collect blood samples from the subjects you want tested . . . finger pricks on slides will do fine. Still, you'll need to hire a phlebotomist used to controlled testing."

"Or a dozen," Steve said thoughtfully.

"Just how many blood samples are we talking about here?" the doctor asked, suddenly concerned.

"I don't know," Steve said honestly. "Maybe half the Native Americans in the Northeast before we're through."

There was dead silence on Dr. Fawn's end. Then she spoke quietly. "You know you're talking about a lot of money here. I could slip in this little bit of work without notice. But a few hundred random typings that will cross-section a few thousand individuals or more. You're talking many thousands . . . more likely hundreds of thousands of dollars."

"Give me the best price you can," Steve said. "I promise you this is for the good of all Native Americans."

Again there was silence. Then she offered, "I can give you a price only based on what the university wants to charge, if they'd even get involved, which they probably won't." Her voice filled with enthusiasm. "How about I set up a small lab right in your backyard? I only need four hundred square feet. I can get a few talented students to do the grunt work."

Paula asked, "And that'll satisfy any possible legal challenges we could get . . . to the results?"

"It'll all be over my signature and scrutiny, for what that's worth. I can commute there weekends if necessary. You're talking the better part of a hundred thousand to set up for equipment alone; a Profiblot, a DNA sequencer, FluorImager, a capillary electrophoresis unit . . . and normal lab glass . . . but some of it will come back, more than half probably, when you sell the equipment and close it down. Maybe I can pick up some of it used, but I doubt it."

"You won't be sorry," Steve said. "Get on to leasing the space, Paula. The empty suite next to you should do fine, and when the lab is finished, you will probably be ready to expand the coalition and need the room. Dr. Fawn, start lining up the equipment. I'll start hustling money."

Meredith Fawn jumped in again. "On your end, start collecting phlebotomist résumés . . . an ad in the paper. But, Drum, I could be on St. Thomas in the sun . . . this had better be good."

"It could be the biggest victory since Greasy Grass."

Dr. Fawn laughed.

Steve excused himself to let Dr. Meredith Spotted Fawn and Dr. Paula Running Fox handle the details.

Now, step two, proving a direct lineage.

Sally walked into his office and set his gym bag on the desk. He still had this little problem to resolve. For a brief moment he considered telling the photographer bastard to take the relatively innocuous pictures to Al Giovanni and tell him to cram them, but then, he couldn't do that to Angela. What seemed innocuous to most wouldn't seem so to Don Aldo Giovanni.

Even though Steve decided he could no longer put up with their situation—not that it seemed Angela wanted to have a situation, or cared if she did—he still would never want to see her hurt in any way.

Not in any way; not for as long as he lived.

No, he had to work out some way to solve the problem of the "photographer" without hurting Angela.

Maybe beating the hell out of the bastard and threatening to break both his legs would solve the problem An Aldo Giovanni solution.

He'd fight fire with fire.

His buzzer blared, and Sally's voice rang with irritation. "Your photographer is on the phone."

CHAPTER FIFTEEN

Per the photographer's instruction, Stephen eased his way through Central Park, watching for the turnoff that passed close to the Bethesda Fountain.

Late September and the leaves were beginning to turn; the park was at its best, reminding Steve of the cottonwoods, alders, and aspens of the Flathead Valley. He wished he could stop, walk, and truly enjoy it. Steve seldom drove. The five-year-old BMW he owned, which he normally left to gather dust in the basement of the condo building, had been hard to start.

Beside him on the seat rode a small black canvas gym bag Thad and Sally had stuffed with twenty-five stacks of faux two-thousand-dollar bundles of cash. However, these had been rewrapped so each contained a twenty top and bottom, with ninety-eight ones in between. What appeared to be fifty thousand was actually twenty-five stacks of one hundred dollars each, or twenty-five hundred total.

And even that he didn't plan to see delivered to the photographer. Two cars behind him, Thad Wintermoose rode shotgun in a hired town car that looked like a thousand others in Manhattan. After a special request to Barry Litcomb, who owned Litcomb's Limo, a highly skilled driver, Freddy Lowenstein, had arrived with a souped-up Lincoln Town Car to handle the driving for Steve's bodyguard. Freddy was six foot plus, built like an athlete, with close-cropped black hair and a goatee to match. Dark, piercing eyes and concentration said he was all business.

Thad was armed with his .38, but also carried a taser dart gun that would drop a perpetrator at twenty-five yards, leaving him immobile, as if he'd been hit with a train, but as unharmed as if the train turned out to be cardboard.

It was Steve's plan to turn the tables on the photographer, to drop him like a rock and scare the hell out of him with a few kicks to the ribs and knots on the head, or at worst with a shot from the taser. And then to force him to hand over the negatives.

He figured that was all it would take to get the man to leave them alone—unless, of course, he actually had something to do with Nick Masticelli. If that was the case, things would be a little more sticky.

Steve had thought a lot about it and decided that the photographer was probably someone from his past who knew he knew Al Giovanni and found out accidentally that he was seeing Angela. And thought he could turn a few easy bucks from the knowledge. He undoubtedly knew of Nick Masticelli because he had followed Steve, or Angela, the night of the Rainbow Dinner.

He was probably a minor player in the Giovanni or maybe even the Masticelli family who'd decided to freelance and pick up a few extra bucks.

At least he hoped that was all it was.

Steve had been confused because he had been getting mixed signals from the threats from the St. Regis contingency and calls from this jerk—threats he mistakenly thought came from the same source.

As he neared the pond, he eyed the crowd, some sailing model boats, some feeding the ducks and geese, some just strolling and enjoying the sunny but blustery Friday afternoon.

I'll be in a hunter-orange scarf, the photographer had said. *Slow at the curb, yell "Hey, paisano" to me, and I'll answer "Your mama wears combat boots" so you know it's me, then hand me the money through the window.*

However, that was not the way it was going to go down, at least not if Steve had anything to say about it.

The hunter-orange scarf stood out like a beacon. The man was tall, unshaven, stocking-capped, emaciatingly thin, and stood rocking back and forth like he couldn't wait to get the next speedball to snort up his hatchet nose. He looked as if a cardboard house over a steam vent would be a vacation paradise at his economic level.

And the imbecile was looking the wrong way on a one-way lane for Steve's car, so Steve slowed as he got within twenty feet of the man, then blew the horn. The man jumped three feet back as if he'd been shot. He glared at Steve, who lowered the window and shouted, "Hey, *paisano.*"

The man hurried over to the driver's window, eyed the car, and mumbled, "Blue beamer." He focused watery, reddened eyes on Steve. "Where da bag, man?"

"That's not the right response."

"Oh, yeah. Uh . . . your mama is a friggin' combat guy."

"That's not it either."

"Jus' gimme the fuckin' bag, man."

Steve was worried. The man he'd talked to on the phone sounded nothing like this, although he knew the man had his voice disguised. But it was the pacing, the tone, all wrong; still, he was too committed not to go forward.

He shoved the gym bag through the window. The man grabbed it and headed toward the pond.

Steve gunned the BMW, passing the man, then braking hard when he got a hundred feet down the lane. He swerved off onto the grass clear of the traffic. He could see the man in his mirror, beginning to run, but the town car behind him had already jumped the curb and started after the man.

Before Steve could get out of the BMW, the big Lincoln had caught up with the blackmailer and the passenger door swung open, knocking the running man flying.

As Steve started running toward the downed man, Thad Wintermoose was out of the car and pinned him in some wrestler's scissors hold, the man squealing like a thrown calf being branded. The money bag lay on the ground where it had fallen, a dozen feet from the two.

Just when Steve arrived, he heard a distant report and the ground at his feet seemed to explode. Confused, he stopped and stared. Thad extracted himself from the hold on the blackmailer and charged Steve, to his surprise knocking him flying and up against the Lincoln.

"Head down, head down!" Thad shouted. He had palmed the .38 revolver.

"Get in the car!" Freddy, the driver, yelled from a position almost prone on the driver's side.

Thad opened the back door and shoved Steve in, scrambling in behind him. Seeing Steve's confused look, he explained. "A shooter, with a rifle on the overpass." The Lincoln peeled away, throwing turf up behind the wheels, dodging scrambling strollers until it returned to the pavement. With only two wheels on the macadam, it shot the wrong way on the one-way lane and sped away from an overpass Steve had barely noticed, fifty yards from where the meeting had been staged.

As Barry Litcomb had said, Freddy could handle the town car.

A hundred honking horns expressed their disagreement. Steve raised his head high enough to see the blackmailer running away with the gym bag, before Thad pulled him back down.

"Keep your head low until we're out of range."

"The son of a bitch got away with the money," Steve moaned.

"That was some bum the real guy paid to make the pickup," Thad surmised. "The real guy was probably the one on the overpass with the rifle."

"A lousy shot," Steve said, a half-smile crossing his face.

"Probably hit exactly where he wanted to hit. He was no more than fifty yards away. Mr. Magoo could hit us with a rifle at that range."

"I've got to go back and pick up my car," Steve said a little sheepishly.

"Let's make a full round of the park, then I'll get it. If we don't make it back in time, better to pay for the impound than to take a bullet. That guy's going to be real mad when he finds those ones in the twenties sandwich."

Steve sighed. "Yeah, maybe it was a bad idea."

"Here's another nice mess you've gotten me into," Thad mumbled under his breath, but with a tight smile as the Lincoln gunned away.

"Stan Laurel?" Steve asked.

"Close. Oliver Hardy. Now what, boss?"

"Now we get my car, go to the office, cut a bonus check for Freddy here . . . getting shot at wasn't part of the bargain, and wait to hear from the 'photographer.' "

"I'm sure you won't have to wait long. He'll be seeing red anytime now."

"Yeah, he'll be mad as hell."

"No, boss, not just mad. I put a dye pack in one of those money bundles. It'll explode when he riffles through it and blow red dye all over him. I talked the security guy at First Federal out of it."

"So, he's not only going to be slow-roasted, but marinated."

"You got it."

"I hope I'm not the one who ends up well done."

"I'm sorry we didn't get him."

"Not your fault, Thad. I didn't give you much time . . . you probably saved my ass, and I thank you."

He'd proved himself. If nothing else had come out of the abortive plan to grab the blackmailer, Steve was sure he'd hired the right man.

And Steve would need him. For what he had in mind, he'd need Thad, and a whole lot of other tough men.

Freddy took Steve back to his office while Thad drove the BMW back to the condo garage.

On the ride there, Steve decided he could make some good out of the trip. "Freddy, you worked for Barry long?"

"Fifteen years, ever since I quit driving stock cars. Got busted up in a wreck, or I woulda gone on to win at the brick track."

"Too bad." Freddy's driving demonstrated his expertise, even on the city streets. "You know, I'm in the gambling biz."

"The Red Ace . . . that's what Barry told me."

"How would you like to drive me again tomorrow night?"

"I got seniority around the company . . . usually take Saturday off . . . but I might make an exception."

"I understand there's a couple of spots around town where a guy might throw the dice, or maybe even roulette."

Freddy was quiet for a moment. "Figured you got in plenty of gambling, being in the business."

"Yeah, I do. I just want to check out the underground competition. You able to find a couple of places?"

"Illegal as hell . . . Got to check with Barry first."

"You got a phone. Check away."

In a few minutes, he hung the phone up. "You're on, Mr. Drum.

I can take you to a half dozen spots, but you're on your own gettin' in . . . but it wouldn't hurt to say you know Barry."

"Great, pick me up at seven. I'll buy dinner, then we'll work the street. Let's start with the biggest."

"That'll be TriBeCa . . . art gallery fronts the deal."

"Okay."

Steve was not surprised when he walked into his office to find Sally with an angry look and the phone four inches from her ear, as if it were trying to bite her.

"Just a minute," she said, poking the hold button. "Who is this asshole who's calling me names because you're not here?"

"The photographer?" Steve asked.

"Yeah," she said, disgusted.

"I'm sorry, Sally. But put him through."

In five long strides he was in front of his desk and had his phone in hand.

"You son of a bitch!" Darth Vader shouted. He was beyond angry; he was explosive. Rage bubbled out of the phone like hot lava.

"Hey, I brought you some money," Steve said calmly.

"That wasn't me, you stupid wooden Indian!" Steve had to hold the phone away from his ear. "Or I'd have kicked your ass and that fat Indian who jumped out of the car."

"So, what now?"

"Now . . . now I'm covered with red dye and have a lousy coupla thousand bucks . . . covered with red fuckin' dye. And *die* is the operative term here, asshole. You're going to die, you prick, and it won't be Papa Al that kills you, it'll be me. Those pics are going to Papa Al, but in my own good time."

"Then you don't want the money?"

"Fuck you and your money. I never gave a shit about the money. I just wanted you to squirm. It's your red skin I want, and I'm going to personally peel it. You won't know when or where, but you're going down, swimmer. You're going to the bottom in concrete shoes . . . or up in a puff of smoke."

Steve listened for a long time to the dial tone, as if the man would come back on line to say more. Finally he set the phone in the cradle. Who the hell knew so much about him, and Angela, and Al? Who knew he had been a swimmer?

Why did this crazy have such a hard-on for him?

Why did this have to happen now, when he had so much to do?

Screw it, he had to get back to work.

He picked up the phone and dialed Alex Dragonovich. He was told to come right on up and walked out of the office and caught the elevator. Melody, the luscious blonde, was at her reception desk.

"Hi," Steve said, stepping over to where she had her head lowered, doing some paperwork. She barely glanced up, keeping her head down.

"Good afternoon, Mr. Drum—"

"Wait a minute, look at me."

She did, a little sheepishly. She had obviously tried to cover a black eye with makeup, but couldn't hide the mouse on her cheekbone.

"What happened, Melody?"

She laughed, but hollowly. "I'm clumsy. Had a little too much to drink at the party last night. Slipped and hit my eye on my own bathroom lav."

Steve could feel the heat begin to caterpillar up his back. "You sure that's what happened?"

She laughed, but he caught a quiver of the lip. She was obviously laughing in lieu of crying. "Sure. Slipped on my own bathroom shag rug."

"Looks like the result of the hard hand of a pile of chicken shit passing for a man to me."

"Oh, no. Who'd do such a thing? Slipped is all." Again, the lip quivered. "Mr. Dragonovich is waiting for you. Please don't mention the eye thingie to him." She looked him right in the face, pleading.

"Wouldn't think of it. He wouldn't *be* the pile of chicken shit, would he?"

She shook her head, but tentatively, smiled appreciatively, and went back to her paperwork. Steve caught her looking at him as the elevator door closed.

"Thanks," Steve mouthed as the doors shut. Obviously he was not going to get the truth out of her. As he rode up the private elevator, he had to calm himself down. He was sure he'd caused that with the pelvic-beating dance he'd had with Melody. That son of a bitch, Dragonovich, had liked it even less than he appeared. Steve silently swore he was going to bury the bastard.

He was shown in without the obligatory twenty-minute wait.

Without a greeting, Dragonovich looked up and said, "When are you going to New Mexico?"

"Haven't gotten it set up yet, but I wanted to come up and assure you that it's going to the top of my agenda next week . . . in fact, I'm leaving Sunday night."

"You're not the only fish in the Native American ocean, you know, Drum."

"Yes, sir," Steve said with feigned humility. "I'm right on it, Monday morning I'm meeting with Hector Alvarez, and he's got me set up with the Navajos on Tuesday. I'll have a report for you by next Friday."

"Make sure you do. Is that all?" Dragonovich looked at him as if he hoped he would say something about his receptionist's eye.

Steve decided to disappoint him. "Wanted to thank you again for allowing me to dance with the help last night. What a great party."

"It was fine. Call me Friday with a verbal report, or before if you have one done. But no later than Friday."

"Yes, sir, Friday." He backed out of the man's office, spun on his heel, and headed for the elevator, glad he hadn't screwed up what took him so long to set up.

But he had to get his butt to New Mexico next week.

God, things were coming down around his head.

And one of those things would be a noose if the photographer had anything to say about it.

The last thing he did that day was brief Thad regarding the photographer's call and ask him to take whatever cautionary measures he deemed necessary.

He told Thad, "I don't have time to die right now."

CHAPTER SIXTEEN

Steve spent Saturday working at the office, except for a trip to the gym and a game of racquetball with Fred Alexander, his real estate broker friend and former client. He did make reservations to fly to Gallup, New Mexico, on Sunday night at six P.M., and hotel reservations for Sunday and Monday nights, returning Tuesday night on the midnight flyer. Then he called Hector "Alvarez" Rodriguez at Monument Mining and set up his meeting. Rodriguez would pick him up at the airport Sunday night and said he'd have no problem making them an appointment with the Navajo Tribal Office attorney for either Monday afternoon or Tuesday.

And Steve was sure he *would* have no problem. He laughed as he hung up the phone. It was the first time in his life that Steve had knowingly set up his own failure. Even though Rodriguez had no way of knowing, Steve knew what his every move would be. The king of the hustlers was being hustled.

After three games of racquetball, Fred brought him up to speed on the recent history of Rockefeller Center and what little he knew about the Asian American Real Estate Trust and its president, Wilber Ian Wong.

Saturday night, Freddy Lowenstein, Thad Wintermoose, Paula Fox, and Steve made the rounds of what were the current decade's answer to the Prohibition speakeasies of the twenties.

They ran the Manhattan gambling gauntlet from the TriBeCa

Player's Club, hidden discreetly in a warehouse behind an art gallery called Foibles. With ten-dollar minimums on two crap tables, a roulette table, a dozen blackjack tables, and fifty or more dollar slots, it was a small Las Vegas casino. From there they visited a half dozen clubs, finishing at an East Side club in the rear of a three-star French restaurant. You had to enter the place through the kitchen or a door labeled JANITOR between the rest rooms. That club featured only four baccarat tables.

They covered seven illegal gambling establishments in all. Each club allowed them in without question when Barry Litcomb's name was mentioned. As whorehouses at one time depended on cabdrivers, it seemed illegal casinos depended on limo companies. Illegal gambling was alive and well in Manhattan, even among the upper crust—Atlantic City was still too far for many of them to travel for an evening's entertainment.

Steve played lightly, managing to lose only a couple of hundred. His mission was knowledge, not gambling. Paula actually made fifty dollars playing the slots at two of the clubs. Freddy lost regularly, and Thad, repeating the Claude Rains *Casablanca* line "I'm shocked, shocked, to find that gambling is going on here" every time they walked into a joint, never risked more than five dollars, and then rarely.

When Steve discreetly inquired as to who owned the clubs, all he received in reply was a polite smile and a not-so-polite glare if he asked again.

Steve knew there were dozens, maybe hundreds, maybe thousands of other card games and crap games around the city, particularly in Chinatown, where more exotic mah-jongg and other traditional Chinese games of chance abounded. But he was interested only in the full casino operations that were connected— highly connected—probably to the families running the city's crime, and most certainly to the city's government and police.

They couldn't operate without governmental and police oversight—purposeful, deliberate, well-paid blindness.

At the end of the evening Steve invited Thad and Paula to a short late-Sunday-morning meeting at the office, bribing them with the promise of being treated to brunch at Tavern-on-the-Green afterward.

He heard no more from the photographer, nor did he get a

call from Angela. He reminded himself for the thousandth time, he would think of her no more.

It was time he let Paula and Thad in on some of what he had in mind. It would help clarify his own thinking to get some feedback from Paula, whom he'd trusted and admired for years, and from Thad, who he was beginning to trust implicitly—with his life, of late.

He finished dictating the agreement between Red Ace and Big Sam's, and had the coffee made by the time they arrived at the appointed ten-thirty and took seats at his desk.

"I've been thinking long and hard about what to do with this valuable and unique document."

Paula sipped her coffee, watching him intently. She'd managed to keep her curiosity at bay for over a week, wondering where Steve was going with what they'd been doing, wondering if she'd done the right thing bringing him the foolscap in the first place.

"As, of course, you know, gambling is my primary business. Gaming, from bingo to baccarat, is the hope of all Native Americans, at least in the short run, to get a leg up and bring us to a level playing field with the white-eye.

"But Indian gaming has always had to take place on the rez, and the rez, most times, is not the ideal location for a casino or any other large-scale traffic-driven commercial endeavor. As my real estate broker friends have told me time and time again, there're three things that make a commercial venture successful. Location, location, and location."

"So, what's the bottom line?" Paula asked impatiently.

"The bottom line is a reservation. One in an excellent commercial location. One near a major population center. It's my intention to bring the rez to the prime commercial location rather than the other way around."

"And you think this document will lead to a rez here in New York State?" Thad asked.

Steve was silent for a second, then smiled. "How about here on Manhattan Island? It may be the nation's smallest rez in terms of acres, but it also may be the nation's most profitable."

Paula laughed aloud, shaking her head, as did Thad, then she muttered, "I think you've been smoking wacky weed in your peace pipe. The white-eye will never, never go for a rez on Manhattan. And you've got to have a tribe before you have a reservation."

Steve smiled. "They won't go for it in the conventional sense, but I plan to hoist them on their own petard. You keep moving forward to prove lineage and bring me a tribe, either existing, or a group for whom I can get federal acknowledgment. Find me someone for whom to negotiate and I'll move forward with negotiating tactics that might just make it happen. . . . No, that *will* make it happen. The treaty we hold is only a pawn in a very large chess game. But I love games, and the white-eye is not going to be dealing with an ancient chief who believes he's worth only what he gives away. It's time we came out on the top of a negotiation or two, and I intend to do so."

Paula leaned forward in her chair and eyed him intently. "Is Red Ace Corporation going to be the big winner here? Is that what you have in mind?"

Steve gave her a hard look, covering the fact she had hurt his feelings, then spoke slowly. "Yes, Red Ace Corporation is going to win, but no more than the Native American Coalition is going to win, than Thad is going to win, and, hopefully, through the coalition no more than all Native Americans are ultimately going to win.

"Believe it or not," he continued with conviction, "I think we'll need the help of every Indian in this country to pull this off."

Paula smiled, relieved but still skeptical. "I think you've got a long, winding river to paddle." Her well-arched brows drew together for a second before she suggested, "I had lunch with David Greenberg yesterday. I didn't mention it last night because I wanted to think it through before I recommended hiring him." She held up her hand to stop any objection until she finished. "And I know, he's not Indian, but that might serve to our advantage." She waited for an objection, but got none. "After we left, it seems he burned his bridges with the archaeology department— probably all of NYU—at the meeting Thursday, lying through his teeth, denying that I left the dig with anything." She smiled. "In fact, Lund called him a liar to his face, and so did the girl. David lost his temper and called Lund, and I quote the best of his recollection, 'a pea-brained pompous ass.' " She laughed. "I like that boy. You know he's a newspaperman by vocation, and anthropology was only an avocation he hoped to meld with his work. He's a great writer, and sympathetic to our cause. It looks like we're going to need a lot of public relations, press relations"—

she smiled thoughtfully—"even more than I thought yesterday, given this vision quest of yours, and I'd like to put him to work. He's quitting school and needs more than he's getting at the underground paper he's been working for part-time."

"Stop selling, Paula. A done deal," Steve said, to her surprise. "We take care of those who take care of us . . . and apparently David has. Get him a desk. You've got room in your reception area until we expand next door. And I want to see him as soon as he starts. I've got a little research for him to do."

"Good. One other thing," she said, her tone more pensive. "How are you going to explain how we got our hands on the treaty? It looks like I may be the sacrificial lamb here."

Again she'd hurt his feelings, but he understood her concern. "Look, Paula. Right or wrong in the eyes of the law, what you did was morally *right*. Remember, if you committed a crime, I'm certainly a co-conspirator. I'll keep you out of jail, and not only that, you'll be a hero to all Native Americans."

"I'll hold you to the 'keep me out of jail' part. Heroine I don't care about."

Steve rose, and cautioned, "Needless to say, this meeting is top secret, for our ears only. I don't know you well yet, Thad, so I'll risk being insulting by repeating it—for our ears only."

"What happens in the bush stays in the bush."

"Sean Penn," Paula said. "And this is war, too, Thad, so keep it to yourself."

Thad eyed her; this time it was his turn to look hard to cover the fact she'd hurt his feelings.

Thad and Paula both nodded, but Thad wasn't quite satisfied. "So, you thinking about Harlem for this rez, where we'd get little objection from city hall?"

Steve eyed them both before shrugging casually. "Actually, Harlem would probably be an easier bet, but remember location, location, location. I'm a good Catholic and I'd like to be closer to my favorite cathedral, St. Pat's, and closer to the park . . . and, you know, Paula, I love the theater. And five's my lucky number. So fives being lucky, and near the theater district and St. Pat's . . . how about, say, Fifth Avenue and Fiftieth? Actually, I'm thinking midtown . . . how about someplace, like, say . . . Rockefeller Center?"

Both of them stood, mouth agape, as he headed for the door.

"Brunch, anyone?"

CHAPTER SEVENTEEN

The tour of Rockefeller Center started at two P.M., and Steve, alone and dressed like a tourist, bought a ticket. He figured it was the fastest way to learn what he wanted to know about the huge complex.

Some sports show was being broadcast by IBC on the giant screen on the front of the building. A downhill ski racer, a story and a half tall, took a terrible spill as Steve watched, but the volume on the giant speakers was cut off and the scene lacked impact. He turned his attention back to the tour.

The guide explained that John D. Rockefeller, Jr., had started the project over sixty years before, during the Great Depression. It was one of the most ambitious urban projects ever undertaken.

Located between the Avenue of the Americas on the west, Fifth Avenue on the east, Forty-eighth Street to the south, and Fifty-first Street to the north, the project was bisected by one of Manhattan's only private streets, Rockefeller Plaza. The street, inspired by the fact John Jr. thought New York blocks too long and consequently wanted the Center's three primary blocks broken in half, was closed one day a year to protect its private stature. The project is cut into thirds the other direction by Forty-ninth Street and Fiftieth Street, still in the public domain.

To the west of Rockefeller Center lies the theater district; across Fifth Avenue to the east rises historic St. Patrick's Cathedral. Eight blocks to the north is Central Park. Trump Tower is only five blocks north and across Fifth Avenue, and the Empire State Building and United Nations buildings only blocks south and east, respectively.

They started the tour in the heart of the Center, at the lower plaza. While the rest of the tour hurried on, Steve paused at the stairway down to the lower plaza and read an inscription beside the bronze bust of John D. Rockefeller, Jr. It read:

> I believe in the supreme worth of the individual and in his right to life, liberty, and the pursuit of happiness.
>
> I believe that every right implies a responsibility; every opportunity, an obligation; every possession, a duty.
>
> I believe that the law was made for man and not man for the law; that government is the servant of the people and not their master.
>
> I believe in the dignity of labor, whether with head or hand; that the world owes no man a living but that it owes every man an opportunity to make a living.
>
> I believe that thrift is essential to well-ordered living and that economy is a prime requisite of a sound financial structure, whether in government, business, or personal affairs.
>
> I believe that truth and justice are fundamental to an enduring social order.
>
> I believe in the sacredness of a promise, that a man's word should be as good as his bond; that character—not wealth or power or position—is of supreme worth.
>
> I believe that the rendering of useful service is the common duty of mankind and that only in the purifying fire of sacrifice is the dross of selfishness consumed and the greatness of the human soul set free.
>
> I believe in an all-wise and all-loving God, named by whatever name, and that the individual's highest fulfillment, greatest happiness, and widest usefulness are to be found in living in harmony with His will.
>
> I believe that love is the greatest thing in the world; that it alone can overcome hate; that right can and will triumph over might.
>
> John D. Rockefeller, Jr.

Steve was slightly taken aback. This didn't sound like the son of a man who was considered by many to be one of the great despoilers of the country, a man who rode his steed of wealth, trampling the bodies of workingmen beneath.

Maybe he'd heard wrong about John D. Rockefeller, Jr.

After all, he did have a statue portraying an American Indian in a most positive light, among the myriad other art of Rockefeller Center. Most wouldn't have acknowledged the Native American's existence.

But, as old Standing Bear had told him many times, *It's not what you say, it's what you do that matters.* Still, if old John Jr. was a good man, he couldn't have expressed it better than in the words on that plaque.

Steve decided to reserve judgment until he was more knowledgeable.

He had to hurry to catch up with the rest of the tour.

The guide, a vivacious little blond girl with a slight Russian accent, was just finishing an explanation of the eighteen-foot-high gilded bronze statue in the plaza. They continued on, spiraling out in a clockwise manner from the plaza. First visiting the lobby of the International Buildings, forty-one and fifty-one stories; then International North, six stories; then Palazzo d'Italia, also six stories.

Steve suddenly became more and more interested. The British Empire Building stood six stories tall. He listened closely as the bubbly little guide explained the history of it, and the French Building, La Maison Française, next door, also six stories. The International Buildings and these two were attempts by John Jr. to attract international tenants at a time when American companies had been hit severely by the Depression, and, of course, an attempt to foster international goodwill. Both these smaller buildings, as well as the lower plaza, were among the Asian American holdings.

The tour continued to One Rockefeller Plaza, the original Time-Life Building, thirty-six stories, then to the jewel in the crown, the GE Building, with its apex being the Rainbow Room.

Now Steve's interest crackled with electricity.

At seventy stories and two million two hundred thousand square feet, the GE Building shadowed the rest of Rockefeller Center. Although the McGraw-Hill Building, at only fifty-one stories, had a larger footprint and was slightly larger in square feet; and the Exxon Building at fifty-four stories was only slightly smaller in square feet—30 Rockefeller Plaza, originally the RCA Building, rose above them all in both height and beauty.

While the rest of the tour group went on, Steve decide he would skip the other buildings. He was too intrigued by the Asian American holdings.

One of the things the guide had mentioned, and he now wanted to explore, was the below-street-level concourse. It was truly a subterranean city—a city below the city. With its own barber shops, banks, pet shops, restaurants, service establishments, and even a post office and greengrocer, the concourse interconnected not only the buildings of Rockefeller Center, but provided a complete below-ground maze of delivery docks and roadways. He wandered for over an hour below street level.

Steve was fascinated by the fact that truckload after truckload of goods could be delivered to the GE Building without being a traffic hazard to the streets above—and more important to his plans, without being seen. These delivery areas, or so said the cute blond Russian, handle seven hundred to one thousand trucks per day. Lined up, they would stretch four miles up and down Fifth Avenue.

He was also intrigued to learn that the consulates of nine foreign nations; the Passport Office; the National Weather Service; thirty-five restaurants; seventy travel, transportation, and information offices; and the subway serve the Center. Altogether the Center totals over fifteen million square feet of rentable footage, and even then, one quarter of the land has been left open for parks and plazas.

Finally, after hours of walking the halls of the GE Building, watching the flood of people even on a Sunday, enjoying one of the world's great collections of art, Steve came to a conclusion— *you did good, John Jr. Right good.*

He also remembered something of which he had to ofttimes remind himself—it takes great fortunes to do great good.

Now all he had to do was figure out how to bring it full circle. To do great good not only for Manhattan, but for its original inhabitants, and those like them all over the country who'd given up so much so edifices like this could rise in the nation's cities.

And he had to smile to himself as he waved a cab down. He actually didn't think old John Jr. would mind a damn bit.

Flying with the sun and time changes, Steve arrived in Denver at seven-forty P.M., and had only a little over an hour layover before he caught a commuter to Gallup, landing right on time at ten-thirty. He wore khakis and a long-sleeved pullover, carrying only his briefcase and a two-suiter that would fit under the seat so he had to check no luggage. Certain that no outsider knew his plans, and making sure they weren't followed, Thad had stayed in New York after driving Steve to Kennedy. He busied himself studying personal protection, helping Paula, trying to figure what the photographer was going to do next, and how to identify the slimeball.

While on the plane Steve read a pair of reports on ICOM, one from Stanley Reporting and one from Jonathan Noble, Steve's friend and stockbroker. The first confirmed that the company was in serious trouble. A Peruvian gold mine they'd bought into was having serious flooding problems and would probably have to be abandoned altogether, causing them to report a ten-million-dollar write-down. A California oil field that depended upon a co-generation project for over half its revenue stream was being cratered by new power regulations, allowing competition in electrical supply. But even more serious was ICOM's biggest money producer, the island of Natonaru, in the Marshalls.

Natonaru was basically an island of bird shit on a coral base; over eons, the birds of this area of the South Pacific had favored this particular one-by-four-mile roost, and had deposited guano there. A literal mountain of it. It was an almost inexhaustible supply of phosphate that had fueled ICOM's growth for over ten years, driving their stock up to thirty-six dollars a share from less than six in that time. It was Alex Dragonovich's greatest business coup, acquiring the rights to the unoccupied island's hidden wealth, then convincing Handai, a major Korean trading company, to build a port and loading facilities on the island's lee side in exchange for exclusive trading rights. But he'd made one serious error.

He'd negotiated the contract for the sale of all the island's phosphate production to Korea. Enough phosphate to provide fertilizer for hundreds of thousands of acres of Korean farmland, with the excess going to other Handai Pacific Rim customers—at a time when it was unimaginable that the Korean currency, the won, would ever go down in value. But only this past week, Korean bank failures had begun to fuel the crash of the won against the dollar.

ICOM, who paid American miners, who bought American mining equipment, who paid interest to American banks, all in dollars, was suddenly confronted with supplying phosphate to Handai for payment in almost worthless won. Should the won fall even further, ICOM would suffer hundreds of millions of dollars in operating losses. And the stock would go in the tank.

Steve had wondered if ICOM could merely shut down its Natonaru operation, but this report confirmed that ICOM had borrowed millions and millions from Handai for other ICOM endeavors, and Handai had the right of offset. They could in fact take over the mining operation and supply themselves, continuing to pay an override in won to ICOM if ICOM didn't perform on the loans.

Dragonovich, Steve thought with a smile, had his nuts in a crack.

This was one of the reasons Dragonovich had jumped on the Hovenweep mine in New Mexico. He needed a major announcement to offset the catastrophic failure of the Peruvian mine, the California oil field and co-gen project, and, particularly, Natonaru.

Dragonovich is won unhappy boy, Steve quipped to himself, laughing aloud until he realized he was bothering other passengers. He lay his head back and closed his eyes. *We're going to rub his nose in it, Pop,* he thought, smiling quietly to himself as the plane began its descent.

Steve had another thought as the plane made its final approach. He wondered if the Korean business and currency failure might have a rippling effect throughout Asia. Would Hong Kong, Taiwan, and Japan be adversely affected? He'd have to watch the markets closely and be ready to move quickly against the Asian American Trading Company. Should they have their own internal troubles, then it was much more likely Rockefeller Center would come on the market.

As promised, Hector Rodriguez met him at the gate. Hector was a prospector and the discoverer of the Hovenweep mine, or at least had represented himself to ICOM as such. A short, stocky man with a head full of wavy salt-and-pepper hair, Hector also had represented himself to ICOM as being Hector Alvarez rather than who he actually was.

They loaded up in a Toyota Land Cruiser adorned with magnetic door signs proclaiming MONUMENT MINING, and Hector drove to the hotel, the historic El Rancho. The place was actually little more than a motel, but in the heyday of western movies it had been second home to production companies and movie stars. Every room boasted the name of a famous star who'd stayed there. Steve was checked into the Betty Grable room. He almost asked for the Cary Grant room just so he could rag Paula by telling her he slept in the same bed as Cary had, but didn't.

He parted ways with Hector, agreeing to one of the bar's famous margaritas after dropping his bags off—the room, it turned out, hadn't been remodeled since Betty stayed there—then walked through the spacious southwestern-decorated lobby to join Rodriguez.

He knew far more about Hector "Alvarez" Rodriguez than Rodriguez knew about him. He'd first come across Rodriguez in Montana, when the man with his brother, Gilbert, in tow, had convinced the Rocky Boy's Chippewa-Cree reservation to put up several thousand dollars in "good faith seed money" to promote mineral exploration on the rez. The scam was he promised that the Indian "seed money" money would be promptly repaid from the millions the mining company would pour into the reservation.

His pickup had sported a magnetic sign proclaiming him to be a part of Alcoa Mining. Rodriguez had been a small-time grifter then, and loved to line his pockets with Indian money. It was an easy matter to check with the man's "clients" and Alcoa Aluminum and discover they'd never heard of Hector Rodriguez. They had no interest or knowledge of any Rocky Boy's exploration project. The tribe had made only a small deposit on the fee Rodriguez insisted on having, and Steve was able to circumvent the real disaster of several thousand more.

Steve had been able easily to squash the man's scheme to rob what was already Montana's poorest rez—at least rob it worse than he already had.

Rodriguez had actually spent a weekend in a Havre, Montana, jail before the county had to release him on bail. They had little or no evidence of fraud, as he hadn't been able to complete his scam. Rodriguez and his brother, a co-conspirator, had hightailed it out of Havre on Monday morning. Their magnetic car signs had been sailed into the plains. The Chippewa-Cree stayed hot on their trail for a hundred miles. The Rodriguez brothers were never to be heard of by the Rocky Boy's tribes again, or by the bondsman who'd gone their bail.

The Rodriguez name had popped up several times over the years in Steve's travels and business endeavors, but Steve had never had occasion to actually meet the brothers until then—and was glad he hadn't.

He was sure that the "Navajo" legal representative he was scheduled to meet would actually be Gilbert Rodriguez, the brother—neither a Navajo nor an attorney.

Steve walked into the bar and climbed up next to Hector and in front of the waiting margarita, the size of a breakfast cereal bowl on a pedestal. He immediately motioned the bartender over. "These are on me."

"That's very kind of you, and ICOM," Hector said, and smiled broadly, flashing pearly white teeth.

"Expense account," Steve answered, and toasted the "Navajo." Hector was doing his best to pass as Navajo for this scam. He wore a balloon-sleeve shirt that looked as if it was woven at the nearest hogan, a ten-gallon Hoss Cartwright hat with an engraved silver band and red feather, and enough silver and turquoise adorning his neck, wrists, and fingers that he'd sink like a rock if he fell in the river.

"So," Hector said, "did you bring a check?"

"We've got to get the agreement with the tribe negotiated and executed, and another series of test holes drilled, before you get another check, Hector. Didn't Rostinburg tell you—"

"That's right. I forgot. We meet with Tobias Nakai, chief counsel for the Navajo-Hopi Mining and Power Consortium, tomorrow afternoon, after I drive you up and show you the discovery. While on-site we meet with an independent driller, High Desert Drilling, out of Cortez."

"Great, Hector. You know this company?"

"Sure, I know them well."

I'll bet, Steve thought, but again merely toasted the man and took a long draw on the margarita.

Hector smiled and downed his. "Another, amigo," he called to the bartender, then turned back to Steve. "Nakai should have a letter of intent on the terms I discussed with Rostinburg, ready for ICOM's signature."

"Already? I thought I was to meet with the tribal council? I was told I'd have to negotiate terms." Steve put up as much objection as he thought any legitimate consultant in his position would. He knew he would never be allowed to meet with the legitimate tribal council. First, it would take months and months, if not years, to get an agreement to mine on Navajo reservation land, if anyone ever could; and second, there was no legitimate discovery. The Navajos were sophisticated business people, already in the mining business with one of the United States's largest coal mines, and they would make their own determination regarding the validity of any discovery long before approving any long-term mining lease.

Only a square mile of the supposed discovery was actually on the reservation; the balance of two square miles of the supposed rich alluvial deposit was on private land north of the rez, and that lease had already been negotiated—at least an executed lease agreement accompanied the package. Steve knew it was also a forged document, as was the accompanying policy of title insurance. Steve knew what ICOM would require, and the groundwork had been laid. The land was actually controlled by the Bureau of Land Management.

"No, no, not the council," Hector said, "I've been working with them for almost a year on this project. We have all the terms negotiated, all acceptable to ICOM, and all you have to do is set up the independent core drilling so ICOM can do their final due diligence, then take the letter back to New York for signature. As soon as we get the half mil deposit from you guys, then with the million on approval of the assays, you take over. I suggest a direct bank transfer of all moneys to our bank in Albuquerque."

"The million comes after," Steve said with a feigned hard look, "we assay and approve our own core samples."

Hector lowered his voice, as if to keep anyone else in the bar from overhearing. Actually there was only one other customer in the bar, and he almost had his face on the table. He must have been on his tenth giant margarita.

"I guarantee"—Hector slapped Steve on the back—"you'll get

the richest core samples you've ever seen ... as much as four hundred ounces of gold to the ton, plus sliver and a substantial lead deposit, for what it's worth."

"Then there'll be no problem." Steve lifted his glass to Rodriguez, then drained his margarita. "Well, Hector, what time in the morning?"

"We prospectors are up and at it early. How about breakfast here in the hotel at seven, then we'll head across the rez to the claim, a few miles from Hovenweep. It's a long drive, but we can be back here in plenty of time for our meeting with Mr. Nakai."

"Mr. Nakai has his office here in Gallup? I presumed he'd be in Window Rock, or Shiprock." Steve was having a little too much fun asking Hector tough questions.

"Oh, no. Nakai is a paid consultant, an attorney, like yourself. He's a Navajo too, but not an employee of the tribe. His office is here."

"Seven it is," Steve said, leaving with the excuse he was tired from the long flight.

As he walked into his room, the phone rang. He answered it on the second ring, smiling at hearing an old friend's voice. Harry Tongue kidded him, "Well, Steve old buddy, you happy with old Harry's hard work?"

Harry and Steve had gone to high school together and been best friends, at least until Harry joined the army, then did a stint in Leavenworth for selling army material to every scrap dealer in California. Harry had always had a little too much entrepreneurial blood for his own good; his high school nickname was Silver. Six years of hard time hadn't made him a lot smarter, only more careful.

Steve had run into Harry on his last trip to Montana, more than a year ago. After a few beers he'd decided he could put Harry to work on his upcoming project—in fact, Harry was exactly the right guy. And Harry had proved himself. He'd been the planner behind the "discovery" at Hovenweep and the prime mover in the involvement of the Rodriguez brothers.

Rodriguez had brought the mine to ICOM at Harry's instruction. And ICOM had jumped on the opportunity to develop a property with assays as high as four hundred ounces to the ton.

Assays of ore samples that Harry had hauled all the way from Montana.

It was the oldest of scams, salting the mine.

Steve had taken the better part of two years to set the whole thing up. Harry had strict instruction never to contact Steve in New York unless it was via a private post office box Steve kept exclusively for mail from Harry. Steve had to keep his involvement absolutely secret. The Rodriguez brothers had no knowledge of it. Harry wanted to leave the country, skip his parole, and head to South America when this was over, and that suited Steve just fine—with any luck, he'd do so with a pocket full of ICOM money. Steve'd had to involve the Navajo reservation, since without it in the equation, ICOM would have no reason to require his consultation. But actually, as it worked out, the rez was out of it, and had never even been contacted.

Steve had worked hard behind the scenes to convince ICOM that should they ever need help in Indian affairs, Red Ace's Steve Drum, the neighbor just a few floors below at 40 Wall Street, was their man.

At first he thought he could just burn ICOM for a million or so—an unsatisfying solution so far as Steve was concerned—but now, with their internal problems, he had entertained thoughts of breaking them, and Dragonovich along with them.

He was taking a great risk, breaking a book full of laws in the process, one he'd sworn to himself never to take again, but he owed it to his father to count coup on Alex Dragonovich, to shame him, to injure him beyond and worse than death.

Before he turned off the motel room light, Steve called his home phone. Angela had called from France but sounded more than irritated, angry, in fact, and left no number.

For a second he had a feeling as hollow, remote, and vacant as an abandoned strip mine. For a moment he felt as if he might throw up, then he swallowed and took a deep, settling breath. To hell with her, he again resolved, then, wistfully, turned off the light.

But sleep was elusive, coming and going all night.

He really didn't like what he was doing to ICOM, and tried to put their thousands of innocent stockholders out of his mind, but thoughts of his father looking up at him from the Long Bar floor, blood bubbling from his mouth, drove him on.

He was very, very close to burning Alex Dragonovich.

CHAPTER EIGHTEEN

They drove north out of Gallup on 666. This desert road, lined with autumn asters, made Steve a little homesick. Snakeweed and chamisa mottled the slopes with gold, khaki, and yellow. He wondered if he'd been too long in the concrete canyons.

Before reaching the town of Shiprock, they turned east on Route 64. The town's namesake stood tall in the Southwest. It was Steve's first time on the Navajo reservation, and he could see why the mountain of rock had gotten its name; it actually resembled a huge ship on the horizon, rising up out of a rolling desert that sometimes, particularly in the evening's gray-blue light, resembled the ocean. It was only a few miles before they departed New Mexico and entered Arizona—although in Steve's eyes they were in neither, they were in the Navajo Nation.

Hector acted as tour guide along the way, pointing out the Chuska Range, the Chaco River drainage, then the Carrizo Mountains. They left Route 64 and turned north on a dirt trail, paralleling a dry creek bed that would eventually lead them to the San Juan River.

An occasional hogan dotted the barren landscape, sheep grazed the sparse hillsides, and once they saw a horseback shepherd and his dog working a small flock of gangly goats toward some unknown destination.

The road became steeper, dropping into the San Juan River

canyon, and Hector stopped, set the lugs on the wheels into position, and they continued in four-wheel drive.

"That's us, up ahead." He pointed across the canyon to a side
canyon and a greasewood-covered alluvial fan stretching out onto
the plain. Russian olives and tamarisk trees rimmed a coulee
winding its way through the boulders and rock-covered desert.

"Where's the reservation border?" Steve asked.

"We're working off the U. S. Geological Survey maps, and this
baby." He popped open the glove compartment and held up a
hand-held GPS. "It's accurate to a few feet . . . and we just crossed
out of the rez into private land."

"That's a global positioning device?"

"That's it. You guys can do a finite survey if you want. It's in
the agreement. But this baby has worked to everyone's satisfaction
so far."

In the distance Steve could see a small truck-mounted drilling
rig, a tent and campsite, and two men waiting. The Toyota
bounced its way to a stop alongside the rig.

Steve and Hector climbed out and shook hands with the driller
and his roustabout, then reviewed a blown-up USGS map with
the claim marked out in red and a grid set up with core hole
locations marked off every three hundred feet.

"You guys got this pattern approved by ICOM?" Steve asked.

"It's their map," Hector offered quickly. "We had a couple of
ICOM engineers here all last week, checking our GPS readings
and making sure we would meet their requirements. We're just
waiting your go-ahead and we'll be drilling."

"As soon as I see the letter of intent and approve its terms, I'll
give you the go."

"When do we get the deposit check?" Hector asked, always
closing in on the money, his only objective.

The driller looked disgusted. "Shit, break out the whiskey, Al.
We could be here for days before we go to work."

"Maybe," Steve said, "maybe not. I should have the letter this
afternoon."

"And as soon as I have the check," Hector encouraged, "I'll
drive back up and give you guys the word to go to work."

The driller hocked and spat on the ground. "This rig is two
hundred fifty a day, standby. I guess I don't give a shit how long

you guys screw around." He turned and headed for a folding chair outside the tent flap, and sat.

"You seen enough?" Hector asked Steve.

"Let's drive the boundaries as close as we can, then head out of here."

They bounced along, Hector pointing out the three square miles of alluvial fan spreading out from a steep, narrow canyon mouth.

"Do we go on up into the canyon with our rights?" Steve asked.

"We've got an option from the Haupt Ranch, which is the private holding, for another two square miles to the north, in case we find the mother lode up that canyon that's been feeding this deposit for eons."

"Good. You've done a great job here, Hector. You've made my job easy, presuming the letter of intent has all the deal points."

Hector flashed his pearly whites. "Then let's head for the attorney's office."

"I'm ready."

The office sported a sign TOBIAS NAKAI, ESQ. SPECIAL COUNCIL TO THE NAVAJO. Steve wondered how fast the sign would come down once he had left. The outer office featured a rotund lady with a cherubic face seated at the desk, reading a romance novel, which found the desk drawer quickly as they entered. She was introduced to Steve as Chipeta, but Steve thought he recognized her from pictures Harry had provided him. She was Nakai's wife, Josephina. Steve smiled. A real family operation.

As Steve had suspected, "attorney" and "Navajo consultant" Tobias Nakai was actually Hector Rodriguez's brother, Gilbert. Gilbert was much taller than his brother, and graying at the temples. He, too, was dressed to convey his "Navajo" background, with a silver Kokopelli, the flute player and fertility god, on a silver chain around his neck. It hung, the size of a man's palm, inlayed with black onyx, dancing across the yellow and red power tie he wore.

Steve sat in a leather chair in front of the "attorney's" desk, impressed, reading a rather well-prepared letter of intent. All the deal points asked for by the ICOM representative, Rostinburg, were covered. Steve looked up with a smile. "You folks are very accommodating," he said to Nakai.

"This is an agreement that serves the Navajo Nation well,"

Nakai said, rising officiously. "If this is satisfactory, I have to go to Window Rock to meet with the tribal council."

Sure you do, Steve thought, but rose and extended his hand. "I've enjoyed our short time together and know we'll meet again."

"I hope so."

Steve smiled along with the lie, and they were out the door and back in the Toyota within twenty minutes of when they'd left it at the curb. "That was almost too easy," Steve said.

"Oh, no, don't get that impression. I've been slaving on this deal for months . . . years in fact."

"I'm going to feel guilty taking ICOM's money," Steve said.

"Don't," Hector said with a laugh. "They got plenty."

Not for long, Steve thought. *Not for long.*

With the phony letter of intent in hand, Steve was able to cut his trip short and catch a flight out. He would make a nine P.M. midnight flyer from Denver back to New York, putting him into Kennedy a little after two in the morning, and in bed at three by the time he got to his condo.

He was dragging when his alarm went off at six A.M. Tuesday.

Pleasantly surprised, he toasted the TV with his orange juice when the financial channel announced currencies all around the west half of the Pacific Rim were falling against the dollar.

Steve was pleasantly surprised again when he walked into his office.

Sally, equally surprised at his early appearance, looked up. "Hey, you took an early flight. Dr. Spotted Fawn is in Paula's office. She took some vacation time and is setting up a lab— What the hell are we doing in the laboratory business?"

"Sally, Sally," Steve said with a laugh. "I sometimes wonder myself. I'll fill you in pretty soon. Hang in there."

With this news, and the money the lab would require, he needed to act. "Get Jonathan Noble on the phone for me . . . then Fred Alexander."

She stopped him as he began to turn toward his office door. "Thad is at a personal protection lecture, but he's going to be mad as hell at you for not telling him you're back. If he's going to guard your body, he has to be near it."

Steve shrugged. "I can't get used to being baby-sat."

"Get used to it," Sally said maternally. "All this hubbub is for naught without your smiling face on the planet."

"Yes, ma'am," he said, giving her a smart salute. He headed into his office and plopped down in his chair. He was about to begin dumping personal assets, mostly stocks and bonds he'd been acquiring for years. It was time to get liquid, because what he was about to do would take every penny he could raise, beg, borrow, and steal . . . plus a hell of a lot more.

When Noble was reached, there was dead silence on his end of the line when Steve announced, "Jonathan, start selling my portfolio out."

Finally, his old friend managed to say, "You retiring?"

"Hardly, my friend. Just the opposite. I'll fill you in soon, but right now, cash is king."

"You're sure about this? If my guess is right, this market is not going anywhere but up . . . unless this Korean bank failure causes a major fallout, but I don't anticipate it."

"Good, I hope for everyone's sake it goes through the roof. But it's going up, or down, without taking me along for the ride, at least for a while. I need cash. Sell it all, and put eighty percent of the proceeds in short-term paper, the best yields you can get, but low, low risk and nothing that'll take more than thirty days to get shed of. I want at least a mil five in cash in my savings and checking, and the rest short-term."

"Okay, but fax me over an instruction. I can't believe this."

"Me neither. Sell it."

Only moments after he hung up, Sally buzzed to say Fred Alexander was on the line.

"Fred, who in your company is best at dealing with Asians?"

"Hell, boy, call The Donald. I just finished reading an interview with Mr. Trump, and he seems to be the best at everything."

Steve laughed. "By God, he's not bad. He owns a major chunk, if not all, of this building I'm in, and the rents keep climbing. The worst of him is the fact he sued the federal government to try and ban Indian gambling. Thank God he wasn't too good at that."

"We all have our own axes to grind. Seriously, Steve. There's no one here who claims fame with Asians. Is this something big?"

Again Steve laughed. "This is Steve Drum you're talking to Fred. No," he lied, "it's just some lease negotiations with some inscrutable Taiwanese."

"Hell, you speak the language. Do it yourself."

"And have a fool for a client?"

"True."

"Don't be so quick to agree," he said, smiling.

"I'd suggest Cookie Yamamoto, but he takes on only the jillion-dollar deals. To be truthful, I have no idea."

"No sweat. Let's hit the court again soon."

"Soon."

He rose as he hung up, then walked out into Sally's office. "Sal, see if you can find a guy named Cookie Yamamoto in the real estate brokerage biz. I want a face-to-face with him."

"You're kidding. Cookie?"

"Serious as a heart attack . . . I m going down to meet the good Dr. Fawn. Buzz me if you need me."

As he walked the hall, he tried to remember where he'd heard the name Cookie Yamamoto. And he wondered if a Japanese would be able to deal with the Chinese. All he knew was his hunch said use an Asian broker to deal with Wilber Ian Wong. He sure wouldn't take a "mud-hut Indian" seriously.

He smiled at Jonathan's recommendation of Donald Trump, even in jest. The last man on earth who'd want to be involved in this deal, and its hopeful conclusion, would be The Donald. He wanted to keep Atlantic City exclusive.

Steve was surprised to come across a sign painter in the hall at the suite next to the Native American Improvement Coalition. Stroking busily, he was just finishing DNA MEDICAL SERVICES on the glass door.

Walking on, he met Paula and a tall, imposing woman exiting the coalition office. The surprisingly young woman, who he presumed to be Dr. Fawn, had coal-black eyes and raven-wing-black hair pulled back to a severe bun accenting her aquiline features. She was strikingly attractive, but in a harsh, no-nonsense way. All business.

"Steve," Paula said, surprised, "we were just on our way down to see you."

"This must be Dr. Fawn." Steve extended his hand, and got a long-fingered, well-manicured, firm handshake in response. "You can't begin to know how much I appreciate your help." Then he turned to Paula, motioning to the sign painter. "You didn't waste any time."

"I was going to try to reach you in New Mexico today to check on naming this new sideline. Meredith suggested that we might help pay the rent by taking in some outside business while we're doing our work."

Steve smiled appreciatively. He couldn't tell them how welcome the thought was, now that he'd just told his broker to sell everything he'd worked all his life to build. "You're both beautiful ladies . . . business persons"—he corrected himself with a laugh—"after my own heart."

"The better news," Meredith Fawn said, "is that I found more than half the equipment we'll need at a bankrupt lab in Connecticut. If I can have a certified check for thirty-six thousand nine hundred dollars, I can rent a van, drive up, and pick it up tomorrow. We have to move fast."

"Made out to?" Steve asked. He wanted her to know she had his full support.

Meredith spun on her heel and headed back into the coalition office, saying over her shoulder, "I've got the bankruptcy referee's name . . ."

"Well," Paula said quietly. "We're off and running. I've composed a letter to all the reservations in New York State, asking for volunteers for a Native American heritage DNA study . . . and giving them a free cholesterol check, that was Meredith's idea, if they let us prick a finger. Those rezes with health clinics can draw blood for us and ship the slides. They can earn a few bucks for the service, say fifteen dollars a slide, and it'll save a lot of legwork."

"That's great. Now, let's pray it all comes to something."

He was surprised to see David Greenberg exit the office with Meredith Fawn.

Steve welcomed him warmly.

Glancing at his watch, Steve saw it was nearing noon, and suggested, "I'm buying lunch. I'd like to fill you all in . . . at least as much as I can, on what this is all about."

Both David and Meredith smiled in anticipation. "We're ready," David said at the same time Meredith said, "All ears." Steve thought long and hard as they all walked to a steak house, Off the Wall, he enjoyed a couple of blocks from 40 Wall Street. When they finally settled in around a corner table and ordered, he decided to take a chance.

"We've discovered a document," he told them, ". . . a three-hundred-fifty-year-old document, that grants certain rights to the tribes of those Native Americans buried beneath the McGuire Building. I can't tell you where I'm going with this discovery, or where it will eventually lead, but I can tell you it could be among the most exciting things ever to happen to benefit Native Americans. It could also be a disaster if not handled with utmost secrecy and utmost care."

He paused, but no one ventured a question. "This is not going to get us back what we've lost over the centuries, but it may go a long way toward gaining some economic advantage. If you'll take that at face value for a while and help me prove up some direct descendency, I promise you'll be in for some exciting, and challenging, times ahead."

"That's it?" David asked, obviously disappointed.

"That's it for now, David. And even that has to stay at this table. Paula has filled me in regarding your interest in this from a journalistic standpoint. I have no problem with her promises to you. I promise you'll have the story of the century, maybe a book, if you hang tight and keep it close to the vest until we give you the word."

"Okay. That I can do."

"And what else you can do is some research for me. I want to know everything there is to know about Manhattan history, both political and natural history, in the mid-1600s. I need maps, documents, a report in a doctoral dissertation format with footnotes— the whole nine yards. What you'll be doing may become supporting documentation for a court brief."

"Okay, I've always enjoyed history."

"Good, because you're going to get a snootful before this is over. I'll be giving you a legal description, written in the mid-1600s, and I want that superimposed as closely as possible onto a current map."

"I'll get right on it."

The waitress brought their lunch, and as soon as she'd put the last plate down, Steve continued. "Now, who do you know in the fourth estate?"

"The press?" David answered. "My uncle is a reporter at *The New York Times*. . . has been for twenty years. I've been dating a writer at IBC, Sarah Birnbalm. And of course I know most everybody in the rags . . . the underground scandal sheets."

"International Broadcasting Corporation? Aren't their offices in Rockefeller Center?"

"They've been there for years, but the rumor is they're thinking about relocating."

God works in mysterious ways, Steve thought. "So, find out what you can about their interest in moving. Pump this source of yours," Steve said, then laughed when he realized the implication, as did the rest of the table.

"My pleasure," David said with a lecherous smile.

"I'm sure you won't mind that assignment. And start developing a file on press contacts. We're going to need all the help we can get from the press, unless I miss my guess . . . and our good relations with them is your direct responsibility." Then he had another thought. "Check the last, say, three years, and find out who has written positive stories about the reservations, Indian gaming, and any other Indian affairs in the press, or TV, or magazines, for that matter. I want to know who's likely to be on our side, and who's not."

"Is that all?" David said, looking a little overwhelmed.

"That's a start. Speaking of sides, and just so all of you know, it's cowboys-and-Indians time all over again. I've had some death threats, just to add a little spice to the mix. Keep on your toes, be ready to duck, and don't catch a ricochet. I won't be offended if, after this lunch, you'd rather keep your contact with me via the phone." He chuckled, but they obviously didn't see the humor.

They all centered worried eyes on him.

"Thad Wintermoose is hired on as my bodyguard. If you notice anything unusual, you might mention it to him."

Shrugging it off as if it were nothing to be really concerned about, Steve turned to Meredith. "So, when do we start drawing blood?"

She took a moment before answering, then gulped and offered, "I've decided that rather than rent one, we should lease a van or panel truck this afternoon and start equipping it, I'll use it to pick up the lab equipment tomorrow. We'll need the van to work out of on those reservations without a health clinic. We can begin drawing quickly, but we need some kind of a program set up—"

Paula interrupted. "I've already contacted a number of tribes and they're waiting for a date to advertise for donors. No reason we can't set up a schedule this afternoon."

Meredith smiled. "Let's get to work ... I've got only two weeks."

Their salads arrived. Steve eyed his team. "After lunch will be soon enough."

Steve worked the afternoon away without incident, completing his report for ICOM and getting a breakfast appointment with Roman "Cookie" Yamamoto, who Sally had finally run down at Pyramid Realty on the upper East Side not far from Steve's condo.

The afternoon was uneventful, but when the day was over and the town car pulled up in front of the condo, the ramp entrance to the garage was blocked by two fire trucks, hoses leading into the opening. A group of uniformed men surrounded an ambulance being loaded with a body on a gurney. A dozen police cars, some with lights flashing, sat askew in the street, two of them cordoning off the block at either end.

Steve leapt from the car and explained to the cop blocking the street that he lived there, then hurried to see what was up.

CHAPTER NINETEEN

He was stopped at the ramp by another uniform.

"What's going on?" Steve asked.

"Move along, sir. We've got things under control."

"I live here. Who's hurt?"

"The doorman. There was an explosion in the parking base-ment. The bomb squad's there now."

Steve felt a shiver rack his back. He didn't attribute it to the chill in the air even though it was cold enough he could see his breath. He made his way to the ambulance, but was stopped again by a uniformed cop.

"Move along, sir," he parroted the first.

"Tuffy's a friend of mine. I'd like to speak to him."

"The injured guy . . . They said he'll live. Check with the hospi-tal later."

"How bad's he hurt?"

"Burns and glass cuts on the arms, chest, and neck, but his face is okay. Maybe some busted bones. He's in shock . . . took a hell of a whack."

The ambulance doors were being shut, so Steve had no chance to speak to Tuffy and offer what encouragement he might. He turned back to the officer, "What blew up?"

"I heard it was a car."

He wanted to get to a phone to find out where they would take Tuffy. "Can I go up to my apartment?"

"Yeah, they just gave the okay. That BMW is toast, but everything else—"

"BMW? What color?"

"Dark blue."

"Christ, that could be my car."

"You sit tight. The suits'll wanna talk to you."

Steve waited while the officer made his way down the ramp,
then returned with a plainclothes cop with a shield hanging out
of his overcoat pocket. The man's rumpled overcoat, suit, shirt,
and soup-stained tie reminded Steve of Columbo, but his hair
was dirty blond and cropped short, his eyes a troubled gray.

He walked up to Steve and extended his hand. "Detective
Rollie Wood."

Steve shook and introduced himself.

The detective looked him up and down. "You connected with
the Red Ace Corporation that the beamer was registered to?"

"That's my company, and a blue, five-year-old BMW parked
on the second level front is my car."

"It's your pile of crap now," Wood said. "It's a wonder it
didn't burn the whole place down."

"What happened?"

"Blew all to hell. You didn't have anything stored in your car
that might . . . ?"

"Nothing. Not even a can of oil."

Suddenly feeling chilled to the bone, Steve suggested they
continue the conversation in his condo, and Detective Wood followed him up. As they rode the elevator, Steve pondered telling
Wood about the photographer, but a hunch told him to keep it
to himself for a while, at least until he could talk with Thad, who
was due back in the office in the morning.

To Steve's surprise, Thad was hunkered down, sitting on his
hocks like a hunter at a campfire, patiently waiting next to his
apartment door.

He rose as Steve approached. "Heard it on my scanner. Recognized the address and thought I'd better be here."

Steve made the introductions, introducing Thad as a coworker,
not a bodyguard, and they entered. Wood immediately excused
himself to the bathroom to wash the crime scene off his hands.

That gave Thad a chance to ask Steve, "What did you tell him
about our boy?"

"Nothing, yet."

"Let's chew on it awhile before we get—" Wood returned and Thad let it lie.

The rather rumpled detective took a seat without being invited and pulled a pencil and little spiral notebook from an inside coat pocket.

But before he could ask a question, Steve did. "How did Tuffy get involved with a bomb in my car?"

"What I get so far is that your doorman was upstairs, delivering something, then came down and the doorman across the street told him some guy had jumped the barrier and gone down into the garage. He went down to check it out and saw the guy running from your car. He said he knew he couldn't catch him—"

"Tuffy's got a bum knee, old football injury. He played in the NFL in the sixties."

"Anyway, he went to the car to check it out, and the next thing he knew he was in the ambulance. We figure it went off prematurely, or was some kind of motion device and he set it off by just touching the car. Luckily it was under the driver's seat, and he was near the back bumper. . . at least that's where he left a shoe. He was blown across the driveway, but we found the driver-side door a hundred fifty feet away. If he'd been next to the door, or if you had, you'd be scorched mush."

Steve spent over an hour fielding questions from the detective about the Red Ace Corporation, but not before he took the phone off the hook. The press was on to who owned the destroyed vehicle and had started calling. Detective Rollie Wood grew far more interested when Steve indicated that he was a consultant to gambling interests all over the country.

Finally, the detective seemed to tire, and rose. "I'm sure you'll hear from our organized crime division, Mr. Drum. Bombs and gambling will catch their interest. If you think of anything else, here's my card."

He left, not seeming satisfied, merely temporarily placated.

Thad returned from the kitchen, where he'd been making tea, and handed Steve a cup. He feigned a slight Australian accent. " 'There is no bomb in that building. I will bet vital parts of my anatomy on that fact.' " He smiled and shook his head in wonder.

"Okay, what's that one from?"

"Mel Gibson, *Lethal Weapon.* I'm glad they weren't *your* famous last words. You sit tight while I go over the apartment with a fine-tooth comb. Our boy may have been more busy than just remodeling your car."

Steve picked up the phone and began calling to try to get a report on Tuffy's condition, but he was unsuccessful. Call waiting beeped, and he clicked over, surprised by Paula's voice. At the same time, the building entry intercom buzzed. Thad responded, telling the reporter in the lobby that Mr. Drum was speaking to no one.

Paula sounded worried. "I saw on the news that a bomb went off, and it looked like your building."

He explained the situation, then asked her to call Sally and put her on to finding out where they'd taken Tuffy, what his condition was, and what they could do to help his family. Then he turned on the financial channel and didn't move from the deep leather couch. He did note, through half-closed eyes, that Pacific Rim currencies were dropping like dead ducks against the dollar. The Indonesian, Taiwanese, and Hong Kong currencies were particularly volatile.

If the Asian American Real Estate Trust depended upon Pacific Rim investment, as Steve suspected they did, then they were in deep trouble. Maybe the mud-hut Indian had a chance. . . .

When Thad finished, he returned to the living room. "I can't find anything that looks out of place."

"I guess our boy is upping the ante."

"I guess," Thad said, his tone disgusted. "You'd better start letting me know when you're coming back to town, so I can do my job. Or better yet, don't leave town without me."

"Yeah, I guess I'd better not. You wanna start bunkin' here?"

"Not really, unless you think I should. I've got a warm spot . . ." He let it drop, then continued. "But I want to be waiting at the door when you're ready to leave, and I want to deliver you home at night. Short of being a bedfellow, I'm going to stick to you like stink on kaka."

Steve toasted him with the cup of tea. "Cheers. I think I'm convinced."

Thad downed his cup and headed for the door. "You're not going out tonight?"

"I'm going to catch up on some overdue zees."

"Okay. Don't answer the door for nobody." He reached to the

small of his back, under his coat, and produced a small but nasty-looking pistol. "I'm going to leave this with you. You know how to handle an automatic?"

"I was raised hunting, Wintermoose. In fact, I pole-axed my first winter moose with an old thirty-thirty at twelve years old."

"Very funny. A bolt- or lever-action rifle is not an automatic handgun."

"Yeah, yeah. I had a Colt sidearm my last year in the Corps at the ripe old age of twenty-two, long before these smooth Indian cheeks were being shaved regular."

"Okay. Nine shots, forty caliber." He headed out the door. "What time in the morning?"

"I've got an eight o'clock breakfast at Chino's about five blocks from here. Town car is picking me up there at nine . . . I was going to walk down. You can either come here or meet me there."

"Steve, remember, you're not going out of this apartment without me. I'll be here at seven-thirty."

"Yes, sir," Steve said, and saluted.

Thad yelled through the door after he closed it. "Bolt this baby." And Steve did.

He poured himself a much-needed scotch, clicked off the TV, put on a Ravel disc, and leaned back in the deep couch, closing his eyes and letting the music take him away from it all. Dropping off to sleep halfway through the drink, he was awakened by the phone. He knew he'd been sleeping, as the disc had played through and stopped.

"So, that wasn't you they put in the meat wagon?" Darth Vader asked. "Too bad."

"Fuck you," Steve said, instantly awake. "Why don't you come on over and face me, you slimy bastard. I'd like to stomp your balls into a grease spot—"

He laughed. "Is the old BMW a little fucked, Farley?"

"You hurt a good man, and you're gonna pay."

"He was a Harlem nigger. It was a red nigger I wanted."

"Just come over, slimeball, and let's finish this."

"You're finished . . . next time."

The line went dead, but as soon as Steve laid the receiver down, it rang again. He jerked it back up. "Just get over here, asshole. I'll knock your dick in the dirt."

"Actually," the extremely sensuous voice said, "I've never been accused of having one."

"Angela?"

There was silence for a second, then her voice took on a sharper edge. "You were expecting another lady, a blonde maybe?"

He didn't answer. His stomach suddenly churned, contradicting the heat flooding his loins. Then he steeled his resolve. "You in Italy?"

"Tomorrow."

They were both silent this time. "Well, I hope you're enjoying yourself, and your time with your family."

"I am. Did you get my letter?"

"What letter?"

"I left you a letter under the doormat the night of the Rainbow Dinner. And I left a message on your machine to call me at the Pen."

"Oh, did good ol' Nick, the high school sweetheart, take the time to drop you by so you could shove a 'dear John' under my doormat? What a guy!"

He could hear her deep sigh. "I knew Nick in college, not high school, and he was never a 'sweetheart.' He's Papa's friend."

"Angela, I'm in the middle of something that requires my full attention, and I think—"

"Oh, is the blonde there? She looked as if she'd require a lot of attention. High maintenance, I'd guess."

"A *business* something, and I think—"

"Stop! Right there . . . I'm going to be home in a week, and we'll talk in person."

"Sure. You'll give me an hour or so right before you run back to Saddle River and Mama and Papa."

"I'm sorry you didn't get my letter."

He paused for a moment. "It must be very late there."

"It's three A.M. But I have to talk to you."

"And I have to talk with you about something that affects the both of us. But I won't worry you with it while your enjoying your trip . . . as you said, we can use a little time apart. I didn't believe it before, but now I agree wholeheartedly. Call me when you get back if you think about it and it doesn't foul up your busy schedule." It hurt him, like twisting a knife in his guts, to say it, but he did. "Don't bother dropping by, just call." He knew if he saw her, he'd weaken and fall completely apart. All his resolve would wash away.

But it didn't seem he'd have to worry about it. All he got was a dial tone.

Reaching for his half-finished scotch, he downed it in a swallow. He rose and walked to his little built-in bar and poured himself another, then flipped the stereo from CD to radio and the apartment was flooded with Diana Ross and "Ain't no mountain high enough, ain't no valley low enough, ain't no river wide enough, to keep me from you."

I guess the ocean's wide enough, and your family sure as hell is enough, he thought, then switched it off and headed to his bedroom. As exhausted as he was, for an hour he tried to sleep, but imagined her scent wafting from the pillow and couldn't.

Rising, he went to the sauna and took a long sweat bath, chanting one of the Salish songs to drive away evil spirits. Then took a cold shower. He switched the water to hot, to drive away the memory of her. But all he could think about were the times he'd washed her back, and even more intimate places, and she'd washed him, always leading to another bout of lovemaking, sometimes on the shag rug in the bathroom or even in the shower.

He grudgingly acknowledged that he thought about her a thousand times a day, and even more at night. When would it stop? He had to make it stop, or he'd be old and gray, with only a few assignations as memories.

Assignations, rather than a family.

It was ironic. Because of Angela's love and respect for her family, they would never have one of their own.

He had to get on with his life.

He awoke to the alarm, something that seldom happened, as he most always turned it off well before it buzzed.

Dressed and making coffee early Wednesday morning, he glanced up as the front-lobby intercom panel buzzed. A strange voice, not Tuffy's, announced Mr. Wintermoose. Steve said, "Send him up."

When he arrived, Thad chided him for leaving the door ajar without making absolutely sure who was coming.

When Thad entered, he carried a package. "I've got a present for you, Steve."

Steve watched curiously as he unpacked a box and pulled out

a black vest. "That won't go with most of my suits," he said with a smile.

"Maybe not, but neither will bloodstains."

"You really think this is necessary?"

Thad unbuttoned his own shirt, showing Steve the patch of black under it.

"Oh, hell." Steve reached for the Kevlar vest and headed into his bedroom to put it on.

Before they left the condo, Steve called Sally at home and caught her before she headed for the subway, finding out they'd taken Tuffy to County General. He was in critical condition and allowed no visitors other than family. Steve asked her to send flowers and find out how to contact his wife to see if there was anything they could do to help.

At 7:40, with the morning gray, the clouds so low they obscured the tops of the taller buildings, Steve and Thad were walking toward Chino's, a coffee shop in the building where Cookie Yamamoto maintained his office.

Yamamoto was not difficult to spot, the only Asian in the place, and built a little like a compact version of a sumo wrestler.

The man rose with some difficulty and extended his thick-fingered hand as Steve entered and walked straight to his table. "You brought someone else," he said, frowning with such force his heavy brows almost touched. Then he waved the waitress over. "Move me to a bigger table," he commanded, and she began gathering up his breakfast. "Sorry I didn't wait," he murmured.

"No problem." Steve introduced Thad, again as a coworker.

When they got resettled and Cookie went back to demolishing the plate of lox and onions, Steve began explaining what he wanted. "I've got a property I want to buy from a group of Asians, and, to be frank, I thought I'd be better off if an Asian represented me."

With his mouth full of salmon, Cookie agreed, shrugging, "I walk the walk and talk the talk."

"Chinese?"

Cookie paused. "A little. Very little. But I do a lot of business with some Hong Kong groups and know their customs."

Steve carefully did not divulge that he spoke Mandarin well. "Well, I want to retain you as a buyer's exclusive agent. Will you work that way?"

"Look, Mr. Drum. I'm very, very busy—"

"This is a very, very big deal."

This caused him pause. The pause was extended by the waitress arriving to lay a plate full of pancakes in front of Cookie and a fruit cup and coffee in front of Steve. Thad was served the oatmeal and toast he'd ordered. The waitress left, and Cookie asked, "So, what is a 'big' deal to you?"

"Let's just say it's probably nine figures."

"That is certainly big enough. I work on commission, not retainers."

"How about a retainer against commission? That way you can't lose, but you'll be obligated to me by contract."

"So, what is the deal?"

Steve reached into his wallet and dug out a twenty-dollar bill. "Here, you're retained."

Cookie laughed and forked in a mouthful of pancakes dripping with maple syrup. He chewed for a second, not reaching for the twenty, swallowed, then said, "I do not work quite that cheap."

"Not a question of how much it is . . . can I call you Cookie?"

"Of course, Steve."

"It's a matter of you accepting the terms of the contract we're forming. I don't want you to divulge your client, not to anyone, until we have a deal . . . in fact, until a deal is *closed* if we can get away with it. Then I may want to take title in the name of a trading company that makes the seller, and everyone else in Manhattan, believe they're dealing with other Asians."

"That is no problem, Steve. Send me over five thousand, and I will give you a week's time, and my silence. So, what property?"

"The twenty? Take it as good and valuable consideration, and I'll send over four thousand nine hundred eighty when I get back to the office, and I'll buy breakfast."

Cookie laughed, but picked the bill up and shoved it in his wallet. "Terms accepted, presuming I am not already working on this property on someone else's behalf."

"Even if you are working on it, Cookie, you're obligated to not divulge our interest, now that you've accepted the retainer. Though you'll still be allowed to continue whatever else you're doing in regard to the specific property . . . understood?"

"Sure, so what is the property?"

"Thirty Rockefeller Plaza."

This caused a pause by the big Japanese. "Ah so, I knew it had been in bankruptcy due to the sour market, and probably some mismanagement, but some trust, Asian American I think it was, bought the primary building and some other Rockefeller Center property, and I presumed it was no longer for sale."

"Thirty Rockefeller Plaza is the primary building. Maybe it isn't for sale at this time, but I presume the trust's source of funds is primarily offshore . . . and with the Pacific Rim banks and currencies in the tank, and 30 Rock Plaza over twenty-five percent vacant, it probably will be soon, and I want to be first in line."

"Good point, I should have thought of it. . . . I pulled some financial info on you, Steve, and your company, after your secretary called yesterday. If you do not mind my frankness, my new friend, you are not in any position to close a deal on even a small part of Rock Center."

"True," Steve said, then lied. "But I represent a group who can. You get it put together at the right price, and I'll close it."

They parted ways with Cookie Yamamoto promising to get back to Steve by the end of the week, after he'd had a preliminary meeting with Wilber Ian Wong and the Asian American Real Estate Trust. But the meeting was to happen only after he received and executed a letter agreement to be prepared by Steve, appointing him as Steve's exclusive agent in regard to the specific property in question and swearing him to nondisclosure.

They walked out to meet the town car awaiting them, and Steve couldn't help but remember a term his father, Bob Lee Standing Drum, often used, and wondered if he'd let his alligator mouth overload his hummingbird butt. He hoped not. But he wondered. . . . Cookie was right, he was in no position to make even a proper deposit on Rockefeller Center, much less come up with the fifty plus million it would probably take for a down payment and start-up capital.

It was time to start calling in every marker he had, all over the country.

It was powwow time.

CHAPTER TWENTY

To Steve's surprise, a mike was shoved into his face when he entered the lobby of 40 Wall Street. The pretty blond-haired news reporter who held it was tethered to a cameraman by the mike cord. Steve didn't want publicity at the moment. The last thing he wanted was the press snooping around when he had so many secrets to keep.

The other side of the coin was he'd soon need all the publicity, the positive publicity, he could get.

"Mr. Drum, Felicia Ann Garrity of IBC. Can you tell me why your car was bombed yesterday?"

Thad waited nearby, watching for Steve's high-sign to step in and escort him away, but Steve motioned him to wait. "No, ma'am, I have no idea."

Steve kept moving to the bank of elevators, but she was relentless, and both she and the cameraman skillfully backpedaled.

"Aren't you involved in gambling?"

"Red Ace Corporation is a consultant to a number of Native American gaming companies all over the nation. We advise them on such innocuous things as how many rest rooms they should provide . . . how to lay out their clubs for optimum efficiency . . . nonconsequential things like that."

"Then can we safely presume someone disapproves of your gaming connections, and wants you dead?"

Steve stopped, carefully weighing words. "No, I don't think

you can assume that. I think you'd be correct to presume that someone made a mistake and got their bomb in the wrong car. I've had no threats, nor have any enemies, nor any business associates who'd gain by my death. I guess you could say I'm merely an attorney who handles a lot of boring paperwork, just not important enough to kill. Nobody dies over bingo." He laughed. "You're tracking the wrong critter, Miss Garrity. Now I have to get to work."

He entered the elevator with Thad close behind. But Thad stopped and turned, keeping the reporter and her cameraman out of the elevator, and in the process missing it himself.

Sally greeted Steve with, "The damn phone's been ringing off the hook, and I've already run off a half dozen reporters this morning."

"Well, keep running them off. Tell them we'll issue a press release this afternoon, and get a list of fax numbers from them to send it to. That should placate them for a while."

As he finished the statement, Thad walked in behind him. "They took another elevator. They'll be here in a minute. I'm a little surprised you didn't invite that blonde into the elevator with you. . . what a looker!"

"So was Lucretia Borgia, and this looker was trying to shove something long, hard, and potentially lethal in my mouth. There's just something about that picture that doesn't sit well with me." He grinned.

Sally looked confused until Thad offered, "A fine-as-wine reporter, trying to shove a mike under his nose."

Steve held up a finger, wanting a moment while he thought, trying to remember the exact words. " 'If I want to bump uglies with someone'—or was it somebody—'I've got plenty of places to go.' Ed Harris in the Patsy Cline movie. Thad, you're authorized to just go ahead and shoot me if I ever ask a woman if she wants to 'bump uglies.' " He smiled again, then walked into his private office, pulling the door shut behind him.

Thad and Sally stared after him, amazed.

On Steve's desk was a DHL overnight envelope from Patrick McGoogan in England marked *Personal* in large letters. He immediately opened it and found a typed translation of the treaty and a number of other documents, all with attached translations.

Patrick's note was concise:

Steve:

As you can see for yourself, we've got great documentation of the Williamson grant to the Canarsee tribe. We also have (copies enclosed) several pieces of correspondence referring to the tribe and their relocation on Manhattan Island.

I'm busily searching the paper trail to determine what happened to the Canarsee in later times: Did they sell? Were they driven off? (more likely) Did they simply die off from the white man's disease? If they sold out, we'll have some trouble, and if they died off, we obviously have no heirs to fight for. Short of those problems, I still think we can write a hell of a Supreme Court brief.

If history holds true, they were shot and run off their land. Not to wish them bad fortune, but let's hope that's the case.

Have you found out anything in the records there?

Give me a call if I can be of more help. In the meantime, I'm not only intrigued, but fascinated, and I'm nose-to-the-grindstone researching.

Keep well,
Patrick

Steve buzzed Sally. "Sal, I don't want to be disturbed for at least an hour. See if you can get me an appointment with Dragono-vich late this afternoon."

Then he sat to study the contents of the envelope, placing the treaty translation in the center of his desk and placing the other translations around it.

There was a clear and concise legal description of the grant, naming creeks and other physical characteristics of the island as was common at the time, including some huge trees. The trees would, obviously, not be still standing, but the rock points and watersheds—at least the basic lay of the land—would surely be the same. Wouldn't they? It was sure as hell good enough to back up a claim.

He studied the documentation, particularly intrigued by a series of letters from a farmer's wife to her sister in Holland, dated in the 1690s. The woman, Rika Van Der Voort, her husband, Ard, and four children had been on a farm in mid-Manhattan with an unnamed Indian tribe as neighbors. She, of course, referred to them only as "the savages." In the last letter in the series, she described a hard winter, failed crops, a lost milk cow, and the fact her husband suspected that the "savages" who resided to the north of their farm, had stolen and, being ignorant beasts, probably eaten the productive animal.

When Steve was finished absorbing the documents, he buzzed Sally and asked her to come make copies, then run David Greenberg down. In moments David stood in front of his desk. Steve gave him a copy of the legal description from the treaty, and the letters.

"There's a letter here dated 1697. . . . I want to know if anything came of Ard Van Der Voort's missing cow. I want to know what happened to the Manhattan Indians, who probably were the Canarsee. If they sold out, died off, or, more than likely, were killed off."

"I'll start with Ard's cow . . . even if its *bobbe-myseh.*"

"Pardon me?" Steve asked.

"*Bobbe-myseh* . . . Yiddish."

"Meaning?"

"Well, actually," he said, a little sheepish, "something silly."

"Just start there, okay? And see what you can do about locating . . . overlaying . . . that legal description."

He walked out, mumbling. "Oy vey, a cow. I'm chasing a three-hundred-year-old cow."

Steve stopped him. "David, what do you know about Felicia Garrity, the news lady?"

David paused a minute, still holding the office door. "Good tits, not great, but the originals, I understand. Best ass I ever saw on a white woman. Sarah, my friend at IBC, writes and researches for her occasionally if she has a special report to do. Since we're on Yiddish, the shiksa's a bit of a *bummerkeh.*" He noted Steve's puzzled look. "A loose woman."

"In order to get what she wants?"

"Exactly. And she's got the equipment to get about anything."

"Okay, just wondering."

"But she loves causes. If they'll get ratings."

Steve sat and pondered after David left. Maybe he could let Felicia Garrity try and pump some information out of him about his destroyed BMW while he tried to pump some information out of her about IBC wanting to move. She looked like she might just be great pumping. He felt a sudden wrenching in his stomach and wondered why. Thinking of another woman shouldn't bother him. Angela had been out with handsome Nick, hadn't she? He reminded himself again that he would think of Angela no more.

And he would entertain bumping uglies with Miss Garrity . . . that is, if Ms. Garrity entertained the same thought.

He was not surprised when Sally buzzed him with, "A detective from the organized crime division of NYPD is on the line. He wants to come over."

"Ask him to come over in the morning, anytime."

"Yes, sir."

In the late afternoon he made his way up the elevator to the ICOM offices. Dragonovich was out of the country, but had delegated Steve's report to his first lieutenant and in-house counsel, Forrest Rostinburg.

Rostinburg's narrow eyebrows, under an extremely high forehead, rose in surprise when Steve slid his two-page report, a letter of agreement, and invoice across his desk.

"I'd feel guilty taking ICOM's money," Steve said, "at least any piece of the deal. When I got there, everything was done. This letter, with all the deal points you wanted, had already been negotiated by Hector Alvarez and executed by Tobias Nakai, who represented himself as counsel for the Navajo—"

"He does represent them. I checked it out."

Steve was not surprised that Tobias Nakai had checked out, because Tobias Nakai actually was retained by the Navajo tribe, and had his offices in Gallup. It was just that the office of Tobias Nakai that Steve had visited was set up by the Rodriguez brothers and Harry Tongue just for Steve's visit. Nakai's actual office was on the other end of town. Now, if ICOM failed to verify the signature . . .

Steve merely nodded, so Rostinburg continued. "That's as I understand it." Sitting back in his chair, interlacing his fingers across his more than adequate stomach, Rostinburg studied him. "Did you get to the site and meet with the drilling company?"

"Yes, I did, but that was also under control. As soon as you communicate your acceptance and wire the money to Monument Mining's bank, Farmer's and Rancher's in Albuquerque, Hector will get the drillers started. He said you already had his company's account numbers." He managed a worried look. "The drillers are on-site, but indicated that if they didn't hear from you by tomorrow, they'd have to pull off. They couldn't get back for at least a couple of weeks."

"Monument'll have their half mil tomorrow. So, you say you can't help us?"

"Looks to me like the job's done. The invoice is for my expenses for the trip, plus a thousand a day for two days. It's itemized. And the letter rescinds our contract for the two percent of the deal. It also includes a hold-harmless as consideration for the cancellation, which you shouldn't mind since I'm no longer involved in the deal."

Rostinburg shook his head. "Well, Mr. Drum, this is mighty white of you—" He paused for a minute, slightly embarrassed by his choice of words. "Let me read this." He studied the document, then executed it with a flourish and returned a copy to Steve. "It's been a pleasure doing business with you."

Steve rose. "Thanks. I wish I could have actually helped. It looks like a hell of a great project. If you ever really need help in the Native American community—"

"I'll call on you."

Steve excused himself. He'd covered himself as well as he knew how.

Now it was up to Harry Tongue and the Rodriguez boys, to keep things rolling toward the big score.

ICOM was obligated to send another million when and if their "personally conducted" assays came in as represented. Everything would have to stay in place for at least two months for that part of the scam to fly.

Then, when the scam was exposed, Steve would make the real money on the deal—five or six million, doubling his net worth. He knew exactly how, but the timing had to be perfect, as fine as frog's hair. And to do so, he had to take a major risk. Even his slight contact with ICOM would be considered insider trading if the profit resulted from the deal in New Mexico. But with all of his small fortune at risk, he had to take the chance.

By late that afternoon the van was ready to roll and the lab packed full of equipment. Meredith had hired four phlebotomists. Within days they had an operating lab and had people in the field, taking blood samples.

Steve's doorman and friend who'd taken the bomb blast had several broken ribs, a dislocated shoulder, cuts and contusions, and a concussion. Steve spent two evenings that week visiting Tuffy, and making sure his family was well taken care of—Tuffy was living up to his name, amazing the doctors with his recovery.

Steve spent his office hours preparing for his upcoming negotiations with Asian American by studying what had transpired in the Manhattan real estate market for the past year. He'd also received the executed agreement back from Joseph Bigsam and spent a lot of time preparing a report and business plan for Big Sam's casino.

He received no calls from Angela or from the photographer. Nor did anyone take a shot at him or try to blow him to smithereens. Late Tuesday of the following week, Cookie Yamamoto finally called and wanted to see him. Steve invited him to dinner at the expensive Sea Grill in Rockefeller Center. Thad, Steve's shadow, accompanied him.

"Those guys are nuts," Cookie said, sucking an oyster out of its shell.

"How so?" Steve asked.

"There is just under a million three hundred thousand square feet of rentable office space in the building, plus two hundred thousand more in the French Building and the British Empire Building, which they also own. Even projecting the rents at today's rate of thirty-six dollars per year per foot, the annual income could be . . . *not is,* but could be, five mil seven for the office space. There is four hundred thousand square feet of commercial space on the first two floors and the other buildings projected at seven dollars a square foot per month or eighty-four a year . . . that's another projected three mil three, or a total projected annual income of nine mil a year. These nuts are asking twenty times the *projected* gross, or a hundred eighty mil for the building. And the actual gross is far less."

"What's it worth?" Steve asked, already knowing close to what Cookie's answer would be.

"A prudent buyer would not pay half that . . . and he would have to be a user. For your information, I had an associate research the records at the bankruptcy court, and they paid just over seventy-five million for the package. They got a deal, but they paid all cash."

"Are they going to actively place it on the market?"

Cookie smiled tightly, shaking his head. "No, the Chinese do not work that way. They will let it be known that they are entertaining offers, but they will not list it for sale."

"What *will* they sell it for?"

"Eventually, assuming the currency markets in Asia stay in the tank and they are forced to sell, they will be economically flogged into selling it for what it is worth. The market will dictate."

"How long will it take . . . them being forced to sell, I mean?"

"If I knew the currency markets, I would be a currency trader, not a real estate broker. Or if I had an intimate working knowledge of Asian American's internal finances, then I might have an answer for you."

"I want to make an offer."

"It is an exercise in frustration right now, but if you want to . . ." He sucked another oyster, far more interested in his plate than in this deal he thought would never come together. "So," he asked, chewing, "you want to offer the ninety mil it is probably worth?"

"No, I want to offer a hundred ten, but I want enough weasel clauses that I'll never have to forfeit my deposit should the deal not make. I don't want anyone else stepping into this deal and outbidding us."

Cookie eyed him, waving the waiter over and ordering another dozen oysters. "There are hundreds of leases to verify and approve, insurance, title, etc., etc. I can work plenty of ways to worm out of the offer. Why would you pay far too much for the property?"

"Cookie, if the use I have in mind comes to pass, it'll be worth what I'm offering . . . and more."

"And that use is?"

"Private, is what it is."

"It is your money . . . What are you suggesting as a deposit?"

"Say, a mil."

"That, my friend, is as thin as an Ethiopian beggar."

"It'll have to do for the time being."

"I will try and make it work. What is in this deal for me, since I do not think it has any more chance of making than a donkey running the Preakness?"

"Bill me another five thousand when you're ready to submit

the offer . . . but remember, these advances are against any commission you might earn."

"How about terms?"

"Try twenty mil down and thirty years on the balance, all due
in ten. Whatever interest rate you think will fly, maybe prime
plus two."

"I will have the paperwork at your office tomorrow."

After they left the restaurant, Thad shook his head. "Sounds
like a hell of a lot of wampum to me."

"It *is* a hell of a lot of wampum. But with that building full of
slots, and crap tables, and roulette, it'll take only a couple of years
to make it back."

"I guess it's all relative," Thad said, but didn't sound convinced.

That evening Steve walked into his apartment at 6:30 with Thad
on his heels. Without thinking, he poked the blinking answering
machine.

The sultry voice that emanated sounded a little stressed. "I'm
back. I'm at the Pen and I'm coming over at seven-thirty. You
can't reach me, as I'll be out of the room. Please be home."

Walking straight to the bar, Steve poured himself a scotch, neat,
as Thad checked out the apartment—a routine that had become
habit with them.

It was probably the hardest thing he'd done in years, but when
Thad returned, he took a deep, steadying breath and said, "I'll
pour you one Jack Daniel's, then how about going out to eat?"

"Supposed to eat with Paula, but work comes first."

"This is social." Then he stretched the truth. "I don't mind
going alone."

"Screw that. You know my rules. I'm going with you."

"Then how about calling Paula to join us. I'll treat."

"You're on . . . I guess the lady on the answering machine is
going to be disappointed?"

"I doubt it. She's got her own life . . . and I'm just a dalliance
for her."

As he pulled the condo's front door behind them, his stomach
was doing cartwheels and his chest burning. His head swam, and
he thought he might be sick.

God, he wanted to stay, wanted to see her again.

But he had to get on with his life.

He wanted Angela with all his heart, but not as a toy—and he refused to continue to think of himself as one. He wanted her as a wife, and mother of his children.

When Angela arrived, she stood at the condo door for a long while, even though the doorman had indicated that Mr. Drum was out for the evening. She had been pleased, especially after their last conversation, when she found her name still at the doorman's stand, still to be admitted without calling the apartment. Now she presumed it was Steve's oversight that it hadn't been removed.

She had a key, but it was hidden in her things at Saddle River. And she was not sure she would have used it even if she had it with her. She'd hate to be waiting for him, enticingly clad only in one of his T-shirts, if he showed up with the buxom blonde in tow.

She knew Steve had been home earlier and he'd obviously gotten her call. She leaned against the wall and her throat began to burn. Then her eyes. Then a tear streaked her cheek.

She mopped it away with the back of a gloved hand. Now, when she really, really needed him, he wasn't drifting away, but racing to leave her somewhere behind.

She dug into her handbag, but her eyes clouded with tears. The bag fell to the floor, dribbling out its contents. Sagging to her knees, she tried to gather up her things, having to feel for them since she could see nothing more than a blur. A run began in the knee of her panty hose, and she felt it creep up her thigh.

"Damn, damn, damn," she said, managing to do so without a choke.

Finally, she collected her makeup, wallet, sunglasses, and papers, and found the tissue she'd been seeking.

"You dumb redskin," she sobbed quietly, "what you claim you always wanted is here for you, and you're ignoring it." Dabbing her eyes with a tissue she rose to her feet and started for the elevator.

"Okay," she said, standing taller, throwing back her shoulders as the elevator approached. "I guess blondes are more fun. So have fun . . . I don't need you or anyone else. I can handle this job all by myself."

By the time the elevator doors opened, she had collected herself.

Erect, shoulders back, she stepped in next to an old, stooped, blue-haired lady and re-punched the button to the street floor, even though it was already lit. "Alone. All by myself," she said aloud.

"Me too, darling," the old woman said. "Alone's not so bad . . . when you're asleep." She tittered, but Angela couldn't work up even a polite smile.

CHAPTER TWENTY-ONE

"I think you know who put that device in your car, and I think you know why." The slightly puffy Detective Max Bartoli studied Steve with watery eyes. He sat back in a wing chair and glanced at Detective Rollie Wood, who sat next to him in the matching wingback.

Leaning against his desk, Steve replied, "I wish I were important enough to kill, Detective Bartoli, but I really have no idea why anyone might have put that bomb in my BMW. I wanted a new car, but I assure you that's the only motivation I can think of for blowing up Old Blue . . . and I sure as hell didn't do it."

It was obvious the detective from the organized crime division was not buying Steve's disclaimer.

"Normally your proclaimed lack of knowledge would indicate that *you* have something to hide, counselor."

Steve merely eyed him, not dignifying his statement with a response.

Bartoli continued. "Oh, well, if you're not talking . . ." Bartoli said, then reached into his coat pocket and pulled out a cigar. "You mind?"

Steve wanted them out of his office, and this was his chance. "Not a bit. Let's go out in the hall and you can smoke up a storm."

The detective narrowed his eyes but rose as Steve did and followed him out. Bartoli bit the end off the cheap cigar, spat it on the hall floor tile, and lit up. He took a couple of long draws, blowing the smoke in plumes before he asked, "You have anything to do with that outfit down the hall . . . the Native American Improvement Coalition?"

"I'm on their advisory board is about all. I helped them find the space here, and I do their legal work . . . pro bono, of course."

Rollie Wood hadn't said two words since they'd arrived, but finally spoke up. "So, what does this Native American Improvement thing do?"

"Lobbies for Indian rights."

Bartoli stepped in. "In New York? I'd think they'd be in Washington, where the action is. Do they get involved in gambling rights?"

"Yes, and all kinds of other rights. New York is the financial capital of the world, detective. D.C. has the highest crime rate in the free world. Wasn't too hard a decision as to where to locate. The commuter airlines get you to D.C. and back in a flash."

Bartoli clamped down on his cigar and spoke through his teeth. "I'll tell you, Drum, you're not on the level with me. I can help protect you—"

Steve laughed, cutting him off. "I don't need protection, detective. What I need is to get back to a ton of paperwork."

"Okay, but I'm not through with this."

Steve nodded. "Good! Glad to have you around for whatever reason. Maybe this guy won't make the same mistake again if you guys are in the neighborhood."

Wood shrugged. "Yeah, maybe he won't make any mistakes next time. Maybe he'll get a major chunk of your hide."

"Nice to have met you, Detective Bartoli," Steve said with a tight smile, then reached out to shake hands. Rollie Wood walked to the elevator without the niceties. Bartoli shook, but the last thing he said as he walked away toward the door was a mumbled, "You're not leveling with me."

When Steve walked back into the office, Sally was on the phone. "No, Miss Garrity, he's not here—"

Steve, on a whim, gave Sally the high-sign that he would speak to the reporter, and headed into his office.

"Good morning, Miss Garrity. My, but aren't you tenacious."

"I've been called a lot worse, Mr. Drum. And some better. Your press release was bland as oatmeal. When can I interview you again?"

"I told you, I'm just a paperwork kind of guy. But if you insist . . . with or without the camera?"

"Without, if you prefer."

"Do you do lunch?"

"Are you offering?"

"I'm offering, so long as there are no cameras."

"Then I'm eating lunch."

"You're in Rock Center . . . how about the Sea Grill?"

"Is one o'clock okay? I've got a gig to shoot at three."

"I'm buying," Steve said, "so you make the reservation. You big-time IBC entertainment types probably have a lot of pull at the Grill."

"Yeah, they'll probably put us in the pantry. Dan Rather has pull; I don't have poop, but I'm working on it."

He hung up the phone and waited for his stomach to roil, but it didn't. Maybe he was getting over Angela. There he went again. He chastised himself. No Angela. Don't think of Angela.

A messenger arrived with Cookie Yamamoto's offer drawn as instructed in the name of Seattle Sino Trading. Only that morning Steve had contacted an attorney friend in Seattle, Howard Wombush, and had a DBA filed in that name in the state of Washington. Wombush was also Native American, but had a Japanese partner. The partner's name, Somogi, was listed as party of record.

Even before reading the offer, Steve called his broker and found out he would have over a million in stock-sale proceeds deposited in his account by late in the afternoon. He had Sally draw the deposit check, then read, and, after taking a deep breath, executed the offer as Seattle Sino's attorney in fact, and messengered it and the check back to Cookie with the instruction to call before it was submitted.

He hoped that Asian American would presume that he had put the offer together with a Japanese trading company after his conversation at the Rainbow Dinner. And now he was acting on behalf of Seattle Sino and with their power of attorney. He posed only as a go-between.

Steve wandered down the hall to find Thad, who now shared a small office off the lab with David Greenberg. David was deep into a pile of history books, and Thad, too, was reading, but his was titled: *Recognizing the Threat*. He looked up as Steve stuck his head in.

"Hey, I've got a lunch date with that fine-as-wine reporter, and I'd as soon be alone with her."

Thad smiled. "I understand that line of reasoning, boss. I'll grab something from a deli on the way over, and stay close but out of your hair."

"I really don't need—"

"Don't even say it. I'm just reading this book by a retired Secret Service guy, and he says these assholes wait purposely before they try again, just so you'll let your guard down. You still got your vest on?"

"Yes, but I hate the damned thing."

"Good. It'll remind you to keep a sharp eye. Hate's a good thing . . . at least for a while. So, until we get this guy, I'm closer to you than a tick in a lamb's tail."

Obviously exasperated, Steve relented. "I'll come back down or buzz you before I leave." Then he crossed the lab to where Meredith Fawn worked. "Hi, how's it going?"

"Fine," she said without looking up. "Don't expect any results for a week. This is a long process."

"Okay." He stood there a moment, but she was lost in concentration. Finally he walked out and next door to Paula's office. As always, the defensive Alice Blackrock, Paula's enthusiastic secretary, jumped to her feet and guarded Paula's door like an ice hockey goalie, as if he were going to charge by her and score in Paula's office.

"She's here, Mr. Drum," she said, hurrying over to stick her head in Paula's doorway, then smiled. "Go on in."

"What's up?" Steve asked. He moved to her desk and took a seat across from her.

"Scheduling blood work. What's up with you?"

"Restless . . . nervous as a French whore in a German church."

"Why?"

He couldn't really tell her the primary reason, that he was missing Angela terribly and was about to go crazy wanting to call her. "Who knows. This blood work, I guess. If you and Meredith don't turn up anything, we've wasted a lot of time and effort, not to speak of the money."

"Cold feet?" She laughed and rose, picking up her coffee cup and walking to the door. "I'm getting a fill-up, you want a cup?"

"The last thing I need is an upper. No, not cold feet, I just signed an offer on the GE Building and a couple of its neighbors, and a million-dollar deposit check."

Alice met Paula at the door with a fill-up, and Paula returned to her chair. She sighed deeply. "That's a lot of money."

"Oh, I'll get it back if the deal doesn't go down. It's not forfeitable as the offer was written."

"That's a relief, for you, I mean. To tell you the honest truth, I'm flabbergasted that you think you can pull this off. And that you're willing to risk so much to do so."

He stared out her window for a moment, wondering if she was right, if he was nuts to try. Finally, without responding to her remark, he sat across from her at her desk. "As soon as you have the blood work scheduled, I want you to go on the road."

"To accomplish what?"

"I want you to visit every one of the forty-three reservations I have as clients, sell the coalition to those who haven't joined, and present a proposal I've prepared."

"That'll take two months or more!"

"Then it'll take two months."

"This proposal is regarding what?"

"I'm calling it the Manhattan Manifesto. But it's actually regarding Rockefeller Center. The trouble is, I can't name it or what I'm actually trying to accomplish until it's tied up and we have blood connection to the treaty. It's really frustrating, trying to move so quickly on this. I keep having to put the cart in front of the horse."

"Then I'll be selling a pig in a poke?"

Alice brought in a pot of coffee and gave her a refill, and Paula waited until she left before continuing.

"If you're having to move too quickly, what's the hurry? Like we said, the bones aren't going anywhere, and neither is the treaty. We can take our time."

"We could, but I want that building in Rock Center . . . it's a . . . a symbol for me, a vision quest. It's turned my whole timetable up to full-speed-ahead." He stared over her shoulder and out the window for a moment, then glanced back at Paula. "And I've got this continuing feeling of doom, dread, like I don't have a lot of time."

"Steve, I haven't asked because it's none of my business, other than the fact you're my brother in spirit, but who's trying to kill you? An irate boyfriend or some antigambling faction?"

"I wish I knew, Paula. I wish I knew."

"Why don't you let the police handle it?"

"The last thing we need right now is a bunch of flatfoots hanging around. We've got our own agenda, and it wouldn't pay to have the law know about it until we're ready for them to know about it."

He laughed and stood. "Hell, I'll take a lot of killing. Got to go. I've got a lunch date."

"A real date?" she asked with a little sarcasm.

"Well, it's business for her, so she doesn't know it's a real date. But I may tell her after I've got her cornered across the table."

"Oh, good. I guess that's a start."

He paused at her office door. "Paula, how's it going with you and Thad?"

"I keep trying to find a reason to not like the big lug, but so far . . ." She shrugged her shoulders.

"I think he's great, one hell of a man, and I sincerely hope it works out for you two." He smiled genuinely, then ducked out the door with a wave.

Paula sat thinking for a long while after he left. She finally concluded that it wasn't business, the million-dollar check, the death threat, or the blood work that had her old friend looking so profoundly sad. She wished she knew what it was. He'd tell her, in his own good time, if he wanted her to know.

She knew one thing—as hard as he was trying to appear nonchalant, something was grating at his very soul.

CHAPTER TWENTY-TWO

Steve knew enough about fine clothes from talking with and being close to Angela that he recognized a two-thousand-dollar St. John's knit suit —particularly when it was perfectly fitted to a million-dollar body.

Felicia Ann Garrity crossed the room, as fashionably late as she was fashionably dressed, with flashing blond hair and feline movements that bulged the eye of every man in the restaurant. She paused at three tables, table-jumping her way toward him; a blinding smile, comment, a quick laugh, and she moved on, all eyes tracking her.

The Sea Grill occupied a prime location in the lower concourse of Rockefeller Center, almost unique in that it, and the American Festival Cafe across the lower plaza, and a deli called Savories to a lesser extent, looked out upon the ice rink. As Steve waited, he was treated to a pair of ice dancers practicing their art. Above them, encircling the rink, waved the colorful flags of all the United Nations member countries.

Steve rose when Felicia reached the table. It was not one located in the pantry, as she had suggested would happen, but, rather, in the center of the room. A CNBC table: See 'n' be seen.

Receiving the same smile that most men in the room had already garnered, Steve extended his hand. She took it with the firm grip of perfectly manicured long, slender fingers, then took her seat.

"So, Mr. Drum, you've decided to speak up?"

Steve laughed. "Nice to see you again too."

"I'm sorry. I thought this was a working lunch." She eyed him mischievously.

"We can throw in a little work if you insist. But first I insist you call me Steve. Can I call you . . . What should I call you?"

"Call me anything you want so long as you occasionally call me to a two-hundred-dollar lunch. . . . You're having a glass of wine. I'd love to join you, but I'm still working. And it's going to be a long day."

"How about Perrier?"

"That's a strange thing to call me . . . then again, I've been called a lot worse." They both laughed. "My good friends call me Leeci. You can if you'll tell me why your BMW now resembles postwar Berlin? And, yes, I'd like a Perrier." Steve waved a waiter over.

The waiter returned with a glass of ice and the bottle of sparkling water. Steve poured for her. Without even looking at the glass, she called the waiter back.

"This is flat, Patrick. Bring me another."

"Yes, Miss Garrity," the thin young man said, and hurried away.

"They know you here?" Steve asked.

"Actually, they do, here and at most of the fine places midtown." For the first time, he caught a hint of ego.

The waiter came to take their orders, and without looking at the menu she said, "No salad, grilled whitefish, steamed vegetables, no butter. A sprinkle of paprika and a little salsa on the side. You know how I like it."

Steve ordered a seafood pasta and house salad, and the man moved away.

They made small talk about hometowns and universities, and he learned she was a Radcliffe girl, imported from Savannah. He thought he'd caught the hint of southern belle in there somewhere. But she'd long-ago polished most of it away.

She learned he was a full-blood Salish and about his life on the rez. She wasn't bashful, and teased him about now being a Wall Street renegade. He admitted to having taken a few scalps by ambush in the concrete canyons.

When the waiter delivered the food, she immediately cut into the fish, then with no more than a glance waved the waiter back. Steve realized that the man had moved only a few feet from the table, and stood waiting, as if he presumed the order would be rejected.

With the curl of a lush red lip, she chopped up the serving of fish. "It's too rare, and I don't want this put back on the grill. Tell the chef to start fresh, and get it right this time."

"Yes, ma'am," the waiter she'd called by name said, and hurried off.

Steve began to get a very bad feeling about Felicia Ann Garrity—great ass or not. Then again, maybe she *was* a great ass.

By the time they'd finished lunch, she was pumping him hard— but unfortunately not physically, just linguistically, regarding the bombing of his car.

He sloughed it off, as he had before, easily claiming to have no idea who the perpetrator was, since it was the truth. When she found she was going to learn nothing, she switched the topic to illegal gambling in the city. For a long while she dug like a badger regarding the fact she'd heard there were hundreds of underground clubs. Finally, realizing that was also a dead end with Steve Drum, she rose, smoothed the St. John knit over sleek but well-rounded hips, and waited for him to reach for the check.

He did, then rose also, and asked, "You want to match for this?"

Blue eyes flashed icy disdain, but he got the well-practiced Sony-DVD-quality-with-surround-sound smile again. "I don't know from matching," she said, all innocence. "How about just flipping a li'l ol' coin?" There it was, sweet southern belle expecting a true gentleman to buy lunch.

Steve pulled a quarter from his pocket and flipped it. She called out heads. Without even looking at the coin slapped against his wrist he said, "You lose." Her look iced over, then he added. "You lose, I sho' 'nuf get to buy."

The well-oiled smile again. "Aren't you the card."

I'm a few cards short of a deck is what I am, he thought, but didn't say so.

As they headed for the door, she said, "We should try this some evening. You probably know all the underground casinos in Manhattan. I'd love to have a handsome escort to do a little gambling."

"Not me. I'm into legal gaming only." *And you'd go with a hide-out camera in your purse.* Then he wondered if she currently had a tape recorder hidden there. He would bet she did.

"Right," she said, studying him for a hint of sarcasm.

"Of course we could do an overnight to Atlantic City."

"Are you propositioning me, trying to take another scalp, Mr. Drum?"

"I don't have a single blonde on my coup stick."

"I'll bet. Not a single one, rather a few dozen."

He let it drop, since he was merely testing the water to see if her interest lay beyond a story. And now he wasn't sure he was interested.

They parted company without him verifying her "do this again some evening" remark.

As soon as she walked away, Thad was beside him. "So, you two gonna get together for some more intellectual *intercourse?*" He smiled knowingly.

"I doubt it, Sam Spade."

"Maybe you should sweet-talk the lady?"

"I doubt that also. Besides, she's the honey-tongued one, so long as you've got something she wants. If I get blown into a million pieces by our mad bomber, she'll drop by to interview the survivors before they've even scraped up all the lumps. Hell, I've never really understood city ladies. I guess I'm still a country boy at heart. I like my women soft, sweet, and all cuddles. She's soft and sweet enough, but underneath I suspect it's curdles, not cuddles."

As they made their way up the stairs to street level, Thad thought for a moment, then quipped, " 'I'm beginning to repel people I'm trying to seduce' . . . Holly Hunter in *Broadcast News.*"

"Probably close," Steve said. "Actually, in my case I'm beginning to be repelled by people I'm trying to seduce. Come to think of it, I'm beginning to think I just don't have the time or the patience for the game."

"Maybe you could get together, hold the talk in abeyance, and just get on with the other kind of intercourse. Whatever happened to the age-old four Fs?"

"I don't remember that one."

"Find 'em, feel 'em, fuck 'em, and forget 'em. I've got a hunch you could use a little noncommittal belly beating."

"With my faithful bodyguard glued to my side, of course?"

"Perish the thought. Miss Fox and her tomahawk would do a little surgery on this young buck . . . change my mind from ass to grass, should I even consider it."

As they hailed a cab, Steve silently shook his head and thought, *Well, Felicia isn't Angela. I wonder if another woman ever will be.*

Angela, Angela, I've got to quit thinking about Angela. It's time I stood up on my hind legs. Steve said, "Hell, it's time I grew up and got citified." He reached over and took the cellular phone out of its carrier at Thad's waist and dialed information. "IBC please." Thad watched him with interest while he dialed the number. "Felicia Ann Garrity please."

When they reached the office, Sally handed him his messages and told him, "Give David a call. He really wants to show you something."

"Buzz him and ask him to come down."

Steve left Thad in the outer office and flopped down at his desk. The first call in the pile was from Agent Nolan Robertson, FBI. The second was from a client in New Mexico, and the third from Joe Bigsam. He returned Bigsam's first.

The deep voice on the other end of the line didn't bother with a hello. "Somebody tried to take you out. I heard it on the grapevine."

Steve sighed deeply. "Marvin Gaye, about 1972."

"What?"

"Nothing. You guys up there on the seaway probably think the raisins wrote and sung it."

"Whatever."

"Yeah, somebody gave it the ol' college try. I wish I knew who that somebody was. You got any ideas?"

"Wish I could help. You want me to loan you the twins?"

Steve appreciated the thought. The twins were his personal bodyguards. The pair Steve had spotted following them around Big Sam's casino. "Thanks, but not quite yet. I'm sending the head of the Native American Improvement Coalition, Paula Fox, up to see you the end of the week, if you're going to be around. She'll have your report and recommended business plan in hand, plus some other things I want you to be aware of. I may be asking you to lend me not only the twins, but half the rez."

"Don't bother sending her up. I'm coming to the city. You said you owed me a drink."

"When? I'll do better than that, I'll buy dinner."

"I'll be down there tomorrow."

He hung up, then dialed the FBI Agent.

"You called, Agent Robertson?" Steve asked.

"Yes, I did, Mr. Drum. I'd like to come by and chat."

Steve had had plenty of dealings with the FBI. They were the primary law enforcement agency to deal with Indian reservations after the tribal police. He knew they never dropped by just to chat. "Regarding?"

"Just a follow-up on this thing about the explosive device in your automobile."

"I think the NYPD, whose jurisdiction this is, is doing a fine job."

"Still, you're high profile in Indian gaming, and bombs always smell of organized crime. Organized crime and Indian gambling *are* in my province no matter where you hang your hat, counselor. On the rez or off. I'd like to drop by."

"Suit yourself, Robertson."

They made an appointment for the following morning. When he hung up, Sally buzzed him that David was waiting. He entered with a broad smile.

"I've got a lot of stuff on the Canarsee. It seems that they lasted until 1704 or so, then the pressure from the white man finally ran them out. There was another incident of missing livestock, and the Indians were blamed. The last the good residents of Manhattan saw over the sights of their long rifles was the entire tribe of some twenty-five or thirty . . . all that were left . . . canoeing across the East River."

David unrolled a small map on Steve's desk. "The best I can figure, this is the boundary of the agreement. The southwest corner is somewhere in the Sheep Meadow in Central Park, say about Sixty-eighth Street, then it follows the course of a preexistent creek almost due northeast to where Seventy-ninth hits the East River, then north along the river to about One twentieth west to about Adam Clayton Powell Jr. Boulevard and One fifteenth, then south to the point of beginning. As the agreement states, it's four hundred twenty-five hectares, or just about one thousand sixty acres. Nowhere near half of Manhattan, but a hell of a chunk of real estate."

Steve sat back in his deep chair. "That's great news, David. Keep looking, make sure there wasn't any conveyance of the land back to the good citizens or the government." Then he laughed. "Hell, it looks like we own the Metropolitan Museum of Art and the Guggenheim, among other things."

David's smile got even larger. "Several billion dollars worth of other things."

"You had any luck researching Rockefeller Center?"

"You want the good news or the bad first?"

"The bad."

"The bad news is I can't locate the guy, of course, or his family, but the good is I found a tiny item in the July 11th, 1931, issue of *The New York Times.* It seems Danny Murphy, a crew boss on a swamping gang, cleaning out some of the excavations for the underground concourse, found—are you ready for this? Ol' Danny found an Indian burial ground right smack-dab in the center of the Rockefeller Center project. Bones, shards, the whole gambit."

Steve was stunned. It was a development the repercussions of which he couldn't even begin to fathom. If he could tie the Canarsee and the treaty to the Rockefeller Center project, even in the most obscure way . . . hell, it was too good to be true.

"Drop everything else you're doing and find out what happened to Danny Murphy. See if he's got any relatives living. And find out what happened to the discovery . . . particularly the bones. God almighty, if we can find those bones, and if those bones might just happen to have the same DNA . . ."

"Slow down, Stephen. I'm already working on it. But leave us not forget, it was more than sixty years ago."

David rose and started out of the room until Steve stopped him. "David. You did good, my lad. Good as good gets."

"I thought you'd like it." Steve had never seen David smile so broadly.

After David left the room, Steve began to sing softly. "Danny boy, ol' Danny boy, the pipes, the pipes are playing."

Only one thing could happen that would make his day complete, other than Angela . . . Dammit, no Angela. Only one thing.

He turned to his credenza and worked the keyboard of his computer a few strokes, then read the monitor. Yes! ICOM was up from seventeen a share to twenty-two. The march was on. He had to be very careful, play it as fine as a Stradivarius.

Just before six, he called Thad into his office.

"Thad, my lad. I've got a date tonight and I don't need an escort."

Thad frowned deeply. "Don't jump the traces and act like a mule-headed—"

"This is serious business, Mr. Wintermoose. I can't remember the last time I got laid." Even as he said it, the vision of Angela dressed only in his blue shirt flashed in front of him. He willed it away. "And I don't need my body guarded so well I'll never get another warm body up against it."

Thad shook his head. "Look, I'll take Paula out, and we'll go to the same restaurant as you two—"

"No deal. I'll pack the forty caliber in the small of my back. I'll wear the vest. I'll not have my old friend Paula giggling at me across the room, and you giving us a lascivious glare."

"So, okay. You're the boss." He feigned a yawn. "Besides, I could use a night off. Where did you say you were going to dinner?"

"I didn't say, Sherlock. And you're not invited."

"Like I said, you're the boss."

That night, dressed to the nines, Steve walked out of his condo to meet the waiting Litcomb's Limo town car. He climbed in the back and said, "Three blocks down and two west." He was happy to have learned that Felicia Ann Garrity lived only a few blocks from his condo.

The big driver turned to the backseat. "Okay, boss," Thad Wintermoose said, and accelerated away from the curb.

"So when did you go to work for Litcomb, Wintermoose? Is this part-time, or did you give notice after I left today?" Steve leaned back in the seat, both a little exasperated and a little amused.

"Actually, you're my first fare, Mr. Drum, sir. Mr. Litcomb was kind enough to start me off with a big tipper. Ms. Garrity won't know I'm not a regular driver."

"I'll tip your butt . . . into the river," he said, but Thad could hear the chuckle in his voice.

"So, do you have the forty in the small of your back?"

"You've caught me. Rumor is, a woman likes to find something long and hard on a man, but cold steel is not it."

"And the vest?"

"Upstairs."

He rounded the block and stopped at the front of Steve's building.

"The vest, at least," he said, and Steve relented, hurrying back upstairs to get it on.

When Felicia answered her door, Steve was glad he'd worn a brand-new Italian suit, even though it felt a little lumpy with the vest under his shirt.

Felicia Ann Garrity looked as if she'd been rolled in honey and then spangles—and smelled even better than she looked. The gown was cut so low he worried she'd bounce out of it merely walking. But it was fitted so tightly, he decided he'd be lucky to have that happen.

Maybe later.

CHAPTER TWENTY-THREE

They went to the theater, then Sardi's, doing the tourist thing and enjoying a prime table downstairs since she was one lady the restaurant would want seen. *Fame pays, at least at times.* As soon as they were seated, she excused herself to the ladies' room, and table-hopped there and back.

He looked around the room, watching heads turn as she passed, enjoying being out with a beautiful woman. It was the first time in a long, long time he'd brought a lady to a place as much in the public eye as Sardi's. He'd love to bring Angela. . . . *Stop it, Drum,* he said to himself. Steve had a Glenlivet and soda gone by the time she returned. The wine he'd ordered for her sat untouched, but she picked it up, toasted him silently, and drank, while he ordered another drink.

They ordered dinner, and not surprising to him, she returned her fish with hardly a second glance. This waiter was not as quiescent as the first, and stated, "You've destroyed that fish, madam. We could have placed it back on the grill."

She eyed him for a moment with those icy eyes before answering. "Had I wanted it placed back on the grill, I wouldn't have 'destroyed' it. Tell the chef to grill me another."

Steve kept his teeth clamped, remembering Thad's four-F advice. For a passing moment he concluded he must have a room temperature IQ for even being out with her. Then he glanced at the generous cleavage again. And she was good company, other than a couple of little ego quirks. And she was knock-down gorgeous. He eyed the honey-blond hair brushing perfectly tanned shoulders. Life is tradeoffs, old Standing Bear would have advised. Patience, jackass, patience. Old Standing Bear would have advised something like *You're not here to teach her how to make the whole world love her, in fact, she's not doing too bad a job all by herself.*

The rest of the meal was pleasant. He delivered her to her apartment building, and was pleased to be invited up for an after-dinner drink.

The apartment was ultramodern, shades of white and burnished chrome, highlighted with touches of blue and cranberry. An ego wall graced the entry hall—two dozen pictures of Felicia with celebrities she'd interviewed, plaques proclaiming her skills. Most would have used a study wall for the purpose. She directed him to a small cabinet that served as bar and excused herself to the bedroom, and he poured himself another scotch, this time neat.

Staring out her window to the street far below, his mind wandered to Angela, but he quelled the thought. Licee's return helped him quell it even further. Nylons and high heels still on, she reappeared wrapped in a clinging Japanese silk robe.

"Spangles, bangles, and beads were biting," she said in a low, seductive voice as she dropped the lights with a dimmer.

"I envy them," he said, tracking her with his eyes over his upraised glass. "You want a drink?"

"Yes, brandy in a snifter, please. And there's no reason to stay envious. Envy's a heinous sin, I'm told . . . and there are others so much more fun." As she spoke, she casually dropped a foil-wrapped condom on the coffee table.

Well, so much for the mystery of seduction, he thought. *Here's a lady who doesn't subscribe to getting there being half the fun.* He poured her the drink while she hit a button on a built-in stereo, then folded herself casually onto a deep white leather sofa. Soft Kenny G saxophone flooded the room. Her gaze followed him across the carpet as he pulled his tie loose, balancing the glasses in one hand, then setting them on the glass coffee table in front of the sofa and sinking into it beside her.

Her lips met his, and he slipped one hand behind her neck, cupping a full breast with the other.

She pulled slightly back. "Don't muss the hair," she whispered, then her lips were on his again.

When he pulled his shirt off, she stopped short. "You always wear a bulletproof vest to the theater?"

"Only when I'm with a beautiful woman every man would be happy to kill for."

"A good answer, but hardly credible, Drum. Don't expect me not to follow up on that—"

He covered her mouth with his.

In seconds they were both naked.

He couldn't ever remember making love to a woman without "mussing" her hair, but he managed, for the first time.

She rode him like she was astride a stallion, both hands on his shoulders, pushing him back into the sofa, throwing her head, knees folded under her, making him keep his hands to himself, using him. Perfect breasts in his face; he lathed them with his tongue, but she arched away from him, so he decided to just lay back and enjoy it.

She was technically wonderful, if slightly antiseptic.

He feared he was a little too quick this first time, but she was more patient with him than she had been with her fish. At least she didn't send him away, destroyed. Rather, she smiled as if she were the conqueror and he the vanquished. Slipping again into the high heels, she brought him hot wet towels, framing herself in the bedroom doorway with the light at her back filtering through her long, blond hair. Pausing there, she gave him a chance to admire her full-length, in all her naked magnificence, for the first time.

And he did.

After she toweled him off, she led him into her bedroom, all overstuffed dark blue and cranberry, and pushed him down on his back, only this time onto her bed.

He was amused at being handled, but it certainly wasn't unpleasant. Finally, he rolled her onto her stomach, and even as she groaned in complaint stood at the edge of the bed and pulled her to her knees, mounting her for a wild ride in complete abandon, cupping a breast in each hand, taking her roughly. Her nipples hardened, peaked, and he knew she was his. With eyes tightly closed, her face deep in the comforter, head turned to the side, hair in complete disarray, she twisted the coverlet tightly into her fists, crying out in shrieking gasps. He drove into her, sparing nothing. Finally rolling from the bed to the floor, driving into her until she shuddered so long he feared she would faint. He joined her with a racking spasm.

After a minute, panting quietly, he left her to her own thoughts, fist to her mouth, mewing quietly, as he got to his feet and headed into the bathroom.

He returned, and she still lay there, a sheen of perspiration glowing on the perfect tan. He reached down, picked her up in his arms, and lay her in her bed; then dropping, fitting spoonlike, he pulled the coverlet over them.

When he finally rolled away, she was deeply asleep. Her sated breathing pleased him.

At four A.M. he rapped on the window of the black town car. Thad shook his head to clear it, then popped the locks. Steve collapsed into the front seat beside him. "Above and beyond the call of duty, Wintermoose," he said with a yawn.

"So," Thad asked, pulling away from the curb, "is the white-eye tan all over like an Indian maiden?"

"Didn't your mama tell you not to kiss and tell?"

"Yeah, she did, and I'm not gonna . . . you are. Was she tan all over?"

"And a natural blonde, with a good trim. What will the much fairer sex think of next? Grooming's reached a new level."

"Normally I'd say you'd be a good enough judge of what's real, but with this one, maybe only her hairdresser knows. Maybe they're getting a bleach with the trim these days?" Thad laughed, then asked, "So, did you stand tall?"

"Red men all over the nations can be proud, Wintermoose, now drop it . . . I took no pictures." Steve laughed and closed his eyes. The smile faded as Angela waltzed through his mind and guilt tried to elbow its way in. He repelled it with thoughts of the Italian stallion. He was tired, having just had his brains balled out by an incredibly beautiful woman. He shook his head, thinking about another. If brains were taxed, he'd be in line for a refund. Jesus, would nothing keep him from thinking about Angela?

Sleep. Sleep would.

Agent Nolan Robertson was there when Steve arrived, uncharacteristically, a few minutes late. He waved the man into his office without pausing for an introduction.

They shook hands, Steve apologized for being late, and Robertson took a seat across the desk from him.

He was a typical agent: close-cut hair, clean-shaven, a nondescript business suit with vest, and a dark tie. He could have been any one of a thousand Wall Street types in the building. Except this one wouldn't say shit if he had a mouthful. They were all Mr. Clean.

The first of the FBI man's inquiries went much as had the NYPD's, then he got to the meat of his reason for wanting the interview, as he called it.

"You're a consultant to Indian gaming?"

"I bet you guys know more about what I do and who I deal with than I do. Tell me the truth, is my file over two inches thick?"

Robertson smiled for the first time. "Your file's all stock information for us, and I'll bet you know I can't tell you how thick it is or what's in it. The good news is yours is no thicker than any other rez tribal officer or casino owner involved in gaming. Since the court allowed gambling on the reservations, we've had a whole new area of opportunity for organized crime to get interested in what should be only Indian affairs. So we watch with jaundiced eye, as the saying goes."

"To tell you the truth," Steve said, and honestly meant it, "I haven't had occasion to be approached by anyone who smelled of mob connections. The respective states and gaming commissions seem to do a great job keeping the casinos clean."

"Then why the bomb?"

"Hell, I wish I knew."

"Are you wearing a vest?"

Steve gained a new respect for the man. He was the only one to notice the tight-fitting Kevlar since he'd begun wearing it. "As a matter of fact, I am. Wouldn't you if your car had been bombed?"

"Yes, sir, I would. Has anyone taken a shot at you?"

"No. And I think the bomb was a case of mistaken identity. Have you guys looked the parking lot over to see if there's another blue beamer?"

"No, I'm at the mercy of the NYPD until we have reason to believe there are mob connections. I'm leaving you my card, and I'd like a call if you have any more trouble of any kind."

"You'll get one."

The agent left and Sally buzzed him. "Mr. Yamamoto is on his way over. I thought you'd like to see him."

"Thanks, Sally. You're right."

When he arrived, Sally served him a cup of hot tea, and he squeezed into one of Steve's wing chairs.

"Well?" Steve asked, both anxious and eager.

"Well, they are a tough bunch of Chinamen."

"So, what's the deal?"

"The deal is countered, and they've specifically instructed me not to bring back a counter to their counter, should you not accept it."

"So, let's hear it."

"They countered the price by fifteen mil, so it is one hundred twenty-five million."

When Steve said nothing, Cookie continued. "Prime plus two is okay, but the downstroke is fifty million. A thirty-year payout with a fifteen-year balloon is okay. But we have only sixty days to close the sale, putting it into this year, and the worst news is, they want two and a half million on deposit, forfeited within two weeks of the date you sign. They have all the leases and documentation, and claim it can be reviewed in that time frame . . . and I couldn't argue the point. I may not be the sharpest knife on the sushi counter, but I could do it alone in that length of time."

Steve sat back, saying nothing, thinking. He would have probably walked away, let the deal die, had David not discovered the article regarding the bones and shards being discovered during the excavation of the building.

And another situation had surfaced in the press during the past week. A decision by the State of New York to allow the Seneca reservation to place a casino outside the reservation boundaries on other commercially zoned land in a more ideal location for its operation. It put a whole new light on what he was trying to accomplish. At the very least, it softened the State and City of New York's ability to argue his proposed location, not that he planned to give them the opportunity. Still, the ice of nonreservation location had been broken.

But he owed it to himself, and the hard work of many years to accumulate what he had, to try to cut the best deal he could.

He turned back from the window and looked Cookie in the eye. "So, no matter what they said, you have an obligation to communicate a counteroffer, by law, isn't that right?"

"I guess, technically, that's right."

"Okay. Since I'm taking the stance of a go-between in this deal. Since Seattle Sino is officially the buyer, I want to go with you to present the counter-counter I'm going to prepare."

"Not a good idea, Stephen. Even though you are acting as an agent, you and I know you are really a principal, and it is never a good idea to bring principals together when negotiating a deal. That is what agents are for."

"Good idea or not, I'm going with you."

Cookie shrugged his ponderous shoulders. "If you insist . . . it is your money at risk."

"Then let's go see ol' Wilber Wong this afternoon."

They made arrangements to meet after Steve had a chance to prepare his counteroffer and to take care of one more piece of business.

As soon as Cookie left his office, he dialed Oscar Petersen at Stanley Reporting. He'd retained Petersen to look into the personal lives of the officers of Asian American. Petersen answered the phone. He said he would have a written report on Steve's desk by the end of the week, but Steve couldn't wait.

"So, what did you get?" he asked.

Petersen's answer made him smile. As soon as he hung up the phone, he grabbed his black book and made another call, this time to Atlantic City. As Garth Brooks so eloquently pointed out, it paid to have friends in low places. He whistled as he worked up the counterproposal.

Just to give him strength, he poked ICOM into his computer just before he left his office. Up from twenty-two to twenty-five. Even though they'd made no announcement, or disclosed anything in a 10K regarding the Hovenweep discovery, their stock was on the move.

He returned to the business at hand. Asian American's offices were in the GE Building, which they owned. Steve took a moment to visit a florist in the lower concourse, ordered a dozen roses sent to Felicia Ann Garrity at her office, and jotted a note:

Didn't want to wake you to say good-bye. In fact, I didn't want to leave.

He'd never been able to send Angela flowers as he'd wanted to so many times. He'd taken them to her, a single rose, when they'd met at out-of-the-way places. *Stop thinking about Angela, dummy, stop it, stop it. There are amoebas with higher IQs than yours.*

It was late afternoon when Cookie, Steve, and the ever-present Thad arrived at Asian American's door unannounced.

The receptionist buzzed Wong's private office, then shook her head. "I'm so sorry, but Mr. Wong is tied up in meetings all afternoon."

Cookie turned to start out, but Steve was not to be refused. "Tell Mr. Wong that Donald Trump insisted he speak with me."

"He really is tied up—"

"He really wants to see me, or will, when you convey that message."

Almond eyes glared at him, but she buzzed again, relayed the message, and to Cookie Yamamoto's surprise, they were shown into a nearby conference room. One by one the three men who had been at the mayor's Rainbow Dinner arrived, Wilber Wong last.

When introductions were made and they all took a seat, Wong began. "I am so sorry to inform you, Mr. Drum, but no counteroffer to our proposal will be entertained."

"Both Mr. Yamamoto and I have a legal obligation to convey all offers our clients make, Mr. Wong. I'm sure you're aware of that."

"What was this about Mr. Trump wanting me to see you?"

"Actually, that's a private matter between you and me." Steve smiled knowingly as Wong's brows furrowed. "Actually, nothing to do with this negotiation."

Wong smiled but paled. "Well, if you must, please state your counteroffer."

Steve spelled out his proposal. "Forty million down, your purchase price is fine. One month to forfeiture of a two-million-dollar deposit if the deal is to go forward A closing date of March first next year. All other terms the same as your proposal."

Wong shook his head and began to speak to his associates in Mandarin. To Steve's surprise, it appeared that one of the other men was the real power. He didn't ask, but rather told Wong what to do. The man, knowing that Cookie didn't speak Chinese, made the mistake of underestimating his adversary, presuming that Steve also did not. Steve was pleased to hear him say, "Actually, it is a very good deal this red man's clients have offered, Wilber. I think this man is a fool. His chopsticks are a little too short to reach the rice. He should never have left his reservation."

The others laughed, and Steve smiled and nodded, but blankly, as if he comprehended nothing. This was the same man who'd referred to Steve as a "mud-hut Indian" at the Rainbow Dinner. The man continued. "And his clients must also be fools. They will never make this property pay at that price, and we will foreclose on them within a few years, and the market will be much better when we take it back. Press for more, but do not press so hard he goes away. Let the fools carry the property through the bad times. But we must close the deal this year, otherwise I have other plans."

Wong, showing himself to be an excellent actor, beat the table and countered exactly as he had before, giving up nothing. They argued back and forth for the better part of a half hour, with Steve knowing exactly what they would do. Finally, he rose to walk out when Wong seemed intractable. It appeared that Wong was going to let him go, driving the hardest possible bargain, not wanting to lose face by not bettering the deal for his boss, but taking a risk in doing so .

But he didn't know that Steve had another card to play. In fact, he was about to trump Wong's ace.

As Steve and Cookie reached the door to the conference room, Steve turned back. "Mr. Wong, be kind enough to walk me out to the elevator . . . that personal matter I mentioned . . ."

Wong rose and followed, and when they got out into the hall, Steve waved Wong aside so even Cookie couldn't hear, then spoke in perfect Mandarin. "Are your associates aware that you have over five million in markers at Trump's Taj Mahal in Atlantic City? This fool red man knows it. Would you like this fool red man to advise your boss, and all of Wall Street of your extravagant debts?" Steve didn't give him a chance to answer. "Would your boss and your stockholders be pleased if your stock went in the tank because Asian American's president was squandering money, even his own? Would the SEC suspend trading until an audit could be completed, to make sure it's *not* the company's money? Or would you prefer I go back to my reservation without having to expose you?"

For a second, Steve feared the man was going to faint. Not only from the shock of Steve's perfect Mandarin, but the fact he had heard the terms they were willing to accept. And worse, he knew of his disgrace at the tables.

"Now I'm going to show you what a gentleman even a fool can be, and not chisel you down below what I've already countered. Maybe you will get the property back, and maybe all my clients will accomplish is to carry it for you for a couple of years, as your boss suggests. Think what a hero you'll be."

Still Wong had not recovered, so Steve finished. "I want a signed letter of understanding on my desk by ten o'clock tomorrow morning, at my counteroffer terms, Wilber."

The man nodded, still unable to speak.

When Steve, Cookie, and Thad, who'd been waiting in the lobby, entered the elevator, Cookie grinned broadly at him. "You speak Chinese?"

"I speak Mandarin, well enough to understand everything they said and to get my point across."

"Looks to me like you shoved your point right up Wilber's ass. No wonder you insisted on coming along! So, what was Wong about to pee his pants over, besides the fact you understood everything they said in that meeting."

"Personal business, Cookie. But, trust me, we'll have a deal in the morning, at my terms."

"Nice doing business with you, Mr. Drum." Cookie laughed, grasping his thick sides and rocking in glee.

"My grandfather always told me, 'Never underestimate the enemy.' I'm glad Wilber Wong's honorable ancestor forgot to teach him that lesson." And he thought, but didn't say, *And another New Jersey gentleman taught me how to fight with the gloves off. Thanks, Papa Al.*

"Remember that, about not underestimating the enemy," Thad cautioned, eyeing Steve gravely.

Steve shook his head in disgust, but tapped the vest through his shirt, garnering a smile and wink from Thad.

As they exited the elevator, it dawned on Steve. *Now all I've got to do is raise forty million dollars down payment to purchase a property not worth what the loan amount is going to be, and another ten million or so operating capital to begin a business that will have everyone in the state and city government up in arms, probably literally. And put two million . . . hell, probably a lot more . . . probably all of my own money at risk to do so. Wong's boss is right, I am a damned fool. I do have a room-temperature IQ, and it's getting chilly in here.*

Steve knew one thing for sure: It was time to get his head down and tail up, to slow down for no one.

As he stepped out of the elevator, he imagined the hot breath of the bear on the back of his neck.

He was about to risk everything he had, and in one way the outcome was completely out of his hands—if the DNA detectives failed, so did he.

CHAPTER TWENTY-FOUR

Steve stopped in his office long enough to pick up his calls and give Sally some instructions. "Get me a meeting room to accommodate forty for late afternoon, say five o'clock, through the evening, somewhere in Rockefeller Center. Schedule it in ten days' time. I want a portable bar and a meat and potato, atomic-cholesterol buffet dinner served in the room. Make sure there's also plenty of fruit and salads for those of us who enjoy life and want to keep living it. I'm going down the hall." He paused in the doorway. "On second thought, see if the Sea Grill has a room." He turned, then paused again and turned back. "And see if you can find me an accomplished Native American architect. I don't care where in the country you find him, just find him."

He turned to find Joe Bigsam standing in the hallway, having just exited the elevator, one of the twins at his heels.

"Joe! I promised dinner."

"You did."

Sally, overhearing as the door was shutting, spoke up. "You better check your messages."

Steve looked down at the pile of messages still in his hand and riffled through them. One was a call from Felicia, thanking him for the roses and inviting him to dinner at her apartment. Perfect body and she cooks too! Almost too much to ask. He turned back to Bigsam. "You mind if a beautiful woman joins us?"

"Do I look like a fag to you?"

Steve didn't bother to grace the question with an answer, but, rather, turned to Sally. "Please call Felicia Garrity and ask if she can join Mr. Bigsam and me at Toby's. If she accepts, tell her I'll send a car for her at eight, then get us a reservation for around eight-thirty." He turned back to Joe. "I've got to run down the hall for a minute . . . in fact, come along and I'll introduce you around."

Joe introduced him to his bodyguard, the bearlike Dave Redfern, and explained that his twin brother, Dan, was minding the car. They went straight to Paula's office, entered, got the normal defensive reaction from Alice, but were soon admitted.

He introduced Bigsam to Paula, then asked him if he'd like to see the lab next door. Saying he'd explain later why the coalition had a blood lab, he asked Alice to take Joe over and introduce him to Meredith. Then he suggested to Paula, "I want you to put off your trip for a couple of weeks. I'm going to call an emergency meeting of the members of the coalition, and I'm going to personally present my Manhattan Manifesto. I'm also going to prepare a nondisclosure agreement for you to send out to every group who agrees to attend. Ask them to RSVP, then advise me of any group who's not coming. I want to personally call them. In the morning I'll have a firm deal on the GE Building and a couple more of the Rockefeller Center buildings, and I've got to get high behind . . . let's see, we need a good name for this meeting. How about Native Nations' Emergency Summit Conference?"

"That's big enough." Paula laughed, then turned serious. "I'm just as glad I'm not going for a few days. I've got so much to do trying to get this blood work finished."

"I'm afraid to ask . . ."

"Nothing yet, but we've done only the tribes in New York State. We've got to get into the neighboring states."

Steve sighed deeply. "Out there somewhere is a multimillion-, maybe a billion-dollar poke in the finger. We've got to find it. I really hoped we'd find a link right here in New York."

"We'll find it, wherever it is, if it's there."

"This afternoon, please get on the phone and call your members and convince them to come to New York in ten days. Sally will have the meeting place. Then both of you get on to making room reservations. The Hilton, right near Rockefeller Center, can probably handle the forty or so rooms we'll need."

"We'll take care of it. You go take care of your guest. By the way, we've now got a Web page online I'm rather proud of. When you get time, check it out. I'll e-mail the members I can and overnight the rest. We're doing a newsletter, for both snail mail and e-mail—"

"Okay, okay. You're doing great, but find that DNA connection—in your spare time."

"Right, in my spare time."

When he wandered back into his office, he punched up ICOM on his computer. Up another dollar, to 28⅜, and over eight hundred thousand shares traded. With over fifty million shares issued and outstanding, and only a few over three million closely held, ICOM could be in for a wild ride. On a hunch, he called Winston, Winston, & Noble, got Jonathan Noble III on the line, and asked him if he could find out who was buying. If anyone could, it was Jonathan.

He hoped against hope it was Alex Dragonovich.

Before Steve arrived home, his answering machine picked up a call, then the tone of one, two, three was punched in. The messages were read off, including one from Felicia Garrity. "Steve, I'd love to try that new Italian place tonight, Fiorini's. It's supposed to be the hottest. See you soon."

The man in the black sedan, a cell phone to his ear, nodded his head, then mumbled, "The dumb asshole still hasn't changed the default code on his answering machine. So, you're going out on the town, Drum. But not with Angela, but that doesn't matter anymore . . . Maybe I'll just be waiting when you come home."

He sped away, then slowed. There was no hurry. He'd find a deli. It wasn't good to work on an empty stomach.

When the day was over, Steve had Bigsam drive him to the condo so he could change for dinner. Dan Redfern was as beefy as his brother; they were obviously fraternal twins, but still difficult to tell apart. Felicia had consented to have dinner with them rather than at her apartment, so it was Steve's plan to send the car for her, leaving Joe there with him at his apartment so they would have a chance to talk. Then he, Bigsam, and Felicia would be driven to dinner. Thad and one of the Redferns would follow in a cab.

He was still hesitant to allow Felicia Ann Garrity, TV commentator extraordinaire, to know anything about what he was up to. Down deep he didn't trust her. Hell, skin-deep he didn't trust her.

When Steve walked in, Li Chung, his houseboy, greeted him in their usual Mandarin, adding, "You haven't had any calls since you got them off the machine this afternoon."

"Li, I didn't pick up my calls."

Li looked puzzled, then said, "Well, someone did. I didn't make it to the phone, and presumed it was you."

That gave Steve pause. He scratched his head. Who the hell could be getting his calls off his phone? He walked over and hit the replay button, even though the light was no longer blinking. He shook his head slowly as the machine said, "I will *replay* your messages." Then he made a few notes, including Felicia's dinner request. When he finished, he yelled to Thad, "See if you can change our reservations to this Fiorini's."

Still puzzled, he wondered again about the messages, then realized it could be the photographer. He hadn't heard from him in over two weeks and had hoped it was over. Pulling Thad aside, he explained the situation. Thad looked worried, then went to the phone and changed the code to the year of Steve's birth. It would be the last time the caller could eavesdrop on Steve's messages.

After the car left, with Dan Redfern acting as chauffeur, Steve invited Bigsam into his bedroom while he changed, leaving Thad and Dave Redfern in the living room to talk.

"So, what's up?" Joe asked, sensing Steve wanted to talk privately about something.

"How are you fixed for dough?"

"I'm doing okay, why?"

"Because I need fifty million, that's why."

Joe laughed. "Hell, why didn't you say so, I'll write a check." He laughed louder. "You crazy walks-backward Indian, I said I'm doing okay. I'm Mohawk, not Arab sheikh."

Steve looked in the mirror, tying his tie. "I didn't expect the fifty mil from you, but I would like to tell you what I'm up to, and I hope you'll want in. Here's the deal—"

He explained to Bigsam his plans, how they were progressing, concluding with, "I'm going to put this deal together just like any other investment."

Joe Bigsam, who'd been reclining on Steve's bed, sat up, shaking his head in wonder. "By God, this ought to get white-eye's balls by the short hairs. And New York is home to some boys with big balls."

Steve laughed. "The money side gets a second position on the real estate—not that that's worth much as it is. Unfortunately the first position is about one hundred percent of value. In addition to forty-five percent ownership in the casino. My people take ten percent, of which I'll keep five and spread the rest around among my key employees. I get a ten-year contract to operate as manager with standard bonus provisions, with a ten-year option if all the money's returned to investors, plus market interest, by the time my first contract is complete. By the way, I'll have everything I own invested, five million at least, by the time this flies. So only a half percent or so of my stock is promotional."

"Still, a bird's nest on the ground for you," Bigsam said, frowning.

"Easy pickings? Hardly. I'm risking everything I own to achieve this. And an opportunity that wouldn't be here were it not for me and my people. Management will be remunerated as is common in the industry. No bird's nest there. A day's pay for a day's work."

"Go on."

"The rest of the ownership is split among all the tribes in the nation . . . with a good chunk going to the blood relatives of the Canarsee . . . when we find them."

"For what?"

"For being handed the shit end of the stick for the last three hundred years. Not withstanding the fact it's the right thing to do. We have to have them . . . all the tribes . . . because this deal is not going to fly unless I get a hell of a lot of help, not only monetarily, but participatory. You think you had trouble with the FBI when you wanted to expand your operation? . . . What do you think they'll do when I want to take over the GE Building and fill it full of tables?"

"Hell, this could be a blood war."

Steve finished tying the tie, and turned to Joseph Bigsam, his voice low and earnest. "But the spoils of war are worth it. Can I count on you?"

"So, what will five mil buy again?"

"Five mil will buy four and a half percent and a seat on the board."

"Then count me in, Drum. But don't fuck this up. I don't have five million to drop. In fact, I'll be scraping the bottom of the barrel to come up with the dough."

"Damn few do. What do you think I can count on the rest of the St. Regis bunch to come with?"

"Maybe another two million, when I tell them how much you've helped my operation."

"That's a start. By the way, I don't have to tell you how critical it is that we keep this to ourselves . . . particularly in the company of a TV lady who's always digging for a story."

"Enough said, Drum. I was born in the daytime but not yesterday."

"Great. Let's go meet a beautiful lady."

"My pleasure," Bigsam said with anticipation, "but it's too bad she's not two beautiful ladies."

They headed for the door just as the buzzer rang and the door-man called up from the lobby to tell them the car was out front.

As they descended in the elevator, Joe added, "I take it you're buying dinner, since I'm now broke."

"I doubt if you're even close to broke, but, yeah, I'm buying."

Angela Giovanni walked the beach, staring at the sand, deliberately placing one foot in front of the other, retracing her own footsteps. The lights of her parents' Maryland beach house shone in the distance. Since she'd returned from Europe, she'd made the excuse that she needed some time alone, and strangely, neither her mother nor Papa Al had argued.

A cold wind whipped over Chesapeake Bay, and she pulled her goose-down coat tighter, finally relenting and zipping it up. She wanted a cigarette, but she'd quit long ago, and it certainly wouldn't do to start again, particularly not now. She wanted a glass of Cabernet, but that wouldn't do either.

Now that it was more than just herself she had to worry about.

Wishing she could go straight to the telephone and call Steve, she walked up onto the deck and stomped her feet to get rid of the sand. Eyeing the chaise longue, now with its pads in storage— bare bones of redwood and sinew of steel bands remained, along with a thousand memories, a warm feeling flooded her. It was on that very chaise that Stephen Drum had first made love to her; that she'd lost her virginity.

It seemed so long ago, particularly now, with him so far away. Physically distant, but more important, emotionally so. A pain deeper than tears racked her. Why had he cast her aside after all these years? Just when she needed him most?

Sighing deeply, she went into the house and made her way to the kitchen. A little soup would be nice, warming. And it would probably come up easier in the morning. Every morning for the last week, she'd greeted the day by running to the toilet and throwing up.

Damn, damn, damn, how was she going to tell her parents?

There was always abortion. She cut her eyes upward. "Forgive me, God." She didn't mean it. It was not an option. She would not kill her baby. Steve Drum's baby. It was unthinkable even if it weren't a cardinal sin.

But knowing Papa Al, would he want to kill the *father* of her unborn child? Hardly productive, but her father had been known to cut off his nose to spite his patrician face before. Would he spite her beautiful little unborn bastard child, his bastard grandchild, by killing the baby's father? Would he or she be half an orphan before he ever had a chance to meet the man who sired him?

It would be a couple of months before she began to show, so she had some time. Maybe she could go to Italy. Hide out and Papa Al would not know until many months from now.

Maybe that was an answer.

She made her way into the house, cold and lonely as the bay outside. She had to eat something. If she were half the Italian her mother was, she'd start a minestrone from scratch, but Campbell's tomato would have to do. If she had someone else to cook for, it would be different.

As she emptied the can into a pan and added milk, it occurred to her she *did* have someone else to cook for. She'd have to start watching her diet.

She stood staring at the heating soup. Steve, Steve, Steve, you fool.

A watched pot, as the saying goes . . . She walked into the living room and switched on the TV. Worrying never helped, so her mother said, still, she couldn't stop. *Seinfeld* would take her mind off Steve Drum, at least for half an hour.

The hell with it. With determined precision, she poked in Steve's number in New York, but the machine answered. She quietly returned the receiver to its cradle without leaving a message. She wouldn't give him the pleasure of not returning her call again.

Probably out with the blond bombshell.

To hell with him. She'd said she could handle this all by herself, and she would.

This job she could handle, but how could she handle Papa Al?

Steve watched his companions at the table.

Felicia seemed fascinated with Joseph Bigsam and the fact he ran a casino. And he was equally fascinated with her, and probably would have been had she been a dishwasher in a hot dog stand that used only paper, as beautiful as she looked tonight. Joe's wandering eyes made it obvious it was not her intellect or her job as a TV commentator he admired.

Before he was halfway through his veal marsala and she her sea bass marinara—already having finished two bottles of Ruffino Chianti— she'd discovered that he knew of several illegal casinos in New York City.

"Oh, wonderful!" she said, toasting him with her glass. "Then we can go there after dinner."

"No way," Steve said, picking at his pasta primavera.

"Way!" Bigsam said as quickly. "I'd love to take you, little missy."

The last thing Steve wanted was to risk being in an illegal gambling den, since he'd already done that and knew what he wanted to know about the competition.

"Oh, come on, Steve," she pleaded, her tone a dare.

"Can't do it, Leeci. For my own reasons, I can't be seen there."

She pouted. "I've been waiting a long time to go."

"I'll bet you have." Steve's tone was almost accusatory.

"Well, this is my chance, and I want to go."

"Joe's a big boy, aren't you, Bigsam?"

"You bet I am." He eyed her hungrily.

"Then you guys have at it. I've got a long day tomorrow."

"Well, okay, we will." She smiled, a hint of defiance in her voice.

"Check, check out," Steve said, employing an old poker term meaning if you don't bet or raise, you fold. He wasn't used to having a woman he invited out not allow him the courtesy of taking her home. But she was a big girl; free, white, and twenty-one, so the old saying went.

"You're not angry?" she asked him.

"Why should I be angry? I hope you win half the town."

"Good."

As soon as they finished, Bigsam was on his feet. "Let's go," he said.

Felicia laughed and rose to follow.

"I'm going to finish my coffee," Steve said quietly.

Felicia rounded the table and bent down to hug him, whispering in his ear, "I've got to do this, Steve. Call me later."

"Have a great time," he said, his tone less than sincere.

"We'll cab it." Joe enveloped her waist with his big forearm, looking back over his shoulder. "You got the check; you and the boys take the car. Tell them I'll call them later if I need them."

"Who?" Felicia asked, but they both shrugged it off. She had no idea the bodyguards, other than Dan who'd driven them, had been in close proximity.

"Joe!" Steve called after him.

Bigsam turned back as Felicia went to retrieve her coat from the check girl. Steve said nothing, but ran a pinched thumb and forefinger across his mouth, like closing a zipper.

"Don't worry," he said with a grin, shrugging it off, then they were gone.

In moments Thad stuck his head into the restaurant, and Steve waved him over.

The big man sat, shaking his head, mimicking the stereotypical Indian speech. "Big Indian Joe stand taller?" he asked, imitating an old western movie Indian.

"Guess so," Steve answered with a shrug. "Actually, I think she sniffs a story. I get the impression she's like a bitch in heat when there's a story around. Hope it doesn't come back on all of us."

"And that Bigsam, he smells a mare on the wind," Thad said,

and Steve was surprised to feel a little twinge of jealousy. Maybe he was getting over Angela Giovanni; then again, maybe it was just macho pride. The truth was, had it been Angela who'd done what Felicia did, he'd be postal.

He finished his coffee and they walked out to find Bigsam's Lincoln double-parked in front of the restaurant, Dave and Dan Redfern practically filling the front seat.

"Where to?" Dan asked as Steve and Thad climbed into the back.

"Home! Back to the condo," Steve instructed.

When they arrived, he offered the Redferns the option of coming up and kicking back in his living room until they heard from their boss on the cell phone, and they agreed. He turned to Thad before he exited the car. "You can call it a night."

"Naw, I want to check the condo out as usual. Maybe I'll have a nightcap with you guys."

"Make yourself happy," Steve said. Dave Redfern, Thad, and Steve entered the lobby while Dan took the car into the condo garage to park it.

The elevator seemed to take forever climbing to the fourteenth floor. Dave Redfern was telling a joke. "You know why the white-eye wants to get to Mars so bad?" Thad waited behind for the punch line as Steve stepped out into the hall. "Because they heard that Indians had some land there." Both men held their sides and guffawed.

Steve had reached back to hold the door open, when he noticed the stairway exit door, twenty feet across the elevator foyer, standing slightly ajar. He no more than realized this, when it burst open and a black-clad man in a ski mask, shotgun at his shoulder, leapt out.

He centered the weapon on Steve's chest.

CHAPTER TWENTY-FIVE

The roar was deafening, the charge taking Steve full mid-chest, propelling him backward off his feet.

As the shooter jacked in another shell, Thad and Dave charged out of the elevator, wild-eyed, automatics in hand. Discharging his weapon too quickly, ski-mask's shotgun roared again, but merely blew ceiling tiles all over them.

It did cause them both to dive to the ground, but both were able to snap a shot off. Ski-mask disappeared behind the metal door into the stairwell.

Grabbing his cell phone, Thad yelled to Redfern. "Take the elevator to the lobby. Get the son of a bitch. What's Dan's number?"

Dave Redfern yelled it out as he backed into the elevator and punched the lobby button.

Steve lay crumpled up against the wall, his limbs askew in distorted positions, unmoving. A terrible rasping, sucking sound echoed across the now otherwise quiet foyer.

Thad dialed 911, talking as he knelt by Steve's side. Did he have on his vest? He ripped the shredded shirt away, exposing the black material, finding only a reddening deep bruise on the sternum beneath the protective Kevlar and a couple of spots of blood in his upper chest, where the vest didn't protect, actually closer to shoulder level. While he reported the shooting and begged for an ambulance, he checked Steve's breathing. Ragged, but regular.

He had to hang up on the insistent operator in order to get off the phone, but did so after repeating the address, then he dialed Dan Redfern's cell phone. Thad instructed, "Shotgun! Guy in a ski mask and black turtleneck. He's coming down the stairs. Watch out for your brother. He's taking the elevator to the lobby. Cover the garage."

Thad checked Steve's breathing again. As satisfied as he could be under the circumstance, he ran for the stairway and started down. He could hear the man's footsteps far below. He took the stairs four at a time, echoes reverberating in the dim light of the shaft.

Then the shotgun roared again far below, followed by a half dozen sharp reports of pistol shots, then the slamming of a metal door.

The man must have been at least five floors ahead of him, if not more. He hoped Dave Redfern had caught him trying to escape into the lobby, and more so, that he hadn't caught Dave Redfern in his sights.

Thad paused for a moment, listening. It sounded as if the man was slowly coming back up the stairwell.

Taking the stairs four at a time, Thad slowed when he'd covered two floors and began creeping. He heard a door again, and again leapt quickly down a flight of stairs, hitting one out of four.

He almost stumbled when he came face-to-face with a big man, almost fired, as did the other man, before realizing it was Dave Redfern.

Puffing, Redfern managed to get out, "The bastard tried . . . to get out through the lobby, but I got a couple of shots off. He came back in here."

They stared at each other, realizing he must have exited on another floor.

"Shit," Thad said. "I think there are three of these emergency stairwells. The one in the back dumps on the alley, this one in the lobby, and the third, on the other side of the building, exits both on the alley and into the garage. Let's hope Dan gets the prick."

"I'm heading for the alley," Dave said.

"I've got to get back to Steve." Thad stepped out of the stairwell and headed for the elevator. "Be careful," he called after Dave.

"You too." Then he was gone.

By the time Thad got back to his boss, Steve was conscious, but still flat on his back, patting himself down, checking to see if he was all there. And seeming amazed he was.

"Don't move. The ambulance is on its way."

"Jesus," Steve said, coughing, then wincing. "I feel like I got kicked in the chest by a mule."

"You did, a twelve-gauge one. You took a couple of pellets high in the shoulder." Another trail of blood wormed its way down his arm. "And a stray pellet in the arm. Just sit tight."

"I can get up."

"Sure. And you can leap tall buildings in a single bound. Stay on your back, Steve, until the medics get here."

Steve lay his head back down. "What the hell, I need a little rest."

"Think about how much you love that vest while you're at it."

"I do, I do, I do love my vest." He coughed again.

Thad couldn't help but smile, even though he still had a quart of adrenaline coursing through his veins and a .40-caliber automatic clasped tightly in his fist.

At the end of the alley fourteen stories below, the man in black leapt into an equally dark sedan, illegally parked in a cab stand. He stripped away the ski mask just as a yellow cab pulled alongside him, the cabbie yelling profanities and giving him the finger. He raised the shotgun and the cabbie immediately floor-boarded it, peeling away in a cloud.

Fumbling with the keys, breathing heavily, he finally got the car started and roared away just as a black-and-white rounded the corner, lights glaring, siren blaring. But the cops paid him no mind. He passed, then jumped on the throttle.

Jesus, what a mess he'd gotten into. At first it was just Drum, then there were big ugly Indians everywhere. For a minute there he felt like General Custer. He'd taken one stairway to the lobby and right into a big Indian, traded shots, then another to the garage, only to find the same big son of a bitch there. The man must be able to fly, he'd moved so fast. He'd made it back up a floor and out into the alley without the man seeing him again.

He had a burn on his arm, a frayed sweater from a close miss, and a clean hole in his pants leg. He began to shake, the adrenaline working its way out of his system. It wasn't fear; he wouldn't admit it was fear. He had to be more careful next time, if there ever was a next time.

At least he'd blown Stephen Drum into the next world. He'd gone down, splat, like the bucket of shit he was. Too bad he hadn't been able to blow his ugly head off with the second shot, as he'd planned to do.

That's one way to scalp an Indian.

Even out of breath, he began to laugh.

By the time Dave Redfern reached the alley, there was no one in sight. He turned to see two carloads of NYPD's finest piling out of black-and-whites in front of the condo building. The door-man was pointing into the entry. One of the cops spotted him, automatic still in hand.

"Gun! Gun!" he yelled, stepping back behind the cover of a parked car. The other three officers did the same, all bringing their weapons to bear on him.

Redfern let the automatic spin in his hand, hanging from a single finger as he raised his arms. Two of the cops ran to him while the other pair charged into the building.

An ambulance pulled up behind the cop cars, lights spinning, siren winding down.

Hours later, Steve, having just awakened, lay quietly in a hospi-tal bed. They'd operated on him to remove two pellets from his clavicle and one from his upper left arm, and since he left the recovery room, he'd been dozing off and on.

He realized someone was sitting in a chair across the dim room.

"Who's there?" he asked.

"Tuffy," a gruff voice answered. "You need anything?"

Steve smiled. After visiting Tuffy twice during his recovery, he guessed turnabout was fair play.

"Doin' okay," Steve said. "Silly operation, really. Nothing like what you went through. Turn up the lights."

Tuffy crossed the room and hit an overhead light switch just as Joseph Bigsam filled the door.

"A little early to start the war," Joe said without bothering with a greeting.

"I didn't start it. In fact, I didn't even get off a shot. The guy in the ski mask threw down the gauntlet . . . and me."

Steve introduced the two men, then Joe brought him up to date. "Your man, Thad, is down in the coffee shop. He's been on the door to make sure your buddy doesn't try to come around and finish his sloppy work, but I told him to take a break now that I'm here. I guess his permit kept him out of the can, but Dave and Dan were both arrested for carrying a concealed weapon and discharging a weapon in a public place."

"That's bullshit," Steve said. "Are they licensed in St. Regis?"

"Hell, you don't have to have a license on our rez. It's bullshit, okay, but a felony in New York, or so I'm told."

"Bail them, for cash. Don't involve a bondsman. As soon as possible, then get them back on the rez. The FBI won't laugh it off, but they won't press it under the circumstances. I'll defend the Redferns if they want to come back and fight it out, but the best thing is to get behind the redskin shield of the rez and out of the hands of the white-eye."

"I'll do it," Joe said.

"What time is it?" Steve asked.

"Three-thirty . . . A.M." Tuffy yawned.

"Felicia get home all right?" Steve asked.

"Blond bitch damn near got me killed," Joe said, shaking his head in amazement.

"How so?" Steve asked.

"She wanted to go by her office for a minute. When we got to the third club, the security guys, half a dozen big gumba boys, grabbed her purse and found a tiny video camera there. The bitch had been taking pictures of all the games. Video camera wasn't any bigger than my wallet. I guess I'd have seen myself big-time on TV with a bunch of other players if they hadn't made her."

Steve laughed, winced, then laughed again. "So, did the no-neck boys chuck you out?"

"Yeah, on my ear, with Felicia right behind me, and I'm not

used to being eighty-sixed from a place . . . not that I'm a virgin to the process. If the Redfern boys woulda been there . . ."

Steve laughed until he hurt himself. Then couldn't help but ask, "So, how was the rest of the evening?"

"Hell, she was pissed at me because I couldn't do anything about it. They beat her camera into pea-size pieces. She took a cab home."

"Are you sure she didn't get out of there with any tape?"

"Not unless she shoved them in her panties, and I sure as hell didn't get to check there . . . much as I'd of liked to."

"Let's hope she didn't, or you *will* make the news."

When Thad returned and took up his post outside the door, Joe and Tuffy called it a night.

When Steve awoke again, Paula, Meredith, Sally, David, and Thad stood chatting in his room, and the nurse was putting a tray on his bed.

"When do I get out of here?" he asked the nurse.

"Doctor will probably sign your release on his rounds this morning. He's gonna be late. Said not to wake you or you woulda had this tray at six."

"Good. Don't let him be too late," Steve said as the others gathered around his bed.

"So," he asked, not bothering with a good morning, "who's minding the office, and did you get a match yet?"

All of them smiled, but shook their heads. Paula said, "Alice is taking care of the phones. Yours is on call forwarding." Satisfied, he turned to David. "What about our Danny boy's relatives?"

"Believe it or not, I think I have a lead on him. I'm going to White Plains this afternoon to the Sunrise Nursing Home. They've got a Danny Murphy there, former Queens resident who matches my guy. Ninety-three years old, which is about right, and alive and kickin'. I actually think he could be our boy."

"Great. What are you doing here?"

"Jesus!" Paula said with a grin. "I'm sorry they didn't bring you to me. I'd have dug those pellets out with my trusty fingernail file, while you were at your desk raising hell with everyone."

"Sorry," Steve said a little sheepishly. "The pressure is really on, and I don't have time for getting shot or anything else. I appreciate all of you coming on down, but I'd as soon have you working. I'll be in the office this afternoon—"

"No you won't!" Paula, Meredith, and Sally all chimed in. Paula continued. "You're going home to rest and rehabilitate."

"I don't have time."

"Then take time. You come in and we're all leaving, got that?" The others nodded.

Steve clamped his jaw, but they held all the cards. "Okay. I'll rest today, but I'm coming in tomorrow."

"We'll see," Paula said.

"What time is it?"

"Eight-thirty."

"So I'll promise not to come in if you'll all go back to work. And if you promise to call me as soon as you hear from Asian American. We should have an executed letter of intent from them this morning."

"Deal," Paula said, and all but Thad left.

Before Thad walked out to take his chair by the door, Steve asked him, "Does anybody have any idea who the guy with the shotgun was?"

"Nope. He got away clean. All of us got a shot at him, but that shotgun had us hunting a hole at the same time. Sorry, boss."

"Bullshit to sorry. You did just right. Had it not been for the vest . . ." Steve shook his head. "If anything, I thank you. Don't ever apologize again for being right."

"Do you have a guess who the shooter was?" Thad asked.

"Actually, I know a guy with those same dark eyes, which was all I saw of his face, and a build just like our boy with the shotgun. When I get out of here, and get right, you and I are going to go see a guy named Nick Masticelli and have a chat with him. In the meantime, I want you to find out all you can about the guy."

"You got it."

CHAPTER TWENTY-SIX

Just before he was discharged, Steve got a call from Sally.

Asian American's letter, executed by Wilber Wong, had arrived. The only change to Steve's counter to the counter, was the closing date and the time to release funds. The two million was to be released in two weeks, not a month, and the deal was to close by December 31, not the following March. It was exactly as Wilber's boss had outlined in Mandarin during the meeting.

Now he was really in the pressure cooker.

He called Sally and instructed her to cut the check and personally bring it to his apartment, where he would execute it and have her deliver it and the purchase agreement to a third party escrow company, to be held until he instructed its release.

Just before he climbed into the obligatory wheelchair to be escorted out of the room, Detective Rollie Wood and Agent Nolan Robertson walked in, both looking very official.

"You guys working as a team these days?" Steve asked before they could speak.

"Ran into each other in the elevator," Wood said. "But we may be working together now."

"Good, maybe you can catch this guy."

Agent Robertson shook his head. "Not without some cooperation from you, Drum. Come on now, don't you think it's time you told us what you're involved in . . . what it is that someone wants to kill you over?"

"Like I said before, I'm just a paper pusher. Somebody has the wrong target, and I wish they'd find the right one and leave me alone."

"I want a formal statement," Robertson said.

"I've just gotten out of the operating room, agent. I've been drugged up, beat up, banged up, and fucked over. How about Monday morning?"

"I'll call your secretary and make an appointment. You be there. You know what obstruction of justice is?"

"Yes, sir, to both. I'll be there, and I probably know better than you what obstruction of justice is."

They walked out ahead of Steve, Thad, and the male nurse pushing the chair.

Just as the nurse began wheeling him out, the phone rang. Thad walked back and picked it up. "It's Felicia Ann Garrity. She says she's on her way over with a camera crew, and she won't take no for an answer."

"Great." Steve flashed him a slightly evil grin. "Give her this room number and tell her to come on over."

Thad smiled and did as instructed.

"Now," Steve said, "let's get the hell out of here."

Even with a stop at the hospital, she almost beat him to his condo. Thad managed to convince her Steve was sleeping, but still she wanted a time to see him, with cameraman in tow. He left her outside a closed front door and stuck his head in Steve's bedroom, repeating the request.

"How about here, midmorning tomorrow," Steve said.

"I thought you said you were going into the office first thing?"

"How about here, midmorning," Steve said, again adopting the slightly evil grin.

Spending the rest of the day at home gave him time to collect his thoughts. By late afternoon he had a wild idea. They had not been able to make a blood match with any of the tribes in New York and were now working on New Jersey and Connecticut.

What if the descendants of the Canarsee were not an established tribe? He knew that sadly, numerous bands of Native Americans were scattered throughout the United States without tribal affiliation, without the benefit of having a reservation or the programs the government provided. If one of those bands were the true descendants, then he would not only be able to aid a specific group of Native Americans, but a group of disenfranchised ones.

He had Thad set up his computer on his bed after Thad threatened to call and rat him out to Paula and Meredith if he even went to his home desk.

In minutes he had his Internet connection fired up and was reading the home page for the Department of the Interior, then the Bureau of Indian Affairs. He pulled up a list of applications filed with the Branch of Acknowledgment. As an attorney, Steve had handled a couple of applications for tribal acknowledgment, the first step in gaining government recognition. He knew the process, and the seven criteria necessary for a tribe to become acknowledged.

After an hour's reading he leaned back and mumbled aloud, "By God, there was another group in New York who had tried to get acknowledgment and failed."

The Scohomac, a small group of just over one hundred, from Yates County, had filed way back in 1986 and been refused for lack of a continuous grouping. It seems they'd drifted apart over the years, then together again, which often happened when a tribe had no land base. Steve searched his memory for Yates County, then remembered a trip he'd taken to New York's wine country a few years before—a wonderful trip with Angela Giovanni. It was way to the west, in the Finger Lakes region of New York State, near Geneva.

He ignored memories of the trip with Angela, and searched his memory for recent tribal acknowledgment rulings. It seemed to him that recently several tribes who had become separated over the years, then reunited, had gained acknowledgment. Criteria had changed drastically since 1986.

Since the tenure of the Bureau of Indian Affairs' first woman assistant secretary, Ada E. Deer, a Menominee Indian from Wisconsin, great strides had been taken to acknowledge worthy tribal groups. No matter what the results of the blood DNA, the Scohomacs should try again. In fact, if Steve's memory served him correctly, when Ada Deer testified before the Senate Committee on Indian Affairs to gain her appointment, she'd said that her own tribe had been terminated, then, twenty years later, reinstated.

In the morning, Steve decided, he would take a phlobotomist with him and drive to the Finger Lakes district to find the Scohomac. If nothing else, he would encourage them to try again for acknowledgment.

That afternoon he called Washington and found an old friend in the Bureau. Gordon Whitebeard was a Cherokee from Oklahoma who had come up through the ranks of the Bureau of Indian Affairs and was now assistant to the assistant secretary. Without Steve having to plow through the normal bureaucracy, and just before five o'clock, Whitebeard called back with what Steve needed. The name of the chief who'd signed the application.

Waiting until seven P.M., Steve got Yates County information on the line and luckily, after checking several towns and villages, found a number for Tom T. Webster in Penn Yan village on Keuka Lake. Tom Webster answered his phone on the first ring. Being purposely vague, Steve made an appointment to meet the chief of the Scohomac tribe for lunch in Penn Yan the next day. Then he arranged to rent a car from Litcomb. He would drive himself.

Thad, refusing to leave his side, spent the night on the living room couch.

He and Thad were waiting at the office when Paula arrived. She stuck her head in before going on down the hall to her own. "So, you couldn't stay away. How's the shoulder and arm?"

"Great, hurts only when I breathe. I need one of our blood guys to take a ride with me this afternoon."

"Can't happen. They're all in Connecticut with the van."

"I'm on to an unacknowledged tribe across the state. I have an appointment today to meet with the chief. How do I get a blood sample?"

"I'll check with Meredith," she said, and turned to leave.

Steve stopped her. "How's the meeting coming?"

"Fine. We're scheduled to meet at the Hilton next Friday. Nine days hence."

"Good." Paula left and Sally arrived. "Did you find my architect?" he asked her.

"Found a guy in San Francisco. A Chumash from the Santa Barbara area who works there and teaches part-time at the University of California in Berkeley."

"Good credits?"

"He's worked as lead designer on a number of San Francisco high-rises . . . one in Portland and a couple in Seattle."

"Get him on the phone."

In minutes, after satisfying himself as to the man's abilities, he had made a deal to fly Howard Talloak to New York for the weekend, with the promise of a rather large fee for some preliminary design work.

Paula returned. "She said come on down and in five minutes she'll teach you and Thad how to use a lancet to draw what blood she'll need."

Before eight-thirty Steve and Thad were on the road to Penn Yan with the sun at their backs. Steve was able to drive for only the first hour, then had to hand the wheel over to Thad. His shoulder and deeply bruised chest pained him, but he didn't want to take a pain pill, needing to be sharp and alert for Tom Webster. Instead, he lay back and napped off and on.

The rolling country was brushed with light snow, but the sun shone clearly and the sky vibrated with blue. The drive went quickly. Finally, nearing the Finger Lakes country, well-manicured vineyards began to wind their concentric rows of now-barren vines sandwiched between heavily timbered hillsides. An occasional creek and the waterfalls Yates County was famous for began to punctuate the forests.

The square logged Tyrol Mill on the outskirts of Penn Yan, long ago converted to a restaurant, had taken advantage of one of those creeks and waterfalls to grind grain and run a sawmill. Now it was a tourist trap, but one in a beautiful setting—still, the huge water wheel turned slowly, creaking a complaint of its uselessness. In mid-November, the restaurant's tables boasted only a few locals.

Tom T. Webster was a tall man, slender, in blue denim, with a ruddy complexion and a workingman's gnarled hands. He arrived in an old red Chevy pickup with a magnetic business sign on the door reading WEBSTER INSULATION. Lanky and rawboned, Webster reminded Steve of his father. Steve liked him immediately.

Not beating around the bush, Steve asked, "Have you been conducting regular tribal meetings over the years?"

"Sure, for a few years there were less than a dozen in attendance, but we meet on the harvest moon. I have minutes, such as they are, for the last twenty-five or so years, and notes before that kept by my father, chief before me."

"How many are you?"

"One hundred sixty-five, but only about forty here. The rest are all over hell and gone."

"I think you should resubmit your application for acknowledgment."

Webster didn't hesitate. "It was very expensive, and we are all workingpeople. Most of us work the grapes. I'm the only one with my own business, and I just invested all I got in a new foam rig. There is *no* money for legal fees."

Steve smiled. He surmised that Webster thought he was ambulance-chasing, looking for a fat legal fee. "I'll tell you what. If I do the paperwork at no charge, will you agree to bring your people together in this?"

"Sure," he managed to answer, still eyeing Steve suspiciously. "What would we have to lose?"

Knowing he would have to handle this with kid gloves, Steve said, "And there's something else." He took a deep breath, because he was about to tell a small lie. "We're conducting a heritage study, and we need a blood sample from a few in your group. As an aside, I represent the Native American Improvement Coalition in New York. They're doing DNA studies of Native Americans. If the DNA works out, it's a new source of evidence that you're who you claim to be. It's almost impossible for the bureau and its hired-gun anthropologists to refuse you."

"None of us are very high on doctors and hospitals."

"This is merely a poke in the finger, worth thirty-five bucks apiece to your people. Thad here is an expert with the finger prick."

Thad eyed him, not wanting to have anything to do with drawing blood, but smiled as he did so.

Steve phrased the next question more carefully. "And if I do this for you, I expect a business management contract with the tribe, taking nothing other than a percentage of what I gain for you . . . a small percentage at that."

"Damn small I hope. Go to work, and bring me an agreement to look at."

They spent the afternoon running down members to have their fingers poked and get the slides needed. While they traveled from spot to spot, Steve interviewed Tom T. Webster regarding the rest of those things he knew the bureau would want to know before even considering the application. By the end of the day, Webster informed them his name was Thomas Thornton Webster, but asked them to call him by his nickname, Tomtom, and it seemed they were fast friends.

Just before Steve climbed into the car, Tom Webster rested a big, gnarled hand on his shoulder and looked him straight in the eye. "This has been a longtime dream of mine, and my father before me. I don't know why you're doing this, other than this management thing, but God bless you."

Steve swallowed, sorry he hadn't been able to tell this man the whole truth. "And you, my friend. Don't worry, if you and your people win in this, I win too."

They were winding their way back to New York by five P.M. In Steve's briefcase was a copy of all tribal documents including the first acknowledgment application.

It was after ten when they arrived at the office. Meredith, as usual, was working late, with Paula helping her in the lab since her assistants were long gone. Having a very strong hunch, Steve implored her to put the slides they brought on top of her pile. Begrudgingly, she did so.

Sensing how exhausted Meredith and Paula both were, Steve insisted they all take Sunday off, and he would again treat for brunch at Tavern-on-the-Green.

When he checked his calls and his desk, he was pleased to find a note from David Greenberg.

> Great news. Danny Murphy is one and the same. When he went into the nursing home a few years ago, he gave the bones and artifacts from Rockefeller Center to Columbia University. What now? He didn't have much, and was a good old guy, so I put a fifty on his account at the hospital store. Can I get reimbursed?

Not only reimbursed, Steve thought, a wide grin on his face, but hugged. He made a mental note to make sure Danny Murphy's account was enhanced on a monthly basis for as long as he lived and Steve had any money to do so. It was great news! Now, if the university hadn't lost or misplaced Murphy's discovery . . .

This was a job for Paula. He went back down the hall and asked her to go after it on Monday.

She shrugged. "Why wait? Tomorrow should work, Saturday

or not. The department head there is an old friend, and I happen to know he's a workaholic. We were on a dig in the Yucatan together a few years ago. A bottle of Cuervo Especial will work wonders with Dr. Volker, since he's a taquilla-holic as well.''

"Get him a case,'' Steve said.

Among the messages he had was one that had been messengered over from Felicia Garrity, sealed in an envelope, and marked in bold letters, *Personal.*

> Are you angry with me? I'm just doing my job. How about seeing me without the cameraman? Do I need to pay back the dozen roses? Seeing me is the least you could do for a girl who's nursing rug burns on her back.

She had a point.

Then he wondered, would she flat-back for a story? Not a very complimentary thought. In fact, an ego-deflating one.

He called her office and left word he would see her Monday— breakfast, lunch, or dinner. And that roses were unnecessary, but he thanked her for the thought.

With the help of a stiff scotch, Steve slept soundly that night, even with his aching chest and shoulder.

On Saturday morning he and Thad picked up Howard Talloak at his hotel—he'd come in on a midnight flyer—then chatted as they drove straight to Rockefeller Center. Talloak was a strikingly handsome man with a suave casual Santa Barbara appearance, gray sideburns belying his otherwise youthful appearance. Most people probably thought his deep-tan George Hamilton complexion resulted from the beach. He could have been an actor in a soap opera.

Steve had managed to get a box full of Rockefeller Center drawings from Asian American, had them copied and reduced to computer files, then returned the plans. He struck his deal with the architect on the way to the job.

After getting Talloak to sign a nondisclosure agreement, they walked the Center over while Steve relayed his thinking on the project and his vision.

The property Steve had placed in escrow consisted of a long rectangular piece extending from Fifth Avenue on the east to the Avenue of the Americas on the west. It was flanked on the sides by Forty-ninth and Fiftieth streets. Almost two-thirds of the site was occupied by the GE Building—two million two hundred thousand square feet rising seventy stories and crowned by the Rainbow Room, with Rockefeller Plaza, the private street, bisecting the parcel. On the southern third of the parcel across Rockefeller Plaza was the lower plaza, and the French Building, or La Maison Française, only one hundred six thousand square feet rising six stories; and the British Empire Building, also a petite one hundred four thousand square feet rising six stories. Both the smaller buildings flanked what was known as the promenade, leading the pedestrian and the admirer's eye directly to the entrance to the much grander structure that was the heart and soul of Rockefeller Center.

From Fifth Avenue, the two smaller buildings seemed almost an introduction, framing the promenadelike gateposts to the majestic crown jewel of midtown, 30 Rockefeller Plaza.

Talloak seemed gushingly enthusiastic and assured Steve he would either overnight some very rough conceptual preliminary sketches, or download them to him over the Internet before the upcoming Friday meeting.

He put Talloak back on a plane to San Francisco that afternoon, laden with pictures and computer disks full of old plans.

Felicia Ann Garrity elected to have lunch with him, saying she had to go out of town that afternoon, but again went away from their meeting unsatisfied. She spent the first half of the meal firing questions at him regarding the attempt on his life, then the second half pumping him about gambling in New York. Steve stayed as shifty as an NFL running back, not giving her any specifics, denying he even knew about illegal gambling anywhere in the state.

He wondered if he'd ever hear from her again.

Spending the afternoon on the telephone, he worked on getting as big a turnout as he could for his Friday meeting without explaining the exact purpose of the Native Nations' Emergency Summit Conference.

It was Tuesday morning, the day before Meredith was scheduled to return to her job in Michigan, when she called him excitedly. "Get down here, Steve, I want to show you something."

CHAPTER TWENTY-SEVEN

Steve almost ran to her office.

She spread out two almost identical strips of DNA illustration material on a lab table. "This one is our sample from the Andrew McGuire Building, and this is your man in Penn Yan, Webster." She grinned at him as if he should be doing an Irish jig.

"So, what does it mean?" Steve asked.

"It means, in your peculiar reservation vernacular, you've drawn a royal flush, baby! There's no doubt Webster's a direct descendant from old Chief Onnegaha, no doubt in any court in the land, unless, of course, O.J.'s being tried. You've *got* your people."

Steve grinned then sighed deeply. He wanted to celebrate, but he felt as if he were one of the pressed bitterroot flowers his mother used to keep in her Bible. Now, with the weight of Rockefeller Center bearing down on him, he really had to get to work.

Still, he couldn't let his people down. "Send someone out for a few bottles of bubbly. We'll have a sendoff party for you tonight, here in the office, then you and I and Thad and Paula will go to dinner . . . anyplace you choose."

That afternoon he called Cookie Yamamoto. "Hey, I need a favor from Asian American."

"You're not going to try to change the deal?"

"No, Cookie, nothing so tough. I need to begin moving some stuff into some of the vacant space *before* we close the transaction."

"Let me see what I can do."

That night he enjoyed congratulating everyone on a job well done, then he had a quiet sushi dinner with his friends and coworkers. Since they'd not picked up enough outside work to justify keeping it open, they made preparations to disband the lab and its crew. But that would follow testing the rest of the Scohomac band. Two of the lab techs were in the Finger Lakes region drawing blood from every Scohomac member they could reach.

The next morning Cookie Yamamoto called and said that the building had two and a half contiguous floors vacant. If Steve would sign a one-year lease, he could move anything he wanted into one or more of those floors. If he closed the escrow, he could, of course, as the new owner, then cancel the lease. They would require a fifty-thousand-dollar lease deposit, but no lease payments until February.

They were being tough, but he had to move quickly, so he countered with the deposit being prorated in the event he closed the escrow, as would all other deposits. They agreed and sent over the lease with another five file boxes full of leases for his approval.

The bad news was he was betting everything he owned on his ability to complete this deal. If he was stuck with a lease and couldn't sublet it, it would be bankruptcy city.

The good news was, come the next weekend, God willing and tribal representatives receptive and generous, he was ready to begin quietly infiltrating Rockefeller Center. All during the week, he, Paula, and David began systematically lining up equipment. New and used, every decent piece of for-sale gambling equipment in the country was negotiated for by the three. Those deals that seemed favorable, Steve solidified with good faith deposits. He had another million bucks laid out by Thursday.

Another piece of good news invigorated him. After hours in the dusty basement of the Columbia anthropology department and the investment of a case of Jose Cuervo Especial tequila, Paula was successful in locating Danny Murphy's donation and the DNA did prove to be compatible with the Scohomac. Another link in the chain was welded shut.

His plan was much closer to fruition, presuming his other critical piece of business was complete—the execution of his "business management" agreement between the Red Ace Corporation and the Scohomac. Without that he had no standing to do any of the things he was undertaking. He had completed the agreement and overnighted it to Tom Webster. It was yet to be returned. He hoped it was just procrastination on Tom's part, and that he had no serious objections to Steve's terms.

But equally important, the most tedious negotiation of all must be undertaken. The State of New York.

He called the New York State attorney general's office and made an appointment for the Monday following his Native Nations meeting the coming Friday. He was pleased he was able to meet with Andrew Upton so quickly. Upton was an assistant to the attorney general and, Steve knew, had political ambitions. Steve had met him before, when hearings were being held on native gambling in the state, and liked the man well enough. He was old-line family money—somehow distantly related to the Duponts—and didn't need the job. But he saw it as a step toward the attorney general's position, and it in turn as a step toward the governor's mansion.

Steve made a mental note to play on that ambition.

Before he and Thad left the office, he realized there was an important piece of business he had let lie too long. Hitting a few keys on the computer, he pulled up ICOM and was shocked to see that a million two hundred thousand shares had traded during the last session, and it was at 33½, almost double from when he'd gone to New Mexico. He had to be ready to move quickly, then he realized he hadn't heard back from his friend in the securities business, Jonathan Noble. He called him at home.

"What's up on the ICOM thing?"

"Oh, Christ, Stephen, didn't I call you? I have a list of buyers and I'll fax it over. Hell, it looked so good, I bought some myself and put some clients in."

Steve was silent for a moment, then said, "Jonathan, meet me at Hollihan's for a quick drink."

"I'm already home, Steve."

"Don't argue, just meet me."

Actually, they had only a half a drink before Jonathan excused himself in a hurry. Steve made his friend promise that he would get himself and his clients out of ICOM gracefully and without affecting the upward spiral of the stock. Due only to their long business relationship, he was able to do so without divulging to him the reason.

That night, to his initial relief, he got a call at home from Tom Webster. His relief was short-lived when Tom began negotiating each point of his management agreement. When Steve questioned him, he said, "It's my responsibility to do my best for my people, Steve. You know that. You've asked for the right to manage any deals undertaken and originated by you on behalf of the tribe. I think that's too much to ask."

Steve thought quickly, then answered with sincerity. "I asked for management rights, only so long as the tribe was profiting. If you're making a profit from a deal I brought you, how can you complain? It's a profit you wouldn't have made otherwise. It's found money."

Tom was silent for a moment. "Still, it gives you almost complete control over any business proposal you initiate—"

"Only if the deal's approved by you and the other tribal elders. No approval, no deal. Don't lose sight of the fact that I'm the guy investing his time and money . . . a lot of money, as you know . . . getting you folks acknowledged in the first place."

"And I appreciate that, still . . ."

Steve took a big gamble. "Okay, Tom. I wouldn't want to do anything that goes against your grain. You think about it, and meantime, I'll put everything on hold. When you call me back, or I receive an executed management agreement, I'll go back to work on your acknowledgment. Until then, it's in the holding tank. . . . If I don't hear from you, it was great meeting you, and I wish you the best of luck."

Tom said nothing. Steve, too, kept silent, making Tom speak first in response to his ultimatum. Finally, he did. "Okay. I'll take some time to think it over. To tell the truth, I think you're being a little one-sided, not willing to even negotiate—"

"I offered you a fair deal . . . a hell of a fair deal under the circumstances."

"Okay, Steve, if that's the way you want it. I'll talk it around to the elders and possibly give you a call back." There was no mistake that Tom Webster's voice rang with irritation.

Steve sounded as sincere as he could. "When I hear from you and we have a deal, I'll go back to work."

They broke the connection. Steve knew Tom Webster was truly

troubled by the management agreement, but Steve was not prepared to divulge his plans to the Scohomac. They wouldn't begin
to understand the scope of his undertaking, and it would be far
too much to expect this deal, which required lightning-fast reflexes
and footwork, to be controlled by any committee. Particularly a
committee made up of folks unsophisticated in business transac-
tions. Hell, even sophisticated business people would think Steve
was nuts, trying to accomplish what he'd set out to do. At best,
committee management had been the downfall of far too many
tribal deals. It was an old saying that a camel was a horse designed
by a committee. And Steve had too much of his own lifeblood at
risk to bet it on the vote of some good-hearted, well-meaning but
basically unsophisticated country folks.

He had to sit back and think about what he'd just concluded,
feeling the hot glare of old Standing Bear heating the back of his
neck. He knew good people generally had good intentions, but
they didn't necessarily make good business decisions. He had to
charge forward, or his own momentum would overrun him.

He would have to wait to hear from Tom. It would be an
arduous time. Waiting was always the worst of any deal, but this
would be torturous.

Steve realized he had made a mistake. In the spirit of expediting
the deal, he'd laid all his cards on the table with the Scohomac
management agreement. He'd left himself no room to negotiate.
He should have gone after the agreement as he would have any
other, time constraints or no, and purposefully included deal
points he was prepared to give up—in fact, expected to give up.
It was Negotiating 101. He'd made his first major error, and it
could cost him everything he'd worked and planned for. A stupid
mistake. *Remember,* he thought, chastising himself, *step once, look
twice.*

The worst news was his two-million-dollar deposit became
forfeitable on the Wednesday following the Native Nations' Emergency Summit Meeting. Steve could bluff his way through the
meeting, present the deal, if he had to, without really having the
necessary management agreement and consequently the standing
to negotiate on behalf of the Scohomacs. He didn't like it, but he
could. He could also end up with a lot of egg on his face. So far,
everything he'd done on this deal had been travois-before-the-

horse. Why should this meeting be any different? He hoped it wouldn't come down that way, but . . .

Could he risk two million dollars on a deal, a piece of real estate that wouldn't work for anything other than a casino at the price he'd negotiated? He'd have to stop short of that if he had any prudence left. Then again, prudence had boarded a train out of town weeks before. He was spending so much money, it would soon be his last two million.

Thursday came and went with no word from Tom Webster. Tribal representatives began to arrive Thursday afternoon.

Steve kept a keen eye out for the Mashantucket Pequots, who had the largest and most successful, and consequently the most profitable, Indian casino in the nation—Foxwoods in Southeastern Connecticut. Steve had no business relationship with the tribe, but had long admired what they accomplished. He did have high hopes to land them as a major investor, but knew they would have one big problem. A good number of their players came from Manhattan. They would have to be concerned with the fact they might lose a number of those players and a lot of business should a casino open in midtown. Steve would have to overcome that objection. He was taking a big risk even inviting them. Should they want to kill his deal, disclaimer or no disclaimer, they could leak what he was planning and have the city and state, and the Bureau of Indian Affairs, all over him in a heartbeat.

Felicia Ann Garrity and a hundred of her cohorts were lying in wait for any tidbit—and the press had a way of turning a tidbit into a gluttonous feast.

Of course, anyone attending the meeting could do the same. All it would take was an anonymous phone call.

Foxwoods was a full-blown casino, with 5,500 slots, blackjack, craps, roulette, and baccarat, plus high-stakes bingo, keno, a poker room, and a race book. Boasting over 1,400 rooms, patrons enjoyed two hotels and an inn. At only two and a half hours from Manhattan and one and a half from Boston, it boasted the best location relative to population among any of the Native American establishments.

By late Thursday they hadn't arrived, but that didn't surprise him, as they had a relatively short distance to travel compared to most of the tribes. They would probably drive in that day.

The Seminoles from Fort Lauderdale did arrive, which pleased

Steve, since he knew they were capable of substantial participation, as did the Cabazons from Palm Springs. The Cabazons were the granddaddies of Native American gaming, having fought the first legal battles to establish the precedents. It would be a major coup for Steve to land them as investors. And their participation would impress other tribal representatives.

Those three tribes alone could take up the major portion of the forty-three million he needed to raise, should they want to undertake a major risk. It would be a lot to ask of them, but they *could* do it.

By Friday noon, all but the Mashantucket Pequots had checked into the hotel, and another man whose appearance pleased him even more. Patrick McGoogan arrived.

The good news was he had a one-hundred-percent turnout of those invited. It was a good omen. The only thing better would be a white buffalo being born in the back of the meeting room! He wouldn't hold his breath on that one. The bad news was Tom Webster still hadn't called.

It could all be for naught.

Checking ICOM, he was thrilled to note that the stock was still being heavily traded and had topped thirty-nine dollars a share. How long could it last?

His guilt about the Hovenweep deal was assuaged when he got a report back from Stanley, who had tracked a number of the names off the list Jonathan Noble had provided him. Two of the biggest stock buyers were merely fronts for Alex Dragonovich. ICOM's president obviously believed that the Hovenweep discovery would drive his stock over fifty dollars, where it had been a couple of years before.

Alex, my lad, Stephen thought, *what a surprise you are in for.*

He prepared himself carefully for his presentation. Dressing, as he had oftentimes, as if going into battle. When he and Thad entered the hotel, Felicia Ann Garrity and her cameraman awaited in the lobby. He'd taken only three steps past the revolving door before she had the mike in his face.

"This is Stephen Drum, head of the Red Ace Corporation, gambling consultant to a number of Indian tribes. Mr. Drum, does the Native Nations' Summit Meeting have anything to do with Native gambling?"

"I'm also a board member of the Native American Improvement Coalition, Miss Garrity. This meeting deals with the mundane. Reservation problems such as education, water, sewers, et cetera."

"Come now, Mr. Drum. This meeting is titled 'Emergency Summit' . . . hardly mundane, I'd think."

Steve brushed on by her, speaking back over his shoulder. "Education and water quality on the reservations is an emergency to us. Nice to see you again, Miss Garrity."

"Then you won't mind if the press attends?" she called to his back.

He stopped and turned, pausing only for a moment. "Yes, ma'am, actually we do mind. It's reservation business. But I'll be happy to issue a press release tomorrow." He started in, then paused and turned back again. "However, on a personal note . . ." Felicia turned to the cameraman and drew her finger across her throat, and he lowered the camera.

Steve continued. "Actually, I would like to see you tomorrow if you have time. I think we might have something to talk about if you're working on the story I think you're working on." He winked at her and walked on inside.

Felicia was left with a frustrated look, but Steve knew her well enough to be certain Godiva would ride this horse till it died under her; she was a long way from finished.

As he suspected, she and her cameraman followed him down the hallway toward the meeting room. He said a few quiet words to Thad, who walked back and intercepted her. But she was not to be dissuaded. Thad continued on to find hotel security. With a little creative thinking, in moments barricades were set up at the end of the hall, and Felicia and her cameraman were forced out into the lobby proper while maintenance men began working the corridor with large floor waxers—making a great deal of noise.

Felicia screamed at the uniformed security man as she was physically placed outside the barriers by hotel personnel. "You can't do this. I know the first amendment. I *know* my business."

Thad, standing nearby, couldn't help but offer aloud, " 'It was great the way her mind works. No doubts, no fears, just the shameless pursuit of immediate material gratification. What a capitalist.' "

Felicia looked strangely at him as he walked away. She had no idea he was quoting Tom Cruise in *Risky Business.* And certainly no idea that Cruise was admiring a prostitute when he mouthed the line.

When Steve entered the meeting room, he spent a few minutes speaking to those he knew and meeting those he didn't, then took the podium and waited for the room to quiet.

After a moment of dead silence, Steve began.

"Your children are dying."

CHAPTER TWENTY-EIGHT

Steve had their attention. No one moved. All eyes were riveted on him.

"As an ethnic group, you have the highest rate of unemployment in the United States, the highest rate of alcoholism, the highest suicide rate . . . particularly among teenagers.

"And I know you know all this, and are desperately trying to do something about it. You need counselors, teachers, doctors, dentists. You need trade and tech schools, and scholarships to the best universities in the land.

"There's only one way to solve these problems, and you know it as well as I. Money. Lots and lots and lots of money.

"Every one of you in this room has taken advantage of the return of the buffalo, of reservation gambling. That's why you've been invited here. But even so, many of you have succumbed to the Bureau of Indian Affairs controlling your income. Consequently, when you need a counselor tomorrow, instead, you send a request to the bureau to free up some of your own funds. And maybe a year later, your request is reviewed. And sometimes, just sometimes, it's even approved. By that time you need a dozen more counselors.

"I don't think that is as it should be.

"I think your children deserve prompt attention. I think your elderly deserve the best possible care. I think all of you, and your children, deserve the best possible education.

"I know the problem with most Indian gambling establishments, and it's the same problem many, many commercial establishments fight. Location. Reservations, by the nature of how most of us acquired them—maybe I should say, in most instances, had them forced upon us—are in poor commercial locations. At best, we may have a major highway passing through, near which we can locate a casino. Some of us don't even enjoy that opportunity. Some of the rezes are so remote that no degree of promotion could bring a truly adequate number of casino customers to the door.

"The State of New York has recently allowed the Senecas to locate a casino *off* the rez, in a much better commercial location. I think it's time we took advantage of that policy, pulled our thumb out of the dike and created a great flood of money by all of us taking advantage of much better locations. Some states will follow suit, but most won't. It'll be an uphill battle for you who try.

"I'm about to show you the way to participate in the best possible casino location. Maybe the best in the world. I want you to keep an open mind. Above all, I want you to keep a positive attitude. You sit here, only a little more than a mile from Wall Street, where I made what little money I've been able to acquire. Where many, many have made huge fortunes. Many if not all of those fortunes made by the white-eye off the spoils of land, and timber, and mineral deposits, which belonged to our forefathers.

"It's time we took some of that back."

Steve paused for a long while to let that thought sink in, then continued.

"I'm now going to introduce you to a member of California's Chumash tribe, and a very skilled architect, Howard Talloak, who's designed a number of the West Coast's most prestigious skyscrapers. He's going to show you a little project we've undertaken, a project in which I want us all to participate . . . all to benefit from.

"When he's finished, you'll hear from Patrick McGoogan, a professor of comparative law from Oxford, and also a Native American. He'll fill you in on the legal aspects of what we're trying to accomplish, and the proof of our claims.

"You're about to see a project in a fairly good location. The difference between us and what the Senecas did is we're not gonna ask. We *have* the right to locate a casino here, on what we'll demonstrate has proven to be an ancient Native American burial ground. And, better yet, in a few days I expect to have a legal right to operate here.

"Legal in the eyes of the white-eye, or not, here's what we plan to do. . . ."

Paula, standing at the rear of the room, dimmed the lights, and Howard Talloak went to the computer projector to switch it on.

Steve could hear audible gasps in the room as the opening drawing projected onto the huge screen. From Fifth Avenue, the shot showed the two smaller buildings and the promenade, with the towering 30 Rockefeller Plaza in the distance. Stretching from the middle of one of the smaller buildings to the middle of the other across the promenade, four stories high above the street, arched a huge sign, THE ALL AMERICAN, in letters over a story tall, with a much smaller NATIVE NATIONS CULTURAL CENTER AND CASINO below. Below that was a billboard upon which Talloak had creatively featured the Native American headliner WAYNE NEWTON IN CONCERT.

"How many of you," Steve asked without expecting an answer, "recognize Rockefeller Center and the GE Building, 30 Rockefeller Plaza, just across the street from where you now sit?"

With the power of computer animation, Talloak began taking the crowd on a journey through the complex. Even so, the sketches were rough and stylized. Still, the concept was plainly discernible. The ground floor of the British Empire Building had been converted to a museum, free to the public, featuring the British involvement in America as it affected Native Americans. Likewise, the French Building ground floor was a museum featuring the French influence and its effect on Native Americans. The upper floors of the British Empire Building were occupied by the executive offices of the All American Casino and the Native American Improvement Coalition. The upper floors of the French Building were occupied by a small child care center for the employees, but by far the majority of the five floors were occupied by a planned Native Nations College, to be funded by proceeds from the casino.

All the fabulous artwork was maintained, and added to. The lower plaza was also basically the same, with the exception of a huge, larger-than-life, sculpture of a Plains Indian chieftain in full feather war bonnet reaching to the ground, with an open book in hand, reading. Kneeling before him were a half dozen Indian children of various sizes in the tribal dress of several nations, looking up at him, soaking in the knowledge he passed along.

The lower floors of the GE Building were the casino proper, with all the attributes of the finest Las Vegas or Atlantic City club: restaurants, concert halls, shops, and, of course, gaming rooms. Above the casino rose twenty floors of offices, mostly rental space.

"We have a lot of folks in the building with long leases. We have to provide facilities for them. I would eventually hope to occupy the total building with a casino and hotel."

Above the offices resided forty stories of prime hotel space, three thousand rooms. Floors sixty-one and sixty-two were suite floors with only eight rooms. Floor sixty-three consisted of only four five-bedroom suites, each with its own bar, theater, sauna, and Jacuzzi. The Rainbow Room still crowned the building on sixty-five, but the floor directly below was designed as an exclusive casino for high rollers.

Steve continued to talk while Howard Talloak ran the computer projector. "The Center was the first project to encompass office, retail, entertainment, and restaurants in one development. Major works by thirty of this century's finest artists grace the walls and gardens of the Center. Rockefeller Center has been called the heart of New York. The Center maintains the city's only private subway station, providing an estimated fifteen million passengers yearly with a clean, well-lighted facility. By agreement with the city, old John Rockefeller, Jr., wanted a subway station he wouldn't be ashamed of, and he knew if you want it done right, do it yourself. That's what we're doing here, doing it ourselves.

"By the way, how many of you have fifteen million people a year passing by, in this case under, your casino? Hell, we'll have a hundred thousand ice skaters a year on our ice rink in the lower plaza. I know some Indian casinos that don't have a hundred thousand *passing* their casinos on the highway each year.

"But I'm getting off the subject. At the time it was built, Rockefeller Center was the largest urban redevelopment project of all time . . . may still be. It has more cleaning people than most of our tribes have on the rolls; twelve thousand work in Rockefeller Center. If it were a city, it would be about the nation's two hundred thirtieth largest."

By the time he, Patrick McGoogan, and Howard Talloak finished, the audience was astounded. They sat in utter silence as the lights came back up. At first Steve thought he had failed completely, then the excited chatter began. Even with a thousand doubts between them, they embraced the project. They fired questions at the three of them until supper was served, then for three hours after they ate. He distributed a business plan and a pro forma profit and loss statement he'd spent the last couple of weeks preparing. By the time the evening was over, Steve had commitments, including Bigsam's and the other St. Regis casino owners, for thirty-five of the fifty million he needed.

And almost as important, he had commitments for the manpower and the unique backup he needed. In two weeks, tribes from all over the country would be awaiting his call.

When they finished for the evening, Felicia Ann Garrity had given up and was nowhere to be seen.

Lying in his bed that night, Steve was both elated and apprehensive. A miss could be as good as a mile in this instance. He'd been conservative in the amount of money he'd need, and if he didn't have enough, could easily fail. He needed forty million and change just to close on the real estate, and a minimum of ten million for bare-bones equipment and operating capital. That would only give the appearance of a casino, would certainly not be anywhere near what they would eventually require. Still, it was a hell of a beginning.

But what now? He needed fifteen million more at the minimum. Whom could he turn to? He had a passing thought of Aldo Giovanni, but put it out of his mind. He knew the cost would be far too great.

He did have two other sources to try, but both would be a long shot. The Arab American Bank had been active in financing Native American gambling establishments, and Steve had dealt with them before. The problem was, they'd want all the t's crossed and the i's dotted. Odds were, this deal, without years acquiring city and state approvals, would scare them to death. His other source, Backbay Ltd., was a Hong Kong company who'd dallied in financing Native gambling projects, but they, too, were astute and would surely not take a huge risk on a project without proper governmental approvals.

This weekend he would have to prepare for both his meetings

with the State of New York attorney general's office and with potential financiers.

The pressure was building, a steam boiler with the needle bouncing off the red peg. Next Wednesday he had to be ready to turn loose two million bucks; he would be almost totally committed.

And he had heard nothing from Tom Webster and the Scohomacs.

Their silence was deafening.

CHAPTER TWENTY-NINE

Bright and early Saturday morning, Steve got a call from Felicia Ann Garrity. He wanted to meet with her, but he needed a strategy meeting with David Greenberg first, and his strong right arm, Paula. David had been working on a public relations plan, and Felicia's obvious interest in gambling could play right into that program—assuming she was sympathetic with the Native American cause. Her interest could also backfire and she could sabotage them. Steve had enough experience with the press to know how fickle they could be. Ratings were everything, and who got run over in the process seemed inconsequential.

He made arrangements to meet her in the afternoon. Wanting a civil atmosphere and knowing how ladies seemed to enjoy the pastime, he suggested high tea at the Plaza.

She laughed. "You afraid next time I'll sue over the rug burns, counselor?"

"No, ma'am. Just thought you'd enjoy a little civility."

"I would, actually."

"Felicia, leave your camera and recorders home. I'll level with you as much as I can, but I want some of that rare commodity, discretion. At least until it's time to bring the dogs out from under the porch."

"You have such a way with words, Stephen. However, you've tickled my discreet button. I can't wait."

"See you at the Plaza at four P.M. This time I'll make the reservations."

He called David as soon as he hung up and made arrangements to meet him for lunch. As soon as he hung up the receiver, Thad phoned to check on the day's schedule. Steve asked him to arrange for a car to drive, and to invite Paula. Thad would join him, David, and Paula for lunch, then act as driver to the Plaza meeting.

It had been a long and eventful week. Steve indulged himself with a steam, then a leisurely shower. He had hoped his ever-present thoughts of Angela would lessen as time went on, but it seemed he thought of her a hundred times a day, and saw her everywhere. Every woman with shoulder-length dark hair, every woman with a slim, shapely figure received a stare, thinking—secretly hoping—it might be Angela.

As he stood in front of his bathroom mirror, he examined his chest. The soreness and bruising were almost gone. Had the photographer given up his attempts on his life? He doubted it. The man had already demonstrated his patience. Steve hoped he might resolve the matter before the man's patience paid off. He had received a verbal update from Stanley Reporting only the day before, and learned, among other things, that Nick Masticelli played golf every Sunday afternoon, weather permitting, at Stamford Glen Golf and Country Club. He planned to have Thad drive him up tomorrow.

Steve was not convinced that Nick Masticelli was the man in the dark suit, but his build and height were the same, and he had to follow up on the possibility. He had to get rid of his threat. He had no time for the breath of the bear scorching the back of his neck.

Thad arrived, checked to make sure Steve had his vest on—and this time Steve didn't complain—and they drove to Mama Gold's deli to meet David and Paula. David laid out his plan for the media campaign, then Steve questioned him regarding Felicia's sympathies. As he expected, David answered, "She's sympathetic—with ratings."

"I'm meeting with her this afternoon, David. I want to give her something to keep her interested." Thad shot him a knowing smile, but he ignored it. "I know she's working on a story on gambling, and I'd like to get that airtime when we're ready to spill the beans about our plans. We're going to need all the public support we can muster."

"Sarah told me they're working on a special, not just a story. The theme so far is illegal gambling in New York City, but she could probably be swayed if the story is big enough."

"I'll do what I can to sway the lady without letting the cat out of the bag." He turned to Paula. "How are the battle plans coming?"

"Great. I've got trucks and deliveries lined up. Two days from the time you give me the word, I'll have those trucks rolling and a division of people on the move."

That afternoon Steve sat in the lobby of the Plaza, surrounded by chocolate- and sugar-adorned silver tea trays and fur- and silk-adorned silver-haired women. He eyed the opulence of the place. The rococo architecture and bold-patterned carpet and drapes reminded him of Europe. *Well, Standing Bear, we're soaring with the eagles now,* he thought, laughing quietly to himself. *Now let's hope we don't get shot down like a goose.* Of course, it was four-twenty before Felicia arrived. Stunning, as usual, in a blue suit with gray fur collar and cuffs, molded to the perfect body. As usual, she made her way from party to party until she finally settled in across a small mother-of-pearl-inlaid table from Steve.

"Okay, counselor, what's all the cloak and dagger about?"

"About the biggest story of the year for you, Felicia."

"Really? I'm working on a pretty big one right now."

"Illegal gambling in the city is a big story, but not a new one. How about one that'll make the national and international news? And a special to end all specials."

"How did you know what I was working on?" When he just smiled, she continued. "All right, I'm all ears."

"I can't tell you yet, but I can guarantee that you'll be the first and only reporter with an inside line on what's happening."

"Sounds like I should keep working on the story I'm on. It's bigger than you might think, counselor. I've got pictures of people who don't want to be seen gambling in an illegal place."

Steve laughed, then was interrupted by a waitress clad in a black dress with a white lace apron. She took Felicia's order for tea, then reappeared with a tray full of decadent goodies. Felicia selected only one, then her attention turned back to Steve.

"So, you see, counselor, your story had better be huge, because mine is going to blow the roof off local politics."

"Bigsam told me you had a video camera in your purse and just about got him scalped. He said the no-necks beat your camera into tinker's trash on the sidewalk. How did you get out of there with tape?"

"Used up a cartridge, then used the bathroom. I got away with three tapes—Bigsam must have thought I had bladder infection. Tapes are little in an eight-millimeter cam, about the size of a music tape. They fit nicely under a bra strap."

"So, what faces did you get?" Steve asked, curious as to whom she'd caught on tape.

"Can't tell you yet." She mimicked his deep voice.

He smiled. "Touché. But I guarantee my story is much bigger. And I'll tell you this much; it'll rock politics both here and across the country and catch the interest of the whole world. It's bigger than Custer's Last Stand, and they're still airing it a hundred and twenty years later. Can you wait awhile to air yours?"

She was silent for a moment. "How long?"

"I have a meeting Monday, then I'll begin filling you in, given your solemn word you won't air anything, or even tell your network about what's coming down, until I'm ready."

The tea arrived, and Felicia waited until the waitress moved away. "So, will I be old and gray before I can roll tape?"

"A week, maybe two."

She smiled mischievously. "Why would I trust a guy who'd call in the hotel wax brigade?"

"Hell, Felicia, you'd have used a Russian tank brigade to get in if one had been handy. Besides, that was Thad's idea. And a good one, you must admit."

"Good for you, maybe . . . Okay, Drum. One week, maybe ten days, then I'm running with what I have."

Steve's face hardened. "Felicia, I've got to ask this. I'm involved in something that has to have good press. The very best, if it's to succeed. Can you get behind something that's for the good of all Native Americans, a lot of people who need a lot of help . . . all across the United States?"

"Sure, if it's what you say it is, and, of course, if it's a superb human interest story. If you watch the news, you know that good news is seldom a great story, but if it is . . ."

That's honest, Steve thought, *not necessarily admirable, but honest.* He extended his hand, and they shook.

Now he had some work to do on his proposed agreement with the State of New York, since a good part of Sunday would be taken up driving to Stamford and confronting Nick Masticelli. At the least, maybe he could ruin the man's golf game.

Then Monday he was off to see the attorney general to negotiate on behalf of a client who *hadn't* retained him. He wondered now if he was putting not only his total net worth but his shingle at risk. Hell, he was in so deep now . . .

Thad picked him up in a Litcomb car at eleven-thirty A.M. and they pulled up at the pro shop of the Stamford Glen club just at one P.M. Masticelli's standing tee-off time was one-fifteen. The weather was broken, with only gray sky peeking through a low layer of heavy cotton-candy cumulus. The hardwood conifers forming hedgerows between the fairways rose starkly, almost denuded of leaves. The frost left a damp sheen on the grass. Rain was predicted.

Steve had briefed Thad on the ride up. Since they were on their way to see "family," Steve had the 9mm in a holster in the small of his back, concealed by the corduroy coat he wore. Thad carried his own Glock, under a loose New York Jets green nylon jacket, and had a pistol-gripped riot gun loaded with double-aught buck under the front seat. Steve thought they were being a little overcautious, then again, he'd hate to be at the bottom of the eleventh-hole water hazard wearing concrete golf shoes. As Thad had informed him, the road to hell is *not* paved with caution; and fire, at times, was best fought with fire.

Steve entered the pro shop while Thad stayed outside.

Anticlimatically, the attendant informed him that Mr. Masticelli had canceled due to the likelihood of inclement weather. About that, Masticelli was right. Light mist began to chill Steve's face as he stepped out of the pro shop door.

Disappointed, Steve and Thad returned to the town car.

"Now what?" Thad asked, turning the engine over.

"Tony Bambino's."

"What?"

"Second choice on a Sunday. It's an Italian restaurant with a card room in the back. If he's not here, he's probably there."

"So," Thad asked as they pulled away, "we're charging into

an Italian den of black hands to accuse one of them of being a lowlife back-shooter? John Wayne all the way."

Steve smiled. "You can wait in the car."

"I wouldn't miss it. Better than any afternoon matinee."

It took them the better part of an hour to locate the place on Stamford's east side. The sign, smaller than a dinner tray, was covered with soot, as were the windows. Steve was surprised when he entered to find the place immaculate. The black-and-white harlequin-tiled floor gleamed. Only a dozen red-checker-clothed, dark, square tables graced the front, each flanked with four straight-back chairs. The mahogany bar couldn't have seated over ten, and was old enough to have had a million red wines, or even redder Camparis across it. Two elderly Italian ladies worked plates of pasta, not their first, judging by their ample waistlines and double chins. Otherwise the place was empty of customers. An aproned gray-haired man stood behind the bar, washing glasses and wearing black-rimmed ones thicker than the bottoms of any he shined. Mandolin music emanated from some hidden speakers. Next to the bar, a pass-through indicated the kitchen, then three doors, the first two marked SIGNORI and SIGNORE making him believe the third must lead to the card room.

As soon as they entered the restaurant, the man behind the bar approached, forcing a smile devoid of one front tooth fairly well camouflaged under a wiry salt-and-pepper handlebar mustache. He extended a pair of menus.

"No, thanks," Steve said, moving toward the third door with Thad close on his heels. "Card room," Steve exclaimed quietly, waving the man off.

"Hey, that's members only." The man's heavy brows furrowed.

"I'm invited." Before the man could reply, Steve had his hand on the knob.

The room was smoky, a thick layer hanging shoulder height, with as many tables inside as were in the dining room and a lot more customers. The odor of workingmen and stale cigars struck him. Two dozen men, some in silk suits, some in work clothes, sat around, most with smokes dangling from their mouths, playing cards. Four, built like longshoremen, their sleeves rolled up above the elbows. forearm veins bulging, played darts.

The room silenced when Steve and Thad entered, and eyes locked on the strangers in faces seemingly devoid of interest. But stares belied the lack. Steve's eyes searched from table to table until he met gazes with Nick Masticelli, who lounged with three other men at his table. A bottle of grappa and scattered playing cards were the table's only adornment. Without hesitation, Steve crossed the room and stopped an arm's length away.

"I need to talk to you."

Disinterested, he shrugged. "I'm playing cards here—"

"Outside, or here?"

Masticelli smiled, and gave the other men at his table a shake of the head, obviously signaling he thought Steve posed no threat. "How about lunch? This place is primo."

"Okay."

Steve spun on his heel with Thad close behind. Masticelli followed them out, then waved them to a table in a back corner. It didn't surprise Steve when two of the men, a pair of no-necks, exited the card room and took a table only a few feet away.

"So, what's on your mind. Drum, wasn't it?"

"Drum it was. This is my friend, Thad. Thad, Nick Masticelli." The two men shook hands.

Masticelli's look was a little too smug to suit Steve, but then, he was well across the line of demarcation onto Masticelli's home turf. The gray-haired waiter immediately brought a plate of antipasti and a bottle of red wine, three stem glasses interdigitated in one hand. He set them down without a word, then returned to his station behind the bar.

"Hope you don't mind, but Enrico knows what I like. Trust me, you'll like it too. What brings you to east Stamford?" Masticelli asked.

Before Steve could answer, a woman with breasts the size of cantaloupes bulging in a peasant blouse, and a face almost as round, appeared in the pass-through. The waiter picked up and delivered a bowl of steaming soup, ladle, and bowls. Masticelli served them, dropping a piece of toast into each bowl before ladling in soup looking like a simple bouillon and a perfect round egg yolk onto the toast. "*Zuppa pavese,*" Nick said, then translated. "Egg soup."

Again he asked, his curiosity obvious, "What brings you here?"

"A little trouble. Nothing I can't handle, but a little trouble."

Nick blew on a spoonful of soup, eyeing him over it, then

sucked it down. He dabbed at his mouth with a checkered napkin. "So, what brings you to me."

"I guess your size and build, Masticelli. Someone's been using me for target practice. I saw the guy a few days ago. He got lucky and put one right here." Steve tapped the center of his chest.

Masticelli smiled. "You heal quick."

"Man of steel," Steve said, returning the smile.

"You still haven't said what brings you here."

"Like I said, you're the same size and build as the shooter."

This time Masticelli laughed out loud. "Over what? Angela? Besides, gumba, if I came for you, you'd be cold meat." He eyed Steve a long while. "We quit that kind of action around here years ago."

"Nevertheless, what's your relationship with Angela?"

Masticelli smiled again, albeit tightly this time. "What's it to you? Angela is Papa Al's daughter, that's enough for you to know. Enough for anyone."

"So, you don't have a bone to pick with me?"

"If I did, it'd be picked clean, gumba." Masticelli's look hardened. "You got some kind of brass balls, coming here to accuse me. You sit at my table and accuse me. If we did still believe in the kind of thing you're talking about, this would be reason enough."

The two men eyed each other for a moment, until Steve broke the silence. "Not accusing, inquiring. . . . I may be wrong. The man had a mask. You hear anything on the street about who might be after me?"

"Shit, chief, could be Wyatt Earp for all I know. Who's wife are you dickin'?"

Steve rose slowly. "*Grazie* . . . for the soup."

"*Prego* . . . the soup. But hang around. You entertain me. *Insalata caprese* is up next."

"No, thanks. Do me a favor and keep your ears open regarding this thing."

"Okay . . . I can do that."

"And another, treat Angela very, very well."

Nick Masticelli laughed again. "I always have. Since college. I wouldn't treat the daughter of Aldo Giovanni any other way."

"See you around," Steve said, heading for the door with Thad on his heels. He glanced back to see Masticelli wave the two men who'd followed them out of the card room over to join him.

When they drove away, Thad shook his head. "Didn't get much out of that. Good soup though."

Steve merely stared out the window.

When they wheeled up on the expressway, Thad spoke again. "Who's Angela?"

Steve shrugged, still looking out the window. "Just a lady. Someone I've known for a long time."

"A pretty lady?" Thad asked, some humor in his voice.

"Shut up and drive, Wintermoose."

"Okay, just one more question. Did we come here because of the shooter, or some lady named Angela?"

"Shut the fuck up and drive."

The tone of Steve's voice being what it was, Thad decided to shut up and drive. When Steve reached the apartment, he checked his answering machine, then called the one at the office. Tom Webster still hadn't called.

Maybe he never would.

Tomorrow he'd meet with Andrew Upton with the state attorney general's office. Another critical cornerstone in the foundation he was trying to build.

Maybe a clay one. Without this piece of business, the whole thing would become a pile of worthless rubble.

CHAPTER THIRTY

Steve, with Thad shadowing him, took an early commuter flight to Albany, and, leaving Wintermoose in the waiting room, was shown into Upton's office exactly on time.

Thin faced with fine gray-blond hair, Upton extended a long-boned hand. His immaculate demeanor seemed a little out of place in a spartan state office. He seemed to be merely passing through, and if Steve judged his ambitions correctly, that was just what he was attempting to do.

Steve took a seat across his desk, refused coffee, and got right to the point.

"I have a client, a Native American group, who's in the process of becoming acknowledged as a tribe."

Upton's countenance became a little pained.

"Of course, since they're not acknowledged," Steve continued, "they have no reservation. No place to call home. It's our hope the state will cooperate with us in establishing a home for these people. They have been almost three centuries without one."

Steve awaited Upton's reaction. "How can the state help?" he asked.

"Certainly it behooves the current administration to help its constituency, particularly those of lower economic levels who really need assistance. The state can begin by recognizing the tribe; of course that's an informal action, since it has no bearing on their federal acknowledgment. Then, if the state has excess land somewhere, it might make that available—"

"You think the state should *give* these people a reservation?" Upton shook his head.

"No one said anything about 'giving,' Mr. Upton. My clients already have a valid historical claim against a substantial parcel of land. Land actually deeded to them long ago, and, if our resources as to the chain of title are correct, was never legally acquired by subsequent owners. In fact, it appears the land was stolen . . . but that's another subject for another time. That land doesn't belong to the State of New York, so you couldn't give it, or sell it, to my client if you wanted to. All I'm looking for at the moment is some recognition by the state . . . some sympathy with their plight. It would be of help to their cause, and, of course, it would be politically expedient for you and your party. There are several hundred thousand Native American voters in New York State"—Steve exaggerated many times over—"and hundreds of thousands who sympathize with their plight."

Upton seemed enticed and relieved at the same time. He cleared his throat. "Of course, if these people are legally Native American, proven to be, then I see no problem with some kind of state recognition of that fact. Where, by the way, is the property they claim?"

"Can't divulge that quite yet. You appreciate the fact there's a pending lawsuit, which I'm not yet prepared to discuss."

"Of course—"

"There was a recent archaeological discovery, you may have read about it in *The New York Times*. DNA material from that discovery has been evaluated, and my clients, from the Finger Lakes region, have proven themselves to be direct descendants." Steve handed him a legal-sized manila envelope. "Here is the scientific proof of my clients' claims. Please have it evaluated in whatever manner you wish."

Upton accepted the envelope and rose, seemingly pleased that this was all Steve wanted in regard to his clients.

Steve rose also and accepted Upton's handshake. "Thank you, Mr. Upton. A mere letter from your office, addressed to the Bureau of Indian Affairs if you so desire, will be a great help in getting this thing moving for my clients. I can guarantee you and your office will receive a lot of positive press on this. The newspapers have been very sympathetic with Native American causes across the state."

"Where exactly are these people now?"

"Way out west in the Finger Lakes area, in the hills near Penn Yan. You know Indians," Steve said with a smile, "they like the deep forests and lakes. Their demands are only for a parcel of a thousand acres or so. And it's not prime farmland." Steve purposefully let the man believe the Scohomac claim would be for a parcel in the Finger Lakes region. He hadn't lied; their demand certainly was not for prime farmland.

"Of course. Hiawatha and all of that."

"And all of that," Steve said, excusing himself.

He paused at Upton's office door. "May I call you the middle of the week?"

"Of course you may call, but I doubt if I'll have anything so quickly."

"Have some DNA expert look at the material . . . maybe the State Forensic Division at the medical examiner's office."

"A good idea. I'll do that. I'll messenger it over this morning."

It was a first step.

As they headed back to the Albany airport, Thad questioned him. "Well, then, are we under way?"

"It took six days for God to create the earth, Thad. I plan to take at least as long bringing this thing to a head."

"And probably making about as much trouble."

Steve smiled. "A chunk, that's for sure. The snake is definitely loose in the garden."

Late that same afternoon, after a quick commuter flight back from Albany, Steve and Thad walked into the Arab American Bank and met with a vice president Steve had dealt with before. He was hindered by the fact he couldn't divulge the deal, and even so, was not surprised when the bank expressed only a passing interest in financing a nonspecific Indian gaming establishment.

The next morning he went to see Backbay, Ltd. Although they expressed far more interest, Steve was still hindered by the fact he couldn't detail the transaction. He was in a quandary, hamstrung by the necessity of secrecy.

Tuesday afternoon he called Aldo Giovanni and found himself

invited to dinner on Wednesday night at the Giovanni compound in northwest Bergen County. He tried his best to get Papa Al to see him immediately, but the older man was adamant.

That afternoon Steve took a deep, calming breath and called Cookie Yamamoto. Or, more correctly, returned his many calls. "Cookie, this is the day, and I'm ready to drop the two mil. But I'm faxing you over an instruction. I want that escrow perfect. I want the assignments of the leases, and the deed in the escrow and executed. I want to be able to walk into the escrow company and close the deal unilaterally, anytime between now and December 31, by merely tendering the money. And more important, I want to be able to waive the requirement to record the transaction. Agreed?"

"That's a strange request."

"Strange, but necessary in this instance. The risk is purely on my side if it's not recorded. Asian American will still have their money and mortgage. I just may need to take the city and county government out of the equation."

"It is a bit of a stretch, but I can make that all happen."

"Then do so. I'm also faxing the escrow company with an instruction to release the deposit funds to Asian American if and only if the escrow is perfect."

There was no turning back now.

He did one more thing before leaving the office. Punching in ICOM on the computer, he was thrilled to see that ICOM had announced the Hovenweep discovery. It had pushed their shares to 40½ and they were being heavily traded.

It looked like it could be headed for fifty dollars a share, its all-time high.

He called Jonathan Noble, his friend and broker. "Jonathan, you've got to be ready to do something for me, and it's got to be done just right. . . ."

It had been years since he'd been to the Giovanni home, but as he suspected, little had changed.

He convinced Thad to stay at a bar and restaurant near the expressway and drove himself the final mile. He had mixed emotions as he drove up the long, winding driveway, particularly when he passed the turnoff to Angela's cottage and caught a glimpse of it across the pond. He both relished and despised the thought of seeing her. He felt like a hollow man, his heart bouncing around inside a shell. He parked the town car near the front entrance, then walked across slate paving stones, the moss covering them now brown and lifeless.

With a deep sigh he pushed the bell and was quickly greeted by a black maid in a simple black dress with a white lace apron. She was new, if nothing else had changed.

"Mr. Giovanni asked me to show ya'll into the men's den, Mr. Drum. Would you care for something to drink?"

"Scotch, neat, please."

Al was not in the room, so Steve picked up a cue and began a game of rotation on the intricately carved mahogany table. He'd just sunk the two ball, when Angela strode in, carrying his scotch.

She wore a simple black sheath, modestly low cut, a gold chain around her narrow waist and a pair of hoop earrings the only accents. She didn't need even those.

"Your drink," she said, handing it to him as if they'd just been talking in the other room moments before.

He took a second to compose himself, along with the drink. "How are you, Angela?"

"Fine, thank you." She moved back around the pool table and leaned against it. "Don't let me interrupt your game."

"You look radiant. Something is agreeing with you." *Not seeing me, probably,* he thought.

"Something is," she said, a slightly sad smile ghosting across her face, then she smiled genuinely. "I've been at the beach house for a while."

"Aw, you always did love the beach."

"It's quiet." *And has wonderful memories,* she thought.

He started to ask if she'd been to the city, but her father walked in and extended his hand. Steve shook, and Angela excused herself. "I'll see you at supper," she said.

Steve merely nodded, watched her walk away, then turned his full attention to Al Giovanni.

"So, Stephen, it'sa been too long."

"You only had to invite me, Al."

"No, I should not have-a to invite you, Stephen. You shoulda come see your friends once in a while."

He was right. Steve should have kept in touch with the man

who had been so helpful to him over the years, no matter what his relationship with Al's daughter.

"We all get taken up with our own affairs, Al."

"That'sa true—"

"Still, I should have paid my respects, and I hope you don't think me ungrateful."

"Mama and I like to see you once in a while . . . so, what brings you thisa time?"

Steve smiled. "Now I'm afraid to say, Al. I feel like a wayward son who comes around only when he wants something."

"We always thought of you as a son, Steve. I'ma used to sons who only come asking. So ask."

"How is Tony?"

Al picked another cue out of the rack and lined up on the three ball. "He's just Tony. We haven't seen him for a while."

Al shot, missing a hard cut to a side pocket.

"But everything's okay . . . between you and Tony?" Steve asked.

"We haven't seen him for a while," Al repeated, obviously not wanting to talk about his son. "So, what brings you to Saddle River?"

Steve was leaning over the table, lining up the three ball for his own shot, but paused and straightened. "I need fifteen million, Al."

Al eyed him for a moment, took a sip of his Campari and soda, then smiled. "You don'ta come just asking, Stephen, you come with a wheelbarrow."

"You want to hear about the deal? If not, we can make this just dinner—"

"I'ma listen."

For an hour Steve spun the background and then his plans. Finally, Al stopped him.

"So, whadda I get for my fifteen mil?"

"Nothing from this deal but interest. This is a *paisano* deal, Al. My *paisans*, not yours. This is a Native American opportunity, and nobody else is going to participate. It's been too long, and Native Americans have given up too much."

Al paused and eyed Steve as if he were a few cards short of a deck, then he shrugged. "Stephen, you know my business well enough to know, I'ma no bank."

"I know that, Al, but I'm gonna put you on to another deal that will make you happy you made me the loan."

"How happy?"

Steve took a deep breath. He was about to give up his last safety net, his last hope to save anything and come out whole if the Rockefeller Center deal went in the tank. Of course, if it went in the tank, he'd probably spend the rest of his prime years in the penitentiary, so what did it matter . . . "Ten, maybe twenty mil happy, and all before the end of the year."

Al took a long drink, then nodded. "I'ma feel more like a bank alla the time."

With only the four of them at a table holding a dozen, Steve found himself seated next to Angela, with Mama across the table and Al at its head. Steve would have rather been across the table from her, as it was conspicuous when he turned to look at her, and he would have liked to continue to stare at her during all of supper.

They made small talk, Steve asking about Europe, them inquiring about his business. Finally, Angela surprised him with a question. "I hear you called on Nick Masticelli, something about some trouble you've been having?"

Steve finished chewing a bite of prime rib, swallowed, and took a sip of wine. "Actually, I did go to Connecticut to see him. I thought he might help me with a small problem I've been having." He felt as if shards of glass coursed his veins, but he asked anyway. "You still seeing Nick?"

"Seeing? I—"

Al quickly interrupted. "Stephen, I also heard you were-a throwing the ivories at a couple of the joints in the city. A little risky for a man in the business, don'ta you think?"

It was all Steve could do to turn his attention away from Angela, but he did, and it was probably a good thing, as the heat was crawling up his backbone. "Yeah, a little risky. But I needed some info about the competition in town, and that particular competition can't be analyzed any other way."

Steve shook his head. "You all amaze me. You know more about what I'm doing than I do."

Al smiled. "It'sa good business to know what your friends and your enemies are up to."

Steve wondered if Al was sending him some kind of mixed message. If his statement was really a question.

"Are you ready for dessert?" Mama asked, then, without awaiting an answer, turned to the kitchen door and called for the maid.

When they'd finished, Al invited him back to the den for a cigar and a brandy. After they'd lit up, Al blew a bellow of smoke. He surveyed Steve and his eyes went reptilian. "You know, Stephen, I consider you family, but you still have to do the right thing." Steve presumed he was about to get some kind of lecture regarding Angela. Even the question about her dating Masticelli probably upset Al, but that wasn't it. "Thisa money you want, this is beyond family. This is serious business. You sure you canna pay this back?"

"Of course I'm sure, Al. If I couldn't pay it back, I wouldn't ask." That was an exaggeration, Steve knew. He wondered if he really could pay it back. So many things could go wrong.

Al drew deeply on the cigar and blew another cloud of smoke. He was very deliberate when he spoke again. "You got to be sure, Stephen. You got to betta your life on this one."

Steve was a bit taken aback. He knew exactly what Al meant, and knew he was betting his *life* on his ability to repay. Al was not a man who could let an unpaid debt, particularly a major one, go unpaid. Still, he was a little disappointed in Al even thinking he had to make the statement. As deliberately as Al had been, Steve replied. "Al, I *wouldn't* borrow it if I *couldn't* pay it back. I understand what's at risk when I come to your family for money."

Al shrugged. "What's the giverish?"

"Ten, hell, twelve percent is the best we can do. Interest only annually, all due in five years."

"Make it three. I may be meeting St. Peter before five. You calla my bank when you want the money, and a tell them where to transfer the funds. I'll wait for your call on the other thing. If it works, okay. If not, okay. But if it don'ta work, I expect you to go back to the old deal, anda find me a source for a few truckloads o' cigarettes, say fifty semi trucks. The feds are about to raise the taxes again, and every carton is gonna be worth maybe ten to twenty-five dollars more in tax."

"The deal is gonna work the way I told you, Al."

"But if itta don't, I want your word."

It was an old fight between them, and one of the primary reasons Steve had parted ways with the Giovanni interests years earlier. In an effort to impress Al, Steve had set up an illegal transaction with some reservation sources and arranged for a few truckloads of cigarettes for Al to sell in his vending machines. The reservations paid no federal tax on cigarettes, and butt-legging them to outside sellers was a common practice, so common it was closely watched by the FBI. Steve had balked when Al wanted him to go into the practice full-time, and it was eventually the wedge that caused him to leave Al's organization. Al, obviously, still wanted to keep his thumb on Steve, wanted him back.

Al was a thumbs-on kind of guy.

It was petty crime so far as Steve was concerned, and the last thing he wanted to become involved in.

But now Al held all the cards.

"If it doesn't work, I'll go to work on the cigarette thing . . . but I won't have to, Al. It's gonna work."

"Okay. Just so we're clear, you betta it all on the loan, and you'll come-a back to work for me if the other thing don'ta work."

"At least for fifty semi loads." Steve extended his hand, and they shook.

When he left, Angela walked him out to the car, garnering a glare from Papa Al for her effort.

"You haven't exactly burned the phone lines up lately," she said as soon as they got out of earshot of the house.

"We never did have much of a phone affair," Steve said, a little sarcasm in his tone.

"No, I guess we didn't."

"I'm glad to see you looking so well, Angela. You are one beautiful woman."

She smiled. "And I'm glad to see your still blind . . . I used to think it was by love."

Steve opened the door to the town car and stepped into the driver's seat without comment. The truth was, he was too choked up to speak. And his reaction made him angry. He put the key in the ignition, then hit the window button. Angela put both hands on the car door, studying him, still awaiting some reply.

"And you were right," Steve managed to say, "I was." He turned the engine over.

"How soon they forget," Angela said, studying his face.

"I'll see you around, Miss Giovanni," Steve said, and slipped the car into reverse. Had he waited another second, he knew he was angry enough that he would leap from the car and take her in his arms, Papa Al and his fifteen million be damned.

Al stood at the window, watching, his hands folded behind his back.

"That would be nice, Mr. Drum," she said, a strange, wistful sound in her voice. Steve started to back up, then she added. "I'll be at the Pen a week from this Friday. Give me a call."

Heat flooded his backbone. "Nick out of town? Obviously you're talking with him regularly!" He immediately regretted his outburst.

She didn't miss a beat; he could see her Italian temper flare. "For a smart Harvard attorney, you can be one dumb, hardheaded—"

He merely backed the car away, spinning the wheels when he sped down the driveway.

To his surprise, there was a faxed letter awaiting him at the office on Thursday morning, from Upton and the attorney general's office. It was addressed to the Bureau of Indian Affairs, but the cover sheet said Upton had mailed it directly to him. It read, in part:

> The New York State Attorney General's office, in cooperation with the New York State Police Forensics Laboratory, has reviewed the evidence provided, i.e., DNA comparison strips, and concluded that Mr. Thomas T. Webster, and other self-proclaimed Scohomac Indians, are in fact blood related to that certain sample identified herein as the Andrew McGuire Building discovery of Canarsee tribal remains.
>
> This office, of course, is not issuing a legal opinion as to the validity of any claim by the Scohomacs in regard to tribal or reservation status. . . .

It went on with a page and a half of disclaimers, but the first step toward acknowledgment had been taken.

Steve smiled as he read the letter, then moments later his smile widened. A FedEx man arrived with a delivery from Tom Webster, and the envelope contained Steve's management agreement, executed with only a small change. Webster had enlisted a half dozen elders to join him in signing.

Steve's ducks were in a row; it was time to act.

Steve called his people together.

When their meeting broke up, things began to buzz around the Native American Improvement Coalition and the Red Ace Corporation.

The next morning Steve called Felicia Ann Garrity and made an appointment to meet her in his office, with a cameraman this time. She arrived promptly at ten A.M. as promised. And as promptly admonished him, "This had better be good, Drum. I'm missing a major announcement at the United Nations to be here."

"Was Mother Teresa good?" Steve laughed. "You be the judge. I want one thing understood, and it's a subject that will determine if you're to be our liaison with the world out there on an ongoing basis."

"So now the bad news?" she asked, her face falling.

"Not really. My stipulation is that there be no editing of my initial statement. Each time you air it, you air it in total. The rest of our interview you can do with as you may."

"You got it, now give it up."

He had them set up the camera, including putting a remote mike under his collar, and first do a shot of Felicia introducing him. "The man you're about to meet," she began, "is New York attorney Stephen Sounding Drum. He's practiced law here in New York and New Jersey for over ten years and is nationally considered an expert in Native American affairs. Mr. Drum?"

Steve remained sitting behind his desk as the camera zoomed in for a head-and-shoulders shot. He spread out the notes of his statement, carefully prepared by David, Paula, and himself.

"Ladies and gentlemen, my associate, Paula Fox, formerly a distinguished professor of archaeology at NYU, recently made a startling and historic discovery in a long-sealed cave adjacent to the basement of a midtown Manhattan building. Subsequent to that discovery, we have called together the finest group of scientists in the country and abroad to verify our findings.

"It has now been well documented.

"The Canarsee Indians, whose direct descendants, the Scohomac Indians of the Finger Lakes area—still a viable tribal entity—once occupied and owned a substantial portion of Manhattan Island. This ownership was many years subsequent to the historically inaccurate reporting of the trade of a handful of beads for Manhattan Island. The Canarsee obtained their land for good and valuable consideration, services rendered, by a valid deed. In my opinion, an opinion I know will be borne out by the federal courts, they still own that land.

"One thousand acres of Manhattan real estate do not belong to some of you watching this news report."

CHAPTER THIRTY-ONE

Felicia's eyes began to widen.

"In a few days," Steve continued, "I'm filing a claim and quiet title action on approximately one thousand sixty acres consisting of a good portion of the upper East Side, all of the Carnegie Hill area, and a good portion of Spanish Harlem. From the center of Central Park to the East River, from Seventy-ninth north to One twentieth. It's my sincere hope the mayor's office and the State of New York will enter into negotiations to settle this claim in a fair and timely manner, before court action is necessary.

"The Canarsee and their direct descendants, the Scohomacs, have already waited over three hundred years.

"Let me assure you, when we prevail, we will deal fairly with all who have been damaged by false deeds and all who are now tenants of those damaged. We don't expect you to just walk away from property you or your ancestors bought in good faith. As soon as this matter is settled, and what is rightfully the Scohomacs returned, taxes will be all but waived, and consequently rents in those areas affected will be lowered by twenty to twenty-five percent to reflect the fact that Indian lands pay no city, state, or federal taxes. I hope that fact softens the economic effects of our claims as to how they impact the good citizens now residing in the disputed area.

"Thank you for your time.

"That's it, Felicia."

"Just a second, let me catch my breath, then I want to interview you."

"I suspected so. But I want your guarantee that you'll not air this until tomorrow, say ten A.M."

She analyzed him suspiciously. "You sure I have an exclusive on this?"

"You're the only fish in the sea, at least until you air this tomorrow, then I expect there'll be a school snapping at the bait." He laughed, then turned serious. "Still, whenever I have an announcement, I'll give it to you exclusively long before the others get it . . . providing, of course, you remain fair and objective, and if you can bring your pretty little black heart to it, sympathetic to the Native American position."

"I'm fair, objective, and oh so sympathetic."

"Good," Steve said, "Now try and stay that way for a while."

She checked her makeup with a compact mirror, smoothed her hair, then stepped up and put the hand mike in his face.

She spent the better part of an hour doing her interview, then left in a hurry to put together what she hoped would be a special, usurping the morning soaps—and it had to be an important story to attain that status.

When she was finished, Steve cautioned her. "Sleep at home tonight, Felicia, and have your cameraman on standby. I'll be calling you about four-thirty A.M. to give you a location to visit at dawn. Then you'll have, as Paul Harvey says, the rest of the story."

"I guess eight-thirty would be out of the question?"

"Four-thirty, Felicia."

As soon as she left, Steve called Tom Webster. "Tomtom, thanks for returning the agreement. You won't be sorry. I've got to see you this evening. I'm chartering a plane, coming your way. I would like to buy your dinner and that of the other elders who executed the management agreement."

"I'll round 'em up," he said.

By midnight, Steve and Thad had returned to Manhattan. Tucked away in Steve's briefcase was an addendum to his management agreement clarifying Steve's position in the deal and appointing him as council of record signed by several amazed, and somewhat mystified, Scohomac elders and their chief. He also carried Tom Webster's promise to come on a moment's notice, and to bring his insulation equipment.

He didn't get much sleep that night, because at three A.M. Steve met with a group of Indians representing four different New York tribes, and shortly after four they had established camp. Carl Schurz Park was Steve's choice of a great camp location in the newly proclaimed village of Scohomac. Stretching a little over a quarter of a mile along the East River, the park was a scenic location. Resting well within the claimed area of the Scohomacs, it boasted one landmark familiar to all New Yorkers, Gracie Mansion. The residence of Mayor William Patrini, and many mayors before him.

Before the real action was to transpire, Steve excused himself, and he and Thad returned to the office. It wouldn't do to be arrested quite yet; he still had a lot to accomplish.

He stopped at a pay phone and called Al Giovanni on his private home office line. He knew Al's habits well, and knew the odds were good at catching him up and in his home office. Al didn't sleep the sleep of a man without worries. He said only a few words. "It's time. Call Noble and some of your own brokers. Remember, you've got to catch it on an up tic. You've got only a week."

At five-thirty A.M. a park policeman—at least one always remained on duty at the mayor's residence—wandered down to the activity to investigate. He was shown a perfectly forged park activity permit. He investigated it, yawned, and returned to his post near the mayor's driveway.

The mayor awoke early, just at dawn. It was his habit to don a sweat suit, and when time permitted, jog around the park at least twice with his chief aide, Terrence Thornburg, reluctantly gimping alongside. Two personal bodyguards followed.

That morning they had to jog only a hundred yards to find a full-blown Indian village. Wigwams were under construction, sheep, cattle, and horses grazed on hay strewn on the park's frost-burned sod and watered along the East River shoreline. Campfires roasted meat and boiled coffee.

As he and his entourage neared, Felicia Ann Garrity nodded to her cameraman and tape rolled.

A Mohawk elder in full tribal regalia stepped forward and greeted the mayor, whose astonishment caused him to pull up short. The old Indian raised his palm in a sign of peace, and said, "Welcome, Mr. Mayor, to Scohomac, ancestral land of the Canarsee and now the home of the Scohomac Indian tribe. You are welcome to visit anytime, but I've been instructed to request that you begin moving out of Gracie Mansion shortly, as we'd like to have it for our own chief."

The whole speech was accomplished while Mayor Patrini's mouth remained open.

Finally, he managed to ask, "You're putting me on?"

"No, Mr. Mayor," the old Indian said, "actually we're putting you out."

A police van and a hundred New York City cops were on the scene by eight A.M. Mounted policemen began herding Indian ponies, sheep, and cattle, while stoic Indians watched and gave advice. By eight-thirty, paddy wagons arrived and the Indians, too, were herded into cages.

Felicia was barely able to get back and get the remaining portion of her story edited into her special and shown to IBC's executive vice president by airtime. As she suspected, it aired at ten A.M. in lieu of the top-rated soap on the East Coast. Within ten minutes of the beginning of the half-hour piece, Steve Drum's phone began to ring. He could have had another one hundred lines and not been able to field the calls.

While he talked, another five hundred Indians from New York, New Jersey, Connecticut, and Pennsylvania began arriving in vans and trucks, pickups and horse trailers, with their stock. Central Park's Sheep Meadow began to fulfill its name and become one of the eastern United States's most populous Indian villages. Certainly the most populous tent village.

As Indians were arrested, more filled their places. They were coming from as far away as California, by the thousands.

And while New York's boys in blue were busy in Central and Carl Schurz parks with the diversion, the real invasion was under way. Since midnight, truck after truck of crated goods had been unloaded in the lower concourse of the GE Building, and freight elevators worked overtime distributing those crates to floors five, six, and seven. Patrick McGoogan and Joseph Bigsam, in city suits, directed a hundred Indians, each in moving-company coveralls. The GE Building maintained its own security force of over one hundred uniformed guards, but only ten worked the graveyard shift. Security had been advised well in advance of the move-in by the Native American Improvement Coalition. It was business as usual.

At ten forty-five A.M. Steve received a personal visit from Terrence Thornburg, the mayor's chief assistant. It seemed he couldn't get through on the telephone, and even had trouble elbowing his way through the reporters in the hall outside Steve's office.

"The mayor wants to see you, Mr. Drum," Thornburg said, his tone brusque.

Steve reached over and pushed his intercom button. "Sally, do we have any time open in the next couple of days?"

"Now, Drum! The mayor wants to see you *now!* There's a limo downstairs and a police escort. Get up, let's go."

Steve smiled. "Sorry, Mr. Thornburg, but I'm booked up. If the mayor would like to drop by, I'll squeeze him in."

Thornburg's face began to redden. "You don't know who you're dealing with, you son of a bitch."

Steve smiled even broader. "Actually, I do. I'm dealing with a man who's now mayor of a thousand less acres . . . or soon will be. A man who thinks that all of us in the United States are immigrants. He's a son of a . . . of an immigrant and a man who forgot that the original immigrants were greeted and helped by we sons o' bitches . . . the true Americans. Still, in spite of the gentleman's ignorance . . . my door's always open to the mayor, Mr. Thornburg."

The mayor's man stomped out, fists clenched at his sides. He was dialing his cellular phone before he reached the elevator.

At eleven-thirty the mayor's office managed to get through to the Red Ace Corporation on the telephone. Steve instructed Sally to wait to put him on until the mayor was on the line. Steve was not about to subject himself to the pecking order of politics.

When the mayor took the line, Steve took the call. "Mr. Mayor, nice to hear from you."

"Mr. Drum. Have we met?"

"Actually, no. I was one of the admiring throng at a Democratic fund-raiser a couple of years ago, and I was privileged . . . maybe that's the wrong word . . . to attend your Rainbow Dinner recently, but we weren't formally introduced either time."

"Well, good. Nevertheless, can you tell me just what it is you and your people are up to?"

Steve remained silent.

"Just what is it you're trying to accomplish?"

"Why, Mr. Mayor, I'd think it obvious by my statement to the press. We want what is rightfully the Scohomacs. I think I described the claim fairly well."

"You're kidding, of course. Work with me on this, Drum. Isn't this some kind of scam?"

"If you saw the Felicia Garrity special this morning on IBC, you saw a copy of the treaty and deed granting the land to the Scohomacs' predecessors, the Canarsee. We only want back what was stolen from them."

The mayor cleared his throat and his tone rang with officialese. "You ever hear of holders in due course, Mr. Drum?"

"I am an attorney, Mr. Mayor. I understand the concept of holder in due course. I also understand that my clients have been damaged."

"Then you're willing to suspend this invasion of Indians. Already we have over five hundred in jails and holding cells all over the city, and our jails were already full. The Central Park precinct has their holding tanks packed and Indians handcuffed all over the halls, as does the nineteenth. This has to stop." He paused a moment, then continued, his voice taking on an ominous tone. "In fact, I've been advised that *you* might be subject to an incitement-to-riot charge . . . and someone forged a number of park activity permits."

"My God, Mr. Mayor, you're not suggesting . . ." The humor was obvious in Steve's tone. "Actually, Mr. Mayor, when is a peaceful gathering of people considered a riot? Only in New York . . ."

"You may think it's small change, Mr. Drum, but—"

"I would think it below the mayor's office to threaten, Mr. Patrini. If you want to have the city attorney drop by and chat with me, that's fine. I would suggest he have a high-ranking gentleman from the state attorney general's office in attendance. In the meantime, I can't do anything about a lot of Indians who want only to come home to Manhattan. Why don't you offer them a handful of beads each, and maybe they'll go away."

"We have a lot of jail space in New York, Drum."

"And there are a lot of Indians in the United States, Mr. Mayor, over one million acknowledged, and many, many more who are not, and most of them are on the warpath to New York City as we speak. And we haven't yet appealed to our other Native American friends in Canada and Mexico. You'd better circle the wagons, Mr. Mayor. It could be a long, cold winter for all of us. Particularly since most of the city's steam vents are already taken by cardboard campers."

Patrini fell silent for a moment. "That crack about lowering rents was a low blow and deliberate ploy, Drum. We've had a thousand calls this morning, most of them from Spanish Harlem. If we don't have riots on our hands, it'll be a miracle."

"Sounds like the Latinos and blacks might join us in our cause. That's surprising." If the mayor could have seen Steve's grin, he would have been incensed. But Steve kept the smile out of his voice. "If that's the case, I suggest your people hurry up the process."

"My man will be available this afternoon. We'll have to have time to get someone from the AG's office. Say four P.M. here in City Hall?"

"Four is fine, but how about the Sheep Meadow in Central Park. Neutral ground. I'll make sure a tepee conference room is set up with a warm fire."

"You're pushing your luck, Drum."

"A bad habit of mine lately, Patrini; however, the press will love it, and you'll have a rare chance to be a hero, if this thing is quickly settled."

There was a long pause. "Okay, we'll sit down with you in the Sheep Meadow at four."

"Call off the dogs until after we powwow. I don't want anybody else arrested, and it would bode well if you released those who have been."

"Not likely."

"Then at least inform the parks people we're setting up there. You control the perimeter, but the Sheep Meadow is ours for the time being."

Patrini's voice rang with sarcasm. "You want I should send some city maintenance people, or maybe some cops, over to help play camp-out?"

"No, thanks, I don't think they'd know the intricacies of tepee erection, or any other kind. And by the way, Mr. Mayor, don't bother packing Gracie yet. Maybe we can resolve this in another way."

Steve buzzed Sally and asked her to hold his calls for twenty minutes. Ignoring the clamor out in the halls, he walked to the tall windows, sat down on his deep pile carpet, and crossed his legs under him.

Standing Bear, I need some council, he thought, and began to meditate.

His negotiations in the next meeting had to be as finely crafted as the most intricate winnowing basket.

CHAPTER THIRTY-TWO

At four-ten P.M., purposely a little late, Thad passed the Tavern-on-the-Green and the pair of black Lincolns parked there. As if he owned the place—which Steve was basically maintaining they did—he wheeled the rented town car through a line of cops up onto the grass and a hundred yards across it, parking directly in front of the tepee set up there and among the crowd of onlookers and participants gathered around it.

Steve stepped out of the back of the long car, having allowed Thad to chauffeur him in true big-dog-in-the-back fashion for a change. He stood for Felicia's camera for a moment, dressed for the first time in buckskins and moccasins, his hair bound in a simple beaded headband, a single eagle feather hanging at the rear. At his instruction, Felicia Garrity was the only newsperson allowed in the meadow. A hundred or more others, and a dozen camera vans with antennae erected lined West Drive, a hundred yards away. The meadow lay completely encircled by police.

Had it not been for the city suits of the negotiators, it would have been a Remington painting. Waiting outside the tent flap, surrounded by Indians in full tribal dress, Terrence Thornburg stood next to Andrew Upton. Both men had clamped jaws, arms folded, and full-length camel-hair coats attesting to the afternoon chill. The third man was introduced to Steve as Anton Fredrick. Steve had heard of the man, but not met him. He was well recognized as the city's toughest negotiator, known as the "Hun" behind his back. True to form, his gray double-breasted greatcoat and short-cropped blond hair looked as if he should have been goose-stepping under the Arc de Triomphe.

A small fire burned in the dim light at the center of the tepee. The men looked around, expecting chairs and a table. Steve smiled inwardly, then sat, crossing his legs on the elk pelt covering the grass.

Finally, the three followed suit.

"I guess coffee is not an Indian thing?" Fredrick asked.

Steve whistled, and one of the Indian women stuck her head into the flap. "Coffee, please," he said. In moments she returned with four blue-speckled tin Hudson Bay cups filled to the brim with scalding black coffee.

"Damn," Fredrick said when handed the hot tin cup. He managed to set it down without spilling it.

After a moment's silence, Fredrick said simply, "Well, Mr. Drum . . . I should call you Mister, not chief or something?"

"Mister is fine. Steve is fine. I'm not a chief of my tribe, although, rest assured, I am chief counsel for the Scohomacs and have the power to negotiate for them. I am retained."

"Good. State your case."

Steve handed Fredrick a portfolio containing all the documentation. "I expect you'll have to return to your own 'chiefs' before you can conclude these talks, and you'll want to verify our claim, so here's some background material." He went on to state the case both in layman's and legal terms, remaining firm on his demands for the return of the thousand acres.

Fredrick began his retort by conceding that there may be some "claim," but he would have to verify that by inspecting the documentation. It certainly wouldn't result in the return of any real estate after three hundred years of continuous occupation by owners who held and acquired it in good faith. He did concede that a small reparation might, just might, be entertained, in order to circumvent a costly legal action. But then, and only then, if the amount was nominal and if all the insurgents would immediately and peacefully leave New York City.

Upton, reacting a little like a jilted lover, reluctantly agreed that the state would participate in any settlement in order to conclude the matter in a hurry.

At six P.M. women brought in plates of roasted meat and fry

bread and set them next to the negotiators, who looked around for utensils, until they watched Steve scoop the meat onto a pad of bread and begin to eat.

Just as he was about to take a bite, Fredrick asked, "This is beef?"

"I imagine," Steve said, containing his smile. As Upton began to chew, Steve added, "It could be horse, Mr. Fredrick, in honor of your German ancestry, or dog, in honor of mine."

Upton casually filled his hand with chewed meat, and dropped it into the fire while Fredrick smiled and took a big bite. "Beef, I think," Fredrick managed with his mouth half full. Upton left his remaining meat and fry bread on the hide next to him, but recovered another piece of bread.

The negotiations continued. The sum of the settlement was put in abeyance until the other terms were agreed upon. Steve was careful to craft the language so Indians would vacate the *parks* of the city, explaining that it was unfair and illegal to exclude any group from the city per se. Parks and illegal gatherings remained the subject of the agreement. He was careful to craft another provision. He got Upton to agree that the Scohomacs could utilize the settlement to acquire land to serve as their reservation, or in lieu of a cash settlement by the state, to select a parcel of state-owned land of equal value. Upton argued and Steve finally agreed that the parcel would have to be one mutually agreed upon by both the state and Scohomacs, should it be a piece of state land they wanted. Otherwise, they could acquire a reservation site *anywhere* in the State of New York.

The language was clear by ten P.M. The Scohomacs would waive all claims against the one thousand sixty acres in Manhattan— billions of dollars in value—given the fact they could use any settlement proceeds to acquire a reservation site anywhere in the State of New York.

The only item left was the amount. And it was a moot point so far as Steve was concerned; still, he fought hard. Finally, at midnight, after Steve had begun with a demand of one hundred million dollars, he reluctantly agreed they would accept the paltry sum of four hundred thousand.

Rising and stretching, Fredrick said, "So, you'll start moving these people out in the morning?"

"As soon as I have a written agreement executed by the city and the state, we'll pull out of the parks."

"The check will take a little time, presuming it's forthcoming and I can validate your claim by inspecting this wad of documents."

"Of course," Steve said, "it's the city and state we're dealing with. The agreement will suffice; the check can follow."

Steve shook hands with each of them. Upton gave him a tight smile. "You were right, I guess the upper East Side is not prime farmland. It's prime real estate, however."

Thornburg turned back as he was exiting the tent. "I'll tell you, Drum. I think this whole thing amounts to blackmail. You might as well move out of this city when this is concluded. There's no place for you here."

"Actually," Steve said with a broad grin, "I plan to be back on the reservation as soon as you folks bring me an agreement the Scohomacs can live with."

"A wise move," Thornburg grumbled, and let the flap close in Steve's face.

Steve laughed. Again, he hadn't lied.

The city negotiators were confident that all the Scohomacs could buy would be a remote piece of mountain land with four hundred thousand.

They would be well rid of them.

The next two days remained relatively peaceful, except for the clamoring of the press and a few small incidents. The morning following the signing, the story made two columns in *The New York Times*, the Metro section, and the headlines of other city papers. *The Afternoon Sun* declared, THEY'RE BACK in seventy-two-point type.

One incident nearly caused a major calamity. One of the mounted policeman's mares wafted a scent that caused some Indian stallions to chase her across Central Park, with the mounted sergeant hanging on for dear life and a dozen yelling Indians giving chase, but only to recover their stock. The scene was misinterpreted by a nearby, standby SWAT team, who charged into the melee with automatic weapons at their shoulders. Luckily, none of the young braves was armed, and the embarrassed mounted sergeant quickly apologized for his overheated mare and promised to keep her stabled for the duration.

Another group of braves, against Steve's orders regarding firewater, decided Flannery's Pub, only a block from Central Park, was an acceptable watering hole. The Irish took offense, and another in a long line of white-eye/Indian wars ensued with a half dozen from each camp ending up in the emergency ward—luckily this one was fought with fists, a few beer bottles, and a chair or two.

In a more serious incident, a pair of young braves, well-watered, decided to scalp a Hasidic Jewish gentleman—at least relieve him of his beard. He and another two dozen of his peers took great offense, and this time it was the Indians who took flight. It took a dozen of New York's finest to break up the shouting match in the Sheep Meadow, where the culprits were finally run to ground. But not before a dozen Jewish warriors in long, flowing black coats and equally staid flat-brimmed hats were engaged in a bout of wrestling with an equal number of buckskin- and feather-clad Indians. Hair, curly beards, and braids were pulled, black clothing and buckskins torn, but no real damage done.

The press claimed this a first in white/Indian relations and the settling of the west, the west end of the Sheep Meadow, that is.

But no shots were fired in any of the skirmishes. So far, little blood had been spilled.

The Indians remained encamped without further harassment by the police. Steve began methodically bailing out those who'd been arrested, and they returned to their new villages adorning the city's parks. All the while, more and more Indians arrived. Tepees, hogans, wigwams, mud and wattle and woven grass all arose in Central and Carl Schurz parks. Herds of horses, cattle, sheep, and goats increased in size. The village in Central Park became a major tourist attraction, and a hundred tour buses a day passed by, videos scanning, electronic strobes flashing.

Finally, an agreement was faxed to Steve's office from the city attorney's. The key elements were unchanged. Steve studied it, then called Fredrick and made arrangements to meet again in Central Park to conclude the signing.

With the press in abundance, strobes flashing, and tape rolling, the tepee amid a forest of TV-van antennae but the mayor and governor conspicuously absent, Steve was presented with an agreement already executed by the state attorney general and the mayor of New York.

The next morning, the *Post* headline read, INDIANS AGAIN ACCEPT A HANDFUL OF BEADS.

As soon as he was back in his office, Steve called Cookie Yamamoto at home. "Cookie, I'll have the funds in escrow tomorrow. I want this deal to close as soon as possible. I want the money tendered and the deed delivered to me. Hand carried, by you, do you understand?"

"You got it."

The mayor's monthly press conference had been long scheduled for that day. In typical condescending politicalese, he stated in an aside to his normal business, "We were able to help, in a small way, some displaced people. We were glad to be able to come to their aid, and wish them the best. I understand they are busily searching for a remote site in Yates County for a piece of land to purchase, a place they can call home. You can't do a lot with four hundred thousand. . . . Wherever it is, the City of New York wishes them well." He smiled. "And we hope they come to visit the Big Apple, but not to camp out."

Steve, watching the TV, smiled, wondering what the mayor's attitude would be the following morning.

That night, after calling Joe Bigsam and telling him to step up his efforts, he moved all his personal necessities out of his condo.

He had one more important call to make that had to be made from a pay phone. Having Thad circle the block, he dialed a man he'd never met. George Thornapple was renowned as *The Wall Street Journal*'s toughest investigative reporter. He was free with his home phone number, and answered.

"Mr. Thornapple," Steve said, "I don't have a lot of time—"

"Who is this?"

"Like I said, I don't have a lot of time. If you don't want this story, the *Post* or *The New York Times* does."

"Go ahead."

"Alex Dragonovich, chairman of ICOM, has pulled off one of the oldest scams in the book. He's salted the Hovenweep discovery, driving their stock up near its all-time high. You'll find out he's been buying shares for his personal account via a couple of shill companies. It's the business scandal of the decade."

"What's your name?"

Steve hung up. He'd made his pitch, now it was up to Thorn-apple to hit it out of the park.

Odds were, it was the last phone call he'd be able to make for a long while from a public phone, where his location couldn't be traced. Stephen Sounding Drum, and another four hundred Indian warriors, were quietly preparing for a long siege.

That same night, with a great deal of activity at the GE Building, only one incident threatened to expose their efforts. A chance meeting seemed a little suspicious to an IBC graveyard shift employee.

When morning-show editor Bob Tobias sneaked out for a smoke to a tenth-floor deck, he was surprised to encounter dribbles of hay in the stairwell, and piles of what appeared to be animal dung. Being a Stephen King fan, he suspected the worst. What kind of smog-breathing, freely defecating mutation had invaded Rock Center? The odor in the enclosed area aroused his suspicion that whatever it was, it wouldn't be a pretty beast. Moving with his back to the wall, he inched up the stairway until he reached the floor he wanted and tracked the mess to a pair of double doors leading out onto a broad deck. It was not difficult, as that was where he was headed for his Camel.

It was pitch dark outside, but still, he had to look. He slipped out the door and stood motionless, waiting for his eyes to adjust to the darkness.

Suddenly, he was shoved from the rear. He screamed, and spun to come face-to-face with . . . a sheep? He leaped again when a voice rang out. "Don't scare the critters." As his eyes adjusted to the one-hundred-foot-square open-air veranda, he discovered a shepherd and several dozen sheep and goats, contentedly grazing on the landscaping in the moonlight. A stack of hay and straw bales nearby, where umbrella tables once welcomed smokers, was fenced off with temporary rails. Only an occasional bleat competed with the sound of jet planes overhead. When he recovered his composure, Tobias questioned the man, and received a terse reply. "Crazy producer wants for show in the morning. Watch the smokes. Straw burns, you know."

Being used to crazy producers and to seeing almost anything around IBC's studios, Tobias accepted the man's explanation. He had his smoke, carefully, among the bleating and baaing animals while watching the goats do their imitation of a high-wire act as they walked the railings next to a hundred-and-fifty-foot precipice, then returned to his desk.

At dawn the following morning, a passing police cruiser pulled up at the curb in front of Saks Fifth Avenue, and a patrolman stared across the wide street to Rockefeller Center. Scratching his head, he climbed out of his car. He'd never seen a banner on his beat quite so large, over a story tall, stretching from the Rockefeller Center's British Empire Building across the promenade to the French Building. It read: ALL AMERICAN CASINO. Under that, in much smaller letters, was spelled out: WELCOME TO THE NATIVE NATIONS CASINO AND CULTURAL CENTER, AND THE SCOHOMAC INDIAN RESERVATION.

He climbed back inside his patrol car and radioed his precinct. "Hey, Sarge, are casinos legal now in the city? . . . And when did we get an Indian reservation?"

"What?" his sergeant replied. When the patrolman finally received a negative answer, he slowly circled the block, then parked on Rockefeller Plaza and strode up to the wide bank of front doors. He tried a door and found it locked, then pulled his nightstick from his belt and rapped on the glass.

Steve Drum stood just inside the front doors of the GE Building, a cup of coffee warming his hands. A hundred or so token slot machines, lights and bells working, had been set up in the lobby of 30 Rock Plaza. Enough to make the point. A thousand more, and other gambling equipment, still slept in crates on the floors above. Steve was flanked by Thad Wintermoose, Joseph Bigsam, and Patrick McGoogan.

"Well, brothers," Steve said, "the gauntlet is thrown. Felicia and IBC won't have to go far to get this story, in fact, just outside their office door."

He walked over and yelled at the patrolman through the locked doors. "We don't open until six A.M.!"

"Are those slot machines?" the officer shouted back.

"Sure are. Come back with a roll of quarters when you get off work. You're welcome here, without the sidearm."

The patrolman looked puzzled, but returned to his car. In moments, sirens were screaming, converging on the GE Building from every direction.

At about the same time, the few workers in the building became aware that coverall-uniformed Indian movers were now carrying nasty-looking automatic weapons. With an unarmed man stationed at every elevator, the fleeing people were cautioned.

"Be calm. Nothing to get excited about. Go out the subway exit if you wish to leave. No one will be harmed. You're welcome to go or stay as you wish."

Anticipating a problem, Steve had a letter delivered to each of the banks in the concourse. It read, in short:

> If you decide to vacate the building, please have adequate security for your funds and records. We, here at Scohomac, do not allow firearms on the premises, however, we will make an exception if your armored car personnel are accompanying your exit. You're welcome to continue business as usual, if not, please vacate by midnight tonight. If you choose to leave your valuables in place, rest assured they will be protected by Scohomac warriors.

The same message was telephoned to the respective banks' headquarters.

All elected to leave. Soon employees from the restaurants and other early morning endeavors were filing out into the subway station.

Steve nodded to Joseph Bigsam. "Well, Joe, you'd better alert your people. The fun's about to begin."

CHAPTER THIRTY-THREE

With a dozen police cars packing the short length of Rockefeller Plaza, and more arriving, Steve stood inside the locked front doors with arms folded. Finally, a precinct captain of generous girth arrived, with six officers following. He placed a ham-sized hand on the mullion and rattled the locked door.

His rather bulbous nose came against the glass, and he spotted Steve. "Hey, you! Open this door."

"The doors don't open until six A.M., Captain."

"I said open them, now!"

"You're standing on the Scohomac Indian reservation, Captain. You don't give orders here."

"We'll see about that." He strode away, his troops trailing. In moments, a squad of uniformed officers approached with a metal battering ram. This time the captain brought up the rear. They lined up to swing the heavy ram, but Steve stepped directly behind the doors and held up his hand, giving the peace sign. The captain walked to the front of the double row of officers and shouted, "Now, open it, or we will!"

Rising up behind a long counter, twenty young Mohawk warriors appeared behind Steve, exiting their cover in a military manner to form a skirmish line blocking entry into the eight pairs of doors leading into the main lobby of 30 Rockefeller Plaza. In lieu of beaded headbands, each warrior wore a yellow cloth headband imprinted with *Scohomac* in bloodred, but more impressively, each carried an AK-47 in the ready position across his chest and had extra clips of ammo attached to his belt.

Two of the uniformed officers hit the sidewalk on their bellies, firearms extended in front of them in both hands, panning back and forth across the line of stoic warriors.

Police eyes widened as many of them stepped back, retreating, palming their own weapons, but the handguns they held were obviously way outclassed. Steve carefully reached into his pocket, produced a key, opened the doors. He stepped out with a smile on his face. He eyed the two officers on the sidewalk.

"You fellas can get up now. There's not going to be any shooting unless *you* start it. And I wouldn't suggest it." Steve pointed up, and they all raised their eyes to see another two dozen warriors stationed at windows overlooking the plaza. Each held an automatic weapon. Angry, but cautious, the prone officers regained their feet. Steve turned to their leader.

"Captain, you're standing in the sovereign nation of Scohomac. This is not New York City and you have no authority here. I'd advise you to check with the mayor and city attorney before you get a lot of people hurt, or worse, and cause an international incident. There are no hostages here, anyone in the building is free to leave, no one's in peril unless the police put them there."

The captain shook his head in wonder. "Firearms are strictly illegal in New York City, particularly automatic—"

"One more time, Captain, you're not in New York City. Keep calm and we'll resolve this without harm to anyone. Have your men retreat to New York—that would be the sidewalks of Forty-ninth and Fiftieth, Fifth Avenue, and Avenue of the Americas, *outside* the perimeter of this building, the French Building, the British Empire Building, the promenade, and the lower plaza. *Everything* inside that boundary is a part of this sovereign nation. By the way, for your information, we don't allow firearms in Scohomac . . . except for those of our people authorized to carry them."

The captain sputtered, "You're full of shit, mister."

"Here, I'm full of authority, mister. Don't make me exercise it. Please, Captain, check with the mayor and city attorney. By the way, Rockefeller Plaza is ours also. Please remove your vehicles."

"You're claiming a *street?*"

"A private street that we now own. Always has been a private street, or didn't you know?"

After a long look at the armed Indians, the captain shook his head in disgust and stomped away toward his car radio, his entourage of uniformed officers backing along behind, keeping their eyes on the armed warriors.

Steve yelled after him, "By the way, if you want to give me a call, here's my cellular number." He gave the captain his number, and one of the officers noted it.

The police pulled their vehicles back, more to get out of harm's way than to obey Steve's order. A half hour went by, then a pair of armored police vehicles arrived and blocked each end of Rockefeller Plaza. No traffic had appeared on Forty-ninth or Fiftieth, so Steve presumed they were also cordoned off. He could see down the promenade to Park Avenue, and morning traffic moved as usual, but two police cars parked on the sidewalk blocked entrance to the walkway. A police helicopter circled overhead, the whack-whack-whack of its rotors a constant reminder of police presence.

At eight A.M. Steve's cell phone rang and a police negotiator introduced himself as Sam Batistone. He requested another meeting, to which Steve promptly agreed. In moments the captain reappeared with Anton "the Hun" Fredrick and another distressed-looking but well-dressed man Steve didn't know. They approached the doors and Steve stepped out.

"Mr. Drum," Fredrick said without extending his hand.

"Good morning, Mr. Fredrick. Welcome to Scohomac."

"Let me introduce you to Thomas McKendrick, executive vice president of IBC."

Steve shook the man's hand.

"Mr. Drum, I've got several thousand people who'd like to go to work, and some already in there I'm concerned about."

"No problem, Mr. McKendrick. You folks are tenants of ours and we honor our commitments. Under the circumstances, since the police seem to have a lot of firearms trained on the front doors, I'll make arrangements for private ingress and egress to an elevator bank. I suggest you enter from the subway, which is the way most of your people working the night shift left. As your people reenter, I'll have a desk set up and we'll make Scohomac ID badges. Only your employees and customers, and those of other legitimate businesses here in the complex, come in and out of the building. We're doing this for every tenant."

Fredrick held up his hand. "Let me get this straight, Drum. You've commandeered this property and are claiming it as some kind of Indian reservation, this Scohomac? And you're opening a casino in the middle of Manhattan?"

"Not commandeered, Mr. Fredrick. Purchased. The Scohomac Nation, pursuant to and in strict compliance with our agreement with the city and state—an agreement you negotiated—have purchased this part of Rockefeller Center, and it is now the Scohomac Nation. It was deeded to a company called Seattle Sino, and that company in turn has transferred the property to the Scohomac Nation. And you're right, it does seem to be in the middle of Manhattan, but we don't mind. We can live with that."

"You've purchased . . . ? With four hundred thousand?"

"Actually, Mr. Fredrick, you haven't paid the four hundred thousand yet, and we could use it. Then again, it was never suggested that we couldn't contribute other funds. We all pitched in our wampum and raised another fifty mil or so ."

Fredrick began to redden. "You son of a bitch."

"That must be some New York City colloquialism, son of a she-dog, a white-eye term of respect, I presume. . . ."

"This won't fly, Drum."

"It's already airborne, Fredrick."

Fredrick spun on his heel. "We'll see about that." The captain followed him away.

McKendrick stood in frustration, not knowing what to do. Steve laid a hand on the man's shoulder. "Mr. McKendrick, you can begin bringing your people in anytime. We anticipated the problem and have made arrangements for them to enter via the subway entrance."

"IBC has schedules to keep, programming to air. There is no being late in our business. I've got to talk to the police."

"Talk to anyone you want. Just don't be late . . . particularly with your rent." When the executive VP got a few feet away, Steve called after him. "McKendrick, I've got a statement, and I promised your reporter Felicia Garrity first crack at it. Tell her to come to the front door with her cameraman, but it has to be live, Mr. McKendrick, or no interview."

McKendrick nodded, then hurried away after the other two.

Steve retreated to his control center.

Within another half hour, semitrucks loaded with concrete barriers began to arrive, then a crane. By midafternoon, a six-foot concrete wall made of highway barriers stacked two deep surrounded Scohomac.

Al Giovanni sat in his den, a cup of coffee in hand, a newspaper in his lap, alternately watching the television, sipping, and glancing at the paper. Angela came in and greeted him, "Morning, Papa."

"You're early."

"I'm going back to the beach today."

"I wish you woulda stay here with Mama. It'sa too cold—"

They both turned to the TV when a newsman interrupted the morning programming and announced a news special. "This morning, Stephen Drum, a local New York City attorney of Native American heritage, and what seems to be a force of several hundred, possibly several thousand Indians, have commandeered Rockefeller Center—"

"My God," Angela managed to say, before being hushed by her father.

"Drum spearheaded the occupation of Central Park, a matter only recently resolved, the city believed amicably. However, as I speak, hundreds of Indians armed with automatic weapons are scattered throughout the GE Building, in windows, and on rooftops. Police have cordoned off the area and advise avoiding it altogether. A negotiator and an FBI team have just entered the building. More on this developing story as it progresses. Now back to our regular programming."

Al promptly switched to IBC's New Jersey affiliate. It, too, had a special in progress.

"—of course, IBC's headquarters are in Rockefeller Center, and the *America Today* show originates there. We've been informed here at KNJ that we'll be hosting the show from our studios, and other IBC programming will originate here and from our White Plains affiliate. Studio One is dark in Rockefeller Center, and the

New York street crowds normally greeting Kathy and Mark are absent, as the whole area is—"

Al switched off the TV. He turned to a stunned Angela and smiled. "Our wild Indian has outdone himself this time."

"What is he thinking? He must have gone crazy."

"He's a crazy. Crazy like a fox, Angela. Crazy like a Montana coyote."

Al began to chuckle.

Another TV was on in Little Italy in the southern end of Manhattan. The photographer stood, half his face still covered with foam, the other shaved clean, a safety razor in hand, watching the news.

"You smart-ass son of a bitch," he said quietly under his breath. "This time you've cooked yourself. Nobody will give a shit when I take you out . . . in fact, I'll probably get the key to the city."

He began to laugh, finished shaving, and pulled on a long-sleeved black knit shirt, then a black sport jacket. Deciding to get something to eat in the Italian deli below his room, he would then drive up to Rockefeller Center and see for himself what was coming down, and how to best take advantage of stupid Steve Drum's situation.

Steve smiled and greeted Fredrick, the city negotiator, and a new face on the scene, Nolan Robertson, the FBI agent who had interviewed him after the bomb attempt. The two men were trailed by two others, Steve presumed other FBI agents. Then one of the men was introduced to him as Sam Batistone, the police negotiator.

Steve walked over and stood beside the FBI man. Thad Wintermoose stood back, an AK-47 across his chest, watching. "Nice to see you again, Nolan," Steve said in a friendly manner.

"I wish I could say the same, Drum. I presume you have some kind of list of demands?"

"Demands? Not at all. We want nothing but to live in peace with the white-eye, a desire that has prevailed among Native Americans since Plymouth Rock. We want only to welcome you all to Scohomac. You know well the rights of Indians on a sovereign reservation. We don't need to make demands of the city, state, or the United States, other than to let us live, work, and play in peace."

"Okay, okay. By what right do you claim this as this Sco—?"

"Scohomac." Steve went on to explain the terms of the agreement he'd reached with the city and state.

Nolan scratched his head. "That's all well and good, Drum. But as far as I know, these Scohomacs are not acknowledged as a tribe. You can't expect—"

"The application is at the Bureau of Indian Affairs, and *will* be approved. They are a tribe, and have been since time began, or close enough for government work. Nevertheless, we have an ethnological and moral right, and an obligation to our people, that precedes the Bureau of Indian Affairs, the State of New York ... hell, the United States of America. We are exercising our right of heritage, of blood, of centuries of possession before you immigrants waded ashore. You know, Nolan, possession is nine-tenths of the law. Actually, we lost it for only a moment in time, considering how much time there has been."

Steve smiled and spread his arms wide. "But we're back."

"Of course you know, counselor, that other tenth rules many times. We deal with the courts now that the 'white-eye' is running the show."

"Not this time, Nolan. We're here. We're staying here. By the way, in addition to the documentation I gave Fredrick, this building is the site of a Canarsee burial ground, proving without question we were here long before you and yours."

Nolan shrugged. "I'm told you actually don't own this building. There's been no deed recorded, and the mayor's man tells me if one appears, it'll be refused."

"Money has changed hands, and the deed is signed and in my possession. I don't give a tinker's dam about recording. It's a done deal."

Agent Robertson shrugged again. The other two agents had been studying everything they could see from the lobby, which wasn't much. Nolan smiled in a friendly manner. "Well, I don't know what to tell you. How about showing us around?"

"No chance, Nolan." Steve turned serious. "I can tell you that a siege of this place would be costly. We have a couple of 'Nam vets here with us who are explosive experts. Every entrance is wired with plastic. Trust me when I tell you that you'll be blocked, should you try to invade—"

"Look, Drum, you're interfering with the operation of the National Weather Service and two federal banks. This has got to stop now. . . ."

"You a fan of big booms, Nolan?"

CHAPTER THIRTY-FOUR

Robertson's look hardened.

Steve continued. "I hope those demolition boys know what they're doing. If not, the whole building could come down around our ears . . . this baby is pretty old." Steve shook his head with mock concern. "As you may know, this complex has an excellent surveillance system. We can see anyone approaching, any hostile activity, from our control room."

Nolan looked a little smug. "I'm sure the city is figuring out how to turn off the power and water to the whole complex. You may be here awhile, Drum, and it's getting a little nippy out. It'll soon be pretty hungry and dirty inside."

It was Steve's turn to smile. "It's their water and power. We're prepared to be here for a while, a long while. But you might mention to them that we pay our bills, and they'd better have damn good reasons to cut us off."

"Okay, that's it for now. But let's keep the lines of communication open."

"Fine, keep our power and water on."

"Can't help you there. That's up to the city." Robertson turned to leave, then turned back, a sincere look on his face. He buddied up to Steve, put a hand on his shoulder, and spoke in a low voice. "You know, the right place to settle this is in the courts. Why don't you and your people just walk out of here now and settle this in a forum you know well? Hell, if you're right, you could be back in here next year."

"Nolan, this has to come down now, or it won't happen. Besides, we've been fucked over by white-eye courts for a couple of hundred years. We have Scohomac. We're keeping Scohomac. The next time I see you here, I want it to be with a roll of quarters in one hot little hand and a martini in the other."

They left, but not before Nolan traded cell phone numbers with him and Batistone, then Steve returned to his second-floor control room, leaving two dozen warriors for a presence in the lobby.

Thad, Joe Bigsam, Paula, Patrick McGoogan, Tomtom Webster, and David Greenberg awaited him. In addition to the gambling equipment, hundreds of crates of food, most of it C-rations, bedding and sleeping bags, firearms, and medical supplies lined the halls and offices of the third, fourth, and fifth floors. Fifty-gallon drums and five-gallon plastic containers of water were everywhere. Two tanker trucks full of diesel oil, guarded by a dozen warriors, rested in the lower concourse next to the emergency generator room, adding to the already abundant tanking. The generators were more than merely adequate, thanks to the federal government. One of the primary tenants of the building was the National Weather Service. IBC maintained another set to make sure they stayed on the air during even the most severe emergency.

The security headquarters and control room equipment had been augmented with four television sets, each turned to a different network, including CNN. Videotape machines were rigged to each set and recorded continually.

Steve stood before his team. "Well, lady and gentleman. I think we've got a long, long wait."

But his cell phone belied his statement. He answered, spoke a moment, hung up, and turned to David. "You've got the notes of the speech you prepared?"

David handed him a short stack of three-by-five cards, and Steve waved to the rest of them as he left. "The press beckons." He studied the notes on the way down.

Outside on Fifth Avenue, a limo pulled up and an Asian man stepped out and headed for the two police cars parked on the sidewalk blocking the promenade.

"What is going on here?" he demanded of a uniformed officer.

"Not your affair, sir. Move along."

"Not my affair? I own this property. I demand to know what this is about."

"Some bunch of Indians have taken over the building. You can't go in there now. Go over to Fiftieth Street. Captain Donovan can tell you more."

Wilber Wong made his way around the corner and down Fiftieth. What in the world was Stephen Drum up to? He had to call the escrow company and see what was going on. Was Drum trying to steal the property from him? It wasn't like a horse that you could steal and ride away.

God, why did he ever get mixed up with a bunch of mud-hut Indians. Even if they had fifty million as a down payment on an overpriced property.

As he strode down to meet Felicia, Steve thought that there was at least one good thing to come of the last couple of tense, hectic days. He hadn't dwelled on Angela. If that *was* a good thing.

Felicia crossed the lobby and walked with him back to where her cameraman awaited.

"You promised to call me when anything happened," she said. "I'd say this was something happening."

He smiled. "I promised to put you in front of all the others, Felicia. At least as far as the news goes. To tell you the truth, I had no idea how serious things might get, and I didn't want any innocent bystanders around . . . not that you press types can exactly be considered innocent."

She laughed, but grudgingly. "So, where do you want to be raped . . . I mean taped?"

He laughed. "Innocent you're not. On you, it looks good. As to the former, probably not in front of the camera, but the latter . . . If you're game, let's go out under the guns."

"Okay, I don't think they'll shoot down a reporter, at least not while the camera's running."

"This is live?" he asked.

She spoke as she attached a remote mike to the underside of

his collar. "See that little antenna on the camera? The van's just down the street, picking it up and putting it out."

"Hold just a second." Steve pulled the cell phone off his belt and called Batistone, who'd taken up a position in a trailer the police had set up at the far end of Rockefeller Plaza. He called Nolan. Steve cleared the fact they would be exiting the building, and advised the FBI and police that they would be out in the open, but well covered by their own people on floors above.

With that done, and giving them time to alert all the officers on the perimeter, Steve led Felicia across Rockefeller Plaza and around the ice rink to the brass placard and John D. Rockefeller's quote.

He stood in front of it when the camera began to roll. After Felicia introduced him, he began:

"The Scohomac Indian Nation, complying fully with an agreement entered into with the State and City of New York, has purchased three buildings here in Rockefeller Center, surrounding and including the ice rink. This is a legal transaction, and is consummated. Again, pursuant to the agreement, they have declared this property to be their reservation. As many of you know, an Indian reservation is sovereign, and subject only to the laws of that Indian nation and the United States of America, not the state or city, unless agreements are reached regarding same. The State of New York might try to challenge the Scohomac Nation as to not being a legal entity, however—and I'll also provide Ms. Garrity with this document—the state attorney general's office has acknowledged the Scohomac Nation in a letter to the United States Bureau of Indian Affairs."

Steve swung a quarter turn and indicated the ice rink below. "Let me assure you that all those wonderful activities that have been a part of Rockefeller Center, and particularly the ice rink and lower plaza, including the annual Christmas tree, will continue for all New Yorkers."

He pointed at the British Empire Building and the French Building. "In addition, the Scohomac Nation plans to develop a cultural center, Native Nations College, and full-service casino on this location. All activities legal and currently in operation on other reservations across New York State and the United States. We want nothing more than is already in place elsewhere."

His demeanor turned serious. "Before I continue, let me apologize to the people whose rents we were not able to lower. The city threatened to tie us up in court for generations should we attempt to take over the area I formerly mentioned.

"So now we've taken the only alternative left to us. Although Rockefeller Center is not a part of the former deeded lands of the Scohomac, it was theirs long before the white man came to this country. The proof of that is the fact it is holy ground and the site of a Scohomac, Canarsee burial ground. Verification of that will be provided the State and City of New York and this reporter.

"We'd also like to apologize for the fact that the businesses located here in the buildings we've purchased have not been allowed to reopen. It appears the city and the New York police have denied them access. Be assured that we welcome their return, and let me assure those business owners that I will guarantee them representation, on a contingency basis, should they wish to bring suit against the City of New York for business interruption. That includes IBC, who I imagine is being damaged at the rate of several million dollars . . . an hour. I also want to assure those business owners that their property is being protected by the Scohomac police force."

Steve paused to let the possibility of a barrage of liability law-suits soak into the mayor's office, knowing they were watching every move he made.

"We're here in front of some of the ideas, thoughts, and aspirations of John D. Rockefeller, Jr., who developed Rockefeller Center during the Great Depression, providing jobs for thousands and thousands of out-of-work and destitute New Yorkers. We want our small portion of his great dream to carry on that tradition here in the project he founded."

Steve turned to the plaque. "Mr. Rockefeller said, among other things, and I quote: 'I believe that the law was made for man and not man for the law; that government is the servant of the people and not their master.

" 'I believe in the dignity of labor, whether it be with head or hand; that the world owes no man a living but that it owes every man an opportunity to make a living.

" 'I believe in the sacredness of a promise, that a man's word should be as good as his bond; that character—not wealth or power or position—is of supreme worth.' "

Steve turned and looked directly into the camera. "All we want is an opportunity to make a living. All we want is for the City of New York to let us work and to honor their word, their agreement, their sacred promise." Steve turned and looked directly at the camera. "It's an agreement you signed, Mr. Mayor. Show some character and honor your word."

Steve paused a moment, his stare into the camera an obvious challenge to the mayor and the City of New York. Then he turned to Felicia. "Ms. Garrity, let's take a walk."

Steve led her around the promenade, past the ice rink, then back to the GE Building. He paused in the middle of Rockefeller Plaza and pointed to the rows of officers and the barriers and armored cars. "Does that look like a mayor and city honoring their word, Ms. Garrity?" Steve shook his head as if saddened. "I think Mr. Rockefeller would be embarrassed for his city."

Entering the GE Building, Steve described the Scohomac plans, pausing in front of a row of slots. "These machines are here for the recreation and enjoyment of all New Yorkers. A good deal of the proceeds will be used to fund the Native Nations College and scholarships to other colleges and universities around the country. By the way, any openings in the college not taken by Native Americans will be available to any New Yorker, regardless of heritage or income. Some of those scholarships I mentioned will be available to non–Native Americans.

"And we'll also be providing jobs to lower-income New Yorkers. In addition, the casino will guarantee that one half of its job requirements will be filled by other than Native Americans."

He closed his talk in the lobby of the GE Building under the wonderful murals by Jose Maria Sert, and in front of his favorite mural on the south stairway to the mezzanine. The painting depicted the five races of mankind, clasping hands in brotherhood. He motioned to the massive piece. "This symbolizes what we're trying to accomplish here. Here you see Caucasian, white; Native American, red; Mongolian, yellow; Malay, brown; and Negro, black; hand in hand, clasped in brotherhood." He paused to let that soak in, then concluded. "We want to go forward, hand in hand with the City of New York, for the benefit of everyone."

He drew a finger across his throat.

"Great," Felicia said. "Now the interview—"

"No interview, Felicia. I'm afraid it would be anticlimactic. I suggest you shoot around the lobby here and outside. You have my cell phone should you need anything else. I'm going up and try to get some rest. I don't know when I last slept."

He turned and started to walk away.

"Steve," she called after him. "I want to stay inside with my cameraman. We can send the tape out."

He stopped and turned back.

"No, Felicia, it's too dangerous."

He started away again.

"Steve," she said with a mischievous smile. "I can be . . . useful."

Steve laughed. "No question. But it's still too dangerous."

Again he moved to leave.

"Steve."

"Yeah?"

"Thanks. It's a great human interest piece."

Steve just laughed and walked on.

Let's hope the NYPD thinks so, he thought as he pushed the elevator button.

When he walked into the control room, he sensed the tension. Joe Bigsam turned to him. "Great job, Steve. However, we've got a force of men, SWAT I think, moving into the lower concourse, near our tanker trucks."

Tom Webster shook his head, the concern obvious on his face. "I swear, this whole thing is nuts!"

"Those fools," Steve said. "Thad, stay with Paula and David. Let's get down there and block them."

CHAPTER THIRTY-FIVE

Steve, Tom, and Joe Bigsam ran from the elevator down a hall of the lower concourse, then through a pair of doors marked private. Entering a long hallway leading to the delivery area of the underground complex, their footfalls echoing in the ominous silence, they paused to evaluate the scene.

A dozen warriors had given ground as instructed and were inside, packed at the end of the hallway, gathered in front of another pair of double doors, exits leading to loading docks where the diesel tanker trucks were parked. The trucks were easy to surrender; they'd finished transferring the diesel fuel into bladders in the lower basement of the building only the night before. Steve hoped the diesel rigs were all the SWAT team was after.

He could hear the thump of a compressor in a side room, and Tom Webster turned into that alcove. In moments, two hoses the size of fire-fighting equipment, both converging at a two-foot-long brass nozzle, were dragged into the hallway. At the exit doors, a gob of yellow material clung, pasted to the door's glass so it could be seen from the outside. It had some wiring and a small black box attached to it and appeared to be deadly plastic explosive. Actually, it was pale yellow Play-Doh in some instances and Silly Putty in others. The detonators placed in the material would blow your fingers off if mishandled, but the material itself was useful only for afternoon playtime.

One of the warriors turned and yelled, "Looks like they're coming in!"

Joe Bigsam yelled to his men. "Okay, guys, beat a retreat. Don't forget to kill the lights."

The warriors ran past them and disappeared out of the hallway, and the lights went dim. The door to the side room housing the compressor and a number of fifty-gallon drums of chemicals was seventy-five feet from the exit doors.

Only Joe Bigsam, Steve, and Tom Webster were left in the side room, with at least two dozen SWAT team members approaching the exit doors, armed and ready for anything—or so they thought.

Slowly, the exit doors swung aside, but no one appeared there. Finally, a tentative shielded and masked face took a quick look, then pulled back. Finally, two men peered inside. One reached up and pulled the detonator from the wad of yellow material. As soon as he did so, Tom Webster, a pair of nozzle-tipped hoses in hand, turned a valve on the nozzle's top. A two-inch-wide spray of material leapt out, crossing the seventy-five feet to the exit doors in a heartbeat. The stream slammed into the two SWAT members before they could raise their M16s and they were driven back by the force. The doors, responding to automatic closers, shut behind them. Immediately upon contact, the combined chemicals began to expand. In seconds, a mass of liquid polystyrene insulation began to harden and take shape, completely blocking the hallway, but Tom Webster didn't pause. He continued spraying, working the expanding mass back toward them until finally he worked the valve and cut the flow. Steve and Joe leapt forward and tilted two pieces of plywood up, jamming them. Each sheet had a two-inch-diameter hole cut in its center. Tom moved forward, fitted the nozzle into one of the holes, and opened it up again. He held it there until the solution began to eke out of the hole in the other piece. Only then did he turn the valve off, laying it down on the concrete floor. He brushed his hands and grinned.

The end fifty feet of the hallway was completely sealed from floor to ceiling, wall to wall, with a giant plug of hardening foam insulation.

Turning to Steve, he slapped him on the shoulder. "Biggest damn insulation job I ever tried."

Bigsam scratched his head. "Reminds me of King Kong pocket gopher, plugging up his hole behind him."

"Call your men back," Steve said, businesslike again. "Let's get this equipment to another location . . . the gopher has more work to do."

Before he got back to the elevator bank, his cell phone rang. "Yeah," he answered, a little out of breath. Tom Webster was with him, while Joe Bigsam remained behind to honcho the equipment move.

"This is Batistone." The voice on the phone rang with concern. "That stuff you sprayed on the SWAT guys . . . is that stuff poison?"

"Yeah, we scraped it from the thyroid glands of a million blue-belly lizards down at the landfill. An old Indian trick. Give them the last rites. . . . Actually, I should tell you pricks it's cobra venom, but all it's gonna do is keep them from catching cold."

"Uh?"

"It's polystyrene insulation. They'll probably be picking it off for a while, but that's the worst of it. It was getting a little chilly in here, so we decided to insulate." Then Steve's voice lost its humor and rang with indignation. "You guys are way out of line. All the entrances to the building are now sealed with a hundred-foot-deep plug, and there are explosives laced throughout the plugs. If you try to tunnel through, you'll be dog meat." Steve's tone hardened. "You're invading a sovereign nation, Batistone. You'd better ask the mayor if he wants to declare war on Scohomac. If so, tell him to get on the TV and do so publicly. I'm curious what his constituents will think."

"Look, Drum, the right place to settle this is in a courtroom. You know that—"

"Okay, I agree." Steve paused a moment before he continued. "However, it's going to be a Scohomac courtroom. I'll get a few volunteers from my warriors to serve as jury and you deliver the mayor to face the music—"

"Very funny."

"I'm serious. New York and the mayor would get as fair a trial in here as Scohomac and I would out there."

Batistone was silent for a moment, then his voice rang with conciliation again. "You know, Steve, Thanksgiving is just a few days away. Goodwill toward men, and all that."

"Actually, I think the goodwill thing is Christmas, Batistone.

And the last day that most Native Americans celebrate is Thanksgiving. It's not high on the reservation list."

Resigned, Batistone asked, "So, what now?"

"Now I want to caution you. I've given a tape to Ms. Garrity, showing how many women and children we have here in Scohomac. I hope you have your SWAT snipers begin picking off the goats on the roof . . . they're here for the milk for the babies."

When Steve hung up, Tom Webster shook his head. Tom said, "You lie as good as a white man. That worries me sometime."

Steve laughed and led the way back to the control room. He'd laughed, but he knew that Tom Webster, too, had everything he owned at risk. It wasn't much, but it was everything to Tom.

When Steve returned to the control room, Paula, David, and Thad were glued to the TV screen. Paula turned to him and Tom as they walked in. "Watch, the mayor's making a statement."

With Terrence Thornburg at his side, Mayor Patrini stepped up to the podium in front of two dozen reporters. The camera zoomed in for a head and shoulders. "You've all heard the allegations made by Stephen Drum regarding an agreement he negotiated with the City of New York, actually with Mr. Anton Fredrick, who's an assistant here in my office. As it happened, I was unavailable to attend those negotiations. That agreement, however, was very specific in that the city and state very generously provided a group of indigent people—"

"I'm not indigent," Tom Webster said indignantly.

"Hush," Paula said as the mayor droned on.

"The fact is, the intent of the city and state was for these people to be able to purchase a modest plot of land for a reservation. We did what was right. It was never the intent of this city for them to locate anywhere within our boundaries. What they're attempting is a travesty of justice, and it's plain wrong. We're not going to tolerate it, and we will remove them by whatever means it takes." He paused a moment as Thornburg leaned over and whispered something in his ear. Then he continued. "Let me remind you that a referendum to allow gambling in the city was soundly defeated in the last two elections. The people have spoken, and as your mayor, I'm going to enforce your wishes. What the people want, the people receive, at least so long as I'm mayor of New York. Thank you."

He turned and left under a barrage of questions. Terrence

Thornburg took the podium, raised his hands to silence the reporters, then offered, "The mayor has a number of pressing issues to attend to. We hope to have this matter at Rockefeller Center resolved quickly, and things back to normal. Thank you." Again the barrage of questions, but Thornburg also made his exit without answering even one.

A reporter came on, summarized the mayor's short talk, then said, "Now, let's go live to Rockefeller Center."

To the surprise of everyone in the room, the news camera that appeared to be located on Fifth Avenue panned over a sidewalk crowded with people just outside the concrete barricades, some of them carrying placards, most of the placards in support of Scohomac.

A line of police stood at easy rest, each with a nightstick held behind him. A chant began. "Down with the wall! Down with the wall! Down with the wall!"

Paula smiled and turned to the others. "Hell, at least a few of the people are with us."

Steve laughed aloud. "Looks like most of them are from Spanish Harlem, still wanting to get their rents lowered."

"I don't care where they're from," Tom said, "so long as they're on our side."

Steve said, "There'll be more there tomorrow, and more yet the next day." He walked to the window of the security office and folded his hands behind him, staring out at the Rockefeller Center garage building across Forty-ninth Street. To his surprise, people still came and went as if nothing were happening sixty yards away. Only in New York.

Thad, studying the security monitors, shook his head without turning away from his job. "You mentioned Plymouth Rock," he said. "We didn't land on Plymouth Rock, Plymouth Rock landed on us . . . Denzel Washington playing Malcolm X."

As they all laughed, the power went off and the room went pitch black. It was Thad who spoke into the silence. "Just a minute, and the portables will kick in." They all waited what seemed an interminable time, then the lights began to come back up and the monitors flickered to life.

"Well," Steve said, "the city crews have been busy. I'm going to check the water. One of you guys pick up an outside line and see if the telephones are still working."

Thad reached for a security line. "Phone is still on . . . no, went dead too."

Steve walked out and directly to a wall-mounted water fountain. He worked the handle and it sputtered for a moment, then it, too, failed. He returned to the security office as his cell phone rang. Terrence Thornburg's voice sounded triumphant.

"I guess things are a little uncomfortable in there?"

"Still a lot nicer than most reservations, Thornburg. Is there something you wanted?"

"The mayor wants to meet with you. Face-to-face, no phones."

"Have him drop over. I can squeeze him in."

"It has to be in a public place."

"Does he ice skate? How about the middle of the rink?"

"You're a real card, Drum. Get serious."

Steve covered the receiver with a hand. "Are all the entrances sealed other than the lobby and subway?"

Bigsam, who'd returned to the room, offered, "Yeah, all sealed up. We left the Forty-ninth Street pipe tunnel as we discussed, but the others are solid as Sears."

Steve removed his hand. "Okay, how about the subway station. It's still rocking and rolling."

"In thirty minutes. The mayor doesn't want to be seen, and you have to agree not to use that damned witch reporter to shout it to the world."

Steve smiled. The power of the press . . . "That's no problem, I wouldn't mind the opportunity to talk straight to the good mayor."

"Thirty minutes. The mayor will have on an old overcoat, gray, and hat. He'll be wearing a beard."

"A beard." Steve smiled, but kept the smile out of his voice.

"A long beard. You might want to be disguised."

"I'll think about it. There are fifty cops in the subway station and a pile of temporary barricades to keep passengers away from the doors."

"The cops will be called out and the barricades taken down."

"I'll see him in the station, near the entrance doors to the GE Building. Thirty minutes."

Everyone in the room overheard his side of the conversation, and they buzzed with questions. He held up a hand, gave them a quick rundown. "I want a video camera down there to record this. This is too good."

Thad hit a selector switch on the monitor in front of him. "Here's the subway entrance. If you stand at the column to the left, facing the entrance from the subway side, we'll have a clear view with this camera."

As he was walking out, he called back over his shoulder, "The power's out, and we've got a number of restaurants in the complex. I suggest you have the boys start making jerky from the frozen meat, and salting or cooking what they can't preserve otherwise. It's back to the woods, boys."

In thirty minutes Steve, Thad, and Joe Bigsam were waiting just inside the subway station doors. When Steve spotted a man with a cane and long gray overcoat, hat, and beard, he stepped out alone and walked ten feet to the column Thad had suggested.

Patrini moved slowly, like an old man. Twenty-five feet behind him, two burly men split up and took positions fifteen paces on either side of where they met.

"Mr. Mayor," Steve said, not bothering to extend his hand, but he was eyeing the two men.

"Don't worry about them, they go everywhere with me. . . . Drum, it's time we put it on the line."

"Oh? I thought that was what I'd been doing."

"What is it you want?"

Steve merely smiled.

The mayor's voice went up an octave. "We all have an agenda, Drum. You're no different. You've had a lot of media exposure here. Everyone in New York knows who Stephen Drum is, you're famous, or maybe infamous is a better word. Now it's time for you to capitalize on it."

Steve wondered just how far the mayor was prepared to go, so he nodded his head as if he agreed.

The mayor continued. "I can offer you six months of easy jail time, no censorship against your license to practice."

Steve laughed. "For what?"

"You and your people walk away. Disband. I don't want to see your people again."

Steve laughed louder. "You're standing fifteen feet from the sovereign nation of Scohomac, Mr. Mayor—"

"You know we'll never, never tolerate this trumped-up reservation, Drum. I couldn't hold my head up in the city—"

"Then you'd better be ready to walk around hangdog, Mr. Mayor."

The mayor paused, seeming to collect himself. "Okay, look. No time served, and I'll get you a quarter-million-a-year job at O'Mellony and Meares in a year or so when this thing calms down. . . . Just get your people the hell out of this icon of New York. Rockefeller Center is the centerpiece of—"

"Mr. Mayor, if I'd wanted a job at some stuffed-shirt anthill law firm, I'd have applied years ago. All I want is for you to acknowledge Scohomac, and let us go about our business in peace."

The mayor looked crestfallen. He sighed deeply. "It'll never happen, Drum."

"It'll happen, Patrini, like it or not."

"Look, Steve. You prefer Steve, not Stephen?"

"Either."

"Okay, Steve. Look, I've got a chance at the governorship. It's important to me, but I've got to have the support of the voters of New York City. Without the city, no governor's mansion."

"What's that got to do with me? The people will vote for you Scohomac or no Scohomac. Just because they voted down the referendum on gambling . . ."

He reddened. "Fuck the people. I want that governor's job. When I get it, we'll have gambling all over the State of New York."

"Did you say 'fuck the people'?" Steve shook his head.

"Fuck the miserable bastards. They've been giving me nothing but misery for a dozen years. All I want is to get out gracefully and end my public life in style."

"Another pension? Is that what you're after, Mayor? Or is it a payoff from a lot of boys in Las Vegas who want to push Atlantic City into the sea? I'd think the mayor's pension would be enough for one immigrant's son. Give it up, Mr. Mayor. I'm going to make this happen. Scohomac is going to be the only game in town."

"I'll see you in hell first," the mayor spat out, his anger showing for the first time.

"That's likely. Are we through here?"

"You're talking bloodbath here, Drum."

"That's your choice, Patrini. I wouldn't want that to come down on my watch if I were running the city, but it's your choice. A lot of good men are going to die."

"Fuck them too, that's what they're paid for. My choice is to have your ass served to me on a platter, no matter how many so-called good men die." Patrini spat out the words, his face growing redder by the second.

Steve started moving back toward the door as Patrini motioned to his two bodyguards, then sidled behind the column out of harm's way.

"Get the son of a bitch!" Patrini yelled.

CHAPTER THIRTY-SIX

Both of the men drew weapons and charged toward Steve, but the doors burst open and Joe Bigsam and Thad stepped out, each with an AK-47 leveled at a Patrini bodyguard.

There was a moment of cold silence, only the buzz of the subway station in the background. Steve studied each man in turn. "You fellows are outgunned. I'd suggest . . ." Both men started backing away.

"Get him, get him!" the mayor yelled, his voice an angry, frustrated falsetto from behind the protection of the column. Just about that time, passersby on the subway platform realized there were men waving guns, threatening each other, only steps away. The screaming and running began.

"You get him," one of the bodyguards said calmly over the growing din, backing away.

Steve and his men disappeared, backing into the GE Building entrance under the watchful eye of two great gobs of yellow Play-Doh punctured with detonators.

When they returned to the security office, Steve picked up one of four cellular phones resting in numbered boxes, each with a phone number stenciled to its side. The phones had been acquired under alias just for this purpose. He was sure his own phone was now being monitored, and was a little surprised it was still functioning, since he'd expected them to cut it off.

He placed another phone call. Felicia answered on the first ring. "What's up," she asked.

"Time for you and a cameraman to put in an appearance."

"Wish I could, but the cops say nobody is going inside. They're turning up the burner."

"Okay, here's what I want you to do."

The photographer stood across Fifth Avenue from the barricades, watching the growing crowds.

This prick thinks he's big-time. He'll go to jail for sure, for causing all this bullshit, but jail's not good enough. I want him to hurt, and what better place than in front of a bunch of TV cameras, with the world watching. His guts spilling out on the sidewalk. We'll see if he looks like a hotshot Indian attorney then.

"Fuck you, Farley," he said under his breath, but aloud.

A big Puerto Rican stood next to him, watching the activity. The big man turned to the photographer, then snarled, "What did you say to me, man?"

"Nothin'. I didn't say nothin'." He moved on down the sidewalk away from the hulking man. Now people completely filled the sidewalks across Fifth outside the barricades. A man he recognized from television, a barrio activist, was being interviewed by a television reporter. He ranted and raved about the inequities of being a man of color. A few feet away, a black woman stood on a makeshift podium, an upside-down plastic milk crate, spewing her rhetoric to the crowd. Most of the people just milled around, some carrying placards. The placards mostly supported Scohomac; a couple were against gambling in general, and a few espoused other causes, including the coming end of the world.

As the photographer stood watching, he eyed the buildings surrounding the GE Building. Across Forty-ninth stood the Simon & Schuster Building, the Rockefeller Center parking garage, and 10 Rockefeller Plaza, which housed, among other things, the now-dark Studio One. It was one of the most famous sidewalk locations in the country, having a major network news show broadcast from just inside its windows there every morning, a show that moved out onto the sidewalk for interviews. Across Fiftieth was the 1270 Avenue of the Americas building and the Guild movie theater.

He wondered if he could accomplish his purpose from any of those locations, then decided upon the garage. Easy ingress and egress, no windows to contend with.

Heading toward the garage, he had to thread his way among the spectators, even across Fifth Avenue from the sidewalk adjacent to the barrier. If this kept up, they'd be in the streets.

Already the cops had a major traffic problem.

If it got worse, it would be pandemonium.

Perfect for an easy getaway.

A tunnel of cardboard boxes had been constructed inside the foam plug in the Forty-ninth Street pipe tunnel. The tunnel was one of six leading into the lower basement of the GE Building. While Steve and Thad waited at the plug end, two of the warriors were inside the cardboard tunnel, waiting for Felicia's signal. In moments they heard a feminine voice reciting the agreed password, "Remember Osceola's head."

In seconds they'd hacked through the remaining foot of hardened foam beyond the cardboard. It took them a few moments more to widen the tunnel so she and the heavily laden cameraman could easily pass through.

Steve greeted her. "Thanks for coming."

"My pleasure. Anything for good old IBC . . . or, should I say, for the Native American cause?"

"Let's go upstairs and find a better place to shoot."

The pair followed Steve and Thad as they climbed three flights of stairs to the area just outside the concourse where the SWAT team had first been thwarted.

They continued up to the second floor via the elevator, entering the security office where the rest of Steve's primary team waited.

Steve motioned to Paula. "Run the tape for Felicia." He turned to the reporter and produced a small tape recorder. "I'm going to play this recorder at the same time, but it'll be out of sync. I'm sure your engineers can put it together. . . ."

As the tape began to roll, Felicia's eyes widened. "My God, that's—" About that time, Steve on tape called the mayor by his title, and the bearded man answered.

Felicia listened to the whole thing, watched the mayor's rather feeble attempt to have his own bodyguards take Steve captive, then, when it was over, began to laugh. She laughed for so long, the rest of them began to wonder if she was under too much stress. When she finally regained her composure, she turned to Joe Bigsam.

"Do you get it?"

"What?" he asked.

"You don't get it?"

"What? What don't I get?"

"You will get it. Just watch my broadcast." She laughed again, then turned back to Steve. "You've got to give me this little jewel . . . at least a good copy?"

"That's the idea, but I want to come to some agreement with you first."

"Anything you want, just so I get to air this tape."

"Okay, that's a given." He turned to Paula. "Copy, please." She handed him a VHS. He removed the audiotape from the recorder and turned to Thad. "We have a copy of this also?"

"We have the original of both."

He handed the tape over to Felicia. "I'll walk you back down. Let's do a short interview in the lobby, then you're out of here."

They paused and again Steve appealed to the people of New York to insist that their mayor honor his agreement with the Scohomac.

As they returned to the lower basement, Steve went through the same "play it only in total" speech he had before, regarding both the tape he'd given her and the interview, and she agreed. As they reached the tunnel, she paused. "I can't tell you right now, Mr. Drum, but this is much bigger than you think."

"How so?"

"My special airs tomorrow evening. Just make sure you're all watching."

"Wouldn't miss it."

She winked at him, then disappeared with her cameraman. At their instruction, she placed a cardboard box against the hole they'd created, and Tomtom Webster did his gopher trick with his insulation equipment.

When Steve got back to the control room, Paula turned to him. "I don't like that woman."

He smiled. "I doubt most women would."

"Horseshit," Paula said, and she seldom swore. "She's a gold digger and a bitch."

"Okay, if you say so."

Thad laughed out loud.

Paula turned on him. "What's so funny, Wintermoose?"

He suddenly got a very straight face. "Nothing, hon."

They were interrupted by Joe Bigsam's urgent voice. "What the hell?"

All of them studied the monitors. A line of police officers, each helmeted and dressed in black, each holding up a shield half the length of his body, each carrying an M16, were forming a line outside in front of the lobby doors. As the camera mechanically panned across the line, you could see a battering ram protruding between a pair lined up in front of each set of doors.

An equally long line of warriors stood their ground inside the doors, but had dropped back to just in front of the wide counter.

"Shit," Thad said. "It's time to see what's behind door number two."

They ran for the lobby.

David Greenberg was not with them, but when they exited the elevator, he stuck his head into the elevator waiting area when they disembarked.

"Are you ready for my Robocop act?"

Steve shook his head. He had his cellular phone to his ear. Sam Batistone answered. "What the hell is going on, Batistone?"

"Nothing I can do about it, Drum. You guys had better lay down your weapons and get your hands in the air . . . the SWAT guys are real nervous."

"It'll never happen. I'm pulling my men out and we're going to the plastic. We've got a remote control device here, with a hundred pounds of that crap attached to it. You tell the mayor, it's on him if half of Rockefeller Center is leveled. I hope you have Saks cleared out, and the streets are vacant." He knew hundreds of people remained outside the barriers, because they were still under the watch of the TV cameras. They now had continuous coverage on a couple of the local channels.

In the hallway perpendicular to the bank of elevators, Steve could see an impressive rig pass by. Its windows were blacked out so you could not see the driver, if there was one. Only a two-inch circular hole remained in the black-painted windshield, so

David Greenberg, at the controls, would not run into a column. On all the windows and across the entire grille of the vehicle was plastered yellow "plastic." Wires coiled from one gob to the next. A wall clock, eighteen inches in diameter, was mounted to the front of the rig, and wires ran from it into the yellow mass.

The clock was ticking, set at three minutes to twelve.

Steve said gravely, "This is your last chance, Batistone. My people are moving out. I hope this doesn't bring the whole damned building down around all our ears."

The Zamboni, the vehicle used to smooth the ice on the rink below, had been moved into the building and painted black. It was an ominous-looking black beast, with yellow warts of death and destruction.

Batistone's voice weakened. "It's what?"

"What?" Steve asked.

"I'm on the radio." As Steve listened, the warriors filed by at a run.

"You're serious . . . Drum?"

"I thought you were talking to someone else."

"No! Not now," Batistone shouted. "What the hell is that thing?"

"It's a remote control police deterrent device. We call it the wasp, and it's got a big stinger. About the same strength as a World War Two B29, I imagine . . . at least that's what my guys tell me. It's ticking, and you've got less than two minutes. Clear them out."

"Hell, they're already out," Batistone said.

"Good." Steve yelled as if he were yelling to someone nearby. "Reset the damned thing! They pulled back." Then he turned back to the cell phone. "Don't try that crap again, Batistone. Tell the mayor to watch the IBC news special tomorrow night. There'll be some information there he'll be interested in."

"What are you talking about?"

"Just tell him."

They all looked at one another in relief after Steve hung up. "That was too close," Thad said.

"This is nuts," Tomtom offered, shaking his head. "We're chasing off a platoon of SWAT guys with Play-Doh and an ice rink toy. Nuts!"

It was all Steve could do to muster a smile. He wondered if the next time they'd be so lucky.

In Saddle River, Papa Al followed Angela out to her car. She carried an overnight bag; a hanging bag was hooked up in the backseat.

"I wisha you'd stay here with Mama, Angela. She needs you. It's cold down at the beach now."

"I told you, Papa, I need some time alone. I wish there were something you could do to get Steve out of that mess he's in."

"An' I tolda you, Steve's a biga boy, and he's doing what he thinks is right."

"He's gone out of his mind. Can't you call him or something?" She opened the door and stepped behind the wheel.

"He'sa doing what he thinks is right."

"Okay, Papa. I'll call you from the beach."

"If you gotta go. Call and let us know you got there safe." She waved and gunned the car away.

When she reached the interstate, she passed the on ramp toward Maryland, went under the overpass, and turned onto the ramp leading the other way.

If Papa Al wouldn't talk sense to Steve, she would.

CHAPTER THIRTY-SEVEN

The photographer, a pair of powerful binoculars to his eyes, stood on the top floor of the parking garage and studied the windows of the GE Building across Forty-ninth Street.

He'd seen several dozen men, each with a yellow headband, moving around inside and lining the railings of the ledges several floors above. Each of them carried an automatic weapon of some kind.

But he hadn't seen his target.

In the trunk of his black sedan lay a Savage 7mm Magnum with a powerful 15x scope. It was the same weapon he'd used to kick up the dirt at Drum's feet in the park, when he'd had thoughts of making a little money off him. Maybe he was up too high. Maybe Drum was staying somewhere lower in the GE Building, to be near the lobby, where the action seemed to concentrate.

He went back to his car and started it. Wheeling down a couple of floors, he found another parking place, then walked to the rail and used the binocs.

He felt heat flood his backbone when he realized he was staring right into the eyes of his enemy. His former friend. His Judas.

Drum was standing at a window, his hands folded behind his back, seemingly in deep thought.

Running across the parking aisle, he popped the trunk of the sedan, pulled on a black ski mask, picked up the weapon, and ran back to the rail.

He worked the bolt and jerked the weapon to his shoulder just as Drum moved away.

Damn, damn, damn.

He could hear a vehicle coming. Jerking the ski mask off, he held the weapon in front of the hood of a parked car while the vehicle passed. Only another car looking for an elusive parking place.

Putting the binocs to his eyes, he studied the window. He marked its location in his mind. He'd watch it until Drum reappeared, then he'd put one right between his ugly Indian eyes.

Steve wandered out of the security office, telling everyone there that he was going up to an office he'd commandeered for his personal quarters. Waving his cell phone at them, he left strict instructions that they should call him if anything happened.

Even though it was only midafternoon, he was tired. Dead tired. He wanted a good rest, because the next night, should everything go right, this thing might just come to a head. He knew it was too much to ask to have this end that soon. They were prepared for months of siege. But it could end without a drop of blood being spilled . . . God willing and if the people of New York were with him.

As he neared the elevator bank, the warriors were busily moving equipment. Every opportunity they'd had, they'd been unpacking and moving slots and tables into place in the lobby, hallways, and empty third floor of the GE Building. It was a long way from what Steve envisioned, but as soon as they had people coming through the doors, they could be gambling.

Steve had his computer set up in his private area, and had a modem there that would attach to a portable phone. He attached his cellular and punched in the proper sequence on the computer. ICOM was off twelve points from a high of 49½, on a volume of over four million shares. He checked the financial news and noted that George Thornapple, the *Wall Street Journal* reporter, hadn't actually done an article yet. He knew Thornapple was a careful man, and he would check Steve's anonymous statements and confirm them as facts before he printed anything. So far the stock was tumbling only on rumor. Steve hoped that Dragonovich was still buying, trying to bolster the price of the stock.

But he had his own problems, he'd done his part to make Papa Al a hell of a handful of money. If Al had been selling short like he'd instructed him, he would already be up several million dollars.

Steve was broke, but at least he'd gotten the loan he needed. He wasn't actually broke, he decided, just fully invested. He had everything he owned at risk, as well as a hell of a lot of the assets and hopes and dreams of others. He would find out soon if it was all for naught.

One thing he knew for sure, come tomorrow night, he was going to have a mad mayor on his hands. In fact, rabid might be a better word.

Then he had a wild thought.

He called the security office and Paula answered. "How many guys do we have who know anything about electronics . . . TV?"

Angela was astounded at the scene. It was almost seven P.M. and the people were still on the street as if it were five-thirty and they were just leaving work. She'd finally found a place to park in the Rockefeller Center garage, after inching her way through the crowds.

Now she stood on Fifth Avenue. The sidewalk across in front of the concrete barriers brimmed with people, and they pushed out onto the avenue itself, as did the sidewalk where she stood. Police were everywhere, trying to keep people on the sidewalk and out of traffic, trying to calm arguments that broke out between different factions, trying to keep the peace. Many of the onlookers were more than just that, they were participants, many carrying signs, most in favor of what was being called Scohomac.

A chant went up, seemingly spontaneous. "Let Scohomac live! Let Scohomac live!"

The whole thing caused her spine to shudder. She hated crowds, particularly crowds that could get out of hand in a moment's notice. And this was one.

What did Steve have to do with all this? Had he lost his mind? She had to get to him, talk to him.

She made her way across the street and tried to find a breech in the barrier so she could sneak inside, but there was none. She moved down Fiftieth Street toward the ice rink and came upon a pair of trailers, but they, too, were barricaded off and the street was blocked.

Finally she approached a uniformed policeman at the barricade. "Sir, I need to get inside."

"Inside the GE Building?" he said, incredulous, and she nodded. He shook his head. "Ma'am, if you owned the place, you couldn't get inside. There's a battalion of crazy Indians in there with enough guns and explosives to level blocks around. If I were you, I'd go home and watch this on TV."

Frustrated, she moved away and mingled with the chanting crowd.

Who were these people? New York had a lot of people of color, but there seemed to be a disproportionate amount here.

Finally, after watching awhile longer, she made her way back to the garage and drove out.

She hoped the Pen would have a room.

She'd try again tomorrow.

The photographer watched the window until the lights were turned so low, he couldn't make out anything going on inside.

The crowds below had dispersed, and only a token number of officers lined the streets. City cleanup crews were busy picking up the street trash and the few placards strewn about.

Finally, tired, he decided he, too, would call it a night. There was always tomorrow. Tomorrow was another day.

This time, however, things were different. Even if he was caught, he would be a hero. At least in the eyes of the police.

Steve awoke well before dawn. He arose, rolled up his sleeping bag, and wandered down to the rest rooms. Happy to note his electric shaver worked, thanks to the generators, he shaved, then wet and combed his hair. He wanted a shower, but so did everyone else, and he had to conserve water. They had filled a tank in the basement, and a pump set up and the tank tied to the fire system so they'd have some chance should an emergency arise. Admittedly a slight chance, but some. He hoped it wouldn't. His own rule to his crew was no water except for drinking, and one flush of the toilets per day.

Alone, he took the express elevator to the sixty-fifth floor, and wandered out and into the Rainbow Room. It seemed like so long ago when he was last there, at the mayor's Rainbow Dinner. Walking to the tall windows, he looked out over the still-sleeping city. Peaceful now.

Far away, he could make out a ship on the Hudson moving slowly south, toward the open sea. For a fleeting moment he wished he and Angela were aboard, then he shook it off. He was too busy to worry about Angela.

Too busy to worry about anything other than making Scohomac into a reality.

He knew the warriors were beginning to feel the pressure of confinement, of being under the watchful eye of the New York City police, under the onus of possibly facing prison sentences for what, so far anyway, was merely trying to better their people's position.

If it ended the wrong way, he would be the one to take the brunt of it.

With the schedule they'd established, he knew that almost twenty-five percent of the warriors would be awake and on guard. He needed the exercise, so he decided to walk down from floor to floor, to visit with every man he could. Sometimes a few words from the boss . . .

By noon it appeared that the mayor's office and the police had decided upon a holding action. Steve knew what they were thinking: Let them stew in their own juice, let them get dirty and hungry, and wanting a little green and a little fresh air.

The day wore on, completely boring except for one piece of news. The financial station reported the business fraud of the decade. *The Wall Street Journal* had reported that ICOM's claim of a major discovery at Hovenweep was a scam. The oldest scam in the world, salting the mine. Alex Dragonovich, company CEO, was not available for comment. ICOM's stock price had fallen to twenty-two and was still plunging. It was suspected that the SEC would suspend trading the next day. Steve hoped that Papa Al had not gotten greedy, and had covered his short sales—the way to take advantage of falling prices. If so, he could have made well over twenty million—more than he'd lent Steve. He would have his cake and could eat it too.

After Steve listened to the report, he stared up at the heavens and thought, *Standing Bear, I hope you're not too upset with me, and, Pop, I hope you're not smiling so broadly, they think you're up to something.* He wondered if one could get thrown out of heaven for enjoying another's worldly misdeeds.

And maybe the worst were to come.

Deciding to make his rounds, he went up to the sixty-fifth floor and started the long walk down, hoping to chat with some of the men who'd been asleep when he'd made the walk earlier.

The photographer slept in. He had lunch at the deli below his room before he climbed into the black sedan and headed out to Rockefeller Center.

This time he lucked out and found a parking place directly opposite the window where he'd seen Stephen Drum the day before. This time he was able to wait in the comfort of his own front seat, the Savage resting beside him.

Late in the afternoon, Drum still hadn't shown himself in the window, and the photographer began to wonder if the window was a one-time thing. He hoped not. Tired and cold, he had to start the car every once in a while and turn on the heat.

Hearing some commotion in the street below, he stepped out of the car and walked to the rail. It wasn't yet five P.M., still the crowds were already larger than they had been any time the day before.

Just as he started back to the warm car, he noticed someone in the window. He brought the glasses to his eyes. It was Drum.

He ran for the rifle.

CHAPTER THIRTY-EIGHT

Angela had driven around Rockefeller Center several times that day, but to no avail. Finally, she decided to park the car, walk around, and try again to find a place to sneak inside.

This time she found a parking spot on the bottom floor of the Rockefeller Center garage, near an alley exit. She parked and made her way outside. Park Avenue, Forty-ninth Street, Fiftieth Street, and Avenue of the Americas, surrounding what was now being called Scohomac, were crowded to the point traffic was beginning to be diverted. As she elbowed her way toward Park Avenue, she noticed a number of bus-sized police vehicles in the distance. Paddy wagons? she wondered. She could end up in jail tonight, maybe that would be the best chance she'd have of talking to Steve before the night was out.

Just at sunset the crowds began to chant in earnest, "Let Scohomac live! Let Scohomac live!" The noise became deafening.

She began to get frightened, and to fight her way back to the garage and the safety of her car.

Steve Drum moved around the security office on the third floor, pacing, waiting for Felicia's news special. Finally, it came on IBC.

"Are you ready to fire it up?" he asked the two Indian technicians who were a part of the warrior band.

They nodded. "Then do it," Steve said.

The giant screen on the front of the GE Building had been dark since the morning they'd moved in. Now it lit up, concurrent with a news flash, and the screen read: *An IBC News Special: Illegal Gambling in New York City.* The crowds outside continued to chant, unaware of the addition to the scene.

He was taking a chance on Felicia Ann Garrity, but he thought it was a good one.

"Turn those giant speakers up, full blast," Steve instructed, walking to the window to check on the crowds below.

Three floors above him, a half dozen warriors rested their AK-47s on a railing. Steve had them all on alert. When the speakers grew in volume enough to be heard over the crowd, they began to fall silent.

At the same time Steve reached the window to see what he could of the action below, the man across Forty-ninth Street rested his 7mm Savage on the parking structure railing.

The crosshairs centered on Steve's chest, but the ski mask interfered with the man's vision.

Steve raised his eyes from the street below, and even at sixty yards he recognized the man jerking the ski mask from his face. Steve's surprise was so great that he didn't truly believe it when Tony Giovanni, Angela's brother, brought the rifle to rest and, at the same time Steve dove aside, pulled the trigger.

The window shattered.

Almost instantly the warriors above trained their AK-47s on the sniper and emptied their clips at the man.

Had the recoil of the big rifle not knocked him back, Tony Giovanni would have been killed in the fusillade of shots. The ricochets spit concrete, then whined and danced all around him. He tried for his car and managed to get under the wheel and turn the key, but then realized that the hood had been stitched by automatic gunfire.

Tony sprang from the car and ran into the parking aisle out of the line of fire from above.

As soon as the gunfire erupted from the heights of the GE Building, several hundred police began to return fire, and spectators began to stampede out of the streets and take cover. Windows all over the GE Building were blown away. Obeying strict instructions, the warriors took cover too and did not return fire.

Steve sat at the wall next to the shattered window, holding his side. All around the room his friends crouched behind furniture, staying out of the line of fire. The vest had deflected the bullet, but still it hurt like hell. He managed to get to his feet. He yelled as he moved to the door.

"I know who that son of a bitch was, and I'm going to get him."

"I'm going with you," Thad said. Outside, the air rang with the echo of gunshots.

"No, you stay here. This could be a real mess. All of you, get all over this building and make sure no one returns fire unless they're in the crosshairs and think they're about to die. Tell them to stay *out* of the line of fire." As Steve ran out, he yelled behind him, "I don't want any bloodshed!" As he said it, he felt the small of his back, making sure the automatic was in place in its holster.

Steve didn't wait for an elevator, but, rather, took the stairs four at a time. He reached the basement where he'd met with Felicia and found the pipe tunnel leading across and beneath Forty-ninth Street. At the end of the cardboard hole, he kicked out the insulation and crawled through. His footfalls echoed as he ran in the dim light. It was a hundred yards to the next Rockefeller Center mechanical room, this one below number ten, next to the parking garage. Without slowing he took the stairs up, bursting out of the stairwell into an employees-only corridor, through a pair of doors with emergency panic hardware leading out onto the alley behind the Rock Center parking garage.

At a dead run he reached the alley entrance to the garage and turned in without stopping. A car, moving fast, hit its brakes. Steve tried to step aside, but it was too late, he collided with it and spread-eagled atop the hood—and found himself face-to-face with Angela Giovanni.

"What the hell?" Steve said, wondering what she was doing there, and for a fleeting moment if she might be helping her brother.

He sprang off the hood and scrambled to the driver's side, just as another car screeched around a turn in the parking aisle fifty yards away.

Tony Giovanni had relieved a commuter of his Honda Accord. He gunned the car toward the opening, where a man was talking with a woman through a car window. There was just room to make it by them, and he didn't slow until he realized the man was Stephen Drum.

He braked the car to a screeching halt alongside the waiting vehicle. Raising the rifle, Tony found himself eye to eye with his sister. For a fleeting second he actually considered shooting her. The bitch was insulting the family again; consorting with Stephen Drum again. Stephen Drum, his archenemy; Stephen Drum, whom his father continually threw in his face.

Instead, in disgust, Tony jammed on the accelerator. He couldn't shoot his own sister, no matter what; he loved her, he couldn't even get in a gunfight where there was the slightest risk of hurting her.

Steve jerked open her passenger door as the Honda peeled out. "Get out!" he yelled at Angela.

"It's my car! You get out." To her surprise, he did, but he merely ran around the car and opened the driver's-side door. Anticipating what he was doing, she slid to the passenger seat and belted herself in before he could drag her out.

"Get out," he commanded. "I'm going after Tony, he's been trying to kill me."

"Tony's crazy, Steve. Go after him, but I'm not getting out."

Steve jumped behind the wheel and looked at her. "Then hang on."

He sped down the alley without looking over at her. "Just what the hell are you doing here?"

"Looking for you, what the hell do you think?" She shrieked and held on as Steve took the corner onto Rockefeller Plaza, then gunned the engine. They could see the Honda just disappearing around the next corner, west on Fifty-first Street.

As they settled into the chase, weaving in and out of traffic, she turned to Steve. "Why would Tony want to kill you? You once saved his life."

"Don't ask me, Angela. He also tried to blackmail me." Steve braked hard, then slipped between two yellow cabs, both of them honking at him with one continuous blast. "And you, in a way. He had pictures of you coming in and out of my apartment building. Not that it would matter to anyone other than your father."

"You know Papa threw him out months ago, won't even speak to him? He cut him off from everything. Tony came to me, he blames you, but it's Papa's fault. Papa's always throwing you up to Tony. And I suspected Tony knew about us. In a twisted way, Tony has always loved me too much."

A block ahead, they could see Tony's Honda, still weaving in and out of traffic.

"Let him go, Steve. I'll have Papa take care of it—"

"You can't do that, Angela. He'd show the pictures to Al and he'd make your life miserable."

"My life's miserable already. Look out!" she shouted as a truck edged out beyond the crosswalk.

Steve wheeled around it. Tony was trapped ahead at a stoplight between two cars, but they, too, had so much traffic, they couldn't move.

"Why's your life so—"

"Because you're not in it, you fool."

He glanced at her a moment, and his hard look softened, then he had to concentrate on his driving again. They were nearing the end of Fifty-first, where it ran into Twelfth Avenue at the Hudson River. The traffic had thinned, and they were up to fifty, then sixty miles an hour.

Tony ignored a light, then tried to make the turn onto Twelfth, but lost control. He was clipped by a produce truck, but managed to regain control. Still on the accelerator, he tried to make the frontage road that ran along the river. He couldn't make the turn. The Honda jumped the curb and crashed through a Cyclone fence, disappearing.

"My God!" Angela moaned. Steve threaded through the cross traffic, to the shouts and honks of a dozen drivers, and slid up to the rift in the fence. He leapt from the car and stared down—twenty-five feet straight down below, and fifty feet out into the water, the Honda was just disappearing under a cauldron of bubbles.

Tony was nowhere to be seen.

"The crazy bastard," Steve said, but his look was not one of triumph, rather of remorse.

"He's a bastard, but go get him, please, Steve."

Steve turned to her. His face a mask of indecision, he remained silent.

"You saved him once."

"I didn't know him them."

"He was your friend once. Go get him. He's sick, Steve. He needs help."

Still, he remained silent, torn.

She took a deep breath, staring at the bubbles boiling the water. "You won't help your baby's uncle?"

"What did you say?"

"I said, he's your baby's uncle."

His jaw dropped, but he stripped off his coat, kicked off his shoes, and dove into the Hudson River's frigid, muddy water.

In moments he reappeared, dragging Tony Giovanni by the collar. A dredging barge was anchored only twenty yards away, and Steve stroked for it. He was able to drag Tony up on a work platform and begin CPR. In moments Tony was spitting water. As soon as Steve could see he was going to make it, he dove back in the river and swam to a ladder leading up to near where Angela stood, anxiously wringing her hands.

Shivering from the cold, taking Angela by both shoulders, he looked into her eyes. "Now, whose baby?"

The approaching cop was shocked by how hard she slapped him, snapping his head around.

He rubbed his cheek, eyeing her as she rubbed her hand. "I didn't mean it that way, Angela. I just wanted to make sure I heard you right."

"You heard me right!"

He looked at her, thought of the child she carried—his child—and felt a surge of joy. "God, you're beautiful," he managed to say, reaching for her.

Her hard look softened and she fell into his arms. He kissed her so deeply and thoroughly, the cop finally had to put a hand on Steve's shoulder to get his attention.

"What happened here?"

Steve raised his eyes from hers. "I got him out. He's out there on that barge."

"I'll call the river patrol." The cop ran for his patrol car.

Steve again took her by the shoulders. "I've got to get back. I can't be gone right now."

"Then I'm going with you."

"No."

"Do you want this baby?" she asked, her voice a little uncertain.

"Of course I do."

Her look strengthened. "There's no taking it without me."

He smiled. "Get in." And they ran for her car.

The cop was returning from his patrol car when they sped away. He shouted after them. "Hey, I need a statement!"

When Steve got within two blocks of the GE Building, the streets were filled with people. There wasn't even sporadic shooting, and the crowds had regathered. Steve glanced at his watch, stopping in the middle of Fifty-second Street and putting the car in park. "I've got to go. You take care of the car."

Angela climbed out and began to follow him. "The car can take care of itself."

By the time he was within a block of the GE Building, the crowds were almost impenetrable, but at least she could keep up with him.

He reached the promenade, realizing the crowd was now dead silent. But the giant speakers weren't. And the huge screen that had been still for so long was now alive with the face of the mayor. The crowd stared, mesmerized.

Steve's timing couldn't have been better. Just as he looked up, the mayor's face was hardly recognizable behind the beard, and a word or so of his voice had been bleeped out; but any fool could see clearly what he was saying, and would recognize the voice. "*Bleep* the people. I want that governor's job. When I get it, we'll have gambling all over the State of New York."

"Did you say '*Bleep* the people'?" Steve's voice from the speakers rang out over the crowd.

"*Bleep* the miserable *bleep*. They've been giving me nothing but misery for a dozen years. All I want is to get out gracefully, and end my public life in style."

The screen cut away to Felicia Garrity. "Now, ladies and gentlemen, I want to take you back to that tape I was able to make while undercover in a local illegal gambling establishment." The screen lit up with tape of one of the places she'd been with Joe Bigsam, the night her camera had been stomped to pieces. In the background, a pair of men entered the room, passing through the light for only a moment. The picture froze, then zoomed in on a laughing, bearded man, just before he disappeared into a back room.

It was the same bearded man who was plainly the mayor of

New York City. They cut back to a head and shoulders shot of Felicia, whose look was triumphant.

"Now, ladies and gentlemen, I won't be the one to accuse any of our local gentry of patronizing an illegal gambling establishment, I'll let you make your own determination." The screen was then split, with the bearded mayor who'd met with Steve on the left side, and the bearded man in the illegal gambling establishment on the other.

The buzz of the crowd intensified.

Steve glanced at his watch. Seven P.M. It couldn't have been better timed if he and Felicia had plotted it together.

Felicia continued. "Just one more item I thought would be of interest to all those men and women out there putting their life on the line every day." Again, the mayor's bearded face lit the giant screen.

"You're talking bloodbath here, Drum," he said.

"That's your choice, Patrini." Steve's voice rang out over the crowd. "I wouldn't want that to come down on my watch if I were running the city, but it's your choice. A lot of good men are going to die."

"*Bleep* them too, that's what they're paid for."

Again, the mayor had enunciated well, and it was very clear to the crowd what he'd said, and neither they nor the hard workingmen and -women in uniforms peppering the area appreciated it.

Suddenly the throngs began to chant, and the chant grew in volume as the mass surged forward. "Let Scohomac live! Let Scohomac live!" The cops, who looked even more disgusted than the crowd, began to give way.

The crowd rushed forward, thousands of them, shoving the topmost concrete street divider, until the first, then several more, crashed to the pavement. Dust flew and the way was clear. They scrambled over the barriers and rushed the gunfire-shattered front doors of the GE Building. Lights began to come on inside and slot machines began to glow and their computer music sang songs of welcome and bring-your-money.

The giant screen on the outside of the GE Building was suddenly transformed to the prerecorded face of Steve Drum in a black tuxedo. "Welcome to Scohomac. We're sorry that we don't have a complete casino here to serve you as of yet, but we will soon."

As the big-screen Steve Drum continued to give a spiel of welcome to the throngs of people filling the lobby and first three floors of the All American Casino, the flesh-and-blood Steve Drum watched from Fifth Avenue.

Finally, when the crowds had thinned, he took Angela's hand and they walked down the promenade and paused at the bronze plaque inscribed with the thoughts of John D. Rockefeller, Jr.

Angela silently read the words, then turned to Steve. "Do you think Mr. Rockefeller would object to all this?"

"Well, he was a pious man. He might object to the gambling, but he sure wouldn't object to the spirit behind it, or where the proceeds are going."

She nuzzled up to him. "So, where are *we* going?"

"How about the condo? I've really been missing you. I think I'm going to be seeing quite enough of this place in the near future. Besides, I need to call your old man and have a talk with him."

"Oh, great, I can hardly wait. Can we have one more afternoon at your place first?"

"Don't worry about Aldo. I think he likes green enough that this time he'll ignore the red."

"What?"

"Nothing. Look, Angela, your father is a lot of things, but he's a family man first and foremost, and I don't mean family in the illegal sense. When you tell him you're having my baby, and that we're getting married, he'll change his whole attitude toward me."

"If that's the case, we should have done this long ago."

Steve grinned. "That's what I've been telling you for years . . ."

She stopped and faced him, pulling him to her, and again they were lost in a deep prolonged kiss.

Inside 30 Rockefeller Plaza several hundred of the thousands of people who'd rushed the casino threw down their placards and put on Scohomac headbands. Some donned food or change aprons.

The same big Puerto Rican who'd challenged Tony Giovanni out in the street gave a curious look at one of them, a short, pretty

Arapaho girl who'd been in the forefront of the "Spanish Harlem" protestors. "I thought you was maybe a Puerto Rican," he said.

She winked at him. "We're all the same under the skin, big boy. You want a roll of quarters?"

When Angela and Steve reached the condo, it was hours before they exited the bedroom. While Angela whipped up an omelet, Steve turned on the financial channel. The lead item was the investigation of Alex Dragonovich for stock manipulation, and the report of his resignation from ICOM. The banks had called his margin loans, and it seems he was millions in the hole and unable to pay.

It was rumored he had fled the country.

It was the best omelet of Steve's life.

Epilogue

A Little More Than One Year Later

Just moments after the Christmas star was placed atop a sixty-foot spruce in the promenade, Steve took Angela's hand and they walked past the huge statue of a Plains Indian chief standing over a seated group of Indian children in the dress of a dozen nations, then into the plush ground floor of the All American Casino.

The doorman greeted them.

"Good evening, Tuffy," Steve said to his old friend.

As they neared the elevator, they passed a bank of telephones.

"I think I'll give the baby-sitter a call," Angela said with a concerned look.

"You called her fifteen minutes ago, little mother. You'll drive the poor woman nuts. Lighten up."

"Okay, okay. Let's go on up."

"Maybe I ought to stop on forty and see how the remodeling is coming along?"

She put a finger to his mouth, shushing him. "You were there this afternoon. You're going to drive those poor workmen nuts, and you've already got them working twenty-four hours a day. Lighten up."

He smiled. "Touché."

As they rode the express elevator to the sixty-fifth floor, Steve eyed his wife of almost a year. The baby had done her figure no harm. It had certainly not harmed her complexion. In fact, she'd seemed to glow. He glanced down at her cleavage, clearly visible in the low-cut, shimmering gown and tugged at the tight collar of the tux shirt. They exited the elevator to a crowd waiting to get into the First Annual All American Scholarship banquet.

Working their way through the crowded entry and across the Rainbow Room, filled with young people awaiting college scholarships and with New York's most prestigious business and social elite, they took their place at the head table.

Seated next to Steve, Mayor Patrini extended his hand, and Steve shook it.

"I want to thank you for coming to present these awards, Mr. Mayor. It means a lot to Scohomac."

"No problem, Steve."

"There's Papa and Mama," Angela said. "You'll excuse me a moment."

Both men rose as she left the table. When she was out of earshot, and the others at the head table seemed engrossed in conversation, Patrini leaned closer to Steve. "You know I'm thinking about running for governor—"

Steve smiled, the mayor's attitude about Scohomac seemed to have taken a complete flip-flop.

Patrick McGoogan, Tom Webster, Joe Bigsam, Meredith Spotted Fawn, Paula Running Fox—all members of the board of directors of the All American Casino—and their spouses and dates shared the head table with Steve, Angela, and Mayor Patrini. David Greenberg, in charge of public relations for Scohomac, was not in attendance—he was on a book tour for his publisher, promoting his new book, *Return of the Red Man.*

Angela gave her mother and father a hug. As soon as she sat, she asked, "How's Tony? I still think you should have gotten him some mental help, Papa."

"Your uncle Angelo says he's gonna make a fine olive farmer, and I thinka Italy agrees with him. And ifa it don't, my older brother and your cousins can handle it. Your uncle can get Tony's head straight better'n any shrink, if it takes a ax handle." Papa Al winked at her, then smiled and asked, "Howsa little Stephen Aldo?"

"Home, Papa, and I'm sure he's unhappy because he couldn't come to see you."

"He'sa only seven months, Angela. He hardly knows hisa grandpa yet."

"What do you mean?" she teased. "He even looks like you."

"A little red version, maybe. You think that red is just because he's a bambino, Angela?"

"Well, Papa, half of it is."

She laughed and returned to the head table as Tomtom Webster took the podium to introduce the mayor of the neighboring City of New York.